THE WRONG HOSTAGE

THE
WRONG
HOSTAGE

Elizabeth Lowell

**Doubleday Large Print
Home Library Edition**

WM

WILLIAM MORROW
An Imprint of HarperCollinsPublishers

This Large Print Edition, prepared especially for Doubleday Large Print Home Library, contains the complete, unabridged text of the original Publisher's Edition.

This book is a work of fiction. The characters, incidents, and dialogue are drawn from the author's imagination and are not to be construed as real. Any resemblance to actual events or persons, living or dead, is entirely coincidental.

ISBN-13: 978-0-7394-6903-3
ISBN-10: 0-7394-6903-7

Printed in the U.S.A.

**This Large Print Book carries the
Seal of Approval of N.A.V.H.**

To the Men and Women
Whose Contributions
to This Novel Are, and Will Remain,
Anonymous

THE WRONG HOSTAGE

PROLOGUE

LANE FRANKLIN TOLD HIMSELF that he shouldn't freak out.

Most fifteen-year-olds would be high-fiving all over the place if they got to spend the summer in Ensenada. Beaches, bims, beer. Life didn't get any better.

Not that All Saints School was exactly in Ensenada's fast lane. Despite the sultry summer heat, no girls wearing butt-floss bikinis were shaking it on the school's beautiful, very private beach. But his cottage was first class and the soccer field was awesome, and with the window open he could hear the surf that broke on the western edge of the campus.

With its scattered four-bedroom cottages, apartments for teachers, dorms for less wealthy students, and a small library/recreation center, All Saints looked like a high-end resort.

It wasn't.

It was a church school where spoiled kids learned how to take orders, how to sit up straight, how to study, and how to be respectful.

Booorrrring.

I had it coming. What I did was a crime.

Even if it didn't seem like it at the time.

Just a little finger time with his nifty new computer and his F's turned into B's in the school's central computer. Too bad he got caught, and way too bad that his father suddenly decided he'd hang around long enough to see Lane registered in a more structured international boarding school.

At least they hadn't caught him when he'd hacked into a military computer, or that bank, and five or six other sacred cows. Once he got inside, he hadn't done anything except enjoy getting away with it.

Then he'd had the bright idea of changing his grades so his mother wouldn't be upset at a row of D's and F's.

Everything's okay.

I've done six months. I can do two more.

So what if his roommates had all moved out three weeks ago. He liked the silence and he didn't have to hide his computer.

So what if the school had enrolled some thugs to play soccer a few weeks ago. So what if the guys looked more like twenty-six than sixteen. So what if they targeted him every time he was on the field. He was quicker and a whole lot smarter than they were.

Lane looked at his watch. Soccer practice would begin in a few hours. Until then he'd do homework. Afterward he'd play games on the computer his mother had smuggled past the school's tight-assed headmaster a few weeks ago.

He still didn't know why they said he couldn't have access to a computer. He hadn't done anything wrong, but suddenly he didn't have phone privileges and couldn't use the library computer. All he could do was write letters.

Like snail mail isn't really lame.

At least Lane didn't have to worry about anyone discovering the forbidden computer. Each student cleaned his own quarters and his own clothes and some even did dishes for the whole school.

It would have been awesome to have an Internet connection, but short of breaking into the school offices . . .

Don't even think about it.

Don't give Dad another chance to push Mom into keeping me here. I haven't had a single black mark in four months.

After his roommates left, he didn't have friends to talk to, but that was okay. He was used to being alone. When he'd first come to All Saints, the only Spanish he'd known had gotten him black marks for saying it aloud. Some of the kids spoke English, some spoke Chinese or Japanese or French, but most spoke Spanish with various geographical accents he was beginning to be able to separate. He'd always been good with languages, but they bored him.

Now that he had a good reason to learn one, he was a whole lot more fluent than anyone guessed. But none of what he overheard made him feel better.

The last three weeks had really sucked. His telephone didn't work. When he asked for someone to fix it, nothing happened. When he asked one of his teachers if he could use hers to call home, she backed away like he'd suggested sex on the desk.

That was the day the two badasses swaggered onto the soccer field and stared at him, silently telling him that he was number one on their hit list.

Something had happened three weeks ago.

Lane didn't know what it was, he didn't know what had caused it. All he knew was that he'd gone from being a student to something else.

Something that felt like a prisoner.

So what? I've held my own with those two pendejos *for twenty-one days. I'm nailing my classes. My room is always clean and neat. The teachers like me.*

Or they did until three weeks ago.

When Mom comes to visit, I'll just casually ask her if Dad has changed his mind and maybe I could come home for a week. Or a few days.

Even one day.

Just a few hours.

Because once I'm across that border, I'm never coming back. I'll live on the streets if I have to.

Lane listened to the relentless surf and

told himself that the waves weren't whispering, *prisoner . . . prisoner . . . prisoner . . .*

But even that hissing chant was better than remembering the voices of the two thugs as they tripped him, elbowed him, kicked him: *You're ours,* pato. *You're dead meat. We're going to sneak into your room, cut off your balls, and make you eat them.*

Lane shut out the sound of the surf and the voices in his memory.

I'm not a prisoner.

I'm not scared.

SOUTHERN CALIFORNIA
LA JOLLA
SATURDAY MORNING

1

THE PHONE RANG FOUR times before Judge Grace Silva pulled her head out of the legal documents she was reviewing.

Maybe it's Ted.
Finally.

It had been years since she'd cared about her husband—newly ex-husband—in any way but as the father of her child. And if there was a persistent personal sadness that she'd failed in marriage, well, she'd just have to live with it. She'd worked hard to make the divorce and all the legalities entailed as civilized and adult as possible.

For Lane.

But she was real tired of getting calls at all times of the day and night asking for Theodore Franklin. Just because he'd kept his legal address as the beach home they'd once shared didn't mean he actually lived with her.

"Hello," Grace said.

"Ah, *señora,*" said a man's voice. "This is Carlos Calderón. I would like to speak to your husband."

Grace didn't bother to point out that Franklin was her ex. If Calderón wasn't close enough to Ted to know about the divorce, she had no reason to announce it.

"Ted isn't here," she said briskly. *And he hasn't been here in three weeks, which you damn well should know because you or one of your employees has called every day.* "Have you tried his Wilshire office, his cell phone, and his Malibu condo?" *Or his bimbo mistress?*

"*Sí,* yes, many times."

"Is it something I can help you with?"

Grace expected the same answer she'd gotten for the past three weeks—a polite thanks but no thanks.

Instead Calderón sighed and said, "Judge

Silva, I am afraid you must come to Ensenada immediately."

Her hand tightened on the phone. As a judge, she was accustomed to giving rather than taking orders. "Excuse me?"

"It is your son, Lane."

"What's wrong?" she asked quickly. "Is he in trouble? He's been so good for the—"

"It is not something to be discussed over the telephone. I will see you in two hours."

"What's wrong?" she demanded.

"Good-bye, Judge Silva."

"Wait," she said. "Give me four hours. I don't know what traffic will be like at the border."

"Three hours."

The phone went dead.

2

Grace barely reached the border by the deadline. Traffic had been heavier than usual, which meant six lanes of stop-and-slow on southbound interstates. The good news was that the Mexican customs officials were waving people through as fast as they could. They might hate Americans, but they loved the Yankee dollar. The only cars the officials stopped held women worth staring at twice.

The customs official in Grace's lane looked half asleep behind his two-hundred-dollar Ray-Bans. With a practiced, languid gesture he started to wave her dark green Mercedes SUV through the checkpoint. Then he saw her through the open driver's window. He leaned forward, hand raised in a signal for her to stop.

The same thing had happened to a convertible three cars ahead of Grace and one lane over. That one had held two California blondes out for a little sin and excitement south of the border.

"Good morning, *señorita*," he said with a smile just short of a leer. Despite the polite words, his glance never got above her breasts. "And where in my beautiful Mexico are you going?"

Anger snaked through Grace, a welcome vent for the anxiety about Lane that made her shoulders and jaw tight. As a teenager, she'd put up with enough macho male crap to last her a lifetime. She really wanted to teach this border cowboy some manners, but it would take more time than it was worth.

Her grandmother Marta had taught her when to fight and when to duck.

You must come to Ensenada immediately.

"Ensenada," Grace said through clenched teeth.

She handed him her passport. Inside the front cover was a laminated Mexican Department of Justice identification card. The Mexican government issued the cards as a courtesy to American judges and other officials.

The customs inspector's thick black eyebrows rose behind the cover of his sunglasses. He handed over her passport and waved her through. "Excuse the inconvenience, *licenciada,*" he said quickly. *"Bienvenido."*

Grace hit the window's up button and left the border behind. Sometimes she didn't know which annoyed her more: Mexico, where men assumed superiority over women and weren't afraid to show it, or the U.S., where men assumed the same thing but the smart ones left it in the locker room.

She wasn't a stranger to the problems of Latin machismo. She had a Mexican grandmother on her mother's side—thanks to the failed 1911 Magonista rebellion in Baja California—and a Mexican great-grandfather and grandfather on her father's side. She had Native American mixed with the pure Mexican, as well as several Scots and a roving Norwegian dangling from the family tree. She also had an Irish-Mexican father and a Kazakh-Mexican mother, plus a pure Kazakh grandmother, refugee from some failed tribal revolt after Communism hit the Asian steppes.

Although bureaucratic types labeled her Hispanic, Grace considered herself the perfect all-American mongrel.

Despite being raised from age thirteen in a Santa Ana barrio by her Kazakh grandmother, Grace was always uneasy in Tijuana. Or maybe it was *because* of her teen years in the barrio that she disliked Tijuana. It didn't matter. She never thought about it and never looked back.

That was another thing Marta had taught her.

La Revo, the traditional entry into Tijuana, seethed with open-air sex shops, girlie bars, and hotels that doubled as whorehouses or holding pens for illegal aliens heading north to the Promised Land. A single woman alone in La Revo was fair game, which was why Grace avoided the whole area by using the new port of entry at Otay Mesa.

Avoiding La Revo took longer, time she didn't have but had to take anyway. Just one more price for being a woman in Mexico, a macho world.

The Otay crossing took her down the Avenue of September 16th through the Zona

Río, past bank after international bank, classy entertainment centers, more banks, and enough upscale international stores to bankrupt a Saudi prince.

Grace paid the glittering shops even less attention than she had the border guard. The brief, chilling phone conversation kept echoing in her mind.

It is your son, Lane.

She turned onto the toll road that led south toward Ensenada and hit the accelerator. The big engine hummed happily. Air-conditioning kept the sultry monsoon air at bay.

There was nothing to do about her anxious thoughts except live with them.

The cell phone in her purse chimed. She grabbed it, glanced at the caller ID window, and pulled onto the shoulder of the road. She didn't want to drive while she had a tricky conversation with a United States senator.

She punched the receive button and tried to sound cheerful. "Good afternoon, Chad, or are you still in a time zone where it's evening?"

Senator Chadwick Chandler made a startled sound. "Oh, yeah, that new ID thing. I keep forgetting that you've got a phone that gets past the usual blocks. For a second there, I thought you were clairvoyant."

"I am," she said, careful to keep any edge out of her voice. "That's how I figured out you've been ducking my calls for the last week, all five of them."

Chandler chuckled. In person, the laugh was engaging. Over the cell connection, it sounded like he was choking on the olive in his second martini.

"I'm not ducking my favorite district judge," he said. "Unlike you rich California kids with your horse ranches and golden surfboard tans, we schlubs in the nation's capital have to work double shifts just to stay even."

"My tan is genetic. I haven't ridden a board in twenty years. As for the horse ranch, that was Ted's idea. He thought it looked good as a backdrop for all the fund-raisers he throws for people like you."

Grace winced as she heard the impatience in her tone. Maybe that was why Calderón had insisted on seeing her in person rather than simply talking on the phone. She didn't have a chatty, schmoozing phone manner. Her work didn't leave her any time for it.

"Ted and you are valuable supporters," the

senator said, "and I've always made sure to express my appreciation, even if I do take a day or two to return calls. What can I do for you?"

"You can tell me if the nomination is in some kind of trouble."

"These things need patience."

"I understand that," she said carefully. "But I didn't seek an appointment on the federal appeals court. It came to me. Now it's been on hold for more than two months, and so has my professional life. If the appointment is a no-go, I need to know now so I can get on with my backlog of cases instead of juggling things while waiting to find out if I'm going to be in place for district trials."

On the other end of the line, the senator sighed silently and looked at the oily bottom of his martini glass. He'd rather deal with Ted than the tiger Ted had married and then found out he couldn't handle.

"Your own district court nomination took three months," the senator said. "An elevation to the appeals court will be more thoroughly examined."

Grace listened to the senator's tone rather than his words. She glanced at her watch. She'd spare three minutes, no more. "Let's cut to the chase. You're waffling, which means something is wrong."

"No, not at all. It's just that at this level the background checks take a lot longer, and the politics get a good deal more intricate. I still have every expectation that you'll be nominated by the White House and confirmed by the Senate as the youngest woman on the federal appeals bench, to say nothing of the prettiest."

"Don't."

Chandler sounded surprised. "What?"

"Don't patronize me. I just had to put up with a leering Mexican customs inspector. Any more flattery like that today and I'll go postal."

Again, Grace winced at her tone. She'd known Chad Chandler for a decade. By the standards of politicians, he'd always been a gentleman.

"Sorry," she said quickly. "I'm being pulled in a lot of directions right now and I'm trying to understand what's going on with the appointment. Is the delay because of the divorce?"

"Hell no, nothing like that. This is the twenty-first century."

The silence spread.

The senator took another sip of his martini.

Grace looked at her watch again. "If everything's okay, what's the holdup? We both know I've already been vetted back to my great-grandparents. There's no new ground for anyone to cover."

Silence.

A senatorial sigh.

"Well," he said reluctantly, "there's something that a few folks down at the other end of Pennsylvania Avenue want to explore."

"Such as?"

"Your son. How's Lane doing?"

A sickening jolt shot through Grace's body, like brushing against a naked, charged wire.

"Lane is fine." She tried to modulate her voice, to stuff down the panic that had exploded just beneath her careful professional surface. "Why? What does Lane have to do with this?"

"When I heard about his drug problems, I was concerned and so were some people in the White House. You know how tricky that kind of thing can be."

Grace heard the words as if they were being pushed through a distorter, tones trembling and booming until there was only sound, not meaning.

Drug PROBlems?
DRug proBLEMS.

"I—" she managed.

"It's a concern," Chandler said without waiting for her to finish. "We had a situation last session that was similar. A judicial nominee's daughter had a cocaine problem and the opposition used it to suggest that the nominee would be soft on drug users. It didn't get much traction, but it was a near thing."

Grace swallowed hard.

"Nobody wants that kind of complication on the appeals court level," the senator said. "These days we have such thin majorities and they shift from hour to hour. Surely you understand the need for caution."

An eighteen-wheeler rocketed by on the toll road, its slipstream buffeting the SUV.

"Lane doesn't have a drug problem," she said.

The senator hesitated, sighed, sipped. "Hey, it isn't a big deal. It happens in all families and nobody's saying it will jeopardize your nomination. The White House just wants to be sure there are no unpleasant surprises."

"Well, I've just had one," she said. "Who gave you the idea that Lane is into drugs?"

"Nobody had to. It's kind of obvious."

"Because he's a teenager from La Jolla?"

"No, because he's down in that rehab center in Ensenada," the senator retorted.

"All Saints School is a private high school on the beach north of Ensenada. It's one of the best prep schools on any continent. The Roman Catholic Church runs it and some of Tijuana's finest families send their children there, as well as wealthy families from South America, Europe, and Asia. It's not a rehab center for junkies."

"Grace, I'm sorry if I offended you. I certainly didn't mean to."

"No problem, as long as everyone understands that we didn't send Lane to All Saints because he needed a drug-free environment. Please tell your informants, whoever they might be, the truth about Lane's school."

There was a long pause, another sip, another sigh. Finally, Chandler grunted. "Odd. I can't say who brought it up. I guess it was just an impression I got."

Even though fear was shifting the world beneath her, Grace made certain her voice was level. "Well, since you haven't talked to me about Lane in months, and no one else in D.C. really knows my son, it must have been Ted who gave you the wrong idea."

"Well, now that you mention it . . ."

"When did you talk to Ted?"

"Two weeks ago."

"Did you see him?" Grace knew her tone was too sharp, but there wasn't anything she could do about it.

"He was in D.C. for a few hours, some kind of hush-hush meeting. He just stopped by the Hill for a few minutes to say hello."

She let out a long, silent breath. Someone had seen Ted in the last two weeks. Progress, of a sort.

"Did he say where he was going?" she asked.

"No."

"Do you know where he is now?"

"No. You sound upset."

"I haven't seen or heard from Ted for more than three weeks," she said. "I was hoping to contact him through you."

"Is something wrong? I mean, between the two of you? I thought the divorce was all very civilized."

"It was. It is. I just hoped that . . ." *Ted would step up and be the father Lane needs.*

That Ted would at least call Lane once a week or even every two weeks.

Another truck roared by, belching diesel into the unusually sultry air.

"It doesn't matter," Grace said. "But if you hear from Ted, please ask him to contact me. I'm tired of being his answering service. A lot of people get angry at me because they can't get through to him."

The senator coughed. "I hear you. Take care, Grace. We need women like you on the appeals court."

"Men, too," she retorted, but she laughed. "Good-bye, Chad. And thanks."

She rushed back onto the toll road, leaving a rooster tail of dirt in her wake and wondering if drugs were what Calderón had on his mind.

3

JOE FAROE CAME OUT the front door of Tijuana Tuck & Roll carrying what looked like a two-foot-long section of vaguely curved abstract art carved from oak. The shop that had made the oak piece had been in the same location for more than forty years. It was a hangover from the days of gringo surfers and hot-rodders crossing the border for cheap custom car work. When angora dice and hand-stitched leather seats stopped being cool, the shop had chosen a different business model.

It made the best smuggler's traps to be

had in a city whose economy was based on smuggling.

The output of Tijuana Tuck & Roll was the kind of open secret Mexico thrived on. The shop was surrounded by a stout chain-link fence topped with lazy, deadly loops of razor wire, the kind that would cut a man to rags.

Joe Faroe knew about wire like that, just like he knew about the auto upholstery shop's real business.

Been there.

Done that.

Burned the T-shirt.

Faroe glanced across the street. The man was still there, still leaning in the shadow of a doorway. The watcher looked away when Faroe stared at him, but he didn't move from his post.

A cop, Faroe decided.

The dude's leather jacket and comfortable belly gave him away. For some cops, life was good.

Okay, is he a Mexican cop or an American working south of the line, trying to figure out the latest smuggling wrinkle?

Is he looking for an arrest or a shakedown?

Faroe closed the chain-link gate behind

him and stared at the cop whose leather jacket was almost as expensive as Faroe's.

The dude pretended he didn't exist.

Faroe kept staring.

Finally the cop looked over casually and nodded. He was an old hand. He knew he'd been burned.

"Have a nice day," Faroe called across the street.

The cop shrugged and turned away to light a cigarette.

Faroe strolled along the buckled, treacherous sidewalk toward La Revo. He'd parked in Chula Vista and walked across La Línea—the border. Now he needed a cab back to the U.S. port of entry. There were always cabs next to the zebra-striped burro on the corner of La Revo and Calle Cinco.

The cop stopped smoking long enough to talk into a cell phone or a radio. Faroe couldn't tell which and didn't care. For the first time in decades he had a squeaky-clean conscience.

Around him the air smelled of broken septic lines and tacos with claws in them. The sidewalks were dirty and cracked, cluttered with hunched *indio* beggars, sidewalk souvenir sellers, and a timeless collection of hustlers, thieves, and ordinary people just trying to get by. They peddled leather boxes, brightly painted wooden toys, and T-shirts celebrating the joys of everything from drugs to anal sex. The shops were ramshackle and poorly stocked. The bars advertised lap dancers. Next door, phony pharmacists in white coats peddled cut-rate Viagra and knockoff cancer drugs.

The tourist district of Avenida Constitución tried to be respectable, but it reeked of shadowy bargains, furtive pleasures, and easy vice. Cheap smokes, cheap liquor, cheap sex; everything the bluenoses had squeezed out of San Diego had migrated a few miles south to Tijuana.

Faroe walked the block that had once held the infamous Blue Fox. Sidewalk bar barkers hailed him every few steps.

"Hey, mister, you want some pussy? How about a little fun? Preeeety girls, right here, come in."

A thin man with a thinner black mustache had incorporated sound effects into his sales routine, pinching one side of his face between thumb and forefinger and jerking the flesh of his cheek juicily to suggest sex.

Faroe had heard all the come-ons since

he was fifteen. Once he'd smiled at the grimy tricks. Then he'd become indifferent. Now he was disgusted.

He didn't know if it was an improvement.

He flagged a passing yellow cab and climbed in the backseat with his parcel. Instantly the driver made eye contact in his rearview mirror and gave him a broad, practiced grin.

"I can find anything for you, *señor.* Girls, mebbe? I know where the clean ones are."

"La Línea," Faroe said. "Go back through the Zona Río."

The driver looked at Faroe's eyes, shut up, and turned north.

In three minutes the taxi left the hustling, squalid streets of Old Town behind. Now Faroe looked out on the broad boulevards of Tijuana's international district. When he'd first come to Tijuana, this river district had been an open sewer over a marshy land. It had been equal opportunity sewage—some stayed south of the border and some emptied with the Tía Juana River into the ocean at Imperial Beach, U.S. of A.

The river still carried sewage, but it was underground now. On top were streets like the Paseo de los Héroes, whose high-end international shopping rivaled that of any city on earth.

Stores. Discos. Nightclubs. Restaurants. Banks.

Lots and lots of banks.

Their business towers were modest compared to those in San Diego, but by the one- and two-story scale of the rest of Tijuana, the banks were giant, glistening, new. A mecca for money.

Just shows what thirty billion dollars a year in outside income can do for a city, Faroe thought. *Too bad the billions came mostly from ghetto addicts and barrio hypes north of the line.*

But that wasn't his problem anymore. Steele and St. Kilda Consulting be damned, he was through with the crisscross, double-cross, black-is-white and white-is-black world he'd lived in all his adult life.

Let some other fool risk his butt to save a world that doesn't want to be saved, fuck you very much.

Yet Faroe still felt sorry for the poor citizens in TJ who weren't in on the money game that was going on all around them. They scrambled for a lousy living while most everyone else fattened on the sugar teat of smuggling.

Too bad, how sad, and there's not a damn thing I can do about it. I've retired my broken lance and put poor old Rosinante out to pasture.

And if Steele doesn't understand, he can just shove it where the sun don't shine.

The cabbie dropped Faroe at the edge of the neutral zone called the port of entry. He walked along another street crammed with pharmacies and souvenir stands. A block south of the physical frontier, shops gave way to storefront travel agencies offering passage to Los Angeles and the Central Valley, Wenatchee and Burlington and Spokane, fifteen hundred miles away. Kansas, Chicago, New York, Colorado, the cotton fields of the South; any and all destinations welcoming cheap workers were represented by hawkers competing for warm bodies to fill their quotas.

Faroe passed the long, snaky line of visa seekers outside the administrative offices of the Border Protection Agency. Like someone who has done it many times before, he pushed through the swinging doors that led to the auditorium-sized processing center.

Last stop before American soil.

A customs inspector wearing a blue shirt and a sidearm spotted Faroe's parcel and pointed to the X-ray scanner.

Faroe put the box on the conveyor belt and waited. A second inspector stared at the scanner screen, examining the contents of the parcels and bags on the belt.

Automatically Faroe stepped through the metal detector and wondered with professional interest what would happen. He might not be in the business anymore but was curious to know how his secret traveling safe stacked up against pros.

The scanner operator stopped the belt to look long and hard at the cleanly sawed oak timber. The outlines of a drawer were clear in the ghostly blue X-ray.

The inspector, whose name tag said "Davison," backed the belt up and ran the oak timber through again. He stared some more, then touched a button at his elbow.

From the corner of his eye, Faroe saw two more blue shirts converge on the scanner.

"This yours, sir?" the scanner asked calmly.

"Yes."

A hand touched Faroe's elbow as a neutral voice said, "Come with me, please."

One of the converging inspectors stood close enough to block Faroe's route back to Mexico. The other barred his path to the United States. Both men had their free hand on the butt of a service pistol.

"Sure," Faroe said to the inspector at his elbow. "You want me to carry the box?"

"That's okay. We'll take care of it."

A supervisory inspector grabbed the parcel off the belt and led the way. Faroe fell in behind, careful to keep his hands in plain sight. Obviously the official X-ray had found one of the compartments. The only real question was, had it found the other one as well?

The sign on the door said "Secondary Inspection." Inside was an interrogation room, a government-issue table, and two battered, straight-backed chairs. The two escorts followed Faroe to the door and made sure he went through. Then they turned and went back to their former posts.

The supervisor, whose badge said "Jervis," put the box on the table and faced Faroe coolly. "You look pretty calm for somebody in a lot of trouble."

During his career, Faroe had made a study of ports of entry; he knew the game. Customs inspectors read body language for a living. Faroe's expression, neck pulse, eyes, hands, and posture didn't give the inspector anything to work with.

"I'm clean," Faroe said, "therefore I'm calm. You saw yourself that the box was empty."

Jervis pointed at the parcel, looked at Faroe's passport, and said, "You want to think about that before you get yourself in any more trouble, Mr. Faroe?"

"Nothing to think about. I'm clean."

"Empty your pockets on this table. Then stand over there and lean against the wall, hands up and flat, legs spread. Got that?"

Faroe could have argued but didn't bother. Jervis was paid for an eight-hour shift. He could spend it on Faroe or he could share the wealth with the next hundred people in line.

"Yeah, I get it." Faroe emptied his pockets, assumed the position, and waited while he was thoroughly, professionally patted down. "Relax, I'm not carrying."

"I'm an old man, Mr. Faroe. I got that way by being careful." Jervis checked for knife sheaths along the calves and ankles before he straightened. "Go back to the table and pick up your pocket stuff."

Faroe went back to where his keys, change,

passport, cash, and package waited. While he filled his pockets again, Jervis ripped through newsprint until he'd exposed the two-foot length of oak. In its own spare way, the wood was beautiful. Jervis shook it hard.

Nothing rattled.

Jervis grunted. "Looked like a hollow log on the scanner. Around here, we don't like that. You're in big trouble, mister."

"Not unless they've changed the rules since I wore a blue shirt," Faroe said. "The box is empty."

"So it's a trap. You admit that."

"It's just what the declarations form says— a jewelry box. A handsome piece of wood for the wife to put her rings in."

Jervis eyed him. "You really were a blue shirt? Where? Here?"

"Yeah." Faroe shrugged. "It's been years, but I was."

Jervis inspected the timber closely. After almost a minute, he pointed to one corner.

"There," he said. "I can see the seam of the lid, barely. Nice work."

Faroe wasn't worried that the inspector had found the outline of part of the box. The whole thing would be installed in the bilge of his boat, which at the moment happened to be lacking a two-foot length of timber. Once Faroe was finished doctoring the oak, even someone who knew the trap was in the bilge would have one hell of a time finding it.

"Jewelry box, huh?" The inspector went over the board again carefully, looking for the catch with his sensitive fingertips. "This is about the only place the catch could be."

"Yeah?"

Jervis poked at a round one-inch knot, the only imperfection in the tight-grained oak. Nothing moved. "Huh."

"It doesn't matter," Faroe said. "You've X-rayed it. It's empty."

Jervis sucked air through his front teeth. "I should confiscate this and burn it."

"Not a good idea. There's this thing called illegal seizure."

Silence stretched while the customs inspector rocked on the heels of his leather boots and watched Faroe's body language.

"Get out of here," Jervis said finally, jerking his head toward the door to America. "But you can fire your proctologist, because if I put your smart ass in the computer, you'll get a body cavity search every time you cross a border anywhere."

Faroe nodded. "Have a nice day."

He picked up the timber and headed out the door. With long strides he headed to his car and an appointment with his safe-deposit box in Oceanside Federal Bank. If his luck held, by the time Steele found another only-you-can-do-this lure to dangle under his ex-employee's nose, said ex-employee would be headed out to sea with several million in D-flawless diamonds tucked in the bilge.

Faroe had earned his retirement the hard way. He planned on enjoying it.

And to hell with saving people from their own stupidity.

4

THE UNEXPECTED ROADBLOCK ON the toll road had cost Grace ten minutes of anxiety while sweating *federales* gripped their automatic weapons and peered into cars. Now she confronted another new security checkpoint on the well-maintained dirt road that led to All Saints.

A clean-shaven young man in Levi's and a loose cotton guayabera stood in the center of the road. A lethal-looking black submachine gun hung across his shirt from a long leather shoulder strap. He supported his elbows on the weapon as he watched her SUV approach. Except for the casual shirt, he looked just like the dark, sweaty men on the toll road.

The gun was certainly the same.

Grace hated guns. She had one, knew how to use it, and hated it just the same, hated what it implied: law alone couldn't protect everyone in all places, all of the time.

In addition to the armed man in the middle of the road, she noted a black Suburban with heavily tinted windows parked off to the side. The driver and passenger-side doors were open. There were two more guards in the vehicle. One wore Levi's and a T-shirt, the other had on a black suit with a white shirt and tie.

Both men held assault rifles across their laps.

Uneasily Grace stopped and rolled down her window, holding out her passport. "I'm here to see my son."

The guard's eyes widened when he read her passport. His right hand dropped to the receiver of the submachine gun. His index finger curled around the trigger guard. He turned and whistled to the men in the Suburban. The man in the suit picked up a hand radio and started talking.

Face carefully blank, Grace waited. Card

players weren't the only people who needed poker faces; judges did too. Hers was as good as any and better than most.

Beneath it she was scared spitless.

It is not something to be discussed over the telephone.

"Windows open, *por favor*," the guard standing in the road said.

Despite the polite tone, it wasn't a request.

Grace punched buttons until Ensenada's hot, humid air filled the vehicle. The sun was hidden behind a gunmetal haze of monsoon moisture, and the temperature was hovering near one hundred.

That's why I'm sweating. It's hot.

But her sweat was cold.

The young guard circled the Mercedes, peering carefully through the open windows, making sure the cargo space was empty.

The man in the suit continued to talk into the radio. Grace couldn't hear him, but she knew from the way he watched her that he was talking about her.

The guard with the submachine gun completed his inspection and looked over his shoulder. The man in the Suburban listened to his radio, then nodded.

"Go ahead, *señora,* but drive immediately to the soccer field," the guard ordered.

"Why? Is there something—?"

"Soccer field," he cut in, curtly waving her forward. His right hand was still curled around the trigger guard of his weapon.

The implied threat turned Grace's anxiety into anger. Just as she started to tell the guard what a rude jerk he was, she saw past his weapon to the square-cut tails of his loose shirt. The tails had caught at his waistband, exposing a shiny badge on a leather holder tucked into his belt.

She recognized the badge. It was issued by the same agency that had provided her Mexican identity card—the Mexican Department of Justice.

"Are you a federal policeman?" she asked quickly.

The guard followed her glance. He yanked the shirttail over his badge.

"Go," he said fiercely. *"Andale. Ahora.* Now, quick!"

When Grace hesitated, the guard shifted his weapon. The muzzle described an arc that came very close to her face. Close enough that she could see into the black eye of the barrel.

She punched the accelerator.

Grit and dust shot in all directions as the SUV's big tires spun in response to the sudden power. The guard leaped back and shouted something Grace chose not to understand.

All she wanted was to see Lane, to hold him, to find out what was going on.

It took her less than a minute to reach the soccer field. It was just inside the school grounds on a shelf of land between the administration building and the sandy bluffs that fell down to the ocean. Large, energetic crowds were gathered along both sidelines of the well-groomed grass, shouting and hooting at the action on the field.

Grace shot into a vacant space behind one goal and shut off the engine. Her dark glance searched the field, frantic to see her son.

There! Thank God.

To his mother, Lane blazed like a torch in the center of the field. He moved with such quickness and poise that he looked more like twenty years old than fifteen. Coolly he tap-tap-tapped the soccer ball between two converging defenders. At the last instant he leaped over their sliding tackles, made con-

tact with the ball again, and headed for the
goal.

Maybe it was the smell of the air, hot, humid, heavy with the coming storm. Maybe it
was Lane himself, lean and fluid, confident in
his own body. Maybe it was the time of the
month. But suddenly Grace found herself remembering what she'd worked so hard to
forget, the days sixteen years ago when she'd
slipped her self-imposed leash and spent a
long weekend with Joe Faroe, the only man
she'd ever met who seemed worth any risk.

**The rhythms of the monsoon storm
surge pounding on the shore, on her,
through her, and Faroe's long, lean body
fitted so perfectly with hers, driving her,
driving him, and the unleashed woman in
her demanded more, gave more, took
more . . .**

Grace shook her head harshly, denying
the memories. When she'd married Ted, she
truly hadn't known who was the father of the
baby growing in her womb—Ted or Faroe.
But she'd known that the odds were heavily
with Ted.

And when she held the baby in her arms,
she didn't care who the father was. For the
first time in her life she was completely in

love. Lane's tiny hands, perfect fingernails, and beautiful, blissful hazel eyes were her world.

He'd grown so fast.

Too fast.

She hadn't wanted him to play soccer, but she'd given in, figuring it was safer than football. Now she was glad she'd allowed her son to compete head-to-head with other healthy young males. Like his biological father, Lane was a natural athlete.

Lane zigzagged deeper into the attacking zone, playing the ball like an extension of his body. Suddenly defenders raced at him from all directions.

My God. They're so much bigger than Lane. Older, stronger.

Even when his own teammates fell back, Lane pushed ahead. A defender wearing a red bandanna rolled into a sweatband threw himself in a sliding tackle that was clearly aimed at Lane, not the ball. Lane leaped, but the other "boy" stuck out his feet, tripping Lane in midair and slamming him to the ground.

Grace was reaching for the car door when the referee's whistle sliced through the air. While his teammates gathered around Lane, the referee drew a yellow card from the hip pocket of his shorts and waved it at the tack-ler. The player came easily to his feet and loomed above Lane, daring him to get up.

Lane rolled over onto all fours, shook his head, and scrambled to his feet. He stepped around the referee, trying to get at his at-tacker. Standing face-to-face with Lane, the tackler was clearly older and bulkier. His red bandanna held his black shoulder-length hair from his blunt, handsome *mestizo* features. He could have been a warrior as easily as an athlete. His smile was calm and cold.

The referee stepped back between the two players, waving his arms and speaking quickly.

After a moment Lane turned and jogged away, joining his teammates to wait for the corner kick that had been called.

Grace felt herself begin to breathe again. Her son had a temper. It made him brave but not always smart.

Like Joe Faroe.

As play resumed she heard a gentle tap on the passenger-side window. She looked over and saw the genial brown face of Carlos Calderón. He grinned around his customary black Havana cigar and gestured for her to unlock the passenger door.

More men with more weapons—long guns slung over their shoulders or submachine guns held casually, muzzles toward the ground—flanked Calderón. They had the same easy insolence and edgy eyes as the gate guard.

Do they have federal police badges too?

But Grace didn't say anything aloud. She touched the switch that unlocked the vehicle doors and picked up her purse from the passenger seat. When Calderón opened the door, she thought about asking him to leave his cigar outside. Then she decided to keep her mouth shut and be the deferential female Calderón expected in Mexico. It grated, but not nearly as much as seeing Lane illegally tackled, tripped, and slammed to the ground.

She extended a cool hand to prevent the more intimate Mexican greeting. "Hello, Carlos. How are you?"

"So nice to see you, Your Honor," Calderón said in unaccented English.

With a nod of his head that was just short of a bow, he took her hand in his own soft, well-manicured one. He held on to her fingers moments longer than necessary. It could have been an accident. It could have been a silent reminder that he was a man of power.

He set the limits of politeness, not her.

"I'm very disappointed that you couldn't persuade Ted to come with you," Calderón said.

Grace withdrew her hand. "I told you that Ted is away."

Calderón gave the graceful shrug that was the hallmark of the Mexican male. He lived freely on both sides of the border, but he'd been born in America. He and Grace had even gone to the same private high school in Santa Ana. Yet here, south of the line, he was *todo mexicano,* formal in the way a Mexican businessman might be.

Grace preferred the American version of Calderón.

"I've been very busy," she said evenly. "I haven't spoken to Ted in quite a while. I haven't had any chance to pass on your message."

Calderón puffed on his cigar. "How disappointing."

"You're a very important client of Edge City Investments," Grace said. "Why don't you just call the firm and ask for Ted?"

Why lean on me and make me afraid for my son?

But she didn't say that aloud. Her Kazakh grandmother had been very clear on that point—never show fear.

"Oh, I've tried many times," Calderón said with a rueful smile.

Thick blue smoke swirled around the interior of the vehicle.

Grace put on her courtroom face, the one that wouldn't notice the smell of sewage if it was shoved up her nose.

Calderón glanced over toward a group of men who stood beyond his bodyguards. He took another deep puff on the cigar. The tip glowed hot and red.

She realized that he was nervous.

Not good. Not at all good. She didn't want to know what it took to frighten a man of Calderón's wealth and power.

"You called me down here to talk about Lane," she said. "Ted isn't necessary for that."

Then she snapped on the ignition switch and ran down every window in the SUV. Cigar smoke had made her hurl when she was pregnant. She didn't like it much better now.

Calderón drew hard on the cigar and blew a plume of smoke toward the windshield. "I'm sorry. I didn't make myself clear. There are some aspects of your son's welfare that only Ted can address."

Grace's heart hammered hard beneath her ribs. "Then speak clearly now. Why is one of Ted's oldest friends and his most important business associate threatening me?"

Calderón looked at her, surprised. "Threatening?"

She gestured toward the armed men. "Telling me to come here among all the men with guns. They weren't here before."

"The guards? They're just a precaution. Some very wealthy people send their sons to All Saints. Unfortunately, in Mexico there are kidnapping and other security issues that rarely trouble American parents."

"Interesting, I'm sure," she said evenly, "but what does that have to do with Ted?"

And Lane.

"Since Ted is the parent who signed Lane into All Saints," Calderón said, "the people who run the school asked me to contact Ted."

"I'm as much a custodial parent as Ted is. Either of us can speak for Lane's welfare."

"Custodial. Such a nice term, a legal term, one that sounds good in your American courtroom. But the legal system isn't quite the same here in Mexico. Other, more realistic considerations hold here."

"Are you saying that I can't speak for my son's interests in Mexico?"

Calderón blew smoke. "At this moment, no. Only Ted may do so."

"In that case I'm taking Lane out of All Saints right now. When you find Ted, you can have a long talk with him about custodial parents."

"Taking Lane with you isn't possible," Calderón said, refusing to meet her glance. "Because Ted signed the papers admitting Lane, only Ted can remove him." Calderón threw her a quick, nervous smile. "So now you understand the importance of bringing Ted here, yes?"

Sweat gathered along Grace's spine. She'd seen that kind of anxious smile before, in the barrio, when young *vatos* curried favor with gang leaders. At that instant she understood that Carlos Calderón, a very, very powerful man in Baja California and all of Mexico, was acting as someone else's messenger boy.

Someone violent enough to make Calderón nervous.

Jesus, Mary, and Joseph. Will I never get free of the gutter? Grace asked silently.

She'd spent her adult life forgetting the gutter, ignoring it, not looking back, climbing high and fast to a place where the air was clean and the nights were safe and women didn't have to be arm candy to be allowed into the halls of power.

"Carlos." Grace's voice was quiet and calm, that of a judge presiding over her court. "Are you telling me that Lane is a prisoner here and only Ted can set him free?"

Calderón looked out at the field, where the referee had just blown the whistle, stopping play. Then he looked toward Grace without meeting her eyes.

"I'm sorry," he said. "This isn't the way I would prefer to do business."

He got out of the vehicle and gestured in the direction of the sidelines. Two men separated from the crowd and strode toward the Mercedes.

"Please," Carlos said urgently, "stand with me to greet him. It is simple respect, something a judge understands, right?"

Reluctantly Grace got out of the car and stood an arm's length from Carlos. One of the approaching men was a black-haired Mexican in clean, creased blue jeans, ostrich-skin boots, and a crisp white pearl-buttoned shirt.

Around his neck hung a heavy gold chain holding a large, diamond-crusted medallion.

It was hard to guess the man's age, except that he wasn't young. He had too much sheer macho confidence to be under forty. He walked with a faint limp, like a retired rodeo cowboy with narrow hips and old injuries. His dark face had the strong, blunt features of the people who had lived in Mexico long before Cortés rode roughshod over the land. The man squinted in the shimmering, hazy light. His left eye was milky. He was no taller than Grace.

Understanding went through her like an icy spear. *I know him.*

Hector Rivas Osuna was head of the most powerful, most violent crime family in Tijuana. Grace had seen his face in newspapers and in U.S. post offices on the ten-most-wanted broadsheet.

No wonder Carlos is sweating.

5

THE MAN WALKING NEXT to Hector was a younger, more polished version of the rough-edged crime lord. He wore a silk shirt, Italian slacks, and thousand-dollar loafers without socks. His hair was styled and blown dry. His skin was lighter, his body less beaten. He hid his eyes behind aviator sunglasses.

But the family resemblance was marked, right down to the narrow hips and swagger. Father and son, perhaps, or uncle and nephew.

"Who is the younger one?" Grace asked quietly.

"Jaime Rivas Montemayor," Calderón said very softly. "He's the heir apparent to the Rivas-Osuna Gang. The ROG. Very violent. Very dangerous."

Grace didn't answer, but now she understood why the federal policeman had been eager to cover his badge. He and his buddies were dancing to a tune called by either Calderón or the most corrupt crime boss in Mexico. Seeing Calderón's nervousness, she was betting on Hector Rivas Osuna being the man in control.

Hector stopped a respectful distance away and bowed his head formally to her. "Your Honor."

There was only the faintest trace of derision in his tone.

Grace nodded in return and kept her mouth shut.

"You tell about her son?" Hector asked Calderón.

Hector's English was close to Spanglish, the border creole, rough but useful. As he spoke, he watched the banker with his good eye, tilting his head in a way that pulled apart the lids of his blind eye. It was obvious that he'd been injured—scar tissue puckered whitely in a ragged line all the way to his thick hair. Most men would have worn a patch to conceal the eye's ruin.

Hector wasn't most men.

"Not completely, *Carnicero,*" Calderón said. "I thought some of the details would be more convincing if they came from you."

Carnicero.

Butcher.

Grace was surprised that Calderón would use such a nickname to Hector's face. She glanced beneath her eyelashes at the nephew. He was watching his uncle with an expression of distaste. Either Hector didn't notice or didn't care.

Hector looked at Grace again, examining her the way the Mexican customs inspector had, but Hector's expression was more complex. Some traditional Mexican males were fascinated by powerful women, so long as that power didn't extend south of the Tía Juana River. Apparently Hector was one of those men.

Grace couldn't decide if that was good or bad.

"I hear you ver' important woman, a judge," he said to her. "That mean you smart, so pardon me if I speak plain. I am a plain man. Do you know me?"

Grace nodded.

"*Bueno.* Tijuana is my world," he said calmly. "I make law. I enforce it. *¿Claro?*"

She nodded again.

"Your husband stole my money. *Mucho dinero.*"

Grace's eyes widened and her stomach knotted.

"He don't give that money to me," Hector said, "I kill *el niño,* the son. Is simple."

Bile rose in her throat. She swallowed it back down.

Hector straightened himself out of his slight stoop, stretching stiff muscles in the middle of his back.

Grace remembered reading somewhere that he'd been badly wounded in a shoot-out on the streets of Tijuana. Yet Hector still had a kind of primitive physical power, the kind of raw charisma that some criminal leaders possessed. A very few men like Hector had come through her courtroom, men who lived violently and often died the same way.

But never soon enough for the innocent.

Hector turned and gestured toward the field where play was winding down. "You saw?"

Grace didn't trust her voice, so she simply nodded, feeling like a puppet whose strings were being jerked.

"*El niño,* he get small bump," Hector said. "A warning, so you unnerstand."

Her stomach knotted more tightly and her throat closed. She couldn't have answered if her life depended on it.

It didn't matter. Hector was still talking.

"The big *hombre,* the one that hit Lane? My nephew. He like to give pain." Hector smiled, showing hard white teeth and a few steel ones. He gestured to Jaime Rivas. "This one, he think we hit your son more hard, make bigger unnerstanding." Hector's smile changed, thin and dangerous now. "Jaime no happy. He talk me into *el banco grande* with Calderón and Franklin. Jaime want to kill *el niño,* but I want *solamente* my money. *¿Claro?*"

Grace glanced at Carlos Calderón. He'd turned his back, plainly showing that he wasn't any part of their transaction.

"Yes," she said.

"*Bueno.* Two days."

"Two days? For what?"

"To find *el cabrón* that is your husband."

"That's impossible!"

"Lo siento." Hector shrugged. "The death of a son *es muy triste.* Ver' sad."

Grace couldn't believe what she was hearing. And she couldn't afford not to believe it.

This can't be happening.

But it was.

"A request, please." She spoke quickly, softly, with a steadiness that came from a soul-deep certainty that she would die before she let this butcher kill her son. If that meant begging a favor from one of the most violent men in any nation on earth, then she'd beg. "I must be able to come to the school and see Lane at any time. Surely you understand why."

"Seguro que sí," Hector said, smiling. "A mother, she must see her son. But today a few minutes *solamente.* Surely you unnerstand why."

Grace didn't miss the mockery in his last words. *A matter of power. He's showing me that getting what I want is entirely at his pleasure.*

The Butcher.

How did this happen?

"Yes, I understand," she said tightly.

Jaime's expression was disdainful, as contemptuous of his uncle as everything else in the world. Especially Lane Franklin, gringo son of a thieving gringo father.

"Thank you," Grace added, throttling her fear.

"Don' be sad," Hector said, smiling almost intimately at her. "I learn much time ago always to offer a choice. *Plata o plomo.* Silver or lead. Smart people, they choose the silver."

Grace drew a hidden breath and vowed not to show any weakness. "Do you understand that Ted and I are divorced? I didn't control him when I was married. What chance do I have now?"

"My people say you have power. Use it to please me."

"Power? Hardly. If I really were powerful, you'd be worried that I'd turn my supposed power against you."

Hector laughed. "They want me in El Norte and in Mexico for murder and a thousand other crimes. *Sí,* I ver' afraid of the law." He laughed harder. "You smart, you work for me."

Grace nodded and hoped her face didn't show her fear. Or her hatred.

"You keep this between us," Hector said, "or I kill the boy. *¿Claro?*"

"Very clear."

Hector turned away.

"Did my husband know this was going to happen?" she asked.

Hector paused, tilting his head as he considered the question for a moment. Then he spoke to her with a combination of respect and mockery that was uniquely his own. "I tell you the truth, the whole truth, and nothing but the truth. Is what you demand, Judge?"

She nodded.

"Franklin know," Hector said simply. "Is part of our deal to have *el niño* in Mexico."

Grace couldn't hide her anger. She didn't even try. "Does Lane know he's a hostage?"

Hector frowned and shook his head. "I no scare children. Two days, *señora.*"

Grace started to ask for more time. A look at Hector's bad eye told her to save her breath. His clothes might have been clean, crisp, fresh; his dead eye was a preview of hell.

"*Sí,*" Hector said, smiling. "You smart woman. *Adiós.*"

The aging crime lord turned and strode away, his sour-faced nephew trailing behind.

As soon as they were beyond earshot, Grace turned on Calderón. She looked at him like she'd never seen him before.

"Is your son enrolled here?" she asked.

Calderón nodded.

"You put him up as a hostage?" she asked in disbelief.

Calderón looked at her blankly for a moment, then shook his head. "It wasn't necessary, not south of the line. He would be as vulnerable on the street in front of our home as he is at All Saints. Besides, my son and I aren't at risk. Hector knows I put a lot of my own money into the investment pool Ted stole."

"How much money are we talking about?"

Calderón hesitated, then shrugged. "My own investment was five million."

"And Hector's?"

"Ten times that at least. Twenty times, possibly." Calderón shook his head. "Jaime never told me the whole amount, but he was trying to sell it to politicians and *narcotraficantes* in both hemispheres."

Grace did the math and felt like throwing up.

Fifty to a hundred million dollars.

The referee blew a long, shrill blast on his whistle, echo of the scream throttled in her throat.

Lane broke away from the celebration of his team's victory and jogged toward her.

Calderón looked at his watch. "I'm sorry, but . . ." He shrugged.

"Only a few minutes." Grace took a deep breath and put a bright smile on her face. "You bastard."

Calderón faded out of hearing as Lane ran up and gave Grace a hug that lifted her off her feet. He was taller than she was. Stronger.

His hazel green eyes and fierce grin were like Joe Faroe's.

When did Lane grow so much?

Where did the time go?

How am I going to get him out of this velvet hellhole?

"We kicked butt," Lane said in a deep voice that was also an echo from her past. "Did you see it?"

"I saw your butt get kicked," she said, running her hands over his sweaty head and shoulders. The ripple of lean muscles on his arms surprised her. *He must be lifting weights when he isn't studying.* "Are you okay?"

He shrugged. "Just a bump."

The echo of Hector's words made ice slide down her back.

"Coach—Father Rafael—told me you'd only be able to stay a few minutes," Lane said. "Something about having to rush back home. Is it Dad?"

"Is that what Father Rafael said?" Grace asked carefully.

Lane swept his sweaty brown hair off his forehead with a gesture that was also from the past.

At least Joe wouldn't have put Lane up as some kind of human collateral.

I only knew Joe a few days, but I know that much.

She wanted to blame Ted for being so unspeakably selfish, for not being able to see the wonderful boy who had grown up right under his nose, calling him Dad. But it was her fault. She'd been so busy with her own career that she'd let the marriage slip away.

Not that Ted had been eager to keep things together. He liked the fact that she was successful, powerful. He liked it because she didn't have time to notice that he was never home.

Damn you, Ted. Even if I deserve this, Lane doesn't. He's the only innocent in the mess we call our lives.

"Where's Dad?" Lane asked.

Grace reached over and brushed his

sweaty hair back so she could see his eyes more clearly.

"On the road," she said. "Why?"

Lane looked away, not wanting his mother to see his disappointment. He knew he shouldn't be surprised. Whenever he needed his father, he was somewhere else. Once, just once, Lane wanted his father to be proud of him, to be there when he needed him.

Like that's ever going to happen.

"No big deal," Lane said, turning back to his mother with a smile. "He asked me something about computers and I have the answer now. But it will keep. I'm sure he's got a lot on his mind."

Grace bit back harsh laughter. "That's an understatement."

For a moment there was silence broken only by the distant sound of men's voices as the crowd at the soccer field dispersed.

"Mom, I want to go home with you," Lane said baldly.

"I want that, too." Grace hugged her son close so that he couldn't see her eyes. She didn't want him to know how frightened she was. "But Mexico is run by men."

"So?"

"All Saints won't let you leave with anyone

but Ted. And Ted . . ." She fought against tears and the screams that clawed at her throat. Gently she released her son and stepped back. "I don't know where he is. I'm sorry, Lane. God, I'm sorry."

He hated to see the shadows in his mother's dark eyes, the tension around her mouth, her voice thick with tears.

"Hey," he said. "No problem. When Dad checks in, just tell him that—"

"Your Honor," Calderón interrupted quietly.

"I know," she snarled. "I know!"

Calderón waited.

She hugged her son fiercely. "I love you, Lane."

His arms closed hard around her. "Love you too."

"Remember that."

"You too." He released her and stepped back, looking at her closely. "You okay?"

Grace's smile flashed brighter than the unshed tears in her eyes. "I'm working on it."

6

"What is it that can't wait, Grace?" Stuart Sturgis asked. "We're having a dinner party and—"

"Have you heard from Ted?" she cut in urgently.

"I told you I would call you when and if Ted contacted me."

"I can't wait that long." Grace's hand clenched the phone until her fingers ached. "I have to talk to Ted *now.*"

"I'm sorry. I'm his lawyer, not his keeper. I just can't help you."

"Stu, it's an emergency."

"Look, why don't you have a glass of wine

or two and relax? Ted will probably call in a few days. He's just a footloose kind of guy."

Grace wanted to scream that she didn't have a few days for a footloose kind of guy to show up. Instead, she said, "Sure. Sure. Sorry to interrupt the cocktail hour."

She hung up and looked at her Rolodex. She'd made thirty calls, talked to twelve answering machines, eight spouses, and ten of Ted's friends/business associates who hadn't heard from him in a while but sure would pass along her message if good old Ted happened to call.

There was only one call left to make.

Two days.

She went to the safe, unlocked it, and pulled out a file it was illegal for her to have. But she had it anyway, and she updated it as often as her CIA source could.

Damn you, Ted. Why aren't you ever here when Lane and I need you?

And damn me for choosing the wrong man.

Ignoring the official stamps across the papers that advised her to do everything but Drop Dead Before Reading, she flipped rapidly through the file, hardly seeing the names—Philippines, Belize, Venezuela, Brazil, Paraguay, Guatemala, Colombia, Bolivia, Peru, and most of all, northern Mexico. St. Kilda Consulting wasn't a government agency, but it had employees in all the hot spots in the world. *Outside the law.*

Not outlaws.

Just not officially sanctioned.

Everything Grace had worked to be rebelled at the thought of being caught in a place where the law she loved was worse than helpless. The courtroom was like a hospital—awful things might happen in it, but the purpose was greater than the blood and pain, and at the end of the day everything was disinfected and ready to work again. Not like the gutters, where nothing rose above the blood and pain, and nothing was ever clean.

St. Kilda Consulting worked in the world's gutters.

Grace memorized the number, locked up the file again, and went to find a minimart that sold phone cards. This was one call she didn't want a record of on her monthly statement.

7

DWAYNE TAYLOR REACHED FOR one of the three landline phones sitting on a desk that was neither messy nor neat, simply well used. "Steele's office."

"This is Mandy in triage," a husky voice said. "I've got a Judge Grace Silva on line four. She won't talk to anybody but Ambassador Steele himself. I've forwarded what we have on her to you. File SK1/17."

Dwayne's broad fingers danced across his computer keyboard, found the file, and opened it. "What's her problem?"

"Kidnap/ransom. Beyond that she won't talk to anyone but Steele."

Dwayne scanned the information he'd retrieved on Judge Silva and made one of the intuitive, incisive judgments Steele paid him very well to make.

"Put her on."

Dwayne took the phone off speaker and switched the sound to the headset he wore. "Judge Silva, this is Mr. Steele's personal assistant, Dwayne Taylor. What can St. Kilda Consulting do for you?"

At the other end of the line, Grace held on to her patience by a very fragile thread. "I made it quite clear to the last four people who wasted my time that it was Ambassador Steele or no one."

"I understand. Are you on a secure line?"

She hesitated. This morning she would have laughed. Now she was glad she'd left her house to make the call.

You keep this between us or I kill the boy.

"I think so," she said. "I'm at a pay phone in a cinema multiplex. I've got maybe two more minutes on this calling card. Then I have to go to the minimart and buy another."

Dwayne almost smiled. Whatever the judge was, she wasn't stupid. "Were you followed?"

"I—" It hadn't occurred to her. *God, I hate this.* "I don't think so."

"Is this a matter of extreme urgency?"

"What's your definition of—"

"A terrorist with a gun held against a hostage's head," Dwayne said calmly.

"I—God—no, it's not. Yet."

"How much time do we have?"

"Two days—no, two days from twelve-thirty this afternoon."

Dwayne breathed out a silent sigh of relief. Compared to most kidnap/ransom situations, that was a decent amount of time. He wrote "RED-2" across the notes he was taking.

"How necessary is secrecy?" he asked.

"Life or death."

His pen paused. He circled "-2." "Are you at your La Jolla address?"

Grace didn't bother asking how Dwayne knew where she lived. The CIA file she'd broken rules to get assured her that when it came to private solutions to problems that simply couldn't be made public, St. Kilda Consulting was the best.

That was what she needed.

The best.

"I'm twenty minutes away," she said.

"Go home. In an hour a woman will pick

you up and take you to a secure place. At twenty-three hundred you will have a video conference with Ambassador Steele. That is eleven o'clock Pacific daylight time. Is that satisfactory?"

Grace looked at her watch and automatically asked, "Can't I just call him from my house?"

"Are you going to say anything that you wouldn't like seeing on the eleven o'clock news?"

"Oh. Of course." Grace felt like a fool. "Sorry. I'm not used to this." *And I hate it.*

"That's why you called St. Kilda," Dwayne said gently. "Do you enjoy reading, watching TV, yoga?"

"Excuse me?"

"The next two days will be hard on you. Find a way to relax that won't fuzz your mind."

Dwayne broke the connection, called San Diego, and got the cell phone on its way to her. Then he went to work on his computer. If he was going to dump someone unexpected on his boss, he'd better be prepared with a more thorough background than he had right now. He launched a program, watched for a few minutes, and pushed back from the desk.

It was only a few steps to Steele's suite. The mammoth mahogany door pivoted at its center and opened into a six-sided room with two walls of glass that looked out over Manhattan. The glass had the special sheen that came from being bulletproof, soundproof, and one-way. It was the kind found in high-tech interrogation rooms around the world.

As usual Steele was facing three walls of video screens, speaking into a headset, and sorting through various documents on his desk. Occasionally he typed on one of the computers that stood by waiting to be used, patient as only machines could be. The sixth wall was taken up by electronics and a huge, colorful clock that divided the world into time zones showing light and darkness. The time zones were made by man; they didn't change. The areas of day and night across the globe did.

Without looking up, Steele covered the mouthpiece of his headset with his hand. "What?"

"You have a video telephone conference at two hundred local," Dwayne said.

"Who?"

"Federal Judge Grace Silva, Southern District of California, San Diego."

"Why?"

"She insisted on speaking only to you," Dwayne said.

"So do a lot of people."

"The number she called belonged to Joe Faroe's cell phone. Apparently Judge Silva didn't have the recent code, because her call was routed through to the public St. Kilda number."

Steele spun around and looked at Dwayne. "Interesting. Do we have a good background on her?"

"I'm working on it."

"Work harder. Get help. Anyone who knows Joe Faroe's cell phone is someone I want to know."

"Yes, sir."

Steele didn't answer. He was talking into his headphone again.

Without a sound Dwayne shut the door behind him and went to work on Judge Grace Silva's background.

8

GRACE LOOKED AT THE woman who was driving her to a destination she hadn't shared. In fact, the woman hadn't shared much of anything but the car. Her bearing was military, but her smile and long nails weren't. The glittering tangerine polish was striking against her black skin. The watch she wore was solid gold. Grace knew, because she'd seen one just like it in the window of one of La Jolla's more expensive jewelry stores.

The driver checked the mirrors as often as the road ahead. Other than making turns without warning, sitting with her lights out, and then taking off in a different direction, the driver was very efficient. So was the car. Dark, Japanese, powerful, anonymous.

Grace had the unsettling feeling that she'd fallen through a hole in reality and was now in a totally different world.

Because I have, she told herself. *It's called the illegal world. What did Faroe call it? The shadow world.*

The world where Lane is prisoner.
This can't be happening.
It's happening. Get over it and deal.

The night guard at the office park waved the car through without a pause.

Three minutes and six locked doors later, Grace found herself in what looked like an ordinary video conference room. One of the three large flat-screen monitors was on. It showed a handsome black man wearing an expensive three-piece suit and what looked like a two-carat ruby in his right earlobe. He was looking at Grace's driver.

"Were you followed?" he asked.

"Possibly, but not for long."

"Just possibly?"

"You told me to keep a low profile," Grace's driver said. "Playing tag on crowded streets doesn't qualify."

The man frowned. "Steele doesn't like un-certainty."

"Then he's in the wrong business."

The woman left the room, shutting the door behind her. Firmly.

"Judge Grace Silva?" asked the man on the screen. "I'm Dwayne Taylor."

"You look awfully good for two in the morning," Grace said, conscious of her own rumpled clothes.

He smiled. "The world runs 24/7. Mr. Steele expects us to do the same."

"How do you manage that?"

"I have two well-dressed clones standing by in the closet."

Despite the tension that made her vibrate, Grace smiled.

"Mr. Steele will be with you as soon as he finishes a debriefing," Dwayne said.

The view switched to the room behind Dwayne. Grace saw walls of video screens, other glass walls with views of the Manhattan skyline, and one with a projection of a global map and time zone clock. A computer-driven terminator line showed the sharp edge between night and day as dawn advanced from east to west across the globe. Computers and other electronic equipment she couldn't identify waited at various workstations around the big room. The floor was wood, polished, expensive.

The best money and blood can buy.

The disdainful thought was reflexive. Grace had spent her life studying the law, weighing its nuances, balancing the larger might of society against the rights of the individual.

St. Kilda went against everything she'd worked for in her life.

The law can't help Lane, she told herself roughly. *Don't look back. Don't have regrets.*

If it would free Lane, I'd cut a deal with Satan and every devil in hell.

A silver-haired man in a wheelchair was talking to one of the screens. Six of the eighteen television sets showed the muted talking heads of American news and business channels. Other screens were tuned to international satellite feeds. On the center plasma computer screen, a sweat-soaked man with a three-day beard and a redheaded woman with a bandanna tied across her forehead talked with tired animation. A line of print ran across the screen.

Grace looked at the conference controls in

front of her. She hit the zoom button. "Ciudad del Este" leaped into focus. She ran up the sound, but it didn't help. Only the man in the wheelchair could hear what was being said. She turned the sound down and went back to looking at the two sweaty, exhausted people on the screen.

St. Kilda employees? Grace wondered.

Plainclothes international cops?

Extreme travelers?

Nothing she saw gave her a clue. From what she'd learned about St. Kilda Consulting, any and all possibilities were on the table.

She zoomed out so that Dwayne was center screen again.

"What's happening in Ciudad del Este?" she asked.

"It's a big world. Lots of things happen."

Right. New topic.

But before she could say anything, Dwayne got up and walked offscreen. So she sat and watched the wall with the global clock, hypnotized by the brilliant edge of dawn advancing across the Atlantic toward New York.

Time made tangible.

And Lane's time is running out.

Steele ended the conference and spun his

wheelchair on the wood parquet floor to face his guest.

"My apologies, Judge Silva," he said as he used both hands to propel himself across the conference area to the desk where Dwayne had been. "One of the few things you can say with certainty about my work is that appointments are only as good as the paper Dwayne writes them on."

"No problem, Ambassador. Considering the hour, I'm grateful that you fit me in."

"People who come to us tend to be at the end of their, shall we say, socially acceptable resources. Your love of and respect for the law is the first thing people mention about you."

"So why am I here, is that it?"

"We aren't criminals," Steele said mildly.

"You sure have made a lot of legal agencies unhappy."

"We operate where they can't or won't. Isn't that why you're here—you have a situation that no legally constituted American governmental agency can handle?"

Grace looked into Steele's clear eyes, metallic blue, deep. She saw intense intelligence and something more. Unflinching ruthlessness, if her CIA file was accurate. His natural coloring was pale, made more so because he had a full head of silver-white hair. His face was handsome in an aristocratic way, with a prominent nose that might have been called a beak on a less civilized, less patrician man.

"You said it was a matter of some urgency?" Steele asked, his voice still soft, gentle, and definitely prodding.

Grace had rehearsed her presentation while she waited for the nameless driver to pick her up. It took less than three minutes to bring the head of St. Kilda Consulting up to speed on Lane.

"Admirably concise, much more so than I would expect from a lawyer," Steele said. "What do you want from St. Kilda?"

"My son. Alive, well, and in the United States."

"Again, concise. How much money has gone missing?"

"Calderón wasn't sure. He said Hector had somewhere between fifty and one hundred million in the fund, some of it his own money, some of it invested for others."

Steele looked like a man making mental notes. "Unless the Rivas-Osuna crime family has had an unusually profitable year, some of that must have come from people outside of the family."

"Jaime—Hector's nephew—would be the one selling the fund outside of the family. He's the one that roped Calderón in." Then the implication of Steele's words sank in. "You sound like you know quite a bit about ROG."

"Drugs are a substantial part of the billions in black money that rolls around the globe every hour. Illegal arms dealing is another chunk. Corrupt, legally constituted governments are responsible for the majority."

Although Steele hadn't emphasized the words *legally constituted,* Grace got the point.

"I know," she said. "Legal doesn't always make it right. But it's better than the opposite, violence and anarchy."

Steele nodded. "On that we agree. You've explained your son's situation and your own desires. What of your husband?"

"Ex-husband. We've been separated—a personal rather than a legal state—for some time. The divorce was final a few weeks ago."

"Does Hector know this?"

"I told him. He still thinks I know or can find out where Ted is."

"Can you?"

"If I could, I wouldn't be here. Ted and I may share an address in La Jolla, but he hasn't spent three consecutive days there in years. Other than an e-mail or two, and a voice mail, I haven't heard from him in three weeks."

"Did any of the communications suggest he was in difficulty?" Steele asked.

"No."

"Was the divorce adversarial?"

"No. We're adults and we behaved like it."

Steele lifted his eyebrows. "Could Hector be your ex-husband's stalking horse?"

Grace frowned. "I don't understand."

"You say the divorce was amicable—"

"It was."

Steele ignored the interruption. "—yet you're a beautiful woman in the prime of life, with a very successful career and a brilliant legal future. Quite a catch by any measure, whether it be physical, intellectual, or social."

She blinked, surprised by his summary. "I don't see myself that way."

Steele's smile was a lot younger than he was. "I know. It's part of your allure. By nature men are possessive creatures. Losing you must have stung. Ted wouldn't be the first divorced man to get even with an ex-wife through a child. Revenge isn't a pretty emotion, but it's very powerful."

Grace looked at her hands. Her nails were short, well kept, businesslike, naked of polish. Hardly the hands of a femme fatale. And if Ted had been hurt by the divorce, he sure never showed it.

Looking back, their marriage had died long before the divorce legally buried it.

"Does it matter why Ted did what he did?" she asked finally.

"It might. Revenge can be a more powerful motivator than fear."

"Then you'll have to ask Ted when you find him."

"Is that what you want?" Steele asked. "For us to find him?"

"If that's what it takes to get Lane home safe, yes. But I was thinking more along the lines of having one of your, ah, employees go to Ensenada and bring Lane home. To be blunt, I want your best Latin American kidnap specialist—Joe Faroe."

9

"COVERTLY REMOVING LANE FROM Mexico is the most dangerous of your options," Steele said neutrally.

"What's the safest?" Grace asked instantly.

"Find Ted, find the money, and return it." Steele ignored the phone ringing on his desk. "Tell me about Hector Rivas Osuna and Carlos Calderón."

"They're both rich and well known, but for different reasons. I suspect you know more about both men than I do."

"My files don't have anything new to teach me. You do, Judge Silva."

Grace stared at the image of Steele while she organized facts in her mind. "Carlos Calderón is one of the most prominent men in Tijuana, and in northwest Mexico for that matter. He's the oldest son of a major Mexican politician, a former minister of the interior. His father, Higoberto Calderón, was a member of the ruling class, a kingmaker, very wealthy and very powerful. He passed all of it on to Carlos."

Steele nodded. "Hereditary power. Is that how Ted met Carlos? Mutual financial interests?"

Grace looked at her short nails. "Carlos and Ted have been friends and associates for a number of years. Carlos owns a bank as well as other businesses. My husband owns and runs an investment fund with worldwide holdings. Their interests naturally coincide."

"From your description, Carlos and Ted are rather like mirror images across the border. Both are wealthy. Both are well connected politically. Both have known you for a long time."

Silently Grace absorbed the fact that Steele knew she'd gone to high school with Carlos Calderón. "His grades were worse than mine."

Steele smiled. "It was the same for everyone at Our Lady of the Immaculate Heart. To put it mildly, you excelled at what was and is an intellectually demanding private high school. Does Calderón still live in the United States?"

"No, but at least two of his sisters do. And his mother, I believe."

"That leaves Hector Rivas Osuna," Steele said. "How long have you known him?"

"If you know where I went to high school, you know that I met Hector for the first time today. Sorry, yesterday, by your time. It's after midnight in Manhattan." She glanced at the clock on the wall. "I'm not as much into global time as you are."

"Globalism is at the very heart of St. Kilda Consulting. What do you know about Hector?"

"He's almost courtly for a thug, ugly, ruthless, intelligent, a careful dresser in his own cowboy style. He has the crude charisma that a few criminal leaders achieve. I suspect he had it before he went into crime. Triple testosterone. Whatever. He doesn't respect anyone's law except his own. He has frightening insight into everyone's own special weakness. In my case, my son."

"What about Hector's business?"

"Put ROG into Google and see what you come up with," Grace said roughly.

"I'm more interested in what you know."

She shrugged, hating every second of the conversation, every word that dragged her closer to the barrio gutter her grandparents, parents, and she herself had spent lifetimes trying to crawl out of.

The gutter Lane was trapped in.

Two days.

And one of those was halfway gone.

"The Rivas clan has long been said to control the smuggling trade in Tijuana." Grace's words were as tight as the line of her shoulders. "That accusation has never risen above the level of hearsay, in Mexico or in America."

"Rumors, shadows flickering on the cave wall," Steele said. "You dismiss them. Is that because the rumors have never achieved judicial proof in either country?"

"What I believe personally and what I believe wearing a judge's robe are two very different things. You've already heard my personal take on Hector."

Criminal.

"Tell me about your view of the relationship between Calderón and Hector," Steele said. "What do you know and what do you suspect?"

"What relationship? There isn't one. Carlos is a businessman and—" Abruptly she stopped.

For a moment she looked past Steele to the glass walls. Far off to the north, through a gap in the picket line of lighted high-rise buildings, was the place where the twin towers of the World Trade Center had once stood. Their absence was a monument to the way the world could change from one moment to the next.

Her world certainly had.

"Sorry," she said finally. "That was an old reflex, very deep. If you deny the monster in the closet, it doesn't exist, does it?"

Steele waited with the patience of a former diplomat.

"Everyone," Grace said, "agrees on one thing about St. Kilda Consulting—what happens here stays here."

Steele nodded.

Her mouth turned down. "In any case, I doubt my former client is in a position to object if I talk out of school. Ten years ago, before I was appointed to the federal bench,

Ted talked me into doing some legal work for Carlos Calderón."

You owe me, Gracie. Without me, you wouldn't be considered for a federal appointment. I'm raising your bastard. If you don't want Lane to know, you'll climb off your high horse and do something for me for a change.

"Carlos wanted to sue two San Diego journalists for reporting there were links between his business empire and drug traffickers like the Rivas-Osuna cartel," she said quietly.

"Men like Calderón often fear a free press more than they do the police."

Grace's smile was more of a grimace. "As I investigated the matter, it became clear that the only basis for the news reports was a federal law enforcement intelligence report that had never been made public. In an effort to demonstrate that the source material was unverified and unproven, my law firm demanded to examine the report. We argued that the entire matter was an unfair effort to discredit a well-known Mexican businessman on the basis of innuendo. Racism of a sort. That was the card we played."

"You weren't the first. You won't be the last."

"That doesn't make it easier to live with now."

Denying the monster in the closet was a child's game, one she'd been playing too long. Yet it was still her first and deepest reflex.

Up to now it had worked.

"Go on," Steele said.

"The government claimed that the Calderón suit was nothing but a fishing expedition," she said tiredly. "They argued that turning over the report would reveal the names of dozens of informants. As a defense lawyer, an advocate, I demolished that idea. We won. The report was turned over. Carlos said he was vindicated and there was no point in pursuing the suit."

"The informants died," Steele said, watching her.

Grace closed her eyes. She'd always been afraid that might have happened. Now she knew.

She swallowed bile, swallowed again.

"When I saw Carlos standing by while a notorious drug lord threatened my son's life," she said hoarsely, "I understood that I'd been played for the fool I was. The monster has always been in the closet and all my denial and shoving against the door won't keep him from getting out."

Steele was silent a moment. Then he looked down at his own legs, wasted to sticks, useless.

"For what it's worth," he said, "you aren't the only person in the room to have been fooled by someone like Carlos Calderón."

Her hands clenched. "I've spent my life climbing out of places where criminals strut and cops tiptoe. I won't be dragged back. I won't let them have my son. Right is right and wrong is wrong and common citizens shouldn't live in fear. That's why I dedicated myself to the law."

Silence stretched before Steele sighed. "I thought diplomatic immunity would deflect the small-caliber bullet that my trusted translator fired into my spine. My mistake. My payment."

Tension vibrated through Grace. "Ted is my mistake. *Yet my son is paying.*"

"That's the real reason you're here, isn't it? To right the wrong being done to Lane? You don't care if your husband is a criminal working with criminals or an honest business-man making honest mistakes."

"All that matters is Lane. If I have to deal with Satan—" Again, Grace shut up. "Sorry, I didn't mean to imply that Joe Faroe is the devil." *Even if he is.*

The phone started ringing again. Another one chimed in.

Steele ignored them. "Your attitude is very much that of the safely legal citizen. That's why St. Kildans don't wear uniforms or talk to reporters. It's one of the reasons that professional counterterrorists hide their identity by wearing black ski masks. They aren't ashamed of their job, but they *are* targets who get tired of trying to explain to people living in the black-and-white world that reality is a thousand shades of gray, yet some things are still worth killing or dying for."

"I—"

Steele kept talking. "St. Kildans work among the shades of gray. All of them. The shadow world. All the places where good citizens don't want to go, don't want to know, don't want even to think about."

"I know."

"But do you know that when reality rears its complex head—and it always does—citizens, politicians, and journalists race to blame the messenger? Mr. Faroe has already felt the impact of just such an exercise in civic piety."

She nodded unhappily. "I first met Joe about sixteen years ago, just before he was arrested and sent to federal prison."

Days before, to be exact. Time enough to fall in love and then watch him turn on me, screaming accusations in gutter Spanish while I cowered beyond the reach of TV cameras and reporters in a shadowy apartment hall.

The flash of steel handcuffs and metal badges was something she'd never forget.

So was the savage hatred in Faroe's face.

She'd done what he wanted—she'd run and kept on running, never looking back, staying the hell out of his life.

Until now.

Ruthlessly Grace stuffed the memories down and locked them in the deepest closet of her mind. It had been sixteen years. She needed Faroe. If he still hated her, she'd just have to suck it up and take it. Lane was all that mattered.

Steele waited while Grace looked somewhere only she could see. He needed to know her state of mind. He wouldn't find out anything useful if his own mouth was open.

"I've kept track of Joe through the same contacts who got me a copy of the CIA dossier on St. Kilda Consulting," Grace said tightly. "When Joe got out of prison he went to work for you. Since then he's been involved in activities in southern Europe, Asia, Iran, and most often, South America. Some of those activities have been termed 'morally ambiguous.' "

"Does that bother you?"

"Yesterday, yes. Today, I don't care. Today all that matters is my son. Joe Faroe is the only man I'll trust with Lane's life."

"I'm sorry to hear that."

"Why?" she asked, startled. "Don't you trust Joe?"

"I trust him far more than either of you can imagine."

"Then what's the problem?"

"A week ago Joe Faroe was exactly what you said—St. Kilda's best operative, especially in Latin American kidnap situations."

"And now?"

"He retired."

"Try again," Grace shot back. "He's way too young for retirement."

Steele smiled sadly. "Where Joseph has spent his years, time isn't the best measurement of age. His last assignment was particularly difficult. Among other unpleasant things that occurred, he was forced to kill a good friend who was trying to kill him."

Grace made a low sound.

"Despite the bloodshed," Steele continued, "the operation itself was a success. Forty percent of the money recovered came back to St. Kilda, as per the contract. Joe took his five percent, told me to go to hell, and walked out. I haven't heard from him since. Knowing him, by now he could be anywhere on earth."

"Knowing St. Kilda Consulting," Grace said, "I'd bet you know exactly where Joe is."

"To what point?" Steele asked. "He's never been motivated by money. The idealism that led him to be an agent for the Drug Enforcement Administration was kicked out of him in federal prison. What does that leave you for leverage?"

"Pride. I can clear his name."

And I should have done it before now. I should have believed in him and searched and . . .

But she'd been married then, the mother of a young child.

Now she was divorced and fighting for that child's life.

"How can you do that?" Steele asked.

"I have the rest of the story, the part that never made the news. Joe was set up and sent to prison because he wouldn't hand over two men beneath him as politically convenient international scapegoats. I have proof, and I have the political clout to arrange a pardon. How's that for leverage?"

Steele raised his eyebrows. "It will be interesting to find out. Your driver will give you a single-use cell phone. It will ring as soon as I'm certain of a few things."

Grace hesitated. "Please don't tell Joe my name ahead of time."

Surprise flickered over Steele's face. "Why?"

"He hates me."

"Interesting," Steele murmured. "You're the first."

"What?"

"Joe Faroe is a man of few emotions. Prison taught him that. How do you feel toward him?"

"He was the worst mistake of my life."

And the best.

But that was something Steele didn't need to know.

10

JOE FAROE WAS HEAD down in the bilge of the *TAZ,* mixing epoxy and watching the resin slowly change color. The oak of the hull where the trap would be concealed was fifty years old. It had been exposed to the waters of two oceans and the pounding of countless waves. Matching the smuggler's trap to the salt-aged and oil-stained wood in the bilge was more art than science.

Faroe had been working on it most of the night and into the day.

In the glare of the halogen work light, the wood was brown, then gray, then brown again. The cuts he'd made to receive the trap revealed fresh, bright wood. He'd dyed the rib from Tijuana with several shades of stain. Now he had to match the color of the epoxy exactly or he would have to start all over.

Again.

Naturally, the moment the epoxy was ready, the satellite phone rang.

Other than cursing, he ignored the interruption. With a foam brush he painted glue onto the ends and the bottom of the trap.

Above him, in the stateroom, the phone rang a third time, then a fourth. The answering device snapped on and played Faroe's new greeting.

"If you reached this number by mistake, hang up. If you didn't reach this number by mistake, hang up."

The caller punched in a digital code that overrode the message. Only three people knew that code. Faroe didn't want to talk to any of them.

He finished applying the epoxy and eased the box into position in the beam.

"Joseph, I need to speak with you. Immediately."

When Steele chose, he could put the bite of command into his aristocratic voice.

Faroe hesitated.

Then he went back to work with a pad of steel wool, rubbing the excess epoxy off the seam.

"If you don't pick up the call," Steele said, "I'll send an Oceanside cop out to your address to conduct a welfare contact. You've been sick, you know, and I'm very concerned that you might be lying helpless, ill, unable to reach the phone."

Faroe cursed again, louder this time. He tried to scrape away the last of the excess epoxy but it had already hardened. Now he would need a belt sander to finish the job.

He rolled over, sat up, and punched the talk button on the cellular phone. "No."

Steele ignored him. "I have a message from an old friend. U.S. District Judge Grace Silva."

Faroe chalked up the hollow feeling in the pit of his stomach to surprise. It sure didn't have anything to do with the flood of memories that threatened to choke him. Some of the memories were the best of his life. Some were the worst.

He didn't know which kind hurt more.

"Joseph?"

"I knew a Grace Silva back when I was with DEA. She wasn't a judge then. She was a federal defense attorney. A good one. Too damn good."

And once, long ago, he'd believed that she'd set him up to be dragged through the gutter with the rest of the criminal slime for the entertainment of the TV cameras.

"It's the same woman," Steele said. "She wants to retain the services of St. Kilda."

"What does a politically prominent federal judge need with a bunch of private, and therefore unsavory, consultants?"

"I'm sure she'll tell you. She's approaching your dock as we speak."

The feeling in Joe's stomach went from hollow to something more complex. "Steele, what do you want with a tight-assed feminist and a very respectable party hack who has been rewarded with a position on the federal bench?"

"Is that how you think of her?"

"It's how she comes across in the newspapers."

And Faroe had been a fool for lingering over the articles, staring at the pictures, trying to find the ghost of the most explosively passionate woman he'd ever known.

"St. Kilda occasionally needs the services of powerful politicians," Steele said.

"So service her."

"Unfortunately, she refuses to be serviced by anyone but you."

Faroe knew he was being baited. Steele was a master at that. But he'd never cast a lure like Grace Silva into the pool.

"I got the feeling the two of you were once very close," Steele said.

"So is a snake to his skin. Doesn't keep him from shedding it."

"Good. The judge made it quite clear that her interest was business only. She has already wire-transferred two hundred and fifty thousand dollars into St. Kilda's accounts."

Faroe went to the refrigerator that was built into the stateroom bulkhead. He looked at the cold beer but took a bottle of spring water instead.

"Silence isn't a useful answer," Steele said.

"I don't need the money."

"Judge Silva said that she was in a position to offer you a presidential pardon."

Faroe drank down half the water before he said, "I don't care whether I can vote or not, and I don't need to worry anymore about carrying a firearm. So I'm pretty much okay with my status as a convicted felon."

"Surely you'd prefer to have your name cleared."

"Actually, my spotted past makes a pretty good pickup line. Woman asks me what I do, I tell her I'm a convicted felon. The dull ones run. The rest move closer."

Steele made an impatient sound. "Judge Silva must have gone to considerable trouble to unearth the story of your unfair arrest and imprisonment."

"Grace always did worry about unfair treatment. In front of a jury she could work up tears on behalf of some of the most brutal smugglers of drugs and human beings on the entire Mexican border."

"Then I'm surprised you had anything to do with her."

"You had to be there to understand," Faroe said roughly.

Monsoon thunder all around, lightning blazing, a kind of hot rain pouring over him that he'd never felt before or since.

He'd spent a long time trying to forget, but it wasn't long enough. In the silence between lightning and thunder, she still haunted him.

"What does Grace need with me or with St. Kilda?" Faroe asked finally.

"Her son is enrolled in some highly regimented private school just north of Ensenada. She wants help bringing him home."

"Send one of your newbies," Faroe said. "It will give him or her practice in the fine old art of bribery."

"Unfortunately, it's not that simple. A Mexican businessman named Carlos Calderón and another man, Hector Rivas Osuna, object to the boy's removal."

Faroe whistled through his teeth. "That's a real pair to draw to."

"You always understand things the first time through, Joseph. It almost makes up for your lack of other graces. Please give the judge a civil hearing. I've already discussed the financials with her. Your cut will be a hundred thousand dollars."

"Back up. I'm not accepting assignments. I quit, remember?"

Faroe was talking to himself. Steele had cut the connection.

A low, haunting voice floated down from the dock. "Permission to come aboard?"

Past and present colliding.

I don't need this.

But part of Faroe sure wanted it. The dumbest part of him. The one that was guaran-damn-teed to get him into trouble.

I turned forty last year. I don't react like this anymore.

The dumb part of him just kept pushing.

"I'll be up in a second, Judge."

11

When Faroe stepped out onto the main deck of the *TAZ,* the morning sun was heating up the unusually humid air. The water in the heavily sheltered bay moved uneasily, echoing the power of the Baja hurricane boiling up from the south. *Chubasco* weather.

Just like the last time.

Grace Silva stood on the dock, looking up at him, shading her eyes with her hand even though she wore sunglasses. She wore a white silk T-shirt and blue jeans. She wasn't thin, she wasn't fat. She was just all woman everywhere a man liked to feel the difference.

Sixteen years hadn't changed her nearly enough.

Damn you, Steele. Did you know or did you just guess?

"Hello, Joe. How have you been?"

For a moment Faroe didn't answer. He didn't trust his voice not to be too rough, too hungry, too angry, too everything. Grace had always done that to him, slid past his defenses and grabbed him where he lived and breathed and hoped.

Son of a bitch.

He shoved his hands into the hip pockets of his jeans and looked out at the ocean beyond the jetty. The surface was gray, slick, almost oily. Waves were breaking with a deceptive, lazy grace that made the jetty tremble.

Not a good time to be out at sea.

Not a good time to be docked.

Welcome to life with Grace Silva.

When Faroe looked back down at Grace, she'd removed her sunglasses. Some of the sixteen years showed around her eyes. She looked tired, tight, almost brittle. She also looked wiser, more mature, less sure of herself, and very unsure of her welcome with him.

"I'm fine, I guess, all things considered," Faroe said. "What about you?"

"Have you talked to the Ambassador?"

Faroe nodded.

"Then you know I'm desperate. Otherwise I wouldn't have the nerve to come here."

"Nerve?"

"Yeah. Nerve. You're not an easy man to face."

"I'd think judges would be used to facing felons."

Grace looked away from Faroe's measuring green eyes, intense eyes shaped so much like Lane's she felt like the dock had been snatched from beneath her feet, leaving her dancing on air. She wanted to scream, to run away, to throw herself into Faroe's arms and find the wild oblivion she'd known only with him.

I'd think judges would be used to facing felons.

"Usually they haven't had sex with them," Grace said bluntly.

Faroe almost smiled, almost swore. Then she squared her shoulders and drew a deep breath. The movement outlined her breasts against the silk of her shirt. Faroe wanted to look away but couldn't. He'd felt a primitive physical attraction to her the moment he saw her sixteen years ago. That hadn't changed.

He wondered if it ever would.

"Do you think this is easy for me?" she asked, her voice too husky.

Faroe stared at the wind vane on top of a sailboat's tall mast. The vane pointed into the wind, helpless to do otherwise. And he, well, he was helpless, too.

Or hopeless.

"My son . . ." Grace's voice failed. "I need you. Lane needs you. Help us. Please."

Faroe turned and looked back at her. She wasn't wearing makeup or high heels or an unbuttoned blouse or tight pants. Nothing to grab a man's attention. Her nearly black hair was short, clean, and shot through with some silver threads a woman with more vanity would have hidden.

"Steele mentioned two names," Faroe said. "I can understand how dudes like that might make you desperate. Steele certainly thought so. He normally doesn't ask for a quarter million, unless you're insured to the gills."

"He could have asked for double that amount," Grace said. "And no, I'm not insured. Neither is Lane."

Faroe blew out a long, silent breath, trying to shake off the past. Whatever else had happened between himself and Grace, her child wasn't part of it.

And that child was in the hands of butchers.

"Come aboard," Faroe said. "We can talk below."

The relief that swept through Grace left her light-headed.

He's not going to turn his back on me. On Lane.

The step up from the dock was more than a foot and the ship moved unpredictably on the restless water. She looked warily at the gap between the dock and the deck.

Without thinking, Faroe held out his hand to her.

Grace ignored it. Instead she grabbed one of the stanchions and pulled herself aboard.

You want me, Faroe thought, *but you don't trust me. That hasn't changed, either.*

12

FAROE LED THE WAY through the hatch into the stateroom. Another hatch was open into the bilge below. The work light was pointed directly at the unfinished beam. Rough epoxy outlined the seams of the smuggler's trap. Casually he picked up the section of the floor and closed off the bilge. The power cord kept the hatch ajar.

"Looks like one of those smuggling things you used to tell me about," Grace said.

"Hell's bells," Faroe muttered. He picked up the floor section again and set it aside. "Go ahead, take a good look. This is going to be the worst-kept secret on the border."

Grace studied the box for a moment. "I take it you won't be smuggling elephants."

In spite of everything he smiled. Her words were the punch line from a customs joke he'd once told her about Indian border inspectors and a devious mahout. Each day the mahout and his elephant appeared at the port of entry. The mahout was searched, as was his elephant. Then they were allowed to go on. This happened for weeks, until some smart inspector figured out that the elephants were the contraband.

"I told that story a year ago," she said. "It was at the sentencing of a Mexican smuggler." She looked into the bilge and added, "You may or may not appreciate the fact that I gave him ten years."

"Then you've learned that there really are smugglers in this world. That's a good thing for a judge to know."

Grace's smile faded. "Oh, I've learned a lot more about the nature of humanity and the shadow world, as you used to call it." *As of yesterday, I learned more than I wanted to know.*

"I still call it that. Nothing's changed, except we're older and the crooks are younger."

Faroe yanked the power cord out of the socket and dropped it into the bilge. He put the floor hatch back in place.

"Can I get you something?" he asked, trying to sound polite. "Water? Beer? There's a little coffee left."

"Coffee would be fine," Grace said. "Black."

That hadn't changed either.

As Faroe rummaged for a clean cup, Grace looked over the rest of the salon. The *TAZ* had at least one computer, video screens, telephones like those she had seen in Steele's office, and a smaller version of the Ambassador's global clock.

"A wooden boat." Grace didn't know whether to laugh or cry at Faroe's stubborn determination to do things on his own terms.

"She was built in Inverness, Scotland, in 1956," Faroe said, handing Grace lukewarm coffee in a clean-enough cup. "She started out as a herring boat in the North Sea. If you dig down between the hull planks, you can still find fish scales."

"I never figured you for a herring fisher."

"I'm rigging her for blue-water cruising. She only does ten knots, but she can keep that up for months at a time."

"Are you single-handing her?" Grace asked, then realized she was holding her breath for the answer. *Stupid, stupid, stupid.*

Faroe nodded.

She told herself she wasn't relieved. But she was. "Steele said you'd retired."

"Yes." The word as closed as Faroe's expression.

She didn't take the hint. "I can't imagine you idling away the next forty or fifty years."

Neither could Faroe, but it wasn't a topic he wanted to discuss with anyone, including himself. If that made him pigheaded, so be it. A man was entitled to the occasional indulgence.

Silence grew.

"We never were very good at small talk," he said, gesturing toward the little chart table in the center of the salon. "Do you have a ransom note?"

Grace sat at the small table. "Nothing that obvious. Carlos and Hector simply made it real clear that Lane wasn't leaving without Ted's—my ex-husband's—signature on the form. Unfortunately, Ted is in the wind somewhere, not returning calls or e-mails. He's not just ducking me, either. I'm getting calls from angry people at all hours of the day."

Faroe nodded. "Tell me about Carlos and Hector and your last visit with your son."

Grace sipped, organized her thoughts, and gave Faroe the same presentation she'd given Steele. Faroe listened intently, his eyes focused on the grounds at the bottom of his own coffee cup, a fortune-teller looking for something in the murk.

He's learned to listen, she realized. *Sixteen years ago, he talked more. At least with me.*

Not that they'd spent a whole lot of time talking.

". . . and then I drove back to the border as fast as I could," she said. She'd been crying silently all the way, but that wasn't something Faroe needed to know. "I wasted hours calling everyone I could think of. Then I called your cell phone. St. Kilda answered."

Faroe swirled the cup, drained the last dregs, and looked up at her.

Grace went still. His eyes were still that astonishing cool green, almost the color of a jade pendant she'd worn the night of their first date. She'd understood from the moment she first saw him that she would sleep with him, even though she knew better. All her life she'd been a dutiful, good girl.

But not with Joe Faroe.

**He's the worst mistake I ever made.
And the best.**

"Sounds like Colombia, not Mexico," Faroe said finally.

"What do you mean?"

"C'mon, Grace. You're not that naïve."

"I've never been to Colombia and only rarely to Mexico," she said.

Faroe shrugged. "Kidnap and extortion are a way of life in Colombia."

She swallowed hard. "You have a way of making it sound so . . ."

"Ordinary?"

"Yes."

"It's much more common than you want to know," Faroe said. "There are a lot of places in the world where hostage-taking is a way of life. Didn't Steele tell you about what he so elegantly refers to as 'the Sanguinary Exchange'?"

"What a grim phrase. I guess he was too much of a diplomat to use it with me."

"Too bad. The term describes what you lawyers might call an exceptional business model."

"Meaning?" she challenged. *He still hates lawyers. Why am I not surprised?*

"When a businessman can't rely on contracts and statutory protections to guarantee performance, he finds other ways. If he fronts, say, a ton of cocaine to a smuggler, he expects the smuggler to put up a son or a daughter or a wife in return."

Grace grimaced. "All right. Yes. Of course I've heard about such things, but not here, not as part of American life."

"And you don't want to know about it."

"Not everyone likes living in the gutter. Most people want more."

Didn't we have this conversation sixteen years ago?

Both thought it.

Neither said it aloud.

"It's all very civilized," Faroe said, his voice neutral and his eyes cold. "The hostage takes a little vacation trip to Bogotá or Medellín or Cartagena. They get to stay in a nice hotel, all the comforts that money can buy, no car batteries wired to their genitals, no cigarette burns. In a month or two, they fly home with a good suntan . . . so long as things go well with the shipment. If something goes wrong, too bad, how sad, you're dead."

Grace put her cup on the table hard enough

to send coffee jumping over the lip. "Blunt. Yes, I remember that about you."

"Pretty words don't make a situation pretty. The Mexicans have been hauling loads for the Colombians for years." Faroe set his own coffee mug aside. "I guess the Mexicans have taken over the kidnap part of the business model. But then, you kind of knew that, didn't you? You're a very bright person. You were usually miles ahead of me in terms of seeing how the world worked beneath the legalities."

With cold eyes, he waited for her response.

"Do you really believe I'm involved with something as twisted and corrupt as drugs and hostages?" she asked.

"That's a no-brainer. You *are* involved. The only question is how much you know."

"You're still a real hard-case son of a bitch, aren't you?" Grace said it calmly, like she'd just discovered he still ordered his steak blood rare.

"It's a hard-case world out there. And isn't that what you're spending two hundred fifty grand for? A hard-case son of a bitch who can deal with this problem efficiently, ruthlessly, few or no questions asked?"

Grace stared at Faroe, trying to see past the cold eyes and expressionless face of a man who'd spent his adult life working undercover against drug smugglers and murderers.

"Right," she said. "I got what I asked for." *Lucky, lucky me.*

"So, are you involved?" Faroe asked, pouring himself a little more coffee.

"In what?"

"In whatever deal Calderón and Rivas are on the other side of."

"You insulting, overbearing, obnoxious—" Grace bit off the rest. She needed him. Lane needed him. "No. I'm not involved."

Faroe watched her closely, searching for the microexpressions of deception. He glanced quickly at the vital triangle at the base of her throat. Her pulse beat steadily beneath smooth skin that was the color of light toast. She faced him without flinching. Her lips were drawn back in a snarl that was much less civilized than her words.

Not lying.

"But you do have some idea of what Calderón and *el jefe chingón* want, right?" Faroe asked.

Grace translated the nickname in her mind and made a face.

"Yeah," Faroe said, watching her over the rim of his coffee mug. *El jefe chingón.* The head motherfucker. That's what they used to call Hector Rivas Osuna, back when I was buying dope in the Pussycat bar on Revolución in Tijuana."

"Delightful." Grace looked at her clenched hands and slowly unlocked her fingers. She didn't know why Faroe was baiting her, but she knew that he was. "There was talk about money, but I don't think it's merely that."

"Merely?" He smiled grimly. "Spoken like the wife of a billionaire."

"Ex-wife."

He shrugged and told himself he didn't care. "So you're half a billionaire."

"Don't count on it," she shot back. "All I got from Ted was the house my salary had been making payments on for ten years, my car, and half of a horse ranch that is a college fund for Lane."

"Then how could you afford St. Kilda Consulting?"

"The old-fashioned way—I mortgaged my house. Anything else you want to know about me and money?"

"If the boys down south don't want money from you, what do they want?"

Grace had thought about that a lot on the way back from Mexico. "Ted."

"Why?"

"They say he stole money from them."

"Did he?"

"I don't know," she said. "He's had dealings for years with Carlos, but I don't know any of the details."

"Yet you let your soon-to-be-ex-husband send your son south. Why?"

Grace made herself ignore the baiting tone and answered the question. If she'd thought yelling at Faroe would do any good, she'd have started screaming the instant she set foot on the dock.

"Lane is very bright, very bored in school, and a wizard with computers," she said. "He's a teenager in full hormonal rush. His judgment isn't all it could be."

"Drugs?"

"No! He hacked into the school computer and changed his grades."

Faroe almost smiled. "I like the kid already."

"Ted had been saying that I was spoiling Lane. Maybe he was right. But someone had to make up for Ted's indifference to—" She stopped, got a better grip on her emotions, and said, "I knew that something had to be done about Lane. He loves me, but he wasn't listening to me or anyone else."

"He's a teenage boy. It's called age-appropriate behavior."

"Is that what you did, kick back at anyone in authority?"

"Pretty much," Faroe said.

"I feel sorry for your mother."

"She was dead before I was fourteen."

"Something else we have in common," Grace said.

"What?"

"My mother died when I was thirteen. So did my brother and my father. I was babysitting a few blocks away or I'd be dead too."

Faroe felt a sympathy he didn't want and Grace didn't need. "Car wreck?"

"My father was an undercover cop working drugs in Santa Ana. One of the drug dealers found out. He shot everyone and fled to Tijuana. By the time I got home . . ." She shrugged.

"You found them?" Faroe asked, horrified at the thought of a thirteen-year-old Grace walking in on a slaughterhouse.

"Yes."

"Jesus."

"That was the moment I dedicated myself to the law. Law was everything the gutter wasn't. Law was all that separated humanity from violence and horror. I wanted to do everything I could to make certain that no more thirteen-year-olds walked into a house of blood and death." Grace looked down at her hands, clenched again. She released her fingers. "Sorry. I don't know where that came from. It was a long time ago."

"You're telling me why the law is your religion, and there's no way you'd sell it out for a handful of silver."

Her eyes widened, revealing both clarity and darkness. "You always saw parts of me better than I saw them myself. It intrigued me almost as much as it frightened me."

"And you saw me. Scared the hell out of me. We're alike in that, at least. Long ago, far away, and nothing to do with today."

"You're right." *And you're so very wrong.* "I went with Ted to see All Saints School. It was, and is, very impressive. A beautiful campus on the beach north of Ensenada, run by the Catholic Church. The teachers are excellent. Until yesterday, I've been able to come and go freely, to see him at least once a week. I could talk to him on his cell phone, until it broke. He used the school computer to e-mail me all the time, until three weeks ago."

"What happened?"

"Something technical about the uplink." She shrugged. "I use computers, but I don't understand them."

Faroe stood up, grabbed a pair of binoculars from a drawer, and went to the porthole. "Where's Ted now?"

"I haven't seen him in three weeks."

Faroe looked over his shoulder at her. "Is that unusual?"

"No. We haven't been close in years."

"You always looked so good on the society pages, the happy and dynamic power couple, out to run the world together."

"Don't tell me you believe everything you read in newspapers," she said coolly.

"Touché. So you and Ted haven't done the nasty recently?"

Grace came to her feet and got right in Faroe's face. "My sex life is none of your business."

"Ease up. I was just trying to figure out whether Ted was the jealous type."

"Why do you care?"

Faroe stepped back from the porthole and

told himself he couldn't smell the woman-scent of her.

His body told him he was lying.

"If Ted was jealous, I'd have a good explanation for the dude up on the dock." Faroe gave Grace the binoculars. "He's got a pair just like these and he's been trying for the last ten minutes to figure out what we're doing down here."

"He's spying on us?" She stepped swiftly away from the porthole.

"Yeah. Now all we have to do is make sure it's you he's after, not me."

13

GRACE JUST STARED AT Faroe. "You think somebody might be following me?"

"Use the binoculars," Faroe said impatiently. "Do you recognize him?"

Reluctantly she went to the porthole again. He made room for her by moving aside. It wasn't enough. She could sense the heat of his body and smell the coffee on his breath. She wanted to tell him to back up, to get out of her space, but she didn't want him to know how much he affected her physically.

Silently she looked through the porthole toward the gangway that led up to the marina parking lot.

"I don't see anyone," she said after a few moments.

"He's smarter than your average mutt," Faroe said, his voice very close to her ear. "He's using the phone booth as a blind."

With her naked eye, she just made out the figure of a person inside the telephone booth at the head of the gangway. When she lifted the field glasses, she came face-to-face with a dark-haired man who was staring at her through his own binoculars.

Startled, heart racing, she jerked away from the porthole. Her back slammed against Faroe's chest. She smelled his skin, yeasty, warm, familiar.

That hadn't changed.

"Easy," Faroe said. "He can't see you behind the porthole glass."

Grace drew a deep breath and inched forward until she could see the gangway again. When she lifted the binoculars, they felt like they weighed ten pounds. Her palms were sweaty. Grimly she focused on the man in the phone booth.

"I don't know him," she said. "And you can't be sure he followed me. Given your line of work, you must have made a lot of enemies."

"This isn't a courtroom, Your Honor. This

is the real world, the one that lives beneath the nice legal world of reasonable doubts. The first thing you learn down here is to go with your best guess."

"You think he's after me."

"The only person stepping on my shadow right now is Steele. So, yeah, I think this bogey is yours." Faroe leaned over slightly, just enough to get a good whiff of her hair. It smelled clean and expensive and sexy. "Which means that he followed you here, which means that you've been under surveillance for an unknown amount of time. Not good, *amada.*"

Darling.

Grace caught her breath. Maybe he called all his women *amada,* but Faroe was the only man who had ever used the endearment with her.

And he was too close.

She could feel his breath stirring her hair when he spoke. She lowered the glasses and tried to turn toward him, to force him out of her space.

He didn't move. He stood there with a faint, irritating half smile on his face.

He knew.

She stepped sideways and held the

glasses like a barrier between their bodies. "Why is it bad that I'm being followed?"

"Because now he knows there's a connection between us."

"He's wrong," she said instantly.

Faroe laughed. "He knows that you're down here with me. That means we know each other. That's all the string he needs. He pulls on that, runs the registration on my boat. That leads him to an overseas corporation in Aruba."

Grace stood very still.

"Then, if he's any good," Faroe said, "the dude finds somebody in Aruba to bribe. He gets the background of that Aruba corporation. That leads him to the lawyer I used to set up the firewall between me and the world. If the lawyer is as crooked as I think he is, he'll sell my name the instant the price is right."

"But—"

Faroe kept talking. "Before you can say 'shuckey darn,' the dude on the dock knows you're talking out of school and hiring a pricey international troubleshooter to help you break your son out of his cozy prison."

Horrified, Grace stared at Faroe. She wanted to argue, to say it couldn't be that way.

She couldn't have signed her son's death warrant.

But the truth was there in Faroe's eyes, Lane's eyes accusing her, her heart beating too fast, her ears ringing, reality a tunnel of light closing down in front of her and darkness roaring around her.

With a muttered word, Faroe shoved Grace onto the banquette seating and forced her head down between her knees.

"You never struck me as the fainting type," he said roughly. "Breathe, damn it. Living without oxygen is only for Hindu holy men."

She took a deep, shuddering breath, then another one, then another. Her ears stopped ringing, the world stopped wheeling, and light came back. She felt Faroe's big hands, one holding her head between her knees and the other stroking her spine with a gentleness that was the opposite of his voice.

"I'm okay," she said. "I can take care of myself."

"Yeah? You could have fooled me. When was the last time you slept more than two hours?"

She shrugged.

"And food?" he asked. "Did you forget that, too?"

She swiped her hair back from her face with both hands. "I'm not hungry."

"Adrenaline wipes out appetite, but it doesn't wipe out the need for calories. It's as basic as blood sugar. You burn, you eat to stoke the fire. You stop stoking, you get light-headed."

He went to the galley refrigerator and came back with a can of Coke. He popped the tab and handed the sugary drink to her.

Grace looked at it.

"I know, I know," he said before she could, "you're the diet Coke type. Drink this anyway. Sugar has its uses."

She took the can and drank a mouthful. Within seconds she felt her body respond. She took another mouthful and shivered, surprised by the physical sensation of sugar hitting her bloodstream.

"I guess . . . I haven't eaten since breakfast yesterday," she said, thinking back.

"Toast and coffee?"

"Coffee, no toast. I was working late."

Faroe went to the pantry and came back with a loaf of sourdough bread, a jar of peanut butter, a bread knife, and a table knife. He cut the loaf in half, then sliced one half horizontally. He spread on a thick layer of peanut butter and handed the open-faced sandwich to her.

"Peanut butter and Coke for breakfast," Grace said. "Add a piece of cold pizza and you're in Lane heaven."

"Your kid has good instincts. Eat."

"Yes, Mother." Grace took a big gooey bite and had no choice but to shut up and chew.

Faroe went back to the porthole. The man was still in the booth. After a moment, Faroe turned away, pulled a stool out from beneath the chart table, and set it down in front of Grace.

"If we're going to do this, you have to learn and learn fast," he said. "First, you live like you're onstage and it's opening night. Somebody's watching you all the time. You just have to figure out who it is and who the watcher is working for."

Grace reached for the soda to help with the peanut butter clogging her mouth.

"Second, protect yourself because nobody else will," Faroe said. "Take care of yourself for the same reason. You're a high-octane woman and you're under a lot of stress. It's doubly important for you to eat."

"Yes, Mother," Grace mumbled, but there

was more peanut butter than sarcasm in her voice.

"Listen up. This is the wrong time to be light-headed from lack of food. Most people, particularly most crooks, make dumb decisions about half the time because they're drunk or stoned or fucked up one way or another. Being hungry is no different."

"Such talk, Mother."

"Another little rule. Don't let anything shock you. Expect the worst and you won't have any rude surprises."

The worst.

Lane's death.

Grace froze.

"Breathe," Faroe growled.

She forced herself to. "If I let myself expect the worst . . ." She couldn't finish.

"Yeah," he said. "If you let yourself expect the worst, you'd go postal and start doing really foolish things, instead of only marginally dumb ones."

"Besides coming to you, what dumb thing have I done?"

"That was enough. Ask Steele for some other St. Kilda consultant. There's too much baggage between you and me."

Surprise showed in her eyes. "But you're

the only one I know well enough to trust. Why do you think I'm here? Do you think this is easy for me?"

"Easy or hard, it's wrong. It was wrong even before I knew we were burned by the dude on the dock."

"So he's seen us together. So what?"

"I've lost the one advantage an operator has to have—secrecy. He's going to be poking a proctoscope up my ass until he figures out who I really am."

"Must you be so graphic?"

"Excuse the hell out of me, Your Honor." The anger in Faroe's voice vibrated inside the *TAZ.* "You'd better get used to the crude things in life because right now you're lip deep in them and headed for a rude dunking."

"You sound almost as angry as you did sixteen years ago." Grace looked at the peanut butter and bread with a complete lack of interest. "That was when you told me to get the hell out of your sight and your life. Is that what you want? Again?"

"You're a lawyer. You know how emotion clouds professional judgment."

"I don't know if I believe that anymore." She took a deep breath. "I believe in blood ties. My child is in terrible danger, and the moment I realized that, the only person I could think of who might be able to help him was you. Joe Faroe. So I sucked it up and came to you. For Lane."

Silence stretched while Faroe studied Grace. He didn't doubt that she was telling the truth.

And his gut said she wasn't telling all of it.

"Sixteen years ago, maybe it would have worked," he said. "But I'm a different man and you're a different woman. That's why you need somebody else. We have too much baggage, the kind that really gets in the way."

Grace watched him. Her eyes were huge, glittering with tears she wouldn't allow to fall.

"I'll call Steele myself," Faroe said, his voice rough with all that he couldn't say, shouldn't think, and didn't want to remember. "There are two men who are as good as I am at this bloody game. One of them could be here by dawn. You and St. Kilda can start over, without the baggage and without the burn."

Grace's eyes dropped to the leather shoulder bag she'd carried aboard. *My God, am I going to have to tell him?*

"I've learned my lesson," she said quietly. "I won't move again without checking over my shoulder."

Faroe let out a rush of breath. "Okay. Good. I'll call Steele."

"No."

"What?"

"No. You said in the shadow world, you have to trust your best guess. It's you or nothing for Lane. It won't be all that easy for anyone to track down your past. If you're good at anything, it's disappearing."

"A really good operative with the right connections could peel my identity in a few days. A week, max."

She looked at her watch. "Lane has twenty-six hours."

"Shit."

"I don't blame you for being angry," Grace said. "I don't know why you quit St. Kilda, but I do know you must have had a good reason. And here I am dragging you back where you don't want to go."

A good reason.

Faroe tried not to remember the feel of a friend-turned-enemy choking to death in his hands, his eyes pleading friendship and his knife still sliding off Faroe's body armor.

It had been a near thing for Faroe. It had been a final thing for Bernardo.

Grace looked at Faroe and wondered what he was thinking that had turned his face into a death's-head. Then he smiled, a smile so cold it made gooseflesh rise on her arms.

"Did Steele tell you?" Faroe asked.

"He said something about you being forced to kill a good man gone bad."

Abruptly Faroe stood up and reached for a three-foot length of rope that hung from a hook above the chart table. The ceiling of the stateroom was just high enough that he could extend his arms above his head, one hand on either end of the rope. Slowly he rotated his arms behind his head and down his back. The tight muscles of his shoulders screamed in protest, then stretched slowly, releasing the tension that had built in them.

Grace watched with a fascination she didn't bother to conceal. The Joe Faroe she'd known a long time ago had been whipcord thin and coiled like a spring, always ready for action. This new Joe Faroe was more muscular and yet more flexible.

He'd learned how to handle the destructive tension within himself.

For the first time, she allowed herself to

hope. Just a little. Just enough so that her throat wasn't locked tight against all the screams she'd swallowed.

He tossed the rope back on the table and looked at her with a quiet expression that said he'd made up his mind.

"You sure it's me or no one?" he asked.

"Yes."

"Two on a tightrope is dangerous, especially when one is an amateur."

Grace glanced again at the purse that held all the pictures of Lane she owned. She was both relieved and oddly sad that she hadn't had to use them.

"What do you want me to do?" she asked.

"Whatever I say, whenever I say it."

She told herself the words only had one meaning. She nodded tightly.

Faroe smiled. "Give me your cell phone."

Without a word she went to her purse, pulled out her cell phone, and handed it to him.

If this was some kind of twisted test, she damn well was going to pass it.

14

FAROE PUNCHED IN THREE digits and hit "send." Then he handed Grace the phone.

She listened to the ring. "Who am I calling?"

"There are only two three-digit numbers in the phone system. I didn't call information."

"You called 911? What am I supposed to say?"

The phone rang a second time.

"Tell them you're reporting a hot prowl," Faroe said. "Somebody tried to break into your boat at Slip F-39. He's up on the dock now."

A third ring.

"And sound scared," Faroe added.

"Nine one one, what is your emergency?"

"I'm at the Oceanside marina," Grace said hurriedly. "A man just tried to break in and I'm here alone. Please help me!"

"A prowler? What's your address?"

"Slip F-39 at the marina. He's gone back up the gangway. He's in the parking lot right now, in a phone booth and he's—he's watching me!"

"Describe him, please."

"Dark hair, a blue shirt, or maybe a jacket. He has a pair of binoculars. I think he's been looking at boats to see if anyone's aboard."

"Okay, ma'am, we'll send somebody right away."

Grace covered the voice pickup and said to Faroe, "They're sending a car."

"How long?"

Grace lifted her thumb and spoke into the receiver. "How long until it arrives? I'm alone and—scared."

The dispatcher hesitated, checking her status board. "Three minutes. You can stay on the line if you want."

Grace mouthed, *Three minutes.*

Faroe nodded, took the phone, and ended the call.

"It really lights a fire under them when the phone goes dead in the middle of a prowler call," he said.

"Clever, but what about me? Doesn't that dispatcher have my number on caller ID right now?"

"Nope," Faroe said. "Cell phones don't trace." *Well, not usually.* "Besides, you haven't done anything wrong. There's a dude out in the parking lot who shouldn't be there and you're nervous."

"You sure you aren't a defense lawyer?"

"I'm a good liar, does that count?"

He grabbed his own leather shoulder bag and checked the interior. All Grace saw before he closed it under her nose was a satellite cell phone like the one on Steele's desk.

"Is there a gun in there?" she said.

"You worried about crossing the border when we go to check out the school?"

"That and the roadblocks."

"Where?" Faroe asked.

"There was one on the toll road to Ensenada and one at the entrance to the school."

"Were they looking for guns?"

"They didn't say, but they could have searched the car, and me, if they wanted to."

"No worries," Faroe said with a thin smile.

"I'm a convicted felon. It would be against the law for me to possess a firearm here or in Mexico. So I don't carry."

"A border cowboy without his gun? Why do I feel that the law is the least of your problems?" Grace muttered.

"Because you know me pretty well."

He led her out the hatchway onto the deck of the *TAZ.* After he locked up the stateroom behind them, he unclipped the safety line and stepped down onto the dock, shouldering the bag. When she was slow to follow, he turned and offered her his hand for balance.

Grace took his hand and stepped down lightly. She was startled when he used her momentum to draw her into an embrace. He looked into her eyes, smiling, ignoring her shocked stiffness.

Whatever I say, whenever I say it.

"There are only two reasons a woman like you would be with a man like me," Faroe said against Grace's lips. "We want the dude up there to think it's the second reason. Hot sheets, not hired help. Okay?"

"Joe—"

"Yeah, I know," he cut in, "you don't want me and you're not used to fooling people. Learn fast, Your Honor. Follow my lead or get your beautiful ass out of the game right now. Which will it be?"

There was an edge to Faroe's voice that told her he meant every word. She resisted for another second, then let her body soften and move toward his.

"Good," he said. "Now put your arms around my neck and let me give you what should look to our pal like a passionate kiss."

"What?"

"Take it easy," he said against her lips. "It doesn't have to be the real thing, just good enough to pass inspection through binoculars."

"A stage kiss, right? All show and no go?"

He smiled. "Yeah, but sell it to the cheap seats. We need this guy to believe I'm the new cock on your walk."

Faroe started the kiss deliberately and discreetly off-center.

Grace mentally calculated the angles between them and the phone booth and let herself sag gently toward him.

Bad move.

Her breasts brushed against his chest. The rest of her body followed without waiting for her command. The kiss went from awkward to explosive as she tasted him and everything changed, past and present mingled like lovers, curling around one another in timeless embrace. She moved closer to him, closer, and felt his erection pressing hard against her.

Slowly, breathing deep, Faroe forced himself back to reality, where time went only one way and someone was watching them through binoculars.

"That's why me taking this job isn't the smartest idea either one of us ever had," he said.

Reluctantly he let go of her.

"I'm sorry," she said. "I don't know what happened."

He gave her a sideways glance. "I do."

"I—it won't happen again."

"Don't bet on it." He put his arm casually around her shoulders and started up the dock. "That kind of need is hard to fight."

They were still walking on the dock when the first patrol car came gliding into the marina parking lot like a killer whale with flashing red eyes. The Latino with the binoculars must have had a guilty conscience. He broke cover and walked quickly toward a black Suburban parked nearby.

The patrol car veered toward the Suburban.

By the time Grace and Faroe reached the top of the gangway, a uniformed officer had the man spread like a blue moth on the hood of the patrol car. A backup unit wheeled into position.

"Remember, we're just a couple of consenting adults walking up to the parking lot after a quickie on the boat," Faroe said softly, tugging gently at her short hair. "Act natural. Look a little at the cops and at the man hugging the hood of the car and trying to explain himself. While you're at it, check out the license plates on the Suburban."

Grace turned and looked at all the action. The license plates were from Frontera Baja California but they had an unusual color pattern.

She tipped back her head and said softly to Faroe, "I saw the same colors on the cars at the second roadblock Saturday, the one in front of the school."

"They're Mexican government tags," he said, nibbling along her cheekbone. "They'll probably come back to the Baja state judicial police. But with any luck those Oceanside cops will run the VIN numbers on the truck. Five will get you ten it was stolen up here."

"Oh, God," Grace whispered. "Policemen driving stolen vehicles and running surveillance for drug traffickers."

"Welcome to my world, tastefully decorated in all the lovely shades of gray. The entrance to that world is down at the south end of Interstate 5. I'll drive."

"I'm a big girl. I can drive myself."

"Can you ditch that dude's partner?" Faroe asked.

"Partner? Where? And stop nibbling. You're distracting me."

"I'll know about the partner as soon as I leave the parking lot."

Unhappily Grace surrendered her ignition key. She was used to being in control. She needed it. Ted had accepted that about her and given her the independence she wanted. At first she believed he'd done it as a salute to her competence. Later she'd realized that once he figured out that she wasn't going to follow his orders, he didn't care enough about her to worry.

From Joe's take-care-of-the-little-woman machismo to Ted's let-the-bitch-do-what-she-wants indifference. Grace let out a frustrated breath. *Isn't there an in-between on the Y gene?*

Faroe tucked her into the passenger seat of her Mercedes and climbed in behind the wheel. He started the engine, listened to the healthy hum, and tapped the accelerator enough to lift the revs above 5,000. There was a lot left before the needle hit the red line.

"Sweet," he said, smiling. "When did you acquire a taste for macho horsepower? Or did Ted pick this out?"

"Ted?" Grace laughed. "He's the kind of guy who'd drive halfway to San Francisco before he realized he was locked down in second gear. I picked out this handsome beast all by myself."

"Ted missed a lot about you."

Grace shrugged. "Maybe I was missing something about him, too."

Faroe doubted it, but all he said was, "Where is Ted's office?"

"He has two. One in La Jolla, on Pacific Coast Highway, and the other in Malibu. But right now he's not at either office and they don't know when he will be."

The tone of her voice told Faroe that she was parroting various receptionists.

"On the way to the border, I'll do a drive-by on the La Jolla office," Faroe said.

"What do you expect to find?"

"Nothing special." *I hope.* "How do I get there?"

Grace bit back what she wanted to say and gave directions instead.

15

LIKE EVERYTHING ELSE IN Grace's life, La Jolla had changed in sixteen years. Once it had been little more than a snotty California beach resort. Now it was a high-end retail and financial center that rivaled Tijuana's Zona Río.

Faroe drove slowly down a side street that dead-ended in the parking lot of Edge City Investments. There was a guard shack at the entrance to the parking lot. Faroe turned the corner and pulled over to the curb, inspecting the five-story stainless steel and glass building.

Silently he read the building directory that had been hand-carved on the marble retaining wall at street level. Besides Edge City, the building housed an import company, an international marketing firm, branches of two Wall Street brokerage houses, and the offices of four financial advisers, three of whom had Spanish surnames.

"There's a lot of black money washing anonymously back and forth across the border," Faroe said.

"You're stereotyping. Just because there are some Spanish names on the building doesn't mean there's something illegal going on."

"Actually, I'm speculating. That's where the big money is, right? Speculation?"

She didn't look convinced.

"Get used to it," he said. "I've seen the ass end of too many aardvarks to be politically correct. Not all male Middle Easterners blow up airplanes, but it's beyond stupid to search everyone's Caucasian grandmother in the name of political correctness."

"The law says—"

"The law is made by politicians," Faroe cut in. "Hell, I know that all Russians aren't part of the *mafiya* or tucked into the trough of a corrupt government, but the chances of Ivan Freaking Innocent coming into big money honestly in Mother Russia is about as great as Juan Freaking Innocent getting big money in Father Mexico without getting real dirty in the process."

She wanted to disagree. It was a reflex she shoved back into the past. She might not like what Faroe was telling her, but if she was arguing civics when the likes of Hector appeared with his heavily armed thugs, she'd be a deadly liability to her son.

"There are lots of places like La Jolla around the world," Faroe said. "Aruba, Medellín, Beirut, Moscow. Fast money, black money, drug money, arms money, terrorist money—it's all pretty much the same. It rolls around this world of ours like a big old sticky ball, picking up outwardly honest bankers and brokers and financial advisers."

"You make it sound like there's no legal money out there."

"Depends on how you define legal. Sort of like provenance in art. Put the goods through three previous owners and you're home free. You'd be amazed at how often art is used as a way to get value—money—across borders and into safe, numbered accounts."

"There *is* a world of law," Grace said fiercely. "I know. I've lived in it."

"The clean tip of a muddy iceberg."

She shook her head.

He looked back toward the steel and glass monument to financial success and let the silence echo.

"Ted didn't start out to end up in the shadow world," Faroe said finally. "It happened one small decision at a time. One light shade of gray. A favor for a friend, then new friends and new favors. These are the people you eat with, drink with, raise your kids with. Close to you."

Grace didn't like where Faroe was going, and she didn't know how to stop him. His calm words were wrecking balls tearing down the world she'd lived in, forcing her to see things she didn't want to see, had fought and worked all her life *not* to have in her view.

"Some of those friends are a dirty shade of gray, and their friends are even dirtier," Faroe said. "The longer you hang with them, the dirtier you get, until one day you wake up and find yourself in bed with the likes of Hector Rivas Osuna. Then you're free-falling in the shadow world with no real idea of how it happened and not a clue about what the landing will be like."

She set her teeth and remembered her courtroom, where the law was a vital, living force, as real as the air she breathed. She turned to tell Faroe about her world, and saw that he was looking past her at something on the street outside. The intensity in him was as tangible as the presence of law in her courtroom. She started to turn around to see what was so interesting but he stopped her.

"No," he said quickly. "We're being watched."

Her stomach pitched. "The Suburban again? How?"

"A sedan," Faroe said, looking away calmly. "He's tucked back in the shrubbery beside that condo down the block. I caught a glint off his glasses. He was trying to eyeball our license plate."

"But who is it?"

"Good question." Faroe reached across and opened the glove box. "You have a map in here?"

Grace pulled a Thomas Brothers San Diego County Street Guide out of the glove box. Faroe flipped through the maps, located a page, and got a confused look on his face.

"Ready to steal an elevator?" he asked without looking at her.

"You have to talk English to me."

"No, you have to listen very carefully and do what I say. The only way to steal elevators is at noon in a busy building. Look lost."

"That won't be hard," she muttered.

He propped the map book on the steering wheel and put the Mercedes in gear. Consulting the page in front of him again and again, he let the SUV roll slowly down the street. When he drew even with the alley where the sedan was hiding, he turned in.

"Joe, what are—" Grace began, moving uneasily.

"Shush, woman," Faroe cut in.

"Don't call me *woman.*"

"Why not? People call me *man* all the time. Or dude. You want to be a dudette?"

Before she could give him the retort he deserved, they were beside the sedan and he was lowering the driver's window of the SUV. The sedan was a full-size four-door Ford Crown Royale, government green. Two Anglos were in the front seat. The one reading the newspaper dropped it on the seat. Both of them looked surprised but were quick to put a game face on.

"Hey, man, do you know where Apollo Avenue is?" Faroe called out. "This map book says it's around here somewhere, but I sure can't find it."

The driver shot him a cold look. "We're strangers here ourselves."

"Well, loosen up and ask directions like a good metrosexual," Faroe said, nudging the accelerator so that the SUV slid past the sedan. "And next time you drop your newspaper on the seat, make sure it covers the antenna on your handy-talkie. Have a nice day."

Faroe hit the gas and turned out onto a city street seconds later.

"What was that all about?" Grace asked.

"Careless cops. I really hate it when the good guys look so bad."

"Cops?" She straightened but forced herself not to glance back. "Those guys were cops?"

"Yeah. Feds, maybe. Their suits were a cut above what a city plainclothes type could afford. Might be customs or what passes for the DEA now. Maybe even part of a task force that includes the locals. I bet if we cruised around we'd find a couple more units back in the bushes. The building's too big for one team to handle."

"What are they doing here?"

Faroe glanced in the rearview mirror. "You want my sworn testimony or my best guess, Your Honor?"

"Whatever gets me closer to Lane's freedom."

Faroe smiled faintly. "You're learning. My best guess is that they're watching your husband's business."

"You can't be certain. There are a lot of names on that building!" Then Grace closed her eyes and took a deep breath. "All right. Sorry. Best guess it is."

"Okay," he said, "we've got Mexican cops in Mexico, who may or may not be working for the crooks, and we've got American cops, who usually work for the good guys but whose definition of 'good guys' is real damn narrow. Then there's you and me."

"So?"

"Either your husband is the most popular guy in two nations, or he's got more trouble than either of us needs."

16

DWAYNE PICKED UP STEELE'S private hotline. "Dwayne here."

"Faroe."

"The Ambassador is talking to a CEO whose assets surpass that of all but a few nations. Shall I interrupt?"

"No. Turn loose the dogs on Theodore Franklin."

"We already have. Steele was certain you would take the job."

"Damn, I hate being predictable. What do you have?"

Dwayne clicked over the computer and

looked at various summaries. "Do you want the long form or the bottom line?"

"Whichever gets me closer to Teddy-boy."

"His hedge fund is in trouble. Big trouble."

"Why?" Faroe asked.

"Bad investments."

"If that was against the law, half the investment experts would be in jail."

"That's just part of the problem," Dwayne said. "Think of a Ponzi scheme crossed with a classic money-laundering profile."

"You're giving me a headache."

"Take two aspirin and call me when I care. Ted's going down. Steele is already smacking his lips."

"I'm trying to imagine that," Faroe said. "It's giving me a bigger headache."

Dwayne laughed. "Nobody gets turned on by hidden numbered accounts like the Ambassador."

"He's not the only one. Some stripe of cop had Ted's La Jolla office staked out."

"Steele won't like that," Dwayne said.

"I'm not doing backflips of joy myself. How close are you to finding Ted?"

"So far he hasn't used any of his accounts or credit cards. When he does, we have him."

"Kick some ass," Faroe said impatiently. "We have a day to get Lane Franklin out of jail."

"We're kicking ass and taking names. No guarantees on the timing."

"Two days, two weeks, two years," Faroe said coldly, "find the son of a bitch who nominated his kid for a Colombian necktie. Men like that need to be taken out of the gene pool."

Dwayne opened his mouth, but he was talking to a dead phone.

17

CARLOS CALDERÓN KNOCKED AT Lane's door and went in without waiting for an invitation. The two guards watching Lane didn't stir from their comfy position propped against a shady side of the cottage. Nothing moved but their dark eyes and the sweat sliding down their cheeks.

Lane was sprawled half dressed on his bed, watching flies walk across the ceiling.

Calderón went to the kitchen, saw the empty orange juice carton, and replaced it with the fresh one he'd brought. A plate of cold tacos and beans sat in the refrigerator next to the juice. It didn't look like Lane had been hungry.

Empty-handed, Calderón went back to the bedroom and roughly hauled Lane into a sitting position.

"Have you heard from your father?" Calderón asked.

". . . uh?"

Calderón gave Lane an open-handed slap. "Your father. Have you heard from him?"

Lane blinked. His eyes almost focused. "No phone."

"The office has a phone. Did he call you?"

Lane's head lolled and his eyes started to close.

A sharp smack across his face focused him again.

"Dunno," Lane said. "Don' . . . tell me . . . shit."

Calderón shook Lane hard enough to make his hair lift. Then he buried one hand in Lane's hair and twisted hard, dragging the boy's face close to his.

"Listen to me, *pendejo*," Calderón said. "I'm not as patient as Hector. If you hear anything from anybody about your father, you tell me immediately or I'll cut your throat and send your head home to your mother. Hector's nephews can have the rest of you. You understand?"

All Lane's fuzzed mind understood was that Calderón really wanted news about Ted Franklin. The rest was a nightmare of funhouse mirrors, sharp pain forgotten in the instant it was felt, and echoes without meaning.

"Unnerstan."

Calderón shoved Lane away so hard that the boy's head thumped against the wall. Lane groaned and slumped onto the bed again. Calderón strode out of the cottage.

The guards were still outside, still sweating.

So was Calderón.

18

SOUTH OF THE CORONADO Bridge, the muggy air began to congeal. American industry and Mexican charcoal cooking fires turned the sky into sludge.

"Use the Otay Mesa route," Grace said. "It takes longer on this side, but it's better than having the tires stolen at a stoplight."

"Talk about not being politically correct . . ."

"Neither is being stared at like I have 'for rent' written on my ass."

Faroe made a sound like a swallowed laugh and watched his back trail. After another quick glance at the mirrors, he shot into the fast lane.

"What are you doing?" Grace asked. "It's a right-hand off-ramp."

"I know."

He kicked down the accelerator and watched the speedometer leap to ninety miles an hour. They raced through the spotty traffic for a half mile. At the last possible moment, he cut across four lanes and drove onto the freeway spur that led up the hill toward Otay.

Grace grabbed the handle in the armrest and looked over her shoulder at the cars Faroe had just cut off.

"Are you crazy?" she said sharply.

"Just careful."

"Careful? You nearly caused a wreck!"

"It's a good way to burn a tail."

Grace went still. "We're being followed?"

"A red Jeep showed up three times in the last thirty miles. Funny thing, but he decided at the last second to go to Otay, too. Reckless, but you know how it is with those Southern California drivers."

She closed her eyes for an instant. "Now who's after us—the Russians?"

Faroe smiled. "Doubt it. Best guess is that

the Jeep is part of the team we picked up at Edge City. These dudes are better than the brain-dead in the sedan. Got to be feds of some stripe. This is a full-on, multiagency surveillance squad."

"I'm so glad you enjoy leading a parade. I could live quite well without the armed attention."

"Don't worry, *amada.* It's only dangerous when they stop watching."

She hoped he was right.

Faroe dropped back to only ten miles an hour over the speed limit, just fast enough to keep from being run over by the rest of the traffic.

"Right now, what I'm guessing is a task force is still in the early stages of the investigation, picking up pieces of string and pulling them to see where they end. Like us."

"Is your world always so . . . active?"

"Bet on it. Things happen right here in the middle of the sunshine world that would probably make the average citizen's hair stand on end and then fall out. That's what crime is, dudes sneaking around, filling their pockets one way or another, and trying desperately to make sure nobody notices."

"The law notices," Grace said.

"Sometimes. Then you have the cops running behind the crooks, usually way behind. The cops are lagging because they have a ball-breaking handicap. Not only do they have to figure out what's happening, they also have to gather legally admissible proof of same, and the courtroom bar is set about as high as the moon."

"There's a good reason for high standards. It separates us from the gutter."

"Judge, the gutter loves your high standards because they make life merry hell for cops."

"You aren't stupid," Grace said curtly. "You know why police actions have to be carefully restricted."

"Yeah, I understand the legal fiction you lawyers have spun in justification. But on the other hand, no, I have no gut-deep sense of why society worries so much about cops."

"Because somebody has to watch the watchdogs."

"Watch them, yes. Pull their teeth and shoot them in all four feet? No."

"Just like the old days," she said, shaking her head. "Me on one side of Justice's scales and you on the other. It's a miracle you didn't become a crook."

"The company sucks sewer water. Be grateful there are noncrooks like me, Your Honor. We keep the biggest turds from ending up on your white linen tablecloth."

Glancing frequently at the mirrors, Faroe followed the road up onto the mesa that was the principal trading post of the NAFTA era. Fresh produce from the interior of Mexico and cheap TVs assembled in *maquiladoras* in Tijuana clogged the northbound roads, swimming against a steady stream of structural steel and manufactured goods headed south. The storage warehouses and import-export brokerages stood shoulder to shoulder with vast fields of used cars and trucks too clapped out for the high-speed American interstates, but okay for the slow, rough roads of Chiapas and Guanajuato.

A gleaming Aeroméxico jetliner leaped up off the Tijuana International Airport runway a thousand yards beyond the barbed-wire and metal-mat border fence. The plane banked out to the south, spewing burned exhaust over the crowded, penniless *colonias* that consumed the rolling coastal hills as far as the eye could see.

Grace felt that old familiar uneasiness crawl through her. "I should be more comfortable with this place. Some of my ancestors came from Mexico. But I always feel alien here."

Faroe touched her hair gently before he put his hand back on the wheel. "Don't worry about it. I know enough about Tijuana for both of us. Tijuana is the model for the shadow world."

"The world you were trying to get out of."

He shrugged.

"Isn't that why you retired," she said, "so you don't have to cross over this line and go back into the Mexico of the mind?"

He braked to a stop at the end of a short line of American vehicles headed south.

"I'm trying to get away from the whole spectrum, light to dark," Faroe said. "That's what my boat is all about."

"The *TAZ*. What language is the name from?"

"It's an acronym dreamed up by a freelance Sufi philosopher named Hakim Bey. The letters stand for temporary autonomous zone."

Grace thought about it for a moment. Each word was familiar, but put together they didn't particularly make sense. "I give up. What does it mean?"

"Bey describes these zones as remote, renegade places scattered throughout the world—Tibet, the South Sea Islands, monasteries high up in the Alps. One of my favorites is an abandoned oil-drilling rig in the English Channel between France and Kent."

"Is St. Kilda named for one of those zones?"

"Not quite. Well, maybe, now that you mention it. Temporary autonomous zones are populated by people like me, dudes who couldn't cut it in the civilized world, burnout jobs, head cases, and fugitives. The zones can be lonely, but they're the only places where misfits have a half-decent shot at being free."

"I see the autonomous part of it, but why temporary?"

"These places only exist as long as they stay under the global radar," Faroe said. "Once the structured world of governments and corporations stumble across a TAZ, they set to work taming it or trying to turn a profit from it. Then the game is over. Any surviving misfits move on to the next TAZ and hope it lasts as long as they do."

A Mexican customs officer wearing Ray-Bans and a brown uniform waved them through without inspection. They crossed the line into Mexico.

"Still Don Quixote," Grace said softly, "the ever-hopeful romantic, looking for the next windmill, the one that he *will* defeat."

Faroe smiled thinly. "You need romance more on this side of the line than you do back there in the sunshine world."

Grace thought about what her life had been even a year ago. She'd been sad about the coming divorce, but safe.

Now I lay me down to sleep . . .

But she hadn't said that childhood prayer in years, because she'd known she would awaken safe in her bed. Alone, but safe. If she ever spent the night in Mexico, she'd be awake praying.

That's foolish. Most of Mexico is safer than the California barrio I grew up in.

At least it had been, before Ted slid down whatever slippery slope he had.

I can't trash him for that. I've started down my own morally greasy slide.

Ted had been furious when he found out he wasn't Lane's father. He didn't believe she hadn't known when they were married. He didn't want to believe her. It gave him the perfect excuse for ignoring the boy who called him Dad, just as he'd ignored Lane from the moment of his birth. It also gave Ted an alibi for all his affairs, which had started years before he knew about Lane. Ted was perfect, she was a deceitful slut, and that was that.

Grace didn't want to think about how Faroe would react when she told him that he had a son. He'd look at her as a liar, a cheat, a thief who had stolen his son's life.

Sooner or later, she'd destroy the fragile, necessary romantic illusions of the man who sat beside her in the car.

Maybe I won't have to.

Maybe pigs sing soprano.

"What's wrong?" Faroe asked. "You look pale."

"Just worried."

It was the truth, if not the whole truth, nothing but the truth, so help me God.

Faroe glanced in the rearview mirror. "You can stop worrying about our tail. The Jeep peeled off at the line. That pretty well confirms that they're cops. FBI, maybe. Or DEA driving a vehicle they seized during a drug bust."

"Why did they stop at the border?"

"Feds don't like coming south. The Mexican government makes them leave their guns on the other side of the line. Not a healthy way to live."

She frowned. "Doesn't it bother you? Going unarmed?"

"I'm not a purist. In some situations I'll carry. But guns have limited uses. Unless you're willing and able to kill, a gun is just iron, lead, and smokeless powder."

Grace drew a deep breath and let it out. "And you're willing. And able."

Faroe gave her a look out of cold green eyes, then went back to staring at the traffic ahead. Silence filled the car.

And filled it.

Pressing against the two people inside.

Faroe lifted one hand, then the other, from the wheel, flexing his fingers.

"There was a guy, a pretty good guy," he said finally. "I thought he was a friend. I would have died thinking it except that I was wearing Kevlar underwear. Body armor."

Grace's breath broke. "Where were you?"

"In a filthy alley behind the Lisboa Casino in Macao. It started out as a drunken fistfight. At least I thought he was drunk."

Faroe looked at his right hand.

Grace's glance followed his. She saw a thin, livid scar that began on the back of his thumb and ran across to the base of his knuckles to his little finger. There were other scars, too, but this one was new.

"After he got me in a clinch, he pulled a knife out of an ankle sheath and said, 'Sorry, Joe.' That's when I understood he wasn't drunk. He was trying to slit my belly and dump my guts on the ground with the fish heads and the prawn fondue."

"A friend," she said, her voice raw.

"We were working an investigation for a major multinational electronics firm. Somebody was tipping off Malay pirates about shipments of high-definition color televisions. Turns out the snitch was my pal, and he thought I was about to figure it out. So I strangled him while he tried to cut off my hand. Then I went back and told Steele I was done."

"That's . . ." She swallowed hard and shook her head.

"Shit happens."

"But you can't blame yourself, not for that," she said. "You were fighting for your life!"

"He was working for the paycheck, same as I was. But after that I didn't want to work anymore for other people or politicians or corporations that could write off lives and black millions as a business expense. I took my winnings off the table and started rigging out the *TAZ*."

"And now I'm dragging you back into it." Her fingers laced together, squeezed. "I'm sorry."

"Consider it a charity gig. We international hired guns do them all the time."

"So you're doing this as a special favor for me?"

He glanced at her for an instant, then back at the jumbled, free-form traffic in front of them. "I don't have a hidden agenda, if that's what you mean."

Avoiding his sideways glance, Grace looked down at her hands clenched in her lap and thought again of what would happen when Faroe found out about Lane.

"That's not what I'm worried about," she said.

"Then what?"

"I can't—don't—won't—"

The dashboard cell phone rang.

Grace could have kissed it.

19

"GOOD MORNING, GRACE, THIS is James Steele." The speaker gave Steele's voice a hollow ring.

Grace glanced sideways, looking for advice.

Faroe nodded.

"Ambassador, I'm here with Joe," she said. "We're just inside Mexico."

"Ah," Steele said, failing to keep the satisfaction from his voice. "From what Dwayne told me, I take it you've signed on."

"Don't take it too far," Faroe said. "While St. Kilda searches under rocks and in cesspools for Theodore Franklin, I've agreed to take a look at the school and give Grace my thoughts about breaking her son out. But all three of us know that it would be better if I bowed out."

"I'm disappointed to hear that," Steele said, "particularly as I've turned up some interesting and pertinent background on the matter."

"Background? If it's one of those cut-and-paste jobs that the research department pulls off Google, dump it in my e-mail. I'll look at it later. Right now we're heading for hip deep in alligators at the school."

"I know you think the research department is of limited usefulness."

"All the clippings in the world didn't warn me about Macao," Faroe said. "And I'm betting they won't tell me what I already know—Grace is caught in a three-corner game."

"Explain." Steele's voice was icy, all irony gone.

"Just before we came south, we did a drive-by peep of Ted Franklin's office. The place is under tight surveillance, probably a task force led by feds. They certainly had all the moves."

For a time the only sound was that of the road and Steele's finger tapping gently on his headset mike. "And the third corner?"

"He looked like a Mexican *federale* to me,"

Faroe said. "He must have put Grace on his radar earlier this morning, at her home. She led him right to me. We've covered ourselves for the moment, but I'm burned. You better get busy on Plan B."

Steele was silent, then sighed. "That is unfortunate. I'll prepare to move Barlow into position."

"Barlow? Are you kidding?"

"I assumed you would want someone who spoke good Spanish."

"Yeah, right, but Barlow lisps like Philip I. He's what *baja californios* call a *chilango.* Border Mexicans treat *chilangos* just about as well as your average Texan treats Yankees like you."

"Who did you have in mind?"

"I don't have a roster in front of me," Faroe said impatiently. "You're the brains of the outfit."

There was a chilly silence on the line. Then Steele cleared his throat. "Judge Silva, you have more experience dealing with adolescent males than I do, so help me out. Joseph won't formally commit to the job but he wants to control how the job is done. It's a classic example of what diplomats and game theoreticians call a no-win situation."

Grace smiled slightly. "Ambassador, I'm not in a position to give advice. I'm alone in a car with said sulky male."

"Well, when he makes up his mind, please do let me know," Steele said, biting off each word.

Faroe was just pigheaded enough not to admit that his mind was already made up. He really disliked being so easily read by his boss.

Ex-boss.

Almost.

"Until then," Steele said, "I'll just continue to perform my administrative and support duties, including the collection of very pertinent intelligence."

Faroe glared at the speaker. "Okay. Fine. I give up. Tell me what you have."

"I was struck by something Judge Silva told me yesterday about the school where her son is being held. All Saints. She said it's run by the Roman Catholic Church, and that the school is very highly regarded."

"So?" Faroe said.

"Well, that raises an obvious question," Steele said. "What is the church doing as hostage-keeper for a well-known Mexican drug trafficker?"

"The Catholic Church is like any other human institution, in Mexico or elsewhere," Faroe said dryly. "If the collection plate is full, the priest is happy."

"Perhaps, but one of St. Kilda's best young researchers came up with several interesting facts. First, All Saints maintains a web site with glowing testimonials from a number of prominent Mexican families, including the Calderóns."

Grace grimaced.

"The Calderóns," Steele continued, "are the Vanderbilts of northern Mexico. The paterfamilias was an interior minister and chairman of the political party that has ruled Mexico since the beginning of the last century."

"I already knew that," Faroe said. "So what? It's like saying the Kennedy family has been entirely straight, except for the days when Papa Joe was a bootlegger."

"I bow to your greater familiarity with the criminal backgrounds of leading families. But the Catholic Church is a somewhat different matter. Our young researcher did a thorough background on the people who run All Saints. She found that the school's rector, a Father Rafael Magón, assumed his post under direct appointment by the Vatican."

Grace's eyebrows rose.

So did Faroe's.

"Father Rafael Magón is a church celebrity," Steele said. "He comes from a famous Baja California family, and had been on the inside of the Vatican fast track before becoming rector at All Saints two years ago."

Grace straightened in her seat. "I've met Father Rafael several times. Even though he's the soccer coach, he didn't strike me as your average parish priest."

"Magón," Faroe said. "I wonder if he's from that family."

"What family?" Steele asked.

"The one with the two brothers who organized a successful Baja del Norte rebellion in 1910," Faroe said. "They captured the only two cities in Baja, Mexicali and Tijuana. Their insurrection became a lightning rod for the wacko left of that day. The Industrial Workers of the World and other anarchist organizations sent in reinforcements, a kind of International Brigade. They had a lot of fun for six months, playing at anarchist government."

"You're talking about one of my grandmothers," Grace said. "When the Magonistas lost, she went north with *federales* hot on her heels."

"Well, that explains it," Faroe said with a sideways glance and a smile.

Grace knew better than to ask what had been explained.

"Mexico City finally got its act together in the summer of 1911 and counterattacked," Faroe continued for Steele's benefit. "The *federales* sent the Wobblies scampering north to San Diego. The Magón brothers and some of their followers went south, into the Baja mountains. Their descendants are still around, still preaching revolution and social change to the mountain peasants and the Indians."

"Thank you," Steele said, and meant it. "I sometimes forget that beneath your relentlessly shit-kicking persona, there lives a serious student of history."

Faroe swung the Mercedes around a slow-moving freight truck that was laboring up a grade, spewing black diesel smoke from its chrome stacks.

"History is a slippery slope," Faroe said. "Things change day to day, sometimes faster. The Magonistas gambled on the support of the international workers' movement. They guessed wrong and they've been hiding in the mountains ever since. Maybe this new

Magón has finally capitulated and thrown in his lot with the crooks, using his robes as cover."

"I wondered about that myself," Steele said. "Do you remember Umberto Meinhof?"

Faroe grunted. "The captain in the Swiss Guards? Is he still in charge of the Vatican's diplomatic security detail?"

"He is. I spoke with him at great length an hour ago. He confirmed that Magón was, and probably still is, a very bright light in the church's diplomatic corps. But when I started to quiz him ever so gently about why such a star was stationed in the backwaters of northern Mexico, he acted as if I'd asked him to procure little girls for the pope."

Faroe whistled softly through his teeth. "And this very bright light is hanging around with traffickers? Interesting."

"I thought so," Steele said gently.

"Maybe the Vatican has decided to bring the Magonistas into the fold," Grace said. "Not to mention the Indians who never really converted."

"Possible," Steele said, "but that still leaves some things searching for an explanation. For instance, I got the impression that the Vatican had gone to some lengths to conceal

Father Rafael's connections to the church hierarchy."

Grace looked thoughtful.

Faroe frowned out the window, trying to order the new piece with the rest of the puzzle in his mind. After a moment, he smiled ironically. "Okay, Steele, I concede your point."

"That being?"

"Maybe there's a reason to spend a buttload of money on researchers."

Steele's laugh was as brief as it was genuine.

"Let's push a little harder," Faroe said. "Call Captain Meinhof back. Tell him we'll keep our mouths zipped, but in return we need a favor."

"And that favor would be?"

"Hold on for a bit." Faroe covered the receiver of the phone and talked only to Grace. "I assume the kids at a Catholic school all have to go to church."

"Of course. There's a regular sanctuary on the campus, plus a small chapel on the bluff overlooking the ocean."

Faroe removed his hand from the receiver. "Tell Meinhof we'll keep his secrets and Father Magón's. But in return the good father has to be in the chapel confessional in exactly"—Faroe checked his watch—"seventy minutes. I feel the need for an honest and complete confession."

"But of course," Steele said dryly. "I'll call you if there's any problem."

The connection went dead.

"I didn't know you were a Catholic," Grace said.

"I have plenty of things to confess. I hope the same goes for Father Magón."

20

SILENTLY GRACE WATCHED FAROE from the corner of her eye. He looked calm and determined, doing what he was very good at doing. She kept forgetting how focused he could be, intelligence like a laser illuminating everything in its path.

Once she'd been the object of Faroe's focus; his strength and intelligence had almost overwhelmed her. Yet it had been electrifying. Erotic beyond anything she'd ever known. When Faroe slipped the leash on his control, he was like riding a storm.

That's why she was frightened of what

would happen if he focused on her in rage and betrayal.

I can't tell him the truth until Lane is safe. Otherwise Lane might not be safe at all.

And every moment she didn't tell Faroe piled up guilt on her side and rage on his.

"Joe," she said softly, "do you mind if I ask you a personal question?"

He glanced quickly at her. "Why should I mind? There are some downright personal things between us."

Grace pushed back the memories of just how personal they'd been. After a moment she asked, "Are you ever frightened?"

"Hell, yes. Every day. Sometimes a lot more often. Why?"

"Right now, I'm so scared I feel like hurling. Yet you sit there like someone taking a Sunday drive. So I ask again. Have you ever been afraid, like I'm afraid right now, a sickening certainty of things spinning out of control?"

"I looked down the barrel of a revolver once," Faroe said. "The barrel was short and the sun was just right. I could see the crosshatching on the blunt end of the round that was about to come under the firing pin. The thirteen-year-old holding the gun was scared, too. I could see his finger so tight on the trigger that his black skin was white."

"What did you do?" she asked in a low voice.

"Same thing you're doing. I swallowed hard. Then I reached out real slow, real careful, and moved the muzzle to one side. I got it through about twenty degrees of arc before the kid flinched." Faroe reached up and touched the hair above his right ear. "The crosshatched round literally gave me a buzz cut. I was deaf in this ear for a week."

"Did you—kill him?"

Faroe laughed roughly. "What for? I helped him clean out his britches. Then he helped me clean out mine."

Grace shuddered and shook her head, wondering how he could laugh about an experience like that.

"So, yeah, I've been scared lots of times," Faroe said. "Fear of death is a natural reaction closely tied to survival. It's a universal part of the human experience."

"You say you're scared, but you don't act like it. Every time I think of Lane and Hector and Ted, I—" Her voice broke. She held out her hands. Fine tremors shook them.

Faroe caught one of her hands, kissed it gently, lightly, and released her the same way. "Up north, you live in a nice, neat, lawful world, but even there, gangs and mafias and terrorists use violence or the threat of it to get what they want."

Grace cupped the hand he'd kissed. "It's not the same."

"No, it's more personal now. A fist in your gut. Breathe, *amada.* You're still a long way from being a Hindu holy man."

She made a sound that could have been a laugh or a throttled cry.

"Just relax and accept what is rather than what you want it to be," he said. "South of the line, violence isn't just a fact of life. It's a *way* of life. Just like it's a way of life in most of the rest of the world, all the places you read about in the headlines, failed states and feral cities. Mexico is veering dangerously close to being a failed state. Tijuana is arguably a feral city."

"It can't be that bad." But there was more hope than certainty in her voice.

Faroe barely suppressed a cold smile. "Let me put things in perspective. When I first came to the border, the weapons of choice were a Model 1911A Colt and the M2 carbine. The Colt had the shock power of a sledgehammer but it rode nicely against the hip, even without a holster. The M2 was popular because with a sharp file and a few minutes it could be morphed from a semiautomatic shoulder weapon into a light machine gun."

Grace looked at him. In profile he looked as hard as the weapons he knew too much about.

"Now the *pistolero*'s tools are different," Faroe said. "Glocks are the favorite pistol, and a Glock would cost an honest Mexican cop half his yearly pay. For long guns, Mexicans prefer H&Ks or Uzis that can rip through a thirty-round magazine in five seconds. Northern Mexico is the new Dodge City. Shoot first, shoot most, and to hell with the bystanders. They should have stayed out of the streets, anyway."

"You're exaggerating."

"Am I? There were some contract killings in Texas, north of the border. That's in the U.S. of A. The murders were carried out by renegade *federales.* If that's happening in the U.S., you know it's worse south of the border. We just don't hear about it. Or if we do, we don't listen."

"You said renegade *federales.* Not official."

"In northern Mexico, police badges are as cheap and meaningful as dime-store whistles. Guns are what count. The borderlands are medieval fiefdoms held by the man with the most money, because money means arms. Power. Entire police departments are for sale to the highest bidder. They become militias for competing bands of traffickers. Police fighting police, *federales* fighting *federales,* and all variations in between."

"I just—"

"Yeah," he cut in. "I know. You just don't want to believe. Neither does anyone else. Yet it's all there for anyone who reads Mexican newspapers. The most notorious of the good cop–good cop battles were between Mexican federal drug agents on one side and Mexican army soldiers on the other. The prize was a jetliner loaded with six tons of Colombian cocaine. The *federales* were outgunned and massacred. People on the inside said the *federales* were more interested in the resale value of the cargo than in law enforcement."

"How can that happen?" she demanded. "Mexico is a civilized country with laws, a constitution, elections, paved streets, electricity, highly developed arts, and—"

"Mexican federal or state judicial policemen are paid a thousand dollars a month by the government," Faroe cut in impatiently. "They can make five to ten thousand a month by riding shotgun for the traffickers. In Mexico, like most of the world, police corruption is common. But here in Baja, the corruption is systemic, institutionalized. Venality is god and there's no lack of money for the collection plate."

"Words," Grace said. "Rumors. Opinions. Prejudices."

"Facts. A federal *comandante*'s badge costs a half million dollars. Of course, the average dude can't come up with five hundred thousand dollars all at once. He has to mortgage his future and use his badge to raise the installment payments. He has to impose his own tax on the criminals in the street, then pass a portion of his earnings up the chain of command. That's how you get hired in the first place. You always kick back part of your street taxes."

Reluctantly, Grace looked at Faroe. He was watching the road with the relaxed intensity that was his hallmark.

"Are you listening, *amada*?" he asked without turning toward her. "Really listening? Despite the crooks that swaggered or tiptoed through your court, you don't know shit from shoe polish when it comes to living in the Mexico that drug money has made."

"I'm listening. I'm just not liking anything I'm hearing."

"Did I ask you to like it?"

"No."

Faroe checked the mirrors. "In Mexico, bribery used to be called *la mordida,* the little bite. Now it's called *el sistema* and the system reaches all the way up the chain of command to Mexico City. And since the system moves anywhere from a quarter to half a trillion dollars a year—"

"Don't you mean billion?" she interrupted.

"No, I mean trillion, as in one thousand billion, the kind of number only astronomers and dope dealers work with. Think of it. One. Thousand. Billion. You could count grains of sand on the beach for a thousand lifetimes and still not get to a trillion."

"It's—it's hard to get my mind around it. Impossible, frankly."

"Yeah. That's how the traffickers get away with it. When the average citizen hears the facts, his eyes just glaze over and he goes back to the TV remote to find a friendlier world. But that doesn't change the other world, the shadow world, where the little bites of corruption get bigger, richer, harder to digest as a society. Money pours through the streets like half-digested banquets washed through the gutters of a Roman vomitorium."

Grace grimaced.

"That's why you don't like going to Tijuana," he said. "At a gut level you know the city is feral. You can't trust it."

"Not all of it. But some of it, surely."

Faroe shrugged. "Drug lords like Hector and his clan live in the best neighborhoods. Just like the mob does in Chicago or Manhattan. The difference is, the mob doesn't actually own whole police departments and judicial courts the way the *narcotraficantes* do in Mexico."

Grace thought of Hector and Lane. "If you know, or even just believe, what you're saying, why did you choose to work in Mexico?"

"It's because I know, and believe, that I wanted to put whatever bit of weight I could on the side of civilization," Faroe said. "To be effective, I had to understand the reality on the streets, to accept the reality of violence. I had to control my own fear of death or fear itself would kill me."

She looked at him. His hands were like his voice, calm and relaxed.

I had to control my own fear of death or fear itself would kill me.

"It's not that I don't care about dying," he said. "It's just that in order to survive, I've become pretty much a fatalist. When it comes, there it is. Until then, it isn't anywhere."

"Like the *chubasco,*" Grace said, gesturing to the clouds slowly seething over the ocean. "The storm is and it isn't. It may never get here, to me. So fearing or anticipating it wastes my energy, my life."

He smiled slightly. "You're getting closer."

"To what?"

"The followers of the Code of Bushido have a saying: The only really effective way to fight is to understand that you're already dead. Accept that and you're free to fight as a warrior of the mind as well as the body."

"But what should I do about my fear for Lane? How would you handle that?"

Faroe was silent for a long time. Then he reached out and slid his fingers through her hair, down her cheek. "I hope I'd do as well as you have."

"Have I?"

"Sure," he said, giving his full attention back to driving. "You found the best help you could and then you went looking for throats to rip out."

21

THE BLACK CHEVROLET SUBURBAN had moved from the shoulder to the center of the dirt road, blocking it completely. The same Mexican in blue jeans and a dusty guayabera leaned against the front fender of the vehicle, his M16 rifle slung muzzle down over his shoulder. A second guard slouched in the driver's seat of the Suburban.

Faroe decided the second guard was the boss—he had the most comfortable chair. Another weapon propped against the frame of the window had a flash suppressor.

Nothing but the best for these boys, Faroe

thought as he ran down the SUV's tinted windows so the guard could see inside.

When the sentry noted the California license plate on the Mercedes, he straightened up and said something over his shoulder. Then he strolled toward the Mercedes looking confident and suspicious. He studied Faroe without expression, then Grace.

Surprise flickered across the guard's face. He slid his hand down the strap of the rifle, lifted the weapon, and let the muzzle move slowly past Faroe's face before stopping at a point somewhere in the neutral territory between him and Grace.

"What you want?" the guard demanded. His English was rude but functional.

"Judge Silva needs to check on the welfare of her son," Faroe said.

"No is possible."

Faroe dropped his chin and looked hard at the Mexican. There was a badge on his belt. Faroe studied the badge like a man memorizing something.

"Of course it's possible," Faroe said.

"No, man," the guard said. "*No es*—is not my order."

"Check your orders again. Señor Calderón

and Señor Rivas assured the judge that she could visit her son at any time. We'll wait while you confer with your superior officer."

With that Faroe turned away, ignoring the guard and his weapon equally. With a wink the guard couldn't see, Faroe reached over and touched Grace on the knee. It was an unmistakable gesture of intimacy, a lover's touch.

"Who are you, *señor*?" the guard demanded.

"A close friend of the family," Faroe said over his shoulder. "Real close."

He turned back to Grace, smiled, stroked her knee, and ignored the guard. Frustrated, the *federale* walked back to the Suburban. He spoke briefly to the man behind the wheel. The supervisor stared across the gap between the two vehicles. Finally he reached for a cell phone and punched in a number. When the call was answered, he spoke for a time, listened, then all but saluted.

"Sí, mi jefe," Faroe said under his breath, reading the officer's lips. "That tells us Hector and his boys aren't interested in pissing you off."

"What do you call kidnapping my son—a playful pat?" Grace retorted.

"In this game, you use anything you can lay your hands on. Did you notice that he didn't even blink when I mentioned Carlos and Hector Rivas in the same breath?"

"That doesn't prove anything," she said automatically.

"Here we go again," Faroe said, shaking his head. "I can hear it dancing on your tongue. 'Carlos is a member of one of the most prominent families in all of Mexico. He couldn't be involved with traffickers. He just couldn't.'"

"Billionaires don't hang out with gangsters."

"Bullshit. There are a lot of places in the world where billionaires and gangsters are the same dudes. Or do you have a better explanation for the fact that we're staring down two members of the Mexican federal judicial police who are actively involved in the kidnapping of an American citizen who happens to be the son of a billionaire and a federal judge?"

"Damn you," she said hoarsely. "It's bad enough to know I'm going up against Hector Rivas Osuna. Add the Mexican government and I'm so afraid for Lane tha—"

"Breathe," Faroe said softly. "That's it. In

and out. You can get through this, *amada.* But you'll have to lose your illusions about a government's invincible correctness. Government is made up of people. Some people are crooks. Pretty simple, actually."

Grace let out an explosive breath, took in one, let one out.

And got through the moment.

The guard gave his boss a casual salute and came back to the Mercedes.

"You visit," he said curtly. "*El niño,* he is in the cottage of the beach."

"*Gracias,*" Faroe said carelessly.

The supervisor glared at them as he started the Suburban and backed it out of the way.

"Have a nice day," Faroe said out the window as he drove past.

Grace almost smiled. She suspected that Faroe's take on the clichéd exit line was about the same as an upright middle finger.

"Turn left here," she said. "Then drive to the parking area next to that big building."

"Those boys are really going at it," Faroe said, gesturing to the soccer field.

She looked at all the players and didn't know whether to be relieved or more anxious because Lane wasn't on the field.

"What?" Faroe asked.

"You read me too well."

"Only some of the time. Now, for instance."

"I'm just surprised Lane isn't out there. You'd enjoy watching him. He's like a gazelle, only not at all fragile. Quick and strong despite being lean."

"Maybe it's harder for his guards to keep track of him on the field, so they're keeping him at the cottage."

"Or maybe he got tired of being thumped on by the big 'boys' that showed up three weeks ago. Hector's relations. Thugs."

"If Hector wanted Lane on the field, he'd be there. Hector doesn't want Lane beaten, or he'd be bloody and bruised. Hector just wants to keep you focused."

"El jefe chingón."

"Don't forget it."

"Carnicero."

"That too. But he loves kids and small animals."

Grace made a sound.

"True fact," Faroe said. "It's just adults he whacks. Usually."

Faroe parked, got out of the Mercedes, and began memorizing the grounds. His eyes swept the grounds, measuring distances and judging angles, a tactical planner looking for fields of fire and killing zones.

Grace joined Faroe, but she watched him, not the school.

"What do you think?" she asked after a few minutes. "Can it be done?"

"I'll let you know. What's the quickest way to the bluff?"

She led him down the paved path to a cluster of cottages at the edge of the bluff.

As he walked, Faroe memorized the grounds. He doubted the beach or the bay had been officially mapped, but he made a mental note to check that possibility. Ocean waves broke cleanly on a reef a hundred yards offshore. Breaking waves humped up beyond the reef. Any rescue boat would have to stand offshore and launch inflatables.

Might be better to hike in from up the coast, with a chopper standing by off- shore to dart in for a fast pickup.

Depending on the guards, of course. How many, how close, how good.

Faroe looked around. Nobody visible but the three Mexican cops around Lane's cot- tage. Two were armed with pistols and as- sault rifles. The third carried a twelve-gauge

riot shotgun. *Pistoleros,* professional gunmen. They handled their weapons like gar-
deners handled rakes, no thought required.

The men had been warned to expect the
guests. One stepped out in front of Faroe
and stopped him with a raised hand.

"What?" Faroe asked.

The guard motioned that he wanted Faroe
to raise his hands. Faroe shook his head as
if he didn't understand. The guard brought
the muzzle of his shoulder weapon up. Faroe
looked surprised, then shrugged and raised
his hands.

The guard patted Faroe down, then looked
at Grace speculatively.

"Don't even think about it," Faroe said
coldly.

The guard looked startled. He wasn't used
to taking orders from civilians.

"Show him your purse," Faroe said to
Grace. "That's as much of a giggle as he
gets."

She opened her purse and handed it over.
The guard grinned at her breasts, glanced
into the leather bag, and waved them
through.

Grace pushed open the door to the cottage and stepped in. The little house once

had held four residents, with a small common area and individual bedrooms. But now, only one of the bedrooms was occupied. The beds in the other rooms had been stripped.

"Lane? It's Mom. Are you here?"

A muffled sound came from the occupied bedroom.

"Jus' a min'," Lane said. He sounded like he'd been sleeping. Hard.

She went quickly to the bedroom door and looked in. Lane was stumbling out of bed, moving with a lack of coordination that frightened her. He looked at her groggily.

"Wha' you doin' here?" he asked, slurring the words.

Faroe joined her in the doorway and measured Lane.

"I had to make sure you were okay," Grace said.

Lane Franklin lurched across the bedroom and picked up a pair of green shorts. He hopped on one foot and then the other, nearly falling as he dressed. Then he straightened up and pushed his shaggy hair out of his eyes.

Faroe saw a handsome teenager, lean and athletic, a boy just growing into a man's body, just beginning to show evidence of peach fuzz on his young jaw. He had his mother's long torso and a pair of strong legs that were well proportioned and suggested speed.

But at that moment, Lane's legs weren't much good for anything. He could barely stand up.

Loaded, Faroe thought. *Screwed up to the max.*

Lane stared at his mother and mumbled something.

"What's wrong, honey?" Grace asked.

She's not used to seeing him like this, Faroe thought. He didn't know whether that was good or bad. It just was. He glanced around the living space.

"I'm fine . . . I guess." Lane's tone was as uncertain as his balance. "Haven't felt . . . good . . . since just after you left."

Grace hugged her son close. Then she held him out at arm's length, inspecting him. His skin was pale and his grin was lopsided. Everything about him was lopsided. She sniffed his breath and gave a relieved sigh. No alcohol.

Unlike Ted, who had become way too fond of booze through the years.

Faroe looked past the boy to the surrounding room. The walls were covered with posters, mostly of soccer players. The exception was one of a musician, Johnny Cash. The country and rockabilly legend was holding his guitar like a machine gun and saluting the photographer with a raised middle finger.

Defiant, maybe, Faroe decided, *but at least he isn't into the usual doper fare of headbanger rock and nihilist roll. Or worse, the* narco-corridas *making heroes out of drug traffickers.*

In one corner several Huichol death masks watched over the desk where Lane did his homework.

Faroe grinned. He'd felt the same way about school.

A blanket covered something underneath the table like a hasty shroud. Faroe lifted the blanket and found a laptop computer.

Lane lunged toward Faroe. "That's mine!"

Faroe turned, catching the boy before he fell. "Take it easy. I'm not hurting anything."

The boy stepped back and squinted at Faroe. "Oh. Sorry. Thought you were one of my *pistolero* babysitters. They're not allowed to come in the cottage. The coach told me."

"Father Magón?" Faroe asked.

"Yeah. Who are you?"

"Lane, this is Joe Faroe, an old friend of mine," Grace said. "Joe, this is my son, Lane."

Lane finally remembered he had manners. He pulled himself together, stepped forward, and offered his hand.

"Hi, uh, Mr. Faroe," he said. "Sorry. I was just . . . taking a nap."

"Nice to meet you, Lane," Faroe said, looking at the boy's eyes. Clear, but the pupils were too dilated. "Where are your roommates?"

"Huh? Oh . . . they all moved . . . three weeks ago. I don' know . . . maybe I have body odor or something." He laughed weakly at his own joke.

"How about those dudes outside?"

"They showed up at the same time."

Faroe nodded. "But they don't come inside?"

"Not allowed." Lane frowned and fought to focus his fuzzy thoughts. "They sit on the benches out there, playing with their guns, talking about girls, smoking cigarettes, eating pork rinds." He grinned. "Their hearts must look like cans of Crisco. I call them the Chicharrones Brigade."

Faroe laughed out loud. Like his mother, the kid was smart and had a wicked tongue.

"Your average Mexican security guard dies before he's old enough to worry about heart disease," Faroe said.

"Of what?"

"Silver or lead. Both can be fatal."

Lane's eyes narrowed. *Plata o plomo. That's the slogan of the narcotraficantes.*"

"It sure is. Makes a man wonder, doesn't it?"

Faroe glanced over at Grace. She was watching him, her eyes wide and intent. When she saw that Faroe had noticed her, she looked back at Lane.

"Are they taking care of you?" she asked.

The boy shrugged. "I can't leave the cottage."

"If you can't go to the cafeteria, what have you been eating?" she asked.

"Whatever they bring me. Alfredo, the *jefe* of the guards, says it's safer for me to eat here."

"What do you think?" Faroe asked Lane. "Is it safer?"

"It's boring."

"So is safety."

Lane grinned, but it quickly faded. "I want out of here."

Grace put her arm around her son's shoulder. "That's why—"

Faroe shook his head sharply. Then held his finger to his lips and pointed to the walls.

Lane stared at Grace, then at Faroe, then at the walls. Faroe put his finger to his lips again and raised an eyebrow. Lane tried to stand straight, but his eyes were almost unfocused. Then he visibly got a grip on himself, held a finger to his lips, and nodded.

Grace brushed her lips against the side of her son's face and whispered, "Trust Joe. We both have to trust Joe."

Lane swallowed, nodded, and drew himself up to his full height. Now he was inches taller than she was.

"Let's go out in the fresh air," Faroe said to Lane. "The Pork Rind Brigade lets you do that, don't they?"

"Most of the time," Lane said. "But wait. I need something to drink. My mouth is dry all the time."

He went to a small bar refrigerator and pulled out an unopened carton of orange juice. Before he could break the seal and drink, Faroe took the carton.

"Hold on," Faroe said. "I'm not a big fan of liquids packaged in Mexico."

Lane opened his mouth, closed it, and waited.

Faroe inspected the waxed carton carefully. The fold-back ears on the "open here" side were still sealed. When he looked inside the fold at the other side of the top, he spotted a tiny hole where someone had slipped a hypodermic needle through the paper. He showed the hole to Grace and to her son. Lane looked confused.

Grace didn't.

"Let's walk," she said to her son. "Fresh air is better for clearing your head than orange juice." *Especially that juice.*

When they walked out into the muggy afternoon, two guards stood up quickly and reached for their guns.

Faroe kept walking.

Grace tugged Lane in his wake.

The guards hesitated, then fell in line about ten feet behind Lane.

As soon as the trail widened, Faroe stepped back and put his arm around Lane to steady him and speed him up. Grace was doing the same from the other side, but Lane was too big for her to hold him up alone, much less to make him walk faster. The three of them moved as a unit to the water's edge, where waves were breaking on the sand.

The guards, once they saw where Lane was headed, slowed down to light cigarettes. They were at least fifty feet behind.

"Keep your voices down," Faroe said quietly. "They can't hear us over the sound of the waves."

Lane nodded that he understood, but he still looked confused.

To Grace he looked terribly vulnerable.

"What's going on?" Lane asked, shaking his head hard, trying to clear it. "Is this as bad as I think it is?"

22

GRACE GLANCED QUICKLY AT Faroe, not knowing how much to tell Lane.

"How bad do you think it is?" Faroe asked the boy.

Lane was silent for a moment, but he was thinking hard. In the ocean air he seemed more alert. He looked at his mother, then at the hard-faced man she'd brought with her.

"I'm really a prisoner, right?" the boy asked.

Grace wanted to soften Lane's words.

Faroe stopped her.

"I know this is tough," he said, touching her hair gently, "but we won't get anywhere by sugarcoating it."

Faroe looked at the boy, who was only a few inches shorter than himself, and said bluntly, "You're a hostage."

Lane blinked. Then he raked his fingers through his hair and yanked, trying to force himself to focus. "I can't think!"

"They're drugging you," Faroe said. "Probably only in the orange juice."

"What?" Lane said sharply.

"Keep your voice down," Faroe said. "It's probably a sedative. It's a common tactic for controlling hostages. They don't want to hurt you. They just want to keep you fuzzy."

"Okay," Lane said. "Okay. That's good. I was thinking I was getting really sick or going crazy or something. The nightmares . . . Jesus. I can't believe people spend money to feel like crap."

"You're not crazy," Grace said quickly, squeezing his shoulders with her arm. "You're the sanest person in a crazy mess."

"Hostage," Lane said, tasting the word, testing the reality. "So what am I hostage for? What do they want? Money from Dad?"

"We don't know for sure," Faroe said. "We should know more in the next day."

"But if you don't know, how can—"

"Honey, Joe's a professional at this sort of

thing," Grace cut in, reaching over to smooth the hair out of her son's eyes. "He's the best there is. But he's only been on the job a few hours. He needs more time to investigate."

Lane glanced at Faroe with new interest. "A professional? Really?"

"That just means people pay me money. But yeah, I've dealt with hostiles like your Chicharrones Brigade. They're just dumb soldiers. We need to find out who the generals are."

That triggered something in Lane's drugged mind. He turned to his mother. "Where's Dad?" he asked urgently.

"I—I've—" Grace began, but her voice cracked.

"We haven't been able to reach him," Faroe said. "Why do you ask?"

"Because Mr. Calderón came to see me yesterday, today too. I think. It's all kind of . . . fuzzy. He brought juice and food and asked me where Dad was."

"Carlos Calderón?" Grace asked.

Lane fought to call up the memory. Like a lot of reality since his mother had left, memory was slippery. He frowned, remembering the past twenty-four hours in bits and pieces, flashes of light and darkness. "Yeah, Mr.

Calderón was kind of pissed, uh, mad when I told him I didn't know where Dad was. Like he thought I was lying. I think he hit me a couple of times. Can't really remember. Nightmare . . ."

Grace's hand clenched hard around Lane's shoulder and she bit back every word she wanted to scream.

"Why isn't Dad here?" Lane asked. "Calderón said I could go home if Dad came down to sign me out."

Grace looked away, hiding the tears and rage and fear in her eyes.

"Your mom's pretty upset about this," Faroe said calmly. "She hasn't been able to contact your dad. It's one of our top priorities."

Lane stared at the sand.

"Do you have any idea where your dad might be?" Faroe asked.

Lane's answer was a shake of the head. Then he looked up at Faroe. "I haven't heard from him in weeks. He used to come down on a helicopter once every three or four weeks, supposedly to drop in to say hi to me, but he spent hours talking with somebody at the school office and barely waved at me."

Grace's heart turned over. No matter how tall Lane was, how fast he was growing, he was only a few months past being fourteen. He was a boy whose world had been turned upside down.

"We'll find your dad, get this thing straightened out," Faroe said. "Don't worry." He reached over and gave the boy a poke on the shoulder, man-to-man stuff that was cover for a quick glance back toward the guards.

They were smoking and laughing. Forty feet away, maybe more.

With the skill of a pickpocket, Faroe pulled a flat, compact cell phone out of his jeans. He palmed the phone and gave it to Lane, shielding the exchange with his body.

"Hide this in your room," Faroe said in a low, intent voice. "We need to stay in touch in a way that the Chicharrones Brigade can't monitor."

Lane looked down at the phone in his hand. "Cool."

"Don't look at it," Faroe said. "Don't look at them. *Look at me.* Don't look away from me when you put the phone in your shorts."

The boy turned his body slightly, slipped the phone into one of the many pockets in his cargo shorts, and never stopped looking at Faroe.

"Good," Faroe said. "The battery is fully

charged, but I didn't have time to get fresh batteries brought in. We have to decide on a communications schedule."

The boy put his hands in his pockets and tried to match Faroe's relaxed stance. "Gotcha."

Faroe smiled. Once the drugs got out of the kid's system, he'd be a pistol.

"Every night, at one A.M.," Faroe said, "pull out the antenna and turn on the phone. It's set to vibrate, not ring, so they won't hear it outside the cottage. If I haven't called you by five minutes after one, shut down and power up again at five in the morning. Can you do that?"

Lane thought a moment. "One might be a little tough but I'm used to getting up early for the twice-a-day workouts. I'll figure something out."

"Set an alarm and put it under your pillow so the guards can't hear it."

"You *do* sneak around for a living, don't you?" Lane said with genuine admiration.

"The first thing I ever needed to hide was a *Playboy* magazine. I know all the teenager tricks."

Lane flushed and gave his mother a quick sideways glance.

Grace didn't know whether to laugh or cry. "It's okay, baby—Lane. It comes with age and the Y gene."

The boy looked relieved and embarrassed at the same time. He glanced back to Faroe. "Can I call you?"

"Only if you're certain you're in immediate danger, the kind of situation my boss—ex-boss—calls a matter of extreme urgency."

Grace flinched, remembering how Dwayne had defined it: *A terrorist with a gun held against a hostage's head.*

"But I don't think that will happen," Faroe said. "The negotiations haven't really opened yet."

Swallowing hard, Lane nodded.

"The other reason to call me is if you hear from your dad," Faroe added. "Just hit the speed dialer. There's only one number in the memory. It will ring in New York, but whoever answers will always know how to get hold of me and your mom. If they can't reach us for some reason, ask for James Steele. You have all that?"

Lane nodded and touched the pocket where he'd concealed the phone. He grinned at Faroe.

"Thanks," he said. "I already know where I'm going to hide it."

Faroe tapped him on the shoulder. "Good. If I'm going to make burros of the bad guys, I need your help."

Grace saw a sudden proud smile spread across her son's face. He was in charge of his own fate now, in a way he hadn't been when she and Joe arrived.

He understands Lane better than Ted ever did. Or ever wanted to.

A familiar mixture of sadness and anger swept through her. She crushed it. Lane needed her focused on helping him, not on her past mistakes.

Faroe gripped Lane's shoulder gently. "Okay. Now I want you and your mom to kill twenty minutes looking at the gulls and the waves and talking about soccer and grades and the girls you never see anymore. If I'm not back by then, go to your cottage. I'll meet you there. And don't worry about the guards. They're on a short leash." *For now.*

"Where are you going?" Grace asked.

Faroe didn't answer. He just headed with long strides toward the chapel.

Grace started talking about soccer.

One of the guards braced Faroe as he walked past.

"Where do you go?" the guard demanded.

"Church," Faroe said. "To pray for the boy's safety."

The guard's smile was as thin as a new moon. "You are wise."

23

FAROE STOPPED IN FRONT of the small chapel whose wooden doors had been burned gray and black by the sun. Salt air from the nearby ocean had corroded the doors' wrought-iron hinges to reddish shadows. A plaque beside the entrance said that Jesuit monks had built the place in 1789, with the help of God and the local Indians. Now the adobe brick walls were slumped like an old priest's shoulders.

The guard who had followed Faroe lounged against the outside of the adobe wall that surrounded the chapel, not crowding his quarry but clearly keeping his eyes open.

The guard's hand was on the Glock he carried butt forward in the waistband of his jeans. It wasn't a particularly threatening gesture—if you were used to seeing armed men.

A pepper tree with a trunk three feet thick filled the side yard of the little adobe chapel. The tree shaded a stone fountain so old that the inscriptions had worn away. Through the lacy green curtain of leaves, Faroe caught a glimpse of a swirling black cassock. A priest was entering the church through a back door.

Father Rafael Magón was a little late, but he was there.

Without a glance at his guard, Faroe walked into the shadowed chapel and pulled the wooden door closed behind him. His eyes adjusted to the dim light coming through four dusty stained-glass windows. The altar was made of tarnished tin and ancient wood. The figure of Christ on the cross must have been carved in the nineteenth century, or even earlier. The Savior's face was dusky, his features thick, his body drenched in blood. He was *muy indio,* like the parishioners he absolved.

The confession booth was set in an alcove beside the altar. Faroe slid onto the rough bench reserved for *penitentes,* but he left the privacy curtain open so he would know if anyone came in the chapel's front door. Through the wooden grille, he made out a swarthy man with black hair and careful blue eyes.

"Father, forgive me, for I have sinned and it's been a long, long time since my last confession," Faroe said. "But then, the same is probably true of you."

The vivid blue eyes focused sharply through the grate. "Confession is a one-way sacrament," the priest said softly. His English was polished, almost without accent. He could have been raised in San Diego rather than Mexico.

"Then where does a wayward priest confess?" Faroe asked.

"Who are you and what do you want?" The voice was still soft, but it was cold with the understanding of power.

"I'm a man who knows you're more than the simple *indio* priest you seem to be. I want to know why a highly placed and well-educated priest, one with powerful sponsors in Rome, finds himself absolving murderers and drug lords."

Behind the grate Magón was like a mosaic of a man rather than flesh itself.

"All of God's children need pastoral guidance," the priest said. "All congregants are human. Therefore they are sinners. The church goes where it is most needed."

"There's a big jump from ministering to aiding and abetting. You seem more interested in your corrupt sinners than in the boy Lane Franklin, an innocent who could die of your neglect."

The wooden grate shot aside. "Who are you?" Magón demanded again, his voice low. "Give me the truth or this charade ends."

What Faroe gave him was a level, unflinching look.

The little chapel was quiet for a long time.

Magón blinked and glanced away, a man thinking, and thinking hard. When he looked at Faroe again, he seemed less certain, more wary. He settled back on his side of the wooden wall.

"You have a good friend," Magón said, "a man I trust as I trust few on earth. He told me to be here but he couldn't say why. He merely said he believed you could be trusted."

Faroe leaned against the wooden wall on his own side of the screen. The air inside the thick-walled little chapel was humid, still, shielded from the restless storm churning up from Cabo San Lucas.

The place smelled dangerous, not confessional.

No risk, no reward, Faroe reminded himself dryly.

"Judge Silva has hired me to negotiate her son's release," Faroe said. "At the moment, we aren't even sure who to negotiate with, since the target of this extortion is Ted Franklin. Lane is merely the pawn. Will you help?"

Magón bowed his head and stayed motionless for several long breaths. Then Faroe heard a rustling sound, like cloth shifting. A thick leather wallet appeared in the little window.

"Cigar?" the priest asked quietly.

"No thanks."

"Do you object if I have one? It's my principal vice. Some of my brethren think I take too much pleasure in them, so I only smoke when no brothers are around."

"Go ahead, I won't report you to the archbishop of Tijuana. Does he realize you're a Vatican spy?"

Magón's only answer was the metallic sound of a lighter being struck. A few seconds later Faroe smelled smoke from a decent Havana cigar.

"Vatican spy?" Magón asked with a faint smile. "Isn't that what is called an oxymoron, like 'military intelligence'?"

"Some of us heathens think the church is as much a political institution as it is a religious one."

"The church does what it must," Magón said.

"So do I. I don't have cathedrals and armies of priests behind me, which makes it a lot easier for me to slide between cracks and disappear into the shadows. That makes a lot of people nervous. What nationality are you, Father?"

The question seemed to surprise Magón. He thought about it for a moment, shrugged, and answered. "I was raised in Logan Heights barrio, in San Diego, but I was born here in Baja."

"Down around El Alamo," Faroe said.

Black eyebrows raised in surprise. "You are clairvoyant?"

"No, but I know that the Magonistas who didn't get their asses shot off in 1911 ended up in the *ejidos* and the mines around El Alamo. There's even a little community called Ojos Azules."

Blue eyes.

"You've been there?" Magón asked.

"Yes."

"Most Mexicans know very little about the Magonistas. It's one of the sad things about my country. Our history is only found in the shadows. You're an odd gringo that you see those shadows."

"I never knew my father very well," Faroe said. "I was born late in his life. The only trips we ever took were to the mountains east of here, between Ojos Azules and El Alamo. My father was either crazy or a shaman, or both at once. The poor people accepted, even celebrated, his differences. He was a marijuana smuggler back before marijuana became an international commodity. He loved to smoke weed and he loved that wild country and its stoic people. After he died, I came down to Ensenada to go surfing. The ocean was the color of his eyes."

Magón studied Faroe's face. There was nothing to see but intent green eyes, wariness, surprising intelligence, and the relaxation of someone who was used to being alert without being anxious.

"Yet here you are," the priest said. "Between the surfer and the man you are now lies much history, yes? You have a hard look about you, the look of a policeman rather than a smuggler."

"I was a cop once," Faroe said, "just like that guy outside with the gun, just like the Chicharrones Brigade keeping Lane in his four-bedroom prison. You don't have to be honest to carry a badge. Or a crucifix."

"So cynical," Magón said wryly.

"It's a dirty job, but if someone doesn't do it, everyone will have to. There are still some innocents in this corrupt world. Lane is one of them."

"And his mother?"

"What about her?"

"I was wondering if there might be some personal relationship between you and the beautiful judge."

It was Faroe's turn to be surprised. News of the hot act in the marina parking lot had made it to Mexico sooner than he'd expected. "Since when do the *federales* report to you?"

Magón looked puzzled. Then he dragged

on the cigar, making its tip glow beneath a pale layer of ash. "I didn't need a *federale* to tell me there is something between you and the woman. I saw the three of you walking down there on the sand. A close relationship would explain why you're trampling where angels fear to tiptoe."

"You have your motives," Faroe said. "I have mine. The only real question is if we can find common ground."

Magón sighed. "I don't want Lane harmed. That's true of all my charges. But Lane is . . . different. Intelligent enough to fear, brave enough not to show it, a natural athlete, a superb student once he realized it mattered, and with surprising insight into adults for a boy his age."

Something in Faroe began to relax. The risk he'd taken was very close to paying off. "Can I count on you to keep Lane safe while I try to untangle this mess?"

"This 'mess,' as you call it, is quite complicated. It's not likely to yield to the efforts of a single man, no matter how skillful or dangerous he is. The outcome is in God's hands."

"My objectives are more limited than yours," Faroe said. "If necessary, I can work alone. Your pope wouldn't like the results."

"This situation has very high stakes. No one controls all the players. No one can guarantee the outcome."

"Not even God?"

"He works in ways we mortals don't always understand."

"Save it for the believers. I hold individual mortals responsible for earthly outcomes."

Magón straightened. "You're threatening me."

"Amen."

The priest's blue eyes stared through the little window, studying Faroe. Magón puffed quickly on the cigar and his face disappeared in a billow of smoke. When the air cleared, his eyes had changed. They were direct, hard.

"If I am as corrupt as you suspect I might be," Magón said, "why wouldn't I run straight to the men who hold Lane?"

"Because you learned this secret in the confessional, Father."

"Only believers are protected by the sanctity of the confessional."

"A lawyer, as well as a diplomat and a spy," Faroe said dryly. "I should have expected no less from the Vatican. Yes, I'm taking a calculated risk with you. I trust our mutual friend in Rome. He may or may not know what you're up to but he knows you're more complex than you appear to be."

"A cynic, yet still a man of some faith," Magón said.

"I've learned to trust a few people. Damned few."

"I, too, have faith in a few people. For the moment I'll keep the confidences of a man who walks into danger by choice."

Faroe almost smiled. Under other circumstances, he would have enjoyed Father Rafael Magón, radical pragmatist and Vatican spy.

"Where can I find Hector Rivas?" Faroe asked.

"Why?"

"He holds Lane's life in his murdering hands," Faroe said.

Savoring his cigar, Magón considered the request for a full minute. A feudal lord and *traficante* like Hector Rivas Osuna had many enemies. A man like Faroe could find many ways to ambush even the highly protected Hector.

"I have nothing to gain by killing Hector," Faroe said, understanding the reason for Magón's hesitation. "With Hector dead, Lane would be in more danger, not less. I'm here to negotiate before anyone gets real nervous. Nerves and guns scare the hell out of me."

Magón looked at the tip of the glowing cigar and sighed a smoke-laden breath. "Normally, I wouldn't be able to answer your question. Hector is always on the move, never sleeping in the same place twice in a row. Sometimes he moves several times in the same night."

"Yeah, well, the man has a lot to worry about," Faroe said sardonically. "History is one long list of people who lay awake wondering who to trust. Some of them guessed right. Others died young."

The priest smiled, then sighed again. "One of Hector's nephews is getting married. I will perform the ceremony this weekend at the Rivas *rancho* east of Jacumba."

"My condolences to the bride," Faroe said under his breath.

"Tonight there's a celebration in Ensenada," Magón said. "Hector is the patriarch of an extended clan. He will attend the party, even if only for an hour or so."

"Ensenada is too big to search in an hour or so. Can you narrow it down?"

"Try the Canción. It's a restaurant on the

grounds of the Encantamar, just off the ocean walk, the *malecón,* in Ensenada. Hector likes the abalone there."

"Thank you, Father."

"Understand that Hector Rivas Osuna is a ticking bomb."

"Anything in particular that will set him off?"

"Everything, at any moment. He has become addicted to rock and nicotine."

The confessional window slid closed.

Shit. A crackhead toking doctored Mexican cigarettes. He could blow up at any instant.

The chapel was so quiet Faroe could hear the gentle trickle of water in the fountain beneath the pepper tree.

The complex Father Rafael Magón had vanished.

24

THE SUN WAS HIDDEN behind a seething silver mass of clouds. Waves humped up man high, higher, then exploded on the beach in a boil of sand and froth. The wind whipped wave tops into a salty mist. Onshore, the wind stripped fine sand from the beach and scored unprotected skin.

Faroe spotted Grace and Lane sitting together, watching the wild waves. The boy's shoulders were hunched in fatigue, his mother's in tension. Neither seemed to notice the seagulls wheeling and keening above them, begging for scraps.

The armed guards lounged twenty yards

up the beach, smoking and waiting, watching, always watching.

Grace sensed Faroe's approach and turned to look at him. Her face was smooth, expressionless. She was working hard to keep her fears under control.

Good for you, woman, Faroe thought, *even if Lane reads you like a billboard. Both of you get points for trying to help each other.*

"Time to go," Faroe said to Grace.

She started to object, then swallowed it.

Lane stood up, disappointed but not surprised.

They walked back across the beach together. Sand peppered cloth and skin. Pretending to turn from a gust of stinging wind, Faroe checked the guards' position.

They couldn't overhear.

"Listen to me," Faroe said in a low voice to Lane. "You can trust Father Rafael, but only up to a point. Don't tell him about the phone or the computer. But if you believe it's all going from sugar to shit, make sure he knows."

Lane nodded.

"Lay off the orange juice," Faroe said. "Pour it down the drain when nobody's looking, act zoned if you want to, but keep a clear head. It's your best weapon. You can help us, but only if you're in control of yourself."

Lane nodded again and gave Faroe an uncertain smile. "Thanks."

"We're going to get you out of this," Grace said tightly. "I promise."

"I'm okay," the boy said. "I just wish . . ." His voice died.

"Go ahead," she said.

"I just wish I knew what Dad's doing in all this."

Sweet bugger all, thought Faroe.

"So do I," Grace said.

When they reached the cottage, mother and son went in. Faroe stayed outside, letting them have their private good-bye. Several minutes later Grace walked out looking furious and frightened.

"He's fine," she hissed under her breath. "He got it hidden." Beneath her fear, there was a bitter kind of anger in her voice.

Faroe didn't say anything until they were back in the Mercedes and leaving the campus. Then he dragged the satellite cell phone out of his bag and punched up a number out of its memory.

When the call was answered, he spoke quickly. "Get me technical support." He only had to wait a few seconds. "This is Faroe. Search the tech inventory. I had an experimental Motorola checked out about a year ago. I didn't bother to return it when I bailed last week. Do me a favor. Activate the GPS pinger on it and get me a lat-lon reading."

"Hold, please."

"Holding," Faroe said.

Grace looked over. "What are you doing?"

Faroe waved off her question. A few seconds later, St. Kilda tech support came back on the line. Faroe listened and memorized.

"One seventeen by thirty-two ten," Faroe said. "Good, it's working fine. Now set an alarm perimeter on it. If the damn thing moves more than two nautical miles, let me know ASAP."

"Twenty-four/seven monitoring?"

"Yes. I know it costs a lot. Call Steele if you have to, but mount that watch *now*. After the monitor is in place, tell research to find out who owns the Encantamar hotel and Canción restaurant in Ensenada. Got that?"

"Yes."

Faroe punched the call off and turned to Grace. "You were saying?"

"What are you doing?" she repeated.

"Just what it sounded like—setting up a

passive surveillance on your son. As long as he can keep the phone within arm's reach, we'll know where he is."

"That's too dangerous. What if they find out?"

Faroe turned onto the toll road and headed south, toward Ensenada. "What are they going to do, spank him? Come on, Your Honor, get serious."

"I am," she shot back. "You might as well have given him a loaded gun."

"Hell of an idea. Did you have one handy?" Faroe gave her a hard sideways look. "I didn't think so."

"You're crazy! If they find that phone, they'll know that I—"

"Look," Faroe cut across her words, telling himself to be patient, she was under a hellish strain. "All they'll know is that someone gave him a way to communicate with Mom. What's important is that Lane feels like he's connected, not cut off, not so much a prisoner."

"But—"

"Despair is the prisoner's worst enemy," Faroe said flatly. "Right now, Lane feels like he has a way of controlling his own fate. We need him level, not panicked or shut down."

"You didn't see how scared he was underneath the drugs and the don't-worry-Mom talk."

"Your son is a tough, savvy kid. Let him use that. It could make the difference between getting free and getting dead."

"He's barely fifteen!"

"A lot of kids don't make it that long. Life's only money-back guarantee is that you die."

Grace simply stared at Faroe and bit back all the words she wanted to scream.

You don't understand! Would you be so damned calm if you knew Lane was your son?

Or is it different for men? Don't they get the importance of children? Sex, yes, that's important to men.

But not babies.

Even their own.

Yet part of Grace was afraid that Faroe would be different. He would care, and in caring, hate her for what he'd never known.

Damned if I do and damned if I don't. So don't.

Don't think about it.

Any of it.

You can't change the past. You can't foresee the future. You can only live now, this moment.

And don't scream.
Whatever you do, don't scream.

But she wanted to scream so much she felt like she was being strangled.

Grace turned away and stared out the window so that Faroe wouldn't somehow sense the bleak warfare pulsing beneath her silence.

25

THE DRIVE TO ENSENADA wasn't long, but by the time Faroe reached the city, he'd had a gutful of the silent tension in the car, an invisible storm waiting to unload.

Grace had barely breathed.

"The first time I saw Ensenada," Faroe said, "it was a lazy resort with a few hotels for gringos and a business district forty years out of date. Now it's a full-speed-ahead port city with seventy-five thousand people, a good seawall, cruise ship docks, and a working waterfront."

Grace didn't even look at him.

So much for a neutral topic, Faroe thought.

In silence he found the hotel overlooking the harbor, parked, and went inside. After a little haggling he rented an ocean-view suite on the fourth floor. He went back to the SUV, pulled Grace out, and herded her up to their room.

In silence.

Faroe shot the bolt behind them and went immediately to the balcony to check out the sight lines. The restaurant Magón said would host a Rivas prewedding celebration was crammed into a corner on the ocean side of the hotel property, surrounded by a head-high wall and a small, well-tended desert landscape. A sign was posted on the wrought-iron front gate, but it was too far away to read from the balcony.

He dug a small pair of binoculars out of his bag and went back for a better look at the sign.

CERRADO

A translation was included for the language-impaired gringos whose dollars fueled Ensenada.

CLOSED FOR PRIVATE PARTY

So far, Magón's information looked good. The Canción was indeed reserved for Hector's clan.

When Faroe turned back to the room, Grace was standing in the center of the suite clutching her shoulder bag. She had the shattered-around-the-eyes look found in psych wards and battlefields. The flat line of her mouth told him that she wasn't going to feel chatty anytime soon.

Faroe went to the telephone, ordered food and a bucket of beers from room service, and came back.

She hadn't moved.

"You want me to throw you in the shower," he asked, "or would a cold washcloth get the job done?"

Without a word Grace went to the bathroom and shut the door behind her. She looked at the toilet and wondered if she could get rid of the cold fear in her gut by sticking her finger down her throat.

You can't throw up the past.

Falling apart won't do Lane any good.

Breathe, damn it.

Just breathe.

She drew a ragged breath, then another, and walked two steps to the sink. The mirror reflected an exhausted woman with a tear-streaked face and wild hair. She dropped her purse on the tile counter and turned on the faucet. Water ran coldly in the sink, sounding loud in the silence. She dipped her hands in the flow, cupped up a double handful, and slapped it against her face. The water smelled faintly of chlorine. It took a few hard, cold splashes, but finally she breathed almost normally without having to remind herself.

The soap was wrapped in paper. It smelled too sweet, like Grandma Marta's pink bath bar, a scent that brought memories gushing back, everything Grace had vowed to leave behind.

Tears much hotter than water ran down her face.

Never look back.

For the first time she wondered if Marta had managed that inhuman feat.

With quick, automatic gestures, Grace fixed her makeup and finger-combed her hair. Despite eyes bloodshot from crying, the new woman in the mirror looked more together. She dug out a bottle of eyedrops. They burned worse than tears, but the next time she looked in the mirror her eyes were clear. She smoothed her clothes as best she could, opened the bathroom door, and went out to face whatever came next.

Sultry, thick air billowed through the open drapes. Boats at anchor moved restlessly, reflecting the power of the distant storm even in sheltered waters. She felt her mood lift. Part of her was looking forward to the violent storm to come. She'd always loved storms. They had a freedom she'd allowed herself only once.

With Joe Faroe.

The man who was leaning against the railing, his arms straight, his attention entirely on the view below.

Memorizing everything, no doubt, she thought with a flash of irritation. *Where does that man get his energy and focus?*

Room service had been uncommonly quick. A handful of plates covered with tin hats sat on the table. An ice bucket on a stand held six long-necked bottles of Corona beer.

Faroe looked over his shoulder as she walked up behind him.

"Better," he said. "Food will help even more."

"Stop mothering me."

He stepped close to her, close enough to stir her hair with his breath. "I don't feel a damn bit motherly toward you."

Her eyes widened. "It's just the wind."

"What is?"

"The wind reminds you of the time when we were . . . together."

"Amada," he said, breathing in her scent, "there are few things on the face of this earth that don't remind me of you."

For an instant she was certain he was going to kiss her. Then he stepped away.

"There's chicken, steak, and cold lobster," he said. "Eat."

He went to the table, opened two bottles of beer, and lifted lids off plates. Three kinds of protein. Baskets of small flour tortillas and a bowl of fresh salsa. He took a tortilla, forked a few bites of roasted chicken into it, and added salsa. Then he folded the tortilla neatly, rolled it in a napkin, and offered it to her.

"Do you have to do everything so well?" she asked, irritated all over again.

"You pay for the best, you get the best," he said, still holding out the food. "Eat. Like I said before, you're a high-octane woman and you're running on empty. If you won't eat for yourself, do it for your son."

She took the burrito. A single bite told her that Faroe was right. She was so hungry she was weak.

No wonder my emotions are all over the place.

Quickly she ate the burrito, looked up, and found another burrito under her nose. Lobster this time, marinated in cilantro and lime, so succulent she almost drooled. She dove in and didn't come up for air.

Watching Grace without appearing to, Faroe ate a few pieces of lobster meat dipped in salsa. Then he made himself a fat steak burrito and added a couple of jalapeño peppers from a separate plate. He grabbed a beer, took the burrito to the balcony, and watched the restaurant.

Grace scooped more lobster into a tortilla, made a defiantly messy burrito, and went out to the balcony.

Four stories below, two workmen were busy inside the restaurant's high fence. There was a pile of flagstones that the men had lifted out of the walkway.

"That's another irritating thing," she said.

"Workmen moving flagstones?" Faroe asked without looking away from the men.

"No. You. You're always multitasking. Eating and talking and watching, yet still completely focused on the job."

"Steele would drive you nuts. He's twice as bad as I am."

"Are those two men really that interesting?" Grace mumbled around a bite of lobster.

"Short of digging foxholes under live fire, I've never seen two men work harder in my life. This is *mañana*-land, yet they're acting like someone is holding a stopwatch on them. I find that curious."

Especially when Hector Rivas Osuna is expected to appear at this very restaurant tonight.

Grace leaned against the railing, licked her fingers, and looked down. Anyone who wanted to watch the men would have to be above them. They were hidden from ground-level people by the high wall and heavily decorated wrought-iron gate. Both men were dressed in coveralls and carrying toolboxes. A pickup truck parked in the alley behind the restaurant held more tools.

One workman tilted a large flagstone on

edge and braced it with his body so that the other man could dig in the sandy soil beneath.

"They look perfectly ordinary to me," she said. "You're just paranoid. You've lived in this hellish world too long. Everything sets you off."

"Could be," Faroe said.

And kept on watching with the intensity of a hungry wolf.

"What do you see that I don't?" she asked finally.

"There's some sort of official decal on the side of the truck."

"So?"

"Even in Mexico, city or state employees don't usually work on private property."

"Maybe they're repairing a sewer leak," she said.

"Ensenada's sewers run the other way, a straight flush to the bay."

"Remind me not to go swimming here."

Faroe went back into the suite and returned with his binoculars. He dragged a chair over to the railing and sat down, peering between the rails with the binoculars.

Grace snuck some of Faroe's beer and waited.

Silence.

"Well?" she prodded.

"Don't go swimming here."

She didn't know whether to smile or smack him. "Do you see anything interesting?"

"They're wearing coveralls, but one of them is wearing a white dress shirt underneath," Faroe said. "In short, they aren't your average dirt-poor Josés living off their brawn."

He offered her the glasses and the chair. She put aside his beer and sat down. The little binoculars were astonishingly strong and clear. Their power magnified the tremor in her hands, visible proof of her underlying tension. She rested her hands on the railing to steady them.

The two men jumped into focus. They looked too soft to be manual laborers. Sweat ran down their full cheeks. One man was indeed wearing a white dress shirt and a heavy gold wristwatch whose diamonds flashed even in the overcast light. He handled the shovel like he wasn't sure which end to use. The second man glanced jerkily around the grounds as he balanced the broad flagstone on its edge.

"Okay," she said softly. "Point made. Shouldn't we be hiding or something? The lookout is twitching like a flea."

"He's at ground level so he's watching at ground level." Faroe took a swallow of the beer, which was barely cool now. "He's an idiot. Anyone with half a brain looks at balconies and roof lines as well. You'd be amazed how many dead idiots there are. Mother Nature's way of chlorinating the gene pool."

"You're just full of good cheer."

"Thank you."

"Here," she said, handing him the glasses. "Even if they're idiots, spying on them makes me nervous."

Faroe switched places with Grace, put the glasses to his eyes, and crouched to look through the railing again.

"What are they doing?" she asked finally. "And why, other than paranoid curiosity, do we care?"

"Hector Rivas Osuna will be eating at that restaurant tonight, along with some members of his family."

"You're kidding."

"Why do you think we're in Ensenada?" Faroe asked.

She opened her mouth, closed it. *Idiot. Did you think he brought you here to tear up the sheets?*

"You could have told me," she said stiffly.

"You weren't interested in talking to me, remember?"

Grace gave him a killing look, but it was wasted. His attention was four stories below.

"So you came to spy on Hector?" she asked.

"I want to talk to Hector. Whether you realize it or not, so do you. Hector is the key to this whole situation. He's the one calling the shots."

He's the one who knows how much time Lane really has.

Grace rubbed her arms like the wind swirling around the balcony was cool rather than hot. "Do we have to be in the same room with that man? Can't you just call him up or something? He scares me."

"Men like Hector are primitive. They understand two things—in-your-face macho or ordering hits behind your back. We have to make Hector think we're macho enough to face him and deliver the one guy in the world he really wants to see, so that Hector won't hit us when our back is turned."

At first Grace didn't understand. Then she did. The food she'd eaten twisted in her stomach.

"Ted?" she asked in a raw voice.

"Your ever-loving ex," Faroe agreed.

"But I don't know where Ted is!"

"You just got a lead on him."

"What?"

"Lie, Your Honor. Hector believes you're his ticket to your husband. We're going to help that belief along, and while we do, we're going to make it real clear you'll play Hector's game only so long as he takes good care of Lane."

Grace opened her mouth to argue, saw the flash of impatience on Faroe's usually impassive face, and reminded herself that he was the expert.

"Kidnapping is all about the safety of the hostage," he said. "We're delivering Hector an in-your-face reminder that it's an issue that cuts both ways. No happy hostage, no happy game."

"But we can't deliver Ted."

"Don't bet on it. There's very little St. Kilda Consulting can't do if it really wants to."

"You're serious, aren't you? About giving Ted to Hector Rivas Osuna?" Grace asked in a rising voice.

"Yes."

"I wouldn't give a handful of dirt to that creature, much less a human being. Ted might not be much, but he's human. I can't do this."

"Can't, won't, or don't want to?"

Grace didn't know what to say.

Faroe lifted the glasses to his eyes again, studying the workmen and then shifting his attention to the alley where their truck was parked. Another vehicle had just pulled in and stopped behind the truck. Two more men stepped out and went to the truck.

"Your child's father or your child," Faroe said without looking away from the alley. "Not a happy choice, but it's the only one Hector put on the table. You knew that from the beginning."

Grace closed her eyes. Faroe was right. She'd known it, she just hadn't *believed* it.

She hadn't wanted to.

She still didn't want to.

"There has to be another way," she said.

"When you find it, tell me."

The room went silent except for the restless wind.

"If you can't decide," Faroe said finally, "go

north and stay there. St. Kilda will do precisely what you hired us for—get your son
back. Just be damned sure not to ask how
we do it."

26

"GRACE," FAROE SAID IN a low voice. "Smile at me, come nibble on my neck, and in general give me a visible excuse to get the hell off this balcony."

The tone of his voice as much as his words told Grace that something was very wrong.

How can he tell me to set Ted up so that Lane goes free, and in the next breath tell me to be a seductive actress?

Because there's no other choice, that's how.

Grace moved stiffly to Faroe, bent over, sank her teeth into his collar, and tugged.

She'd rather have gone for his jugular, but she knew better.

He put down the binoculars, looked at her, and smiled. His eyes were cold. "New workmen arrived. They aren't sloppy. They look up."

"If you had a tie, I'd pull you into the room by it." *And strangle you.*

"Squeeze my butt. Same effect and it will send a message." His smile changed, more real, and his eyes weren't like stone. "Yeah, I know you're wishing for claws you could sink into me."

She reached around him, smoothed her hand over a hard butt cheek, and sank in. "Note to self. Grow claws."

Smiling, Faroe used his body to crowd her inside.

"Close the curtains," he said. "Make it look like a perfume ad."

"You're enjoying this."

"Only part of it, *amada.*"

She was smart enough not to ask which part. Plastering what she hoped looked like a lusty smile on her face, she grabbed the billowing curtains and closed them like a stripper playing with a G-string.

As soon as Faroe was out of sight behind the drapes, he went to the window beside the balcony and parted the cloth just enough to give him a narrow slit. Slowly he lifted the glasses and watched.

Weary and edgy at the same time, Grace sank down on the bed. Three minutes clicked past on the digital clock on the table beside her while Faroe watched the four men from his blind. Then he lowered the glasses, stepped back, and grabbed a notepad from the drawer in the bedside table. He tweaked the curtain again, saw that the men were all in their vehicles, and eased back out onto the balcony with the binoculars.

Grace followed like a weary, wary shadow.

Two vehicles left the alley and turned onto the waterfront street. After they disappeared Faroe scribbled down notes. Then he turned to study the restaurant entrance. The flagstones were all in place again. There was nothing to show the landscaping had ever been disturbed.

Faroe lowered the glasses and stared out at the rolling, wind-whipped ocean beyond the breakwater. Finally he turned back to Grace.

"Where were we?" he said. "Oh yeah, we were weighing choices and moral implications. Nasty business, but necessary in this line of work. Now we've got another choice to consider."

"We do?"

"Yeah."

She didn't want to ask.

She didn't have any choice.

"What is it?" she said.

"Which benefits Lane more—Hector alive or dead?"

"Are you talking about killing Hector?" she asked, shocked.

"Me? Not at this point. But those four dudes, the ones who were driving vehicles with Baja state government tags, likely they have murder on their minds."

Grace just stared at Faroe.

"They left a calling card under the flagstone that's the front doorstep of the Canción restaurant," Faroe said.

"A calling card? What do you mean?"

"An IED."

"Translation," she said impatiently.

"Improvised explosive device."

"Like a pipe bomb?"

"That's one kind. I can't be sure without

going over to take a closer look, but this one looks like a cellular telephone wired to a standard-issue claymore."

"Claymore—isn't that some kind of explosive left over from World War I?" she asked.

Faroe smiled slightly. "In the good old days before black powder, a claymore was a big, double-handed broadsword, perfectly designed for splitting a man from crown to crotch in a single stroke. But nowadays, a claymore is a bomb that would do the world a real favor if it went off within ten or fifteen meters of the Rivas family. So is Lane better off with Hector alive or dead?"

Grace opened her mouth, closed it, opened it again. "You're the expert."

He drew a deep breath and blew it out slowly. Thinking about Hector's remains decorating three square blocks made Faroe want to smile. "I should recuse myself. I despise drug dealers."

She waited and wondered again if she should tell Faroe the truth about Lane, if that truth would affect Faroe's decision either way.

"Shit," he said, blowing out another long breath. "I hate it when this happens."

"This?"

"When I have to save a filthy son of a bitch

like Hector so that I have a better chance of saving an innocent like Lane."

"What are you going to do?"

"Disarm the damn thing."

"That's crazy! You could be killed. Call in a specialist."

"No time to bring in St. Kilda. So who do I call? Who in the Mexican government do you trust?"

She started to speak, stopped, and stayed silent. She hadn't the faintest idea who to call.

Or who not to.

Faroe smiled grimly. "You're learning, *amada.* Wish I didn't have to be the teacher."

"Why?"

"Nobody loves the bad-news dude."

The cell phone in his pocket vibrated. He pulled it out, read the text message, and shook his head.

Grace was afraid to ask and more afraid not to. "Now what's wrong?"

"The hotel and restaurant are part of a major corporation which is part of the biggest business conglomerate in Baja. Grupo Calderón. Your old friend Carlos Calderón is one of Grupo's major owners."

Her hollow, down-the-rabbit-hole feeling increased. "That doesn't make sense. Carlos Calderón is in business with Hector. Why would he put out word to Hector's enemies that he'd be at this restaurant tonight?"

"Maybe Carlos wants to dissolve the partnership."

She frowned. "So are we better or worse off than before?"

"I don't know."

"But you're supposed to . . ." She heard her own words and sighed instead of finishing the sentence.

"Know everything?" he finished sardonically. "My name is Faroe, not Yahweh. The other news St. Kilda sent is less ambiguous."

"Is that good?"

"You tell me. They're closing in on Ted. The fool used his corporate credit card."

Grace ran her fingers through her wind-blown hair. "For what? Booze or bimbos?"

Faroe looked interested. "Ted have a problem with booze?"

"As far as I'm concerned, yes. Ted doesn't think so."

"You have a problem with his bimbos, too?"

"Only that I was that stupid once."

"He made you his wife, not his arm candy."

"My mistake," Grace said. "Too bad I'm not the only one paying for it."

Faroe saw the turmoil of emotions beneath her calm words and changed the subject. "Ted was buying something worse than booze—a lawyer."

"Stuart Sturgis of Bauman, Sturgis, Bauman, and McClellum?"

Faroe nodded.

"He handled our divorce," Grace said. "He and Ted are old college friends and business partners. And no, every time I called Stu, he hadn't heard a word from Ted, and if he did he'd get back to me instantly, yada yada."

"Who was your lawyer for the divorce?"

"I didn't have one."

"No wonder you ended up with nothing."

Grace's eyes narrowed. "I ended up with a car, a college fund in the form of half ownership in a fake horse ranch, and a house in La Jolla for my son. That's all I wanted."

Faroe didn't point out that the home was now mortgaged to pay for her son's rescue, and no one might be alive to use the college fund.

"St. Kilda has a tail and a tap on good old Stu," Faroe said. "Sooner or later, he'll lead us to Ted."

"A tap? A phone tap? That's illegal."

"I don't know what you're talking about, Your Honor, and it will never happen again."

"Nolo," she said.

"Bingo. Stop asking questions. Either I lie or I tell you about activities that a judge shouldn't have personal knowledge of without calling the cops. An enemy who wanted to make a federal case of your guilty knowledge could do just that."

Grace didn't argue. She was skating so close to the edge of the legally permissible that it would take a miracle to keep from falling off.

"How long will it take you to"—*blow yourself up*—"disarm that bomb?" she asked.

"I won't know until I get a look at it. If it's beyond my skill set, I'll leave it alone."

"Take your cell phone."

Faroe laughed. "Why? Believe me, if I screw up, you'll be the second one to know. The chance of a little 'oops' like this is why St. Kilda insists on having a full DNA panel on all operatives. Makes positive ID a lot easier."

Her eyelids flinched. "You'll need someone to warn you if those men show up again."

He weighed the idea. Despite her calm words, her eyes were too dark and her skin was unusually pale. But her hands weren't shaking and she was remembering to breathe.

Most of the time.

"Give me your cell phone," Faroe said. "I'll punch in a number."

"Haven't we done this before?" she muttered, reaching for her purse.

"Sometimes once just isn't enough."

Grace looked up suddenly. Faroe's expression was bland and his eyes were a smoldering green. Knowing that her thoughts were written on her face, she ducked her head and pulled the cell phone out of her purse.

"Now your color is better," he said.

"You're a—"

"Hush, woman," he cut in, grinning and taking her cell phone. "Think how bad you'd feel if your last words to me were insults."

"I'll take a rain check, *man,*" she retorted.

"You see someone coming, hit this button," Faroe said, handing her back her phone.

"My phone will vibrate against my package and I'll think of you."

"Two rain checks."

Faroe was still laughing as he shut the hotel door behind himself and headed toward the IED.

27

WHEN FAROE WALKED OUT of the hotel toward the restaurant, the wind was easing, but still strong enough to cover every sound but the constant blare of horns. Local custom insisted that brakes weren't macho. Horns were.

A huge white cruise ship lay at anchor just inside the small harbor's breakwater. Dinghies shuttled passengers ashore for an artificial foreign "adventure." Faroe wondered why anyone bothered with a herd's-eye view of anything.

But then, he'd never understood people who thought adventure could be safe.

Looking casual, even idle, he wandered over to the garden gate outside the restaurant. The gate was locked. Through the metal grille and iron ivy, he could see the two-by-three-foot flagstone the fake workmen had lifted. The sandy soil around it had been brushed to conceal any signs of their work.

If Faroe hadn't seen them plant the claymore, he wouldn't have suspected a thing.

He looked back over at the hotel and let his gaze travel up to the fourth floor. Grace was leaning against the balcony railing like a woman enjoying the view. The cell phone in his pocket was calm.

Faroe ambled around the corner of the wall to the service entrance the workmen had used. Locked.

They must have had a key. Inside job? Maybe.

Maybe not.

Hard to tell the players without a scorecard.

Grace held on to the railing and tried to look as relaxed as Faroe. While he casually tested the quality of the wrought iron, she looked at balconies and rooftops. Nobody seemed to be watching anything but the scenery.

He must have trusted the wrought iron, because in a matter of seconds he'd scaled the eight-foot gate and was out of sight behind the wall. If she'd sneezed, she would have missed it.

He turned and looked up at the roof of the hotel, a place Grace couldn't see from the balcony. No glass glinted into the falling sun, revealing binoculars. No one but Grace seemed to be interested in him.

After a final quick search, he focused on the restaurant. It was deserted, but the cooks would start arriving soon to prepare for the 9:00 P.M. dinner rush. Quickly he walked around the corner of the building to the flagstone walkway. He checked the ground for trailing detonator wires.

Nothing.

That meant the standoff trigger had to be the cell phone he'd seen the men put into the trap.

Kneeling, he pushed his fingers under the flagstone. It weighed at least thirty pounds but rocked up easily on its side, revealing what was beneath.

For long, long seconds Faroe stared at the convex belly of a U.S. government-issue claymore mine. There was nothing elegant or high tech about this beast. Just a pound of C4 plastique and six hundred steel ball bearings that would explode in a directional, fan-shaped pattern of death. The mine was aimed straight into the air. It would blast ball bearings in a deadly half circle that began at ground level.

It would have killed dozens, maimed dozens more.

He stole a quick glance at Grace. She hadn't moved. He went back to studying the bomb. The initiator on the claymore had been removed and replaced with a blasting cap. The cap was wired to the battery of a cheap Mexican cell phone.

So far, so good.

Very gently he moved the claymore aside to get a better look at the cell phone. On the back of the phone, someone had written seven numbers with a black marker. Again, nothing unexpected. A bomb maker assembled the device, then turned it over to others to use. Not rocket science. Simple instructions for simple men.

Faroe memorized the number. Then he slowly, tenderly turned the claymore over so that its belly was pointed into the sandy soil instead of into the air. Softly, gradually, he laid the heavy flagstone back in place.

Ninety seconds later he walked back into the hotel suite.

Grace ran across the room and threw herself into his arms. She was shaking.

"Breathe, *amada,*" he said. "Nothing happened."

"But I could tell by the way you handled the thing that it was really dangerous."

He inhaled the sweet scent of her hair. "It's a decently made IED that would have turned Hector Rivas Osuna into a shocked eunuch for the microsecond before his asshole went through his skullcap."

Grace let go of Faroe like he'd kicked her. She backed away, hugging herself instead of him.

Faroe told himself that it was a good thing. He really didn't need the distraction of her fear for him, her breasts pressing against him as she trembled.

At least that's what he told himself, but he didn't believe it.

"The really interesting part is that somebody has access to what looks like U.S. Marine Corps hardware," Faroe said. "I was tempted to get a serial number, but I'm not down here to police stolen gear. I'll tell Steele, who will drop a word to someone who wears enough stars to make sure Camp Pendleton inventories its arsenal."

"Did you disarm it?"

He shook his head.

"Then what are we going to do?" Grace asked. "Call the police?"

"Since Hector seems to have the federal cops sewed up, it probably was the local police bomb squad that planted the damn thing. Or maybe the state." Faroe shrugged. "Either way, Hector is red graffiti sprayed on every wall in three blocks."

"But you said Lane would be safer if Hector lived."

"Yeah, he would. Dammit."

Faroe pulled his cell phone out of his pocket and hit speed dial. The call was answered on the second ring in New York.

"It's Faroe," he said. "I need two things fast. First, the phone number at All Saints. It's a private church school on the toll road south of Tijuana and north of Ensenada, both in Baja California, Mexico. There should be a listing in the Ensenada directory or at a web site."

Grace handed him the notepad and pen he'd left on the bed.

He gave her the surprised look of a man

used to working alone, smiled a silent thanks, and started writing.

"Got it," he said after a moment. "Now work your magic on the Telmex cellular supplier for Ensenada. Try like hell on fire to find out who bought a cell phone, probably in the last day or two, that was assigned the following number."

Faroe read back the number that had been written on the phone beneath the flagstone.

Even Grace heard the squawk from the other end of the line.

"I know, I know," Faroe said impatiently. "It's a lot to ask, but a boy's life depends on it. Spend what you have to, but get the info. Yes, it's on my tab. And call me back the instant you get lucky."

Faroe cut off the call and punched in the number of Lane's school.

Grace listened while he talked with Father Rafael Magón, coaxing and threatening by turn. Abruptly Faroe cut off the call, opened a cold beer, and sat on the balcony staring down at the restaurant with the single-minded focus of a predator watching prey.

Grace wanted to ask questions, a lot of them, but knew she wouldn't get any answers. Not when Faroe was like this, consumed by whatever he was planning.

I paid for the best, so I should just shut up and let him work.

And I won't think about how good it felt to be held by him again, if only for a few seconds.

The phone on the bedside table rang. Instantly Faroe was on his feet and standing next to the bed.

"It will be for me, but go ahead and answer," he said.

Grace picked up the receiver on the third ring. A male voice demanded to speak with Faroe. She held out the phone. He took it but put his hand over the receiver.

"Hector?" he asked Grace.

She shook her head. "Some lackey."

Faroe took his hand off the receiver and spoke curtly. *"Bueno."*

The conversation went back and forth in fluent, colloquial Spanish. Faroe finally cut it off with a string of epithets and blunt threats.

Despite herself, Grace was impressed. She hadn't heard language that specific and colorful in a long, long time. Intimidating, too.

There was a pause in the conversation.

Grace looked at Faroe.

He shrugged and waited. Then he started speaking English, a power move that only a diplomat or a judge could appreciate.

"No, Hector, you don't know who I am," Faroe said. "But you know a very good friend of mine, Judge Silva."

At the other end of the call, Hector looked around the classy condo, just one of the several places he'd "borrowed" for his stay in Ensenada. Men and weapons were everywhere. One of his younger nephews worked over a rock of cocaine, shaving it down. Cigarette smoke was thick in the air. Dirty dishes were stacked in the kitchen. The curtains were drawn so tight that not even a slit of daylight made it in.

Except for this odd call, everything was perfectly normal.

"*Sí,* I know her," Hector said. "So?"

"Her business is my business."

"Is she with you?" Hector asked, suddenly wary.

"Yes, she's here, and no, she doesn't have anything to say to you except that you should listen to me. We're going to save your life."

Hector drew hard on the burning cigarette his nephew handed him. "I listen."

In the hotel, Faroe glanced at Grace, mouthed the words *cell phone,* and pointed to his pocket.

She hesitated only a moment before she put her hand into the deep pocket of his slacks. The first thing she found was hard, but it wasn't a phone. She looked up at him, startled. His smile told her he'd been looking forward to this moment.

Obviously he could focus on more than one thing at a time.

So could she.

She removed the phone very slowly, dropping and retrieving it more than once, checking out the pocket very thoroughly.

Faroe's breath came in and his eyelids lowered to half-mast. "You heard me, Hector. The judge and I can save your life."

Grace handed him the phone with a feline smile. She might not be able to scale walls and play with bombs, but she knew how to bring Joe Faroe to attention.

He punched in a number on his cell phone but didn't hit send.

"I am safe," Hector said, unimpressed. "I need nothing from you."

Faroe looked out over the balcony railing to the front of the restaurant. The building was dark. The grounds and the gardens were deserted.

"You're going to a wedding party tonight at the Encantamar in Ensenada," Faroe said. "Dinner at the Canción."

Hector straightened. "Who tell you this?"

"Listen very carefully." Faroe held the receiver of the room phone toward the balcony door, then punched the send button on his cell phone.

Grace's eyes widened. She would have run to the balcony, but Faroe dropped his cell phone and blocked her with his body, holding her close and hard, staying between her and the coming blast.

"One one-thousand, two one-thousand," Faroe counted aloud. "Three—"

A hard white light burst from the restaurant garden, brighter than the sun. An instant later the air was ripped by a sharp, flat explosion. The concussion slapped off the walls of the hotel. Flocks of terrified pigeons exploded from the rooftops of adjacent buildings.

For a few seconds the world went silent, listening. Waiting.

The explosion echoed and re-echoed before it turned to shadow noise in Grace's ears. Stunned, she watched a cloud of dust rise from the courtyard. In that instant she knew what war was like. She swallowed hard against fear and helplessness.

"Did you hear that?" Faroe asked Hector evenly.

"¡Madre de Dios!"

"The mine was buried beneath the flagstone entrance to the Canción. If you don't believe me, send over some men to check it out."

In the expensive condo, Hector was silent for a few seconds. He watched every man in the room with new eyes, wondering if one of them could be the traitor. With a curt command, he sent one man to check out the restaurant. Before the man left the room, his bodyguards' cell phones started ringing. Thirty seconds later, he knew that the man on the telephone was telling the truth.

Whether that made the man friend or enemy didn't matter. What mattered was that he'd had the ability to kill Hector and hadn't.

Hector took a deep hit on his doctored cigarette. "What do you want from me?"

"Meet me tonight, in person. Name the place, name the time. If I get lucky, I'll have the names of the men who laid the trap. If not, we still have a lot to talk about."

In the hotel, Grace forced herself to breathe deeply, then do it again, and again, until her ears stopped ringing. She went to the window and stared down.

It looked like a war zone. Stucco had peeled off the front of the restaurant building. Smashed flagstone was scattered around. The wrought-iron gate had been blown off its hinges and lay in a twisted pile twenty feet away. The restaurant's windows were gone. People were pouring out of the hotel and running to stare at the damage.

She turned to the man who had triggered the bomb.

"Okay, you've got a deal." Faroe hung up and looked at Grace. "Ready?"

"You—I saw—" She tried again. "You just casually triggered that bomb!"

"It was calculated, not casual. We now have an inside track with Hector. He doesn't know if I'm a friend, an enemy, or the Easter Bunny. But he's damn sure I could have killed him and didn't. Given that, he's likely to be real titty-fingered about pissing me off, which means that Lane is safer now than he has been since Hector locked down the school. Let's go."

Grace fastened on the one thing that mattered: Lane was better off than he had been. That was worth a few windows and a wrought-iron gate any day.

Listen to yourself, Judge. Blowing up things is a felony.

So is kidnapping. If it benefits Lane, I'll help Faroe commit as many Class A felonies as it takes.

If the law can't protect my son, screw it.

She fell in step beside Faroe as they headed out of the room. She didn't ask where they were going.

28

GRACE SLEPT FROM ENSENADA to Tijuana. The sound of traffic became part of her, transformed into a relentless, primitive beat. Maybe it was exhaustion that let down her barriers, maybe it was simply that she fell asleep breathing the same air as Joe Faroe, but she slept deeply, dreaming of him. The images and sensations were frank with sexual need. Hot. Heady. Hungry. She woke up with flushed cheeks and a feeling of disorientation.

Faroe was driving in four-abreast traffic on a three-lane street. Newspaper vendors, flower hawkers, and lottery shills danced in and out of the stop-and-go traffic. Astride polished Harleys, pairs of big-bellied cops tried to maintain order. Cars parted around them like water around river boulders.

Many laws were ignored, yet beneath the appearance of chaos there obviously was an informal system understood by the drivers. The result wasn't orderly or neat, but it worked well enough to keep traffic moving.

Off to the north Grace saw the blazing lights of San Diego, a few miles and half a world away. She longed for a bath, longed to strip off the years and start all over again in a new, raw world, where past lies wouldn't exist.

"Where are we going?" she asked.

"Ah, she lives, she breathes. How do I know this? She asks questions."

She smiled, found herself watching his mouth, and flushed, remembering her dream.

"We had such a good time at the Encantamar that I thought we'd try a new hotel," Faroe said dryly. "We're going to the Hotel del Fiesta Palace. It's out by the world's most famous dog track."

"Are we meeting Hector at the hotel or the track?"

"The track, in about three hours. The hotel offers a good view. I've worked the track before, so I've got the layout memorized. But the hotel room will give me a chance to make a long-distance recon before I meet with that crazy bastard."

"We," she said. "I'm going with you."

"I thought you didn't want to be in the same room with him."

"I don't. So what? I didn't want any of this, but here it is anyway."

They drove on, fighting into the Zona Río traffic. As they negotiated the roundabout at the foot of the statue of Abraham Lincoln, Grace spotted the Plaza Río.

"Hector is a clotheshorse," she said. "Ironed jeans, pristine white shirt, ostrich-skin boots, and a hunk of neck jewelry that would choke a horse."

"So?"

"If this is all about macho and command presence, we lose. We look like dog crap. Is there time to shop?"

Faroe looked at himself in the mirror. Dog crap looked back. "Good point. We can afford half an hour."

He drove to valet parking and slipped the attendant half of a twenty-dollar bill.

"Half an hour," Faroe said to Grace as they got out.

"Do we synchronize our watches?" she asked sardonically.

"Better move, *amada.* You're wasting seconds."

She left him behind before they reached the entrance. He started to follow her, then remembered how he looked and went shopping instead. He barely made it back to the valet stand in time. She was already there, three shopping bags on her shoulder, waiting for him. He handed the valet the other half of the twenty and showed another five.

The Mercedes appeared with impressive speed. Not a scratch, a nick, or a dent anywhere.

Even so, Faroe breathed a sigh of relief after he'd fought through traffic to the thirty-story Fiesta Palace and handed the keys over to a bellman. Nobody who knew what Faroe knew drove a car as expensive as Grace's SUV into Mexico and expected to bring the vehicle home intact.

The hotel's stainless steel and gleaming glass turned the reflected skyline of Tijuana into something mysterious and beautiful. While Faroe checked them into the hotel,

Grace stared at the colors of the city. They rippled and flowed, unearthly, and she was floating with them, everything spinning away.

A shower. That's all I need. A long hot shower. Then maybe a short nap.

Or something.

The hours between now and the meeting with Hector stretched in front of her like an eternity. Nowhere to go. No way to forget. Nothing to do but wait until waiting was an animal eating her alive from the inside out.

Lane, are you all right?

"Stop thinking about your son," Faroe said.

Her head snapped toward him. "How did you know?"

"The way you looked. Thinking about him doesn't do any good and can do a lot of harm." He took her arm and led her toward the elevator.

Grace's hands clenched. So did her whole body.

"See what I mean?" Faroe said. "You went from looking blindsided by life to vibrating like a wire stretched to the breaking point. You're wasting energy."

"How do you not think about something?"

"Do you want to hurt Lane?" Faroe asked, sticking the key in the lock.

"No!"

"Then think about something else."

Like how much I want to touch you? Grace thought raggedly. *And how much you don't want to touch me? God knows you've had plenty of opportunity.*

And every time, you don't follow through.

She'd done the same, but she wasn't feeling charitable about it at the moment. Given the choice of thinking about Hector, Lane, or Faroe, Faroe was the least of the three evils. It was easier to feel angry than rejected, so anger was the flavor of the moment.

Faroe opened the door and nudged her into the suite overlooking the dog track. He dumped her packages in one bedroom and his own packages in the other and went to stand at the side of the window. After a long look, he turned and walked to his bedroom.

"Shower," he said without looking at her. "That's what I'm going to do. No dog crap allowed near Hector Rivas Osuna."

Without a word Grace went to her bedroom, walked straight into the bathroom, and began stripping. Moments later she was

alone in a fancy marble and chrome bathroom with an orgy-sized, double-headed
shower.

She told herself that it didn't matter to her
that Faroe hadn't even tried to talk her into
sharing a shower. Her body told her that it
did matter, and that she was a fool to be lath-
ering herself with fragrant French milled soap
just to crawl into bed for another nap.

Alone.

But it beat the alternative, which was to lie
awake trying not to think about things she
couldn't change.

Right. Think about Faroe.

The son of a bitch.

She washed her hair with French sham-
poo from the suite's complimentary supply.
Then she washed it again. Like the sham-
poo, the conditioner smelled like sin and sex
in paradise. She wanted to rub it all over her
body, but settled for just her hair and hoped
that the body lotion was half as appealing as
the rest of the toiletries.

It was. Cool, fresh, perfumed but not over-
powering, the lotion vanished into her skin.

**Eat your heart out, Mr. Feel-Nothing
Man. Shower alone until you turn into a
pink prune.**

She toweled her hair thoroughly, shook her head, and finger-combed the result. Her ancestors had given her smooth, thick hair that required only a good cut to behave.

Faroe knocked on the bathroom door. "Supper's ready."

Obviously he didn't linger in the shower, wishing that he wasn't alone.

"Okay" was all she said.

"Better hurry. It'll get cold."

In the presence of a deep freeze, what wouldn't?

Part of Grace knew that she was being unfair, that she hadn't exactly jumped Faroe's bones or even tried to. But most of Grace just wanted to smack Faroe for never following through on the smoldering looks and equally hot touches.

Screw him.

She almost laughed out loud. That was the problem, wasn't it? She could hardly screw an unwilling man.

With a muttered word, she pulled on one of the hotel's terry-cloth robes, buttoned it at the neck, and cinched it firmly around her waist. Barefoot, she walked into the suite.

A candlelit meal for two waited. The golden flames flickered over plates of steak, salad, fruit, cheese, and puffy rolls. The scent of food told Grace that she was hungry for more than sex.

You're a high-octane woman.

As usual, the son of a bitch was right.

The SOB in question was sitting deep in the shadow of an easy chair he'd dragged over to the window, staring through binoculars. The floor-to-ceiling glass looked out on the grandstands and the dirt track of Hipódromo Tijuana. Beyond, the city fell away into the bright lights of commercial and high-end real estate. The dimly lit shadows that pocked the glitter were *colonias* and barrios, where trash and poverty, rage and hope lived in unholy matrimony.

The candlelight wasn't for a romantic dinner. It was to keep anyone from seeing Faroe at work with the binoculars.

"See anything useful?" Grace asked.

"Not yet."

She sat at the table, poured herself a little red wine from the uncorked bottle, and began eating. A bite of steak told her that it had been seared over a wood fire. The Caesar salad was delicious and authentic down to the raw egg in the dressing. The wine was a Mexican varietal she didn't recognize but liked at first taste.

Faroe walked over, poured himself a glass of wine, and sat across from Grace. A single look told her that he'd showered, shaved, and was dressed in new jeans and a dark green guayabera that was the exact color of his eyes. The same soap she'd used must have been in his shower, too. He smelled of sin and sex.

One out of two ain't bad, Grace told herself bitterly.

Silently the two of them devoured the food. Not until the last savory bit was gone did Faroe say a word.

"We have two hours until we meet Hector," Faroe said. "Unless whatever you're keeping from me is really complicated, that should be plenty of time."

Grace's head snapped up. "What are you talking about?"

"You. You're hiding something, something that has to do with this case. Not good. Not good at all. I don't want to go up against Hector with a partner who's lying to me."

Her stomach knotted. She pushed away from the table so fast that she nearly knocked over her wine.

"Where are you going?" Faroe asked.

"To get dressed."

He moved quickly, blocking her, forcing

her to meet his eyes. She backed away like she'd been burned.

"What is it?" he asked. "You're acting like you're afraid of me."

"I'm the one who tracked you down, remember?"

He shrugged. "You were desperate. I was the only outlaw you knew."

She watched as he took a gliding step toward her. Candlelight flickered over his face, his eyes, heightening the intensity that was so much the core of him. She wanted to back up more. She wanted to step forward until she could taste him.

She didn't move.

"At first I thought that it was the outlaw in me that scared you," Faroe said, watching the pulse in her neck. "But the longer we've been together, the less that flies. You're not a woman to be frightened without reason."

"You're an intimidating man."

"Bullshit, *amada.* Not where you're concerned. You wrap me around your little finger with a smile or a tear."

Her eyes widened. "You could have fooled me."

"I could have, but I didn't. And I won't. Can you say the same to me?"

She was in the middle of the room and she felt like her back was to the wall.

"I thought so," he said softly, watching her frantic pulse. "What are you hiding from me?"

"I can't tell you."

"Why?"

She just shook her head.

"When we face Hector, there won't be any room for secrets or games between us," Faroe said. "It's called divide and conquer. Don't do that to us. Don't do that to Lane."

29

Silence grew, strangling Grace. Numbly she watched Faroe circle her, blocking any escape to the hallway. She couldn't move. She could barely think.

Then rage burned through the numbness. **He could have made this easy.**
He didn't.

"I misjudged you," she said through thin lips. "You're brilliant, ruthless, skilled in things I'd rather not imagine, and a blind idiot who couldn't see the truth when you put your arm around it!"

Faroe picked through her words, looking for meaning. "I don't understand."

"Ya think?" She glared at him and thought of how sweet it would be to just smack the ignorant, arrogant man.

Faroe blocked Grace's open hand before her palm hit his cheek. Then his fingers circled her wrist and held it, restraining her without hurting her.

Shocked, she looked at her hand as if it belonged to someone else. "I wanted to smack you, but I can't imagine I actually tried to. What's happening to me?"

"Good things."

"Good? *Good?* I tried to hit you!"

"I didn't know how hard I was pushing you. Now I do." He kissed her hand and gently forced it back to her side, held it there, keeping her close. "You're too tightly wrapped, *amada.* You're going to explode if you don't let out whatever is eating you alive."

"Whatever is—my son is a hostage! Isn't that enough reason?"

"I thought so. I was wrong. Tell me the rest of it."

She tried to wrench her hand out of Faroe's grip. He was too quick, too strong. She tried to turn against his grip. His arm circled her, held her still.

Close.

"And the next time you want to clock someone," he said, smiling slightly, "don't think about it. Just do it. That way your body language won't telegraph your intentions."

He was only inches away. She could feel his breath across the damp strands of hair that clung to her face. The dreamy, delicate kiss he brushed over the curve of her neck made her shiver. In the shadowy light his expression was calm, focused, and his eyes watched her much too intently.

She wasn't as good at cat and mouse as he was.

"A long time ago, you told me that you weren't a very good liar," he said. "Remember?"

"No," she lied.

"You said you doubted that you could fake anything important, particularly not in bed."

A ripple of emotion went through her. She closed her eyes so that she wouldn't betray herself.

Her lies.

"That was a long time ago," she said in a low voice. "Things change."

"Not everything. Not your core."

His hand opened the button at the neck of

her robe, then dropped to the sash. The bow-knot came undone with a single tug.

She grabbed the lapels of the robe, holding it closed. Part of her wanted Faroe so much she ached. Part of her still wanted to smack him. All of her was in chaos. Caught between conflicting emotions, she trembled.

Faroe's left hand tugged at the edge of the robe and pulled it slowly aside. The terry cloth was rough against the back of his hand. Her skin was smooth, warm, her nipples dark pebbles eager to be touched.

"You were right," he said. "Your body doesn't lie."

"Damn you," she whispered.

"I can live with damnation if I have you."

He shifted so that both hands cupped her breasts, teased her nipples. Then his right hand slid down and across hot curls, found moisture, dipped lightly, then again. Heat spilled into his hand.

"This is truth, *amada*," he said against her lips. "In this we don't have secrets and never did. That's why you haunted me. No other woman came close to what you gave me in those few days."

Grace didn't have to say there had been

no other man like Faroe for her. The truth was hot and wet in his palm.

"See?" he murmured, brushing kisses over her lips, her chin, the taut tendon in her neck. His free hand took one of hers and pressed it against his erection. "No secrets. I want you. You want me. Same as sixteen years ago. One look and neither of us looked anywhere else."

Her eyelids lowered halfway as she slid her palm down his hard length. She didn't try to conceal the hunger shivering through her.

"The only difference between now and then," he said against her mouth, "is that I'm smart enough not to let you slip through my fingers again. This time I'm going to see where it goes."

Grace took his kiss and gave it back to him with interest, until both of them were breathing raggedly and struggling to get closer still. Then she tore her mouth away.

"Is this what you want?" she asked.

"You know it is."

"Is it all you want?"

He smiled almost sadly, kissed her eyelids, tasted the faint salt of tears she hadn't shed. "No. I want the rest of the truth. Sixteen years ago I believed you set me up. It was the only thing that made sense, until after the trial, when I was quietly told the setup came from my side of the street."

She leaned her forehead against his chin. "I know. Now."

"My fault," he said, rocking her slowly in his arms. "I went crazy when they put the cuffs on me. I had a lot shorter fuse back then. Prison taught me to keep a lid on it."

She almost laughed wildly. She really hoped he'd learned, because when she told him about Lane . . .

If she told him about Lane.

When she told him about Lane.

This gentle, tough, sexy son of a bitch was right—they couldn't face Hector when there was a time bomb ticking between them.

"*Amada,* I don't know what you want from me," Faroe whispered into her hair.

She lifted her head and looked at him. He saw clarity and fear, sadness and determination.

"I want to make love with you," she said. "I want to forget for just a little while what year it is, what hour. Then no more secrets. But you have to promise me one thing now."

"Name it."

"No matter what the secret is, you won't

walk away and leave Lane in Hector's hands."

"I can't think of anything you could say that would make me do that."

Her smile slipped and turned upside down. "I can. Your word?"

"Yes."

Grace didn't wait for Faroe to change his mind. She undid his jeans and slipped a hand inside, burrowing and rubbing until she freed him from his clothing.

And all the while she kissed him the way she wanted him, hard and deep and hot. *Now.*

"God," he said hoarsely.

After that he saved his breath for what they both wanted. He pulled a condom out of his jeans, unwrapped it, and sheathed himself. Then he lifted one of her legs around his waist. She made a wild, hungry sound and climbed him until she could feel his erection sliding close to home. A wall slapped against her back. She welcomed it because it forced her closer to him.

She came when he entered her, came again as he drove into her to find his own fierce climax, came a third time while he leaned against her and tried to breathe past the wet fist squeezing him, pleasuring them. She gave a final shudder, tried to speak, couldn't. Her legs slid bonelessly from him. She would have kept on going to the floor if he hadn't been holding her between himself and the wall.

He laughed as he felt his own strength returning, but the bed was still too far away. He let them slide down the wall onto the thick rug, and began moving inside her again.

Her eyes opened. They were dark, dazed by spent passion and the new need building in her.

In him.

"Joe?"

"Like I said, *amada.* For some things, once just isn't enough."

30

GRACE LAY SPRAWLED ACROSS Faroe's chest, listening to the faint ticking of the old-fashioned analog clock on the bedside table. Sultry wind billowed the heavy curtains. The sound of the restless ocean slid between the insistent honking of vehicles looking for space where there wasn't any.

Like her, looking for time when there wasn't any.

"Do you remember when we took one look at each other and just, well, dove in?" Grace asked softly.

"I remember the smell of the match you used to light a cigarette afterward."

"It was a joint. I was tired of being a good girl."

"Yeah, I remember that too." Faroe smiled. "I should have busted your naked ass right there. Maybe we'd have had a better chance of making it stick if we both were convicted felons."

She almost laughed, almost cried, and wished she could make time run backward.

"One first dance, one last dance," she said in a low voice. "I guess that's more than most people get."

He wanted to ask what that meant, but didn't. He wasn't sure he wanted to know.

She pushed away from the shelter of his arm around her shoulders. Then she sat up and looked at him, memorizing the moment and the man, savoring the taste of him in her mouth and the scent of him sliding into her with every breath.

In the faint light from the city, Faroe saw the fullness of Grace's naked body. He reached out to trace the line of her collarbone, then the curve of a breast. It wasn't a demanding touch. He simply enjoyed feeling the heat and weight of her on his palm, the difference between male and female.

"What happened after they hauled you away?" she asked softly.

He rose to one elbow, caught a loose strand of her hair, and pushed it aside so that he could see her eyes, her expression.

Dark, withdrawing, waiting to speak the words she was so afraid of giving him.

"That was a long time ago," he said. "Do you really want to live through it again?"

"Want to? No. But we need to. We can't understand how we got here tonight unless we understand where we were sixteen years ago. I was a girl whose IQ and drive to get out of the barrio fast-tracked me through every school I ever went to. I passed the bar exam when most twenty-one-year-olds were planning how many ways there were to get drunk, high, and laid."

"A lot of them still are doing the same thing."

"Well, one day I looked around and decided I wanted to be like they were. So I told my boyfriend that I needed space. Not a whole lot. Just a week. I didn't want to be fast-tracked into marriage the same way I'd gone through my childhood."

"Another thing we have in common,"

Faroe said. "An unusual childhood. My father was almost old enough to be my grandfather. Not that he was frail. Far from it. He was just a little . . . crazy. Too much weed, maybe."

Faroe traced a fingertip around Grace's shadowy smile.

"Tell me more," she said. "You never talked about yourself."

"Neither did you."

"I guess we didn't talk much the first time, did we?"

He smiled and kissed the hand that was stroking his cheek. "We were too young and too hot to know any better."

"We're older now. Talk to me."

"When other kids played baseball, my father took me out in the desert and taught me about tracking, shooting, hiking, camping, seasons of rain and sun and dust and hail, bandits and wetbacks, and never really trusting anybody but yourself."

"Why was he such a loner?" she asked.

"When he was young, he ran drugs. Maybe he still did when he was older. I never asked, but I don't think so. He hated what marijuana had become, the change from a playful girl to a ball-busting bitch running a billion-dollar business. He grew his own, smoked it, and watched the seasons change."

"Your mother?"

"Left him shortly after I was born. Left me, too, I guess. I don't remember. None of the women after her stayed long. It was just Dad and me."

"No wonder you assumed I'd set you up for a fall," Grace said. "Women have been disappointing you all your life."

Faroe shrugged. "I'm not the only kid who was ever dropped on a doorstep. Things happen. You survive and learn and walk on."

"And after they dragged you off to prison?" she asked. "What happened then?"

He swung his legs off the bed and sat up, turning so that he could face her. "I spent a night in the lockup. The Department of Justice wanted to make an example of me, show how tough they were on civil rights violators. The next day a judge released me on my own recognizance. You weren't around when I went back to my apartment."

"You didn't want me anymore. You made it clear in the kind of gutter Spanish I hadn't heard since I left Santa Ana."

He would have smiled, but the memory

was too painful. "You didn't want to be around me. Before my arrest, I believed in the DEA the same way you did in the law. Complete, unquestioning faith. The DEA was the family I never had. After the arrest . . ."

"You felt betrayed and shaken and furious, like I did when I realized that the law I loved so much couldn't save the son I loved more than anything else."

"Yeah." Faroe's smile was a cold curve of light. "Guess I was really young for my age."

"Belief isn't a bad thing."

He shrugged.

Wind sighed through the room, smelling of past and present, ocean and badly tuned engines.

"What did you do after the arrest?" she asked. "Did they offer a plea bargain?"

"Don't they always?"

"Six months in prison isn't much of a bargain," she said. "I've seen drug dealers and rapists get off with less."

"Oh, the U.S. Attorney offered better than six months."

"What happened?"

"A month after the arrest, I told the U.S. Attorney to take his plea bargain and shove it. I pled guilty to a single count because it was the quickest way to get the mess in my rearview mirror."

She waited, barely breathing.

"I did my six months in the federal day-care camp," Faroe said neutrally, "came out the front gate, and didn't look back. There was nothing back there I wanted." He touched her cheek. "At least, that's what I told myself. I signed up with St. Kilda Consulting and saw every part of the world that had shadows."

"Maybe you should have looked back. Did you ever think of that?"

He stood up and went to the window. She could see him outlined against the night sky, echoes of past anger and pride in his posture.

"Did you look back?" he asked softly.

Silence. A long, ragged sigh.

"No," she said in a low voice. "You made me out of control, wild, desperate for things a good girl couldn't even imagine."

"You could, and did. I wasn't alone in that bed."

"That's what really scared me. When I saw you hauled off in handcuffs, reality came crashing in."

"Which reality?"

"I was a young woman whose amazing

career was the result of years of clawing and striving and sacrifice—my own, my dead parents', my dead grandmother's. All of those lives had been devoted to one thing and only one thing: giving me what was needed so that I could leave the violence of the gutter behind." Her hands clenched and a tear left a gleaming trail down one cheek.

"Go on," he said.

"There's nowhere to go but where I did. Was I supposed to turn my back on three generations of sacrifice because I'd met an outlaw who gave me the best sex of my life?"

"That's what really confused me," he said.

"What?"

"You shouldn't have been in my bed, but there you were. If you were working for the opposition, it made sense."

"Only to you," she shot back. "It made no sense at all to me. When they were dragging you off, you looked right into the lens of a television camera with such rage that the cameraman nearly fell down running away. Even with your hands cuffed behind your back, you scared him. And me. I ran and never looked back. Except . . ."

"Except?"

"You say I haunted you."

"You did."

"It went both ways. At night I'd dream and I'd wake up abandoned, crying. If Ted was there, I'd just say it was old nightmares left over from the day I walked in and found my family murdered. It was halfway true."

"Only half?"

"Maybe less," she whispered. "But you hated me. I could no more have you than I could bring my family back to life. Love was a bait-and-switch game, and I wasn't going to play it anymore. I couldn't. I wouldn't survive."

Faroe caught the second tear before it reached her cheekbone.

"I went back to Ted, told him I didn't need any more space. A week later he hustled me to a JP. The week after that, I missed my period."

Faroe tried to breathe, tried to speak, but there was a fist in his throat he couldn't get around.

"Since birth control pills made me hurl," Grace said evenly, "and Ted was careless with condoms, I figured there was a much better chance that he was the father than you. And once I held Lane, it didn't matter. I took one look at his wrinkled face and tiny fists, and I fell hopelessly in love."

Breathing was all Faroe could manage.

And listening.

"I don't think I've ever seen you speechless," she said.

He could feel his heart beating in his chest. The blood roared in his ears. He began to breathe again. "Finish it."

"You do the math."

He just watched her with green eyes that looked dark, feral.

Grace drew the sheet across her breasts, suddenly aware of her own nakedness and vulnerability. "The age-old male problem— how do I know the bitch is telling the truth?"

Though he didn't move or speak, the pulse at his throat beat hard and fast. His expression was closed, blank, bleak.

"A year later I wanted more children," Grace said. "Ted didn't, but he sure did like sex better without a condom. Lane turned five, and no siblings in sight. By then I'd nagged enough that Ted went to a doctor to shut me up. He discovered he was a few sperm short of meaningful fertility. We were very, very lucky to have conceived once. It must have eaten at Ted, because after a few more months he quietly took a swab of his mouth, and of Lane's, and sent both to a DNA lab."

She stared at Faroe through eyes blind with tears.

"Say it." Faroe's voice was as grim, his whole body vibrating with suppressed emotions.

"Lane, a sweet, beautiful boy who called Ted Daddy and followed him every chance he got; Lane, the innocent who idolized his daddy even though Ted barely bothered to notice him . . ." Her voice frayed.

She drew a deep breath and slid off the bed, pulling the sheet with her, wrapping it tight around her. She walked to the bathroom door, opened it, and snapped on the lights. In the white glare, her face was streaked with tears. She turned and looked at the man who seemed to cast shadows even in darkness.

"Say it."

"Lane is your son."

31

"Well?" Steele demanded.

Dwayne typed on the computer keyboard quickly, then touched the screen with his finger. Documents flew by in a kaleidoscope of information. Narrow-eyed, he watched them, then touched the screen again.

"No calls from any number registered to Ted Franklin."

Steele made a frustrated sound. "Apparently he's smarter than his previous actions would suggest."

"That wouldn't be hard."

"This is an inconvenient time for Mr. Franklin to improve his criminal IQ."

Dwayne bent over the computer again. More documents flew by. He tapped on several, read, shook his head.

"What?" Steele asked.

"A lot of nothing. The team watching the La Jolla house is suffering terminal boredom. No one coming or going. The hostiles watching the house are equally bored and equally determined. Gotta give it to those feds. They're real bulldogs. Some wild-card Mexicans cruised the place. No point in following them, because if they're sniffing around the judge's house, they're as lost as we are."

"Telephone? E-mail?"

"One of our people took the judge's computer and hacked it. So far, nothing helpful and no e-mail but the business kind. No physical mail but bills. No phone calls to the house except from people looking for Ted. No point in following up on them, because they know exactly what we do about his whereabouts. Zip. Zap. Zero. Did I mention zilch?"

"Keep everyone in place. Ted might run for familiar ground."

Dwayne nodded and continued his update. "The team watching the lawyer's house hasn't learned anything except how the rich and ridiculous shop. The team that black-bagged the lawyer's office has an eye-popping list of clients, but none of them connect in any obvious way to our Teddy-boy."

"Try for a subtle way."

"I'll need hundreds of people to backtrack the clients and stake them out."

"Pick the top five prospects. Follow them."

"Pick them how?"

"That's why I hired you. For some things, your instincts are better than mine. Pick five. And get Faroe on the phone. We need to make some plans for the rendezvous."

"I tried. He's not answering his phone."

"Try again."

32

G RACE WATCHED F AROE WITH the kind of intensity he often used on her. In the three minutes since he'd backed her into a corner and dragged the truth about Lane out of her, Faroe had calmly pulled on his clothes, gathered up his cell phone, adjusted something on the unit, and put it in his pocket. Then he'd turned his back on her and stared out the window.

He hadn't said a word.

Not one.

His cell phone rang. He ignored it.

"Say something," she said finally.

"You don't want to hear what I'm thinking."

"Try me."

"How would you feel if I'd shown up with a teenager, introduced you, and said, 'Oh, by the way, this is yours. Little souvenir of three days of jungle sex and a bad rubber.' "

"You look at Lane and see a *bad rubber*?"

Faroe spun toward her. The raw fury on his face was the same as she'd seen sixteen years ago. His voice was deadly calm. It made the hair on her neck lift.

"I look at Lane and see a son I never had the chance to know," Faroe said in a voice that was as quiet as his eyes were wild. "I look at Lane and see a son who never knew his biological father. I look at Lane and see fifteen years gone, fifteen years I'll never get back. Neither will he. Then I look at you."

Instinctively Grace backed away from Faroe.

He matched her step for step, inch for inch.

She'd known he would be angry. She hadn't known how it would feel to be the focus of that rage.

"I look at you," he said softly, "and see an ambitious female who used a stud for sex and a billionaire to raise her bastard."

"I didn't know you were Lane's biological father!"

A wall hit Grace's back. This time she didn't welcome it. She ignored the tears blurring her vision and lifted her chin as Faroe closed the last inches between them.

"You didn't care," he said. "You had a baby and a billionaire and a fast-track career and you just didn't give a damn about the dumb sperm donor."

"The dumb sperm donor threw me out of his life, remember? I didn't know, Joe. I swear it!"

"The dumb sperm donor remembers that you could have found out at any time and you damn sure have known for, what, ten years now? And you still didn't tell me."

"By the time I tracked you down ten years ago, you were in Belize, well out of cell range."

Faroe looked at Grace's bitter black eyes and trembling lips. Part of him admired her for standing up to him when most men would have cut and run.

But most of him was too furious to care.

"How did you know where I was?" he asked calmly.

Too calmly.

"I used my connections to track you to St. Kilda Consulting. I even got your cell phone number, the really private one only Steele has."

"I told Steele he should change those numbers more often."

"I didn't call you," she said roughly. "You were undercover in hostile territory, your life at risk every second. Just imagine how you'd have felt if a woman you hated told you that she'd had your biological son, who by the way was legally the son of a man you'd never met."

Faroe didn't say anything.

"Speechless again?" she said. "A rare double."

"Don't push me, Grace."

"I'm the one with my back to the wall," she said through her teeth.

There was a tight silence.

Then he stepped away, giving her room to breathe.

"Besides," Faroe said neutrally, "Ted was much better father material, right? Rich, successful, socially acceptable, and best of all—not an ex-con."

"You're wrong."

"Which part?"

"The important one. Ted should have been good father material, but he wasn't. Even before he discovered that there wasn't a genetic connection between himself and Lane, Ted didn't care about his son. Ted was too busy with his hedge fund to take time for a baby, a toddler, a young boy, a—"

"Wife?" Faroe cut in.

"The wife was too busy to care about the husband. Balancing a demanding career and a baby took everything I had."

"You're breaking my heart."

"You don't have one. If you did, you'd be more worried about Lane than any other part of this mess."

The smile he gave her was as cold as his eyes. He turned and headed for the door.

"Where are you going?" she asked. "You promised that—"

"I need some space," he cut in. "A whole fucking universe of it."

The door shut softly behind him.

She wished he'd slammed it.

Her shoulders slumped against the wall.

I'm sorry, Lane.

No matter what I do, it's wrong.

When her fingers went slack, the sheet slid to the floor, leaving her naked again.

But Lane shouldn't have to be the one to pay for it.

Grimly Grace kicked aside the sheet and went to the shower. She didn't have much time to pull herself together before she met Hector Rivas Osuna, the Butcher of Tijuana.

Faroe might have walked out on her, but he'd given her some good advice.

Lie, Your Honor. Hector believes you're his ticket to your husband.

33

DWAYNE SHOOK HIS HEAD. "Not answering."

"Hang up and call again. Do it until he answers."

Three calls later, Faroe picked it up. "What."

The word was a snarl rather than an invitation to talk.

Steele answered before Dwayne could. "Where are you?"

"Outside a dog track, feeling sorry for the muzzled greyhounds chasing fake rabbits for the amusement of drunks and drug lords."

"Feeling like you're a greyhound?" Steele asked.

"How long have you known?"

"That you're tired of running in circles?"

At the other end of the line, Faroe watched dogs run in circles and said nothing.

"When Judge Silva insisted on you and only you," Steele said evenly, "I suspected Lane was yours. You're very good, Joseph, but so are many of my operatives. St. Kilda Consulting has high standards."

"But you didn't say anything to me."

"You had more facts at your disposal than I did. When you didn't say anything, I respected your privacy."

"More like my stupidity."

"So you really didn't suspect, even after you spent time with the boy?"

Faroe watched dogs race in circles, chasing something they'd never catch.

Stupid sons of bitches.

"I saw Grace in Lane," Faroe said. "The shape of the eyes, the quickness, the fierce intelligence underneath the drugs they'd poured into him."

"Look at a picture of Ted Franklin, then look in a mirror," Steele suggested. "Lane's nose is yours, as is the width of his jaw and the ears tight against the skull. If you don't believe me, I'll bring photos."

"I don't spend a lot of time looking in mirrors."

Steele sighed and watched the line of light marching across his global clock, time sliding away into the unreachable past.

"What really pisses me off," Faroe said, "is that if Lane hadn't been in danger, Grace never would have told me."

"She would have told you on Lane's eighteenth birthday, the same day she told him."

"Says who?"

"Grace. I just talked to her."

"Suddenly she's just running off at the mouth," Faroe said sardonically.

"Her voice was very strained. This isn't easy for her."

"Call someone who cares. She kept her mouth shut this long, she should have kept it shut for two more days."

"Did you give her a choice?"

Silence was Faroe's only answer.

It was enough.

Steele looked up as Dwayne handed him a shot of scotch, neat. He sipped, sighed, sipped again. When he spoke, his voice took on some of the liquor's smoky flavor. "I suspect Grace was crying, or had been."

"She was always able to turn on the tears

when she needed to. They teach it in Defense Attorney 101."

"She must have skipped that class. Everyone but you regards her as passionless, nothing but a legal and intellectual machine."

Faroe closed his eyes. *Passionless* was the last word he'd use to describe Grace Silva.

"As much as I'd like to indulge your hissy fit," Steele continued, "the clock is running very quickly on this matter."

"You think I don't know that?" Faroe asked roughly.

Steele ignored the interruption. "The more people who suspect or confirm Lane's biological parentage, the sooner it will leak to Hector. He won't be pleased when he finds out that he's holding the wrong hostage."

Faroe had already thought about that.

A lot.

"One, it's not likely to leak before the deadline runs out," Faroe said. "Two, even if it did, Hector won't care. As long as he has Lane, he has Grace, and Grace has the kind of connections that could find Ted. I wouldn't put it past the bastard to know that she would run to St. Kilda."

"The bastard being Ted?"

"Hector, but don't let that stop you. There's more than enough bastards to go around. Come to Tijuana and take your pick."

"Thank you, I will. What is the U.S. airport nearest Tijuana?"

"Brown Field, about two miles north of Tijuana International. But watch out for *mojados* crossing the runway."

"What are *mojados*?"

"Wetbacks. These get that way by swimming the sewage of Río Tía Juana. Anybody willing to do that doesn't deserve to get run over by a jet."

"I'll tell the pilot to take unusual care. We should be there by dawn."

Steele listened to the silence and wished he could see Faroe's face.

"You're not kidding, are you?" Faroe said. "You're actually coming out here."

"Right now, you need somebody you can trust. However our personal styles might clash, trust has never been a problem."

"You're coming. Here."

Steele laughed. "You make it sound as likely as the Second Coming of Christ."

"Close enough. I can't remember the last time you left your Manhattan aerie."

In his Manhattan aerie, Steele smiled and sipped fine scotch. It was rather amusing to know that Joe Faroe had been bowled over twice in one night. If he suspected why Steele was really coming out, it would be three in one night. A tidy hat trick.

"Then you'll go back on the job?" Steele asked.

"I never left it."

"Grace thought you did."

"Grace was wrong. Again."

"What are you doing now?" Steele asked.

"I'm watching a caravan of Chevrolet Suburbans and Cadillac Escalades punch through traffic and turn into the seamiest little sports venue I've seen since they shut down the jai alai fronton in Mexicali."

"Do we know anyone in the parade?"

"Oh yeah," Faroe said. "Hector Rivas and his merry band of *federales,* state cops, and *rurales.* The man must be worried about something. His honor guard looks to be at least company strength."

"That would explain why the phone number you fed to research earlier today traces back to a member of the Ensenada municipal police force. So do the license plates you noted, though the information comes with the usual caveat that second-world record-keeping isn't always accurate."

"Close enough for horseshoes and claymores," Faroe said. "I wouldn't want to be an Ensenada cop when Hector hears the news."

"You're going to the meeting?"

"Hell yes. So call the judge and set her devious mind at rest. I'm on my way to Hector right now."

"You call her, or at least coordinate your moves with her."

"You do it, and there aren't any moves to coordinate. She's at the hotel. I'm at the track."

"Then you should see her rather quickly. She headed for the track as soon as she hung up on me."

"Right now I don't want to be in the same room with her, much less in the same charade."

"Did anyone ask what you wanted? She's going to the meeting. Might already be there, in fact."

"Shit."

The phone in Steele's hand went dead. He passed the unit off to Dwayne. "Brown Field, two miles north of Tijuana."

"I'll tell the pilot. Your car is waiting. The San Diego team is assembling."

Steele smiled like the shark he was. "Excellent."

34

FAROE WATCHED GRACE WALK down the steps beside the lobby entrance to the hotel and strike out for the traffic light that would allow her to cross the chaotic surge of vehicles. She was dressed in a tight sheath skirt, a slinky blouse, and four-inch stiletto heels.

All red.

Where did she get that outfit—Hookers "R" Us?

Faroe waited just down from the point where she would cross the street. When she walked by him, he counted to ten and stepped out to follow.

Jesus. Do her hips always move like that?

She must have heard him moving up behind her. Warily she glanced over her shoulder. When she recognized him in the half darkness, she turned away and kept striding along the uneven sidewalk.

"Slow down," he said, putting a hand on her arm. "You'll break an ankle."

"I'm late."

"Blame the shoes."

Grace shook off his hand, hiked up her skirt, and tried to balance on one foot while she removed a shoe.

"You don't want to walk around in Tijuana barefoot," Faroe said. "Your antibodies aren't up to it. Just what in hell do you think you're doing?"

Grace shook out a small pebble she'd picked up, slipped the shoe back on, and started walking. "I'm going to meet Hector."

"Alone?" Faroe asked, striding alongside. "Dressed like that?"

"You weren't answering your phone. My clothes are left over from Plan A, when you were supposed to be the new cock on my walk and I was a judicial tart gone slumming. Your tart, to be precise. That was your plan, right?"

"It'd be tough for you to make that plan fly without a man to snuggle up to."

"There will be a roomful of men with Hector. I'll ask for volunteers."

"Are you crazy?"

"No. I'm determined. Get with the program or get out of my face."

Faroe looked her over the way every man in that room would. "Tijuana lap-dancer makeup, red leather skirt, red-on-red flowered silk blouse, red shoes—all screaming sex. How'd you find that getup in a strange department store in under fifteen minutes?"

"A salesgirl and a fifty-dollar tip. I told her I wanted to look like a *narcotraficante*'s girlfriend."

"Better undo the top buttons on the blouse. Hector's *muy macho,* the kind that likes a lot of cheap cleavage."

She gave him the response he deserved. "Screw you."

"You already did a world-class job of that, in every meaning of the word."

"As you so kindly pointed out in a similar case, I wasn't alone in that bed."

They walked a few more steps.

"Do you know where you're going?" Faroe asked.

"Unlike a man, I'm capable of asking directions."

"But you sure don't take them worth a damn."

"Since when does it require a penis to be pigheaded?"

Faroe fought against a smile and gestured toward a parking lot. "This way, my little piglet."

She made a sound that could have been choked laughter or a curse. He was too smart to ask which.

Silently he led the way along the fenced parking lot that spread out from the lighted entrance gate of the track. Several hundred cars were parked in ranks behind the fence. In the distance came the rumble of the crowd cheering and cursing the dogs.

"I just got off the phone with Steele," Faroe said. "He's flying out. I think he wants to make sure we don't kill each other before we get Lane back."

"That would be lovely."

"Get real, Grace," he shot back. "Did you think I was going to be happy?"

"I didn't think you were going to be so full of righteous rage. For a moment there, I thought you were going to hit me."

"Oh, Christ."

"You should have seen your face," Grace said.

"What is it that everyone suddenly wants me to look in the mirror?"

Silence.

"Relax," he said after a minute. "For now we're on the same side. After Lane's free, all bets are off."

She stopped sharply and spun toward him. In the half-light from the dingy parking lot, her face was shadowed and unreadable.

"That sounds like a threat," she said quietly.

"It's a fact. You had Lane for fifteen years. It's my turn. I have at least as much claim on him as you do, particularly if you end up in a federal prison for whatever part you've had in your crooked husband's schemes."

"Listen to me, Joe, and listen well."

"I'm listening."

And he was. There was a deadly edge to Grace's voice that he'd never heard before.

"I have no more secrets, nothing more to hide," she said. "I don't know anything about my husband's business. I never did. Don't ever threaten to take my son away from me again."

Faroe looked at her eyes, as cold and clear as her voice. He rolled his shoulders, trying to loosen the tension that had grown in him every second since she'd told him Lane was his son.

"This whole situation sucks donkeys," he said. "I wish to hell you'd kept it shut for a few more days."

"Who backed me up against the wall and kept pushing? You just had to know, didn't you? The great Joe Faroe just couldn't wait another bloody second to—"

"We have to stop fighting." Despite the hard beat of his pulse in his neck, his voice was calm. "For Lane."

Grace drew a deep breath and blew it out. "Then stop taking cheap shots at me."

"I still find it hard to accept that you and Ted were on different planets. You're too smart. You couldn't live with a guy and not know what he's up to."

"We haven't lived together in the way that you mean since he gave me gonorrhea nine years ago. I told him he could have the sluts or he could have me. He chose the sluts."

"Why didn't you divorce him?" Faroe asked.

"Lane called him Daddy. I could put up

with being cheated on if it meant that Lane had two parents."

"I'm surprised you didn't cut off Ted's balls."

"Why? They weren't any use to me."

Faroe whistled softly. "Did you ever love him?"

"He was safe. At the time, that was enough."

"And now?"

"What are you asking?"

"I don't know," Faroe admitted. "Question withdrawn."

They walked along the parking lot fence in silence.

"Did Ted have any enemies?" Faroe asked finally.

"Like grains of sand on the beach. He screwed over a lot of people in business and in politics."

"I always thought politicians were glad-handers."

"Ted isn't a glad-hander. He's a kingmaker. There's a difference. That difference is money."

"I'd like a list of the top twenty," Faroe said.

"No one will talk to you. Ted's a monster

when it comes to business, and for him, politics is business. Most of his associates and employees are scared to death of him."

"But you weren't."

"If you're asking if Ted knocked me around," she said, "the answer is no. If you're asking if he hit Lane, the answer is I'd have put Ted in jail and he knew it."

"Sounds like you wouldn't mind feeding Ted to Hector now. What changed your mind?"

"Watching you play touchy-feely with a bomb."

In silence they walked on toward a side gate that was guarded by a small shack.

Fifty yards from the shack Grace asked softly, "Did you like Lane?"

"He's a good kid, tough, smart. He held it together better than most men in his position would. I like that."

"Yes, that would be the most important thing to you," she muttered.

"What do you want me to say? I spent half an hour with him."

They didn't speak again until they were almost to the guard shack. At the last moment, Faroe said very quietly, "Lane loves his mom a lot. She loves him the same way.

Seeing it made me . . . hungry. Until that moment, I didn't really know why I quit St. Kilda."

Before Grace could say anything, two men in black windbreakers stepped out of the shadows of the guard shack. Both men carried pistols. The barrels were pointed slightly toward the ground, but not nearly enough for comfort.

Faroe stepped to the side, away from Grace.

The gun muzzles tracked him.

35

"Yᴏᴜ ᴡᴏʀᴋ ғᴏʀ Hᴇᴄᴛᴏʀ Rivas Osuna?" Faroe asked calmly.

One of the men snapped on a flashlight. *"Sí, señor. Manos up, por favor."*

Faroe held his hands up and his arms out.

The guard frisked him with quick, neutral efficiency.

"Very polite, these two," Faroe said to Grace. "Show them your arms."

Grace stood in a hip-shot pose while the Mexican ran his flashlight over her costume.

"Satisfied?" she asked sweetly.

The guard's mustache twitched in what could have been a smile or a sneer.

A pair of black utility vehicles roared up the street. With his flashlight the guard gestured toward the lead vehicle, a Cadillac Escalade.

"¿Qué pasa?" Faroe said sharply. "Hector is meeting us at the track."

"Hector, he change his min' *mucho,*" the guard said in the Spanglish of the border. "Get in."

Faroe looked at Grace. "You don't have to risk this. Go back to the hotel."

Without a word she walked toward the Escalade in a skirt so tight he didn't see how she breathed, much less moved. He opened the vehicle's back door, put his hand on her leather-clad butt, and gave her a boost up into the Escalade.

Heavily smoked windows made the interior dark. Grace settled into the middle bench seat. An instant later she realized there was someone on the jump seat behind her. She could smell him, a mixture of sweat, hair oil, and gun oil. When she turned to look, light from the street gleamed faintly on the barrel of the assault rifle that lay across his lap.

"Don't worry about him," Faroe said. "He just suffers from testicular insufficiency."

"You recognize the symptoms, right?"

"In others."

The guard with the flashlight shoved his pistol into his belt and climbed into the front passenger seat. *"Andale."*

The driver bulled his way back into traffic. Behind them brakes screamed and horns shouted. The driver of the Escalade stuck his arm out the window and pumped up and down, the Mexican version of a raised middle finger.

"In Tijuana, working for Hector Rivas means never having to say 'Excuse me,'" Faroe said.

"You're enjoying this," she muttered.

"It's like a hockey game. You don't have to wonder where you stand."

"Lane feels the same about soccer, especially the games at All Saints."

"If he learned that, his time in Mexico wasn't wasted."

"But it goes against everything I've tried to teach him," she said.

"So does Hector. Guess who has the best chance of surviving?"

Mouth flat, Grace watched the nightscape

flash by. The driver passed a police patrol car like it was painted on the street. The officers looked sideways, then straight ahead.

"Like Washington, D.C., where Secret Service Suburbans and FBI vehicles have immunity from traffic laws," she said.

"Down here, the boys have immunity from everything."

"Where are we going?" she asked, straining to see road signs.

"*¿A dónde vamos?*" he said to the guard in the passenger seat.

"Señor Rivas."

"Now you know as much as I do," Faroe said to Grace.

"I doubt it."

"If this is like every dope deal I've ever seen, we'll ride around for an hour while these dudes make sure we aren't being followed. Then they'll call somebody and find out where Hector has decided to be at that moment. That's the problem with living in the shadows. All you have time to think about is covering your own ass. Everything else comes in second."

"I thought Hector owned Tijuana," she said.

"He does. But there's always somebody

out there with a gun and an itch to be the new Hector. Both men know that the change-over would happen in the space of time it takes a slug from a .44 Magnum to travel from one side of Hector's skull to the other."

Grace flinched.

"I'm not trying to disgust you." There was an edge in Faroe's voice. "I'm trying to teach you. Here and now, not one of your beloved laws and regulations are worth cold spit. We're in the middle of a guerrilla war. All that counts is guns and money."

She didn't say anything.

He leaned over, put a gentle, immovable hand under her chin, and turned her face toward him.

"Hector has lived this war for a quarter of a century," Faroe said in a low voice. "He's stayed on top by making sure that nobody gets a clear shot at him. Like every warlord, every tyrant, every outlaw from Bonnie Prince Charlie to Osama bin Laden, Hector has learned to live unpredictably. And richly. He owns players on both sides of the war."

Faroe glanced into the front seat. *"¿Correcto?"*

"Sí, es correcto." The Mexican half turned and gave Faroe a weary, wary smile.

"What a hellish life it must be," Grace said.

"It's better than hoeing a field of pinto beans on some communal farm in the mountains," Faroe said. "Hector is what I'd be if I'd been born in Ojos Azules."

"You sound proud of your barbaric instincts."

"They've kept me alive and allowed you to argue how many legal motions can dance on the head of an indictment."

"Motions are better than bullets."

"In the sunshine world, yes. We aren't there."

"Then it's too bad we don't have any bullets," she said tightly.

"Yeah. I've been thinking the same thing."

The Escalade bored on through the evening traffic, circling back and forth through the Zona Río, past nightclubs and restaurants and cheap upholstery shops and high-end retailers, through slums and shantytowns, and finally past middle-class *colonias* that would have been at home on either side of the border.

Silently Grace admitted that she was seeing the city with different eyes. Tijuana wasn't as alien as it had been. She didn't know if that was good or bad, but she knew it was real.

"What are you thinking?" Faroe asked softly.

"Tijuana and San Diego aren't as separate as I thought they were."

"How so?"

She shrugged. "The U.S.-Mexico border is a legal artifice. It's necessary, but it isn't real. Life and death, hope and fear, drugs and money—they all wash back and forth without much regard for national laws on either side."

"All borders are like that."

"And you like it that way," she said.

"I wasn't given a vote. I was just born into a Hobbesian world and made what I could of it for as long as I could take it."

"Then you looked for a temporary autonomous zone and I found you before you could escape," she said grimly.

He released her chin, caressed her cheekbone with his thumb, and said, "I didn't have anything to escape to, but I didn't know it then. Now I do. I just don't know what the hell to do about it."

The big Escalade tunneled through the

evening crowds along Avenida Revolución, past the tourist bars and shuttered *farmacias* advertising cut-rate Viagra. Drunken sailors from San Diego and wide-eyed tourists from Nebraska shuffled along the crowded sidewalks, staring and fending off the vendors and hustlers or accepting them with as much anxiety as pleasure.

The black Escalade drove on through the crowded streets and alleys of the Zona Norte, past cheap hotels that served as brothels or as consolidation warehouses for the forwarders of human freight, the smugglers whose cargo was illegal immigrants.

"It's odd," Grace said.

"What is?"

"This is a slum, you can see the poverty and dirt, but . . ."

Faroe waited.

"It's so alive," she said finally. "People laughing and shouldering on the sidewalks, eating tacos from corner stands, drinking beer. They don't look oppressed and exploited."

"A lot of them are on their way north. They're smiling because they're on the threshold of the Promised Land."

"I've handled cases involving the immigrant smugglers. They're treated like heroes by the very people they exploit."

"The smugglers *are* heroes," Faroe said. "They offer hope in exchange for money. A good deal for both sides."

"And Hector?"

"They sing his praises in *narco-corridas.* He's a god because he was once as poor as anyone from the hills and now he owns the plaza, which is to say he owns the city."

"The plaza?"

"A slice of the border. Everyone who smuggles anyone or anything through Hector's plaza pays for the privilege. Since his plaza runs from the ocean well out into the desert, Hector is one rich son of a bitch."

"Outlaws paying outlaws," Grace said, shaking her head.

"Even outside the law, there's always some kind of order. *Plata o plomo.*"

As the Escalade forced its way through the Zona Norte traffic, the driver reached for the electric switches and opened every window. Cool, damp air poured in. Grace wasn't dressed for it. She shivered and rubbed her arms.

"I'm cold," she said loudly. "Please raise the windows again."

The guard in the passenger seat shook his head. "No."

She looked at Faroe. "Why?"

"Any *pistolero* on the street can shoot into the car," Faroe said, pulling her close, sharing his body heat, "but our boys here would have a hell of a time shooting back through closed windows."

The guard held up his thumb and forefinger. He aimed the imaginary weapon out the open window and dropped the hammer. Then he turned and smiled at Faroe, showing two front teeth covered in stainless steel that reflected light like the metal of his pistol.

A cell phone rang. The driver snatched the unit off his belt. He listened, then punched the call off and muttered something to the guard.

The guard grunted in surprise, then looked back over his shoulder. "You mus' be *muy importante.* We go righ' now to see *el jefe.*"

"How long will it take?" Faroe asked. "She's freezing."

Silence was his only answer.

36

FAROE HELD GRACE FOR fifteen minutes before the Escalade turned off a fast thoroughfare and slowly climbed a coastal hill. Once the wind stopped pouring through the windows, he expected her to back away.

She didn't.

He told himself he should let go.

He didn't.

The neighborhood was quiet, expensive, and overlooked the Pacific Ocean. They passed two Tijuana police cars that formed a casual roadblock. The officers didn't quite salute, but they sure didn't offer to stop the big SUV. The road wound up the hill to the top, where a big house was surrounded by an even bigger fence. The automatic gate opened. As the Escalade pulled into the driveway, the garage door lifted. It closed the instant the vehicle's bumper cleared the electronic beam.

The three bodyguards waited. They hustled Faroe and Grace out of the car and into the house. The place was expensively furnished, etched glass and buttery leather couches, fine art on the walls and fine stone tiles on the floor.

And it smelled like the barracks of an unwashed army.

Grace wrinkled her nose.

Faroe memorized everything he saw.

The jock-strap smell couldn't quite conceal the sharp tang of tobacco and marijuana smoke. Male voices called back and forth, ragging on each other and the world. A half dozen bodyguards lounged in front of a huge wide-screen television set, smoking and watching a soccer match. Four more men sat at a dining room table eating a meal of roasted chicken with tortillas and pickled peppers.

Weapons lay everywhere. Black assault rifles with loaded magazines stood at attention on a long rack against one wall. Chrome and black semiautomatic pistols hung in shoulder harnesses on a clothes tree, along with an old but still deadly sawed-off shotgun on a shoulder strap.

The man chopping up the chicken used a machete as long as his arm.

Faroe felt naked.

Grace's sheer silk blouse, skyscraper heels, and tight skirt shocked the place into silence for a moment. Then several of the men made remarks in Spanish.

Faroe gave them a long look before he said to the Mexican from the car, "Your *compadres* are pigs. Tell them to mind their mouths in front of my woman."

The guard shrugged. "You tell them."

"If it happens again, I will."

"I no think it happen. They don' like you look."

"Do I want to know what they said?" Grace asked. "My gutter Spanish isn't as current as yours."

"They like your shoes."

"Great. I'll swap them for one of those rifles."

The guard's mustache twitched. Definitely a small smile.

They were escorted through the barracks to a separate wing of the house. Two men armed with Uzi submachine guns blocked their way.

The Mexican with the mustache barked out staccato orders and used Hector's full name.

The guards stepped back and let them pass.

Faroe, Grace, and Mustache walked down a long hallway lined with bedrooms. Each had been turned into some kind of work space. Through the open door of one bedroom, Grace saw three young, well-dressed women working at machines on a table.

"They look like bank tellers," she said softly to Faroe.

"They are. Banco de Hector. The machines are mechanical currency counters."

Bales of counted, sorted, and banded bills were stacked waist high along one wall of the room, like so many yards of green paper.

For an instant Grace couldn't believe what she was seeing. There was more money in this upscale suburban bedroom than she'd ever seen short of the Federal Reserve Bank vaults in Washington.

"So, Judge, what you think? You like my *pinche casa de dinero*? Huh?"

Hector Rivas stood in the hallway in front of them, smoke curling up around his face from a cigarette in the corner of his mouth. He looked like a character out of a noir magazine.

And every instinct Faroe had told him that Hector was screwed up on something—as unpredictable as hot nitroglycerin.

The Butcher.

Jesus, Grace, why didn't you go back to the hotel when you could?

"Is ver' *grande,* no?" Hector said.

"I've been inside the Federal Reserve Bank in Washington," she said calmly.

Hector stared at her, sucked in a breath, held it, smiled like a fallen angel, and let the smoke trickle out. One of his eyelids drooped almost shut. The other eye glittered in the light like a snake's. When Grace didn't back up, he grinned and stepped out of the doorway.

"Bienvenido," Hector said, with a bow and a flourish.

And a close appreciation of her body.

She swung her hips past him into a big room with a twenty-foot ceiling, brick walls, and a huge fireplace at the far end. Despite the heat inside the house, the elaborate gas logs were burning fiercely. The furniture in the room was dark, oversize, and too ornate for her taste. One of the walls was covered with hand-painted tapestries depicting bloody scenes from the bullring. Another wall was loaded with Spanish art depicting various moments of the Crucifixion.

A blond boy sat near the hearth, working over something on a silver tray. He could have been an acolyte or a sacrifice.

"Do we pray or laugh?" Grace asked Faroe very softly.

"Pray."

There was an obviously new addition to the stately room. In the far corner, a high-tech communications center gleamed with glass, plastic, and status lights.

Hector's nephew, Jaime, sat at a long desk talking softly into a telephone and staring at one of the three computer screens in front of him. As he talked, he scrolled through web pages, reading figures into the phone. There were two more hardwired phones within his reach, as well as a handheld radio and a satellite cell phone on their charging cradles.

Slowly Grace walked into the room. As she

watched, Jaime hung up the phone and hammered intently on the computer keyboard. He looked more like an international business technocrat strumming the threads of an electronic spiderweb than a drug smuggler.

When Faroe moved past Hector to follow Grace, the drug lord grabbed Faroe by the arm and turned him toward the light.

"Hey, mon, don' I know you from the joint?" Hector asked.

"No, *jefe.* I would remember you."

Hector turned his head to bring his good eye to bear. "Din' you one time try to buy some *chiva* from *un hombre* named Ramón Posada in the back room at the Blue Fox? I sure I see you."

Faroe smiled slightly. "*Jefe,* you're remarkable. That was more than seventeen years ago. There was a deal with a man named Posada, but I was just along for the ride. The buyer was an East Los Angeles dope dealer named Jorge Chula. But I don't remember seeing you there."

Hector smiled, revealing a rich man's teeth—gold and silver and steel replacing teeth lost to brawls. "I watch by a *pinche* hole in the ceiling because I din' trust *el cabrón* Chula *nada más que* I can piss on him."

"I heard later that he was some kind of a snitch for the gringos in San Diego," Faroe said. "Whatever happened to him?"

"I take his balls and feed them to a dog."

With that Hector turned and walked into the great room.

Grace didn't look at Faroe.

He didn't look at her. Jorge Chula had indeed been an informant. Faroe's informant. He'd been using him as a stepping-stone to Posada, who dealt ounces and half kilos of heroin from various Tijuana bars. Faroe hadn't known that Hector was running Posada. Hector hadn't known that Faroe was running Chula.

When *el jefe* came closer to the hearth, the fair-haired boy glanced up anxiously.

Hector ignored him.

Without seeming to, Faroe examined the *jefe de traficantes.* In some ways Hector was old-fashioned, like the guard outside the chapel at All Saints. Hector wore a full, bushy mustache that curled down either side of his mouth, *bandito* style. He carried his Colt pistol backward in his belt, like *pistoleros* had done for fifty years.

The solid gold diamond-studded pendant he wore on a heavy gold chain around his neck was stamped with the likeness of Jesús Malverde, El Narcosantón, Mexico's patron saint of drug smugglers. Although the Catholic Church disavowed Malverde, there were roadside shrines honoring him everywhere in northern Mexico, and every shrine had its pilgrims and whispers of miracles.

As Hector crossed the room, he moved with the faintly dragging gait of a drunk or an aging rodeo rider, someone with old injuries that had never fully healed. Yet his shoulders were still powerful, his hips narrow, his belly under control. His head seemed too large, like a bull's, but it only added to his impact.

Faroe decided that Grace was right. Hector had a raw, animal charisma that was perfectly suited to his life. His self-assurance alone would draw lesser men to him like pilgrims to a shrine.

Hector gave Grace a sideways look as he circled her, squinting past the smoke curling from the cigarette in his mouth. His black glance ran over her like hands.

"Your Honor, you have changed," he said.

Grace's smile was a double row of teeth. "Not really. This is what I usually wear under my black robes."

Hector gave a drunken hoot and looked at

Faroe. "Gringas. Sometimes they think they smart, yes?"

Faroe nodded and shot Grace a quick look of encouragement. She'd found precisely the right tone to charm the *traficante*. Faroe didn't know how long it would last, but he'd take every advantage fate threw him.

Hector took the half-smoked cigarette from his lips. His fingers opened, the cigarette dropped to the glossy marble floor, barely missing a beautiful Persian rug. He ground out the ember under the heel of his ostrich-skin boot. His next move was to reach for a leather cigarette case in the breast pocket of his white linen cowboy shirt. When he discovered that the box was empty, he cursed savagely.

The blond boy leaped up and rushed over with a silver tray holding ten filter-tipped cigarettes, a small pile of tobacco, and a smaller pile of white powder. The cigarettes were an inch shorter than normal. Their white tips had been twisted like those of a hand-rolled joint.

Faroe recognized the doctored cigarettes and knew his instincts had been right—Hector was an explosion looking for a fuse. The special cigarettes had different names in

Mexico, Colombia, Peru, and everywhere else they were smoked. In Tijuana, the cigarettes were called *cocaína a la mexicana.* Their crimped tips were loaded with powdered crack cocaine.

They were bad news.

Hector tossed the empty case to the boy, selected a smoke from the tray, and stuck it in the corner of his mouth. As the acolyte carefully transferred the rest of the cigarettes to the leather case, Hector fired up a gold Zippo and sucked in vaporized cocaine. He held the smoke in his lungs. An angelic smile spread across his blunt features.

Instant bliss.

Faroe hoped that Grace didn't understand just how slender their hope of survival was. Hector finally had fallen in love with the white lady. Traffickers lived frantic, pressure-filled lives. Cocaine gave them the feeling of endless energy, endless strength.

But the white lady was a bitch mistress, all black lips and whips, bloody spurs and knives. She could keep a man like Hector aroused and focused for days.

Then she'd drop him off a cliff.

Faroe wondered where the smuggler was on the inevitable arc from euphoria to murderous irrationality. Then he wondered what had driven Hector into the deadly lady's arms. There had been no hint in any files that the *narcotraficante* had become slave to his own wares.

Hector drew again on the cigarette, sucking the last residue of crack from the tobacco. Then he dropped the half-smoked butt on the tile and ignored it. His good eye flickered open. He grinned drunkenly. He looked at Grace's breasts like a boy who had just discovered girls were different.

"So you have *un amado,* like *su esposo,*" Hector said.

"My ex-husband has many women." She shrugged. "I stopped caring a long time ago."

"Ah, but your husband mus' be ver' angry. Tha's why he no care for his son. Maybe he punishes you?"

"He stopped caring a long time ago, too."

Faroe thought fast and mean. At the rate Hector was blazing through crack cigarettes, they didn't have much time left to work with even a marginally sane man.

"We saved your life," Faroe said, "because we have a deal to offer you. You interested?"

Hector's hand paused on the way to his cigarette case. *"Dígame."*

"We'll trade you Ted Franklin for Lane. Straight across. No side deals." Faroe's voice was calm. The rest of him was on red alert. It was make-or-break time, and he didn't know how well Her Honor could lie.

It had to be good.

Hector looked skeptically at Grace. "You can do this?"

"Give you Ted?" she asked.

"*Sí.*"

"On a golden platter, with a roll of hundred-dollar bills in his mouth."

It was good.

37

H
ECTOR LAUGHED ROUGH AND loud. *"Aiee,*
a ball-breaker."

"You'll never get the chance to find out,"
Grace shot back, her face a cold mask.

"No, no, Your Honor, I say it *con respecto,"*
Hector said.

"Bueno, jefe," Faroe said evenly. "Now
speak to me, because I'm the one who will
cut off Franklin's head and carry it south in a
box. *¿Comprende?"*

For several long seconds Hector studied
Faroe. Then he nodded. *"Usted es un hombre fuerte y formal.* We make deal."

"Good. Why do you want Franklin?" Faroe asked.

Hector didn't bother to hide his surprise. "The judge? She don' know?"

"She was never part of Ted's business. He was never part of hers."

Hector squinted at both of them for a long time. He pulled the leather case from his pocket and stuffed another cigarette into his mouth. He toyed with the lighter like a pipe smoker buying time to think.

"*¿Es verdad?*" he asked Grace. "Is true?"

"I tried to tell you that the other day," she said. "Ted's business with you and Carlos is his own."

Hector made a face, as if hearing Calderón's name left a bad taste in his mouth. "He is *un hijo de la chingada,*" Hector said bitterly. "Carlos cause this, him and *todos los jefes politicos.* Strong men like me take all the bullets and *los politicos* sit clean and pretty and collect *la mordida*—the bite, you know?—for the plaza."

"I understand," Faroe said.

Hector hissed through his teeth and stared down the hallway toward the counting room.

Faroe wondered if the explosion had finally found a fuse.

"You are *politico*," Hector said to Grace. "How much you take for the rent of the plaza?"

"Bribery?"

"Sí, sí," he said impatiently.

"We don't do business like that in America."

"Boolsheet! All government like that. How much you take from men like me?"

Grace looked at Faroe. *What now?*

Fortunately Hector kept talking. *"Los politicos* in Tijuana and Mexico City bite me good. That room has more than twelve million gringo dollars, if the smugglers and *facilitadores* don' cheat me much. You hear me, Judge?"

"Yes."

"That is—*¿cómo se dice?* Loan?"

"Rent," Faroe said, hoping to defuse Hector's rage.

"Rent. Two weeks." Hector's voice rose. "That is what the plaza de Tijuana cost me. Two focking weeks."

Grace's eyes widened. She looked at Faroe.

"That sounds about right," Faroe said evenly. "The politicians charge Hector six million a week so that he can risk his life and the lives of his family running a dangerous, violent business."

"*Sí, sí. ¡Exactamente!* I pay *todo el mundo.* Guns and men and food and women—these not free. I am a great milking goat," Hector yelled. "And then they put horns on my head and fock me in the ass. *¡Aiee!*"

Grace tried to look sympathetic, but doubted her acting skills were up to it. Hector screwed the men beneath him and the politicians screwed Hector.

She wouldn't give a pile of dog turds for any of them.

"Where does Ted Franklin fit into this?" Faroe asked.

"He stole from me, the *pinche* money *los politicos* don' take!"

With that, Hector erupted into the kind of Spanish Faroe didn't want to translate for Grace. Instead, he provided a running commentary on the core of Hector's rant.

"Carlos and Jaime talked Hector into buying a bank from Ted," Faroe said softly. "Hector didn't want to. He has a cash business, so he 'don' need no focking bank.'"

Hector took a breath, spotted Jaime, and yelled, "Jaime, Jaime, *¡andale pues!*"

Jaime spun around in his high-backed executive chair. He looked angry but he kept his mouth shut. Obviously he had experience with his uncle's drug-fueled rage.

Hector gave his nephew a one-eyed glare. "Jaime, tell your plan *grande,* the plan you make with that *cabrón* Carlos and his *cabrón amigo,* Franklin. Tell how el Banco de San Marcos feex everything."

As he spoke, Hector made moist, scornful noises and pumped his hips to demonstrate his contempt for his nephew and his big ideas.

Faroe had been watching Grace. She'd ignored Hector's crude sign language, but her eyelids flickered at the mention of Banco de San Marcos.

Jaime came to his feet like a feral cat. He glared at Faroe, then at Grace, but when he turned to his uncle, his face was neutral, blank.

"This Jaime here, he genius," Hector went on sarcastically, his accent getting thicker the madder he got. "Beesness degree. *Aiee, cabrón.* He need machines to make a beesness I make out of my head."

"Times have changed, *jefe,*" Jaime said evenly. "We can't compete with other organizations if we don't—"

"No," Hector said, waving his cigarette wildly. "You want to own this beesness I shit bullets to make."

"I simply want to rationalize it," Jaime said. His eyes said they'd been around this track as many times as any greyhound.

"Boolsheet! Beesness is blood and fear and power!"

"I don't think our business should be discussed in front of strangers, people who do not wish us well," Jaime said.

Hector turned a torrent of Spanish on his nephew.

Faroe translated the meat of it for Grace. "Listen, *pendejo,* you don't have any problem talking about our business to Carlos Calderón. Who are you to tell me who I can talk to?"

A man hurried into the room, a burrito in one hand and a piece of paper in the other. He circled the shouting Hector to put the paper on Jaime's desk.

"You talk to that *cabrón* Ted Franklin," Faroe continued translating. "These people—that's you and me, Grace—aren't dangerous to ROG. We have what they want. They have what we want. So tell them our secrets, just as you have already told our enemies."

Jaime looked uncomfortable. "Uncle, you are tired. Your judgment is—"

Hector drew his pistol and fired four times at the man armed only with a burrito. He was dead before he hit the floor.

Grace made a choked sound.

Faroe grabbed her and pulled her away from Jaime, who had the look of a man marked for immediate death.

Armed men poured into the room.

"Uncle, I swear to—"

Hector backhanded Jaime across the mouth, sending the younger man staggering.

Faroe went back to translating Hector's words in a voice only Grace could hear. "Don't, burro. Don't presume to talk to me. You are very bright. You have a very good education that I paid for. Someday you might make a good man in our business, but you are not ready yet to take over from me. Until you are, never again question my judgment. Never."

Faroe waited.

So did everyone else in the room.

Hector shoved his pistol back into his belt and gestured toward the body on the floor.

Faroe murmured along with Hector's words. "Take that *cabrón* and dump him with the garbage. A little warning for other traitors who walk past me to do Jaime's work."

Flushed, all but choking on rage, Jaime waited for whatever came next. He watched Hector with the eyes of a man looking for the best place to slide in a knife.

While the body was hauled away, Hector dug out the leather box and stuck a new cocaine cigarette in the corner of his mouth.

"You okay?" Faroe asked Grace very softly.

"No."

"Can you keep it together a little longer?"

"Yes."

He squeezed her arm and wondered if she understood the dynamics of cocaine intoxication. Irritability and irrationality were just the beginning. Paranoia and delusions followed close on.

Then things would get ugly.

Hector turned toward Grace and Faroe and said in English, "So, wha' you think?"

"You're very efficient," Faroe said, ignoring the trails of blood on the white marble floor and the grim humor of the men dragging out the body. "Shall we set up the details of our trade?"

"*Sí,* but first, you come with me. I show you efficient. Then you know don' fock with Hector Rivas Osuna."

Faroe didn't have any choice, so he started after Hector.

Grace followed.

"No," Hector said, waving her off. "You puke."

Grace looked at Faroe.

"Stay here," he said instantly.

"Why? What could be worse than seeing a murder?" Though her voice was steady enough, her skin was pale beneath all the makeup.

"Plenty. Stay, *amada.* You don't need new nightmares."

"What about you?"

"I'll squint." Then he added very softly, "Work on Jaime. Find out what pushes his buttons."

38

Faroe followed Hector through a door leading to a short, brick-lined hallway. At one end of the hall a circular metal staircase wound down to the lower level of the house, which was also walled with brick.

Hector, less angry now but getting higher with each toke, reverted to Spanish. "This is a wonderful building. Very expensive, very solid. It belongs to a wealthy judge here in Tijuana, although he has decided to let me borrow it for a few months."

The *traficante*'s amused smile told Faroe that the judge hadn't had any choice.

"He would like it back someday, but he is

not man enough to ask," Hector said with a laugh. "Not like the ball-breaker upstairs. *Aiee,* that is a strong woman."

Faroe hoped that Grace would continue to amuse Hector . . . but not too much. Hector's reputation with women depended on how high he was.

There was a heavy metal door at the base of the staircase. The door was guarded by a blank-faced man carrying an assault rifle. Without a glance Hector brushed by the man.

Faroe followed and found a spacious wine cellar converted to a torture room. Beautiful wooden wine racks were attached to the walls with heavy wrought-iron supports. A big, unshielded lightbulb dangled from the ceiling. The intense glare fell on the slumped body of a man dangling from chains strung up over the wine racks. The prisoner had longish dark hair that was slick with sweat. He was dressed in a white shirt that was red, covered with his own blood.

Faroe recognized him instantly—the bomb layer from Ensenada. One of the guards was wearing his solid gold diamond-rimmed watch.

Hector grasped a handful of the prisoner's

sweaty black hair and jerked his head upright.

The bomber's face was a swollen, gross
balloon. Bruises had gathered below and
around his eyes, closing them darkly. His jaw
hung slack and awkward. Broken.

Hector twisted his handful of hair and the
bomber grimaced in pain, showing bloody,
broken teeth.

"Are you ready to talk?" Hector asked, his
voice gentle.

The hair on Faroe's neck stirred. He would
rather Hector had screamed.

The bomber made a ragged sound. Be-
hind swollen lids, his eyes glittered dryly, like
those of a coiled rattlesnake. His tongue
worked behind bloody teeth. He tried to spit
in Hector's face.

His mouth was too dry.

Hector patted the bruised and bloody
cheek and said tenderly, "There, there, it is
almost over. Just tell us who paid you and we
will take away all your pain."

Faroe felt the chill of danger and the heat of
adrenaline sliding into his blood. He wondered
what his chances were of getting one of the
automatic weapons before they got him.

Hector was nuts.

"So, what you think?" Hector asked Faroe. "Is this the man who tried to kill me and my family?"

Faroe's face was a mask. He carefully studied the man but finally shook his head. "I doubt his mother would recognize him now."

Hector laughed and nodded. Then he signaled to the shadows.

One of the waiting men stepped into the cone of light. He had a barrel chest and the emotionless eyes of a picador in the bullring. He mustn't have been as stupid as he looked—he wore tight latex gloves to protect him from his victim's blood.

The torturer held a stripped electrical wire in each hand. He looked at Faroe, then at the bomber, and touched the two copper conductors together. Dazzling blue-white sparks arced and showered over his hands. He grinned and waved the two wires in front of the bomber's face. He touched them together again.

"Would you care for a little of this, perhaps?" he asked, polite as a waiter presenting a dessert tray.

"This man, Tomás, he really enjoys his work," Hector said, clapping the man on the shoulder. "My Torquemada."

Faroe looked into the torturer's eyes and knew Hector wasn't bragging. It was the simple truth.

"This one has been disloyal for a long time," Hector said, gesturing toward the prisoner. "He works for a band of marijuana farmers down in the mountains between Sierra de la Laguna and the ocean. They use my plaza but they do not pay. I think I will hang his body from an overpass on the Ensenada toll road for all his friends to see on their way to work tomorrow morning."

Faroe waited, wondering if Hector had a point or if he simply got off on blood and death.

"Should I bring my Tomás upstairs and introduce him to your judge?" Hector smiled. "Should I tell her that her son will be my gift to Tomás?"

Only years of living undercover kept Faroe from going for Hector's throat. Only hard-won discipline kept Faroe's voice neutral.

"As you pointed out, the judge is not without her own power," Faroe said. "If Lane is harmed, there will be an international crisis. That is not good for business."

"Ha! You think that will save the boy? I have many eyes reading the diplomatic telegrams between the gringo government and Mexico City. I have many ears listening to embassy conversations for the first sign of intervention."

Faroe agreed with a calm he was far from feeling. "This is so."

"The boy would live only as long as Tomás and I decide to keep him alive. And after we finish with him, somebody will tell the gringo authorities that the boy was a bad one who simply ran away and, like so many other unfortunates, was never heard from again."

Faroe didn't doubt a word of it.

And if Lane got hurt, Faroe would hunt Hector down and execute him where he found him.

"What you said is true," Faroe said, "but it will not get you Ted Franklin on a golden platter with a roll of hundreds in his mouth."

"Yes." Hector ground the spent cigarette beneath his heel. "That is why you are still alive."

39

STEELE SAT IN THE part of the Learjet that had been transformed into a flying office for the use of whichever St. Kilda consultant needed it. The wheelchair was a tight fit in the working space, but it didn't matter. If he needed anything, Dwayne would get it before Steele even knew he wanted it.

Dwayne handed over a satellite phone. "It's Mazey with the land and cell phone taps. Something is going down."

"Steele," he said calmly, taking the phone. But his heart kicked in the hope that they'd caught a break. "Go ahead, Mazey."

"We've had multiple hits on her home and

cell phone, all from Ted Franklin, all within the last hour."

"Messages left?"

"He wants his ex-wife to go to Lomas, where he'll call her at midnight."

"What, where, or who is Lomas?"

"We're working on that, sir. It's a fairly common name in the area."

"Midnight." Steele looked at his watch and folded his lips unhappily. "We're not going to be on the ground in time to help you with this one. Call Faroe and see what Grace knows."

"His phone is off. Hers is 'out of area.'"

"Mother of—" Steele bit off the curse. "Where is Faroe?"

"Assuming that he's still carrying the phone, our satellite monitor puts him in Tijuana."

"That's a large place. Do better. What about the boy?"

"Still at All Saints. Assuming—"

"That he has the bloody phone with him," Steele finished impatiently.

"Yes, sir."

"Anything else?"

"The team watching Sturgis's office saw him get in a car whose plates came back to the U.S. government. The driver shook the team. We didn't have enough assets in place to tail a real pro. No one has seen or heard from Sturgis since."

"Bloody hell."

"John told me the feds have withdrawn surveillance from the La Jolla house, but the Mexicans are all over the place like a rash. He left a message on Dwayne's phone, but—"

"The phone is turned off," Steele finished. Since John was Mazey's husband and the head of all surveillance teams on this consultation, Steele knew that the information was solid. "Dwayne is with me. Forward all intelligence to the number he'll give you."

Steele handed over the phone to Dwayne, called up the satellite monitor, and split the screen. One dot stayed put above Ensenada. One dot was mired in Tijuana.

He tried Faroe's number himself.

Nothing.

Grace's number.

More nothing.

"Anything on Lomas?" he asked Dwayne.

"Too much. We'll never get it sorted out by midnight California time."

"Can you override Faroe's off switch?"

"If he hasn't dicked with it, yes," Dwayne said. Then he told his frustrated boss what

Steele already knew. "But if Faroe shut down his phone, he had a good reason. The life-and-death kind."

Steele didn't argue. "What do you make of the fact that the feds withdrew from the La Jolla surveillance?"

"It means they know more than we do."

"Precisely. Get someone monitoring all government communications channels within sixty miles of the border. Key words ROG, Hector Rivas Osuna in any combination, Faroe, Grace, Judge Silva, Ted or Theodore Franklin, Calderón, Lane Franklin, All Saints or Todos Santos, Bank of San Marcos, Banco de San Marcos."

Dwayne leaned against the desk, punching in numbers, waking up the St. Kilda consultants who specialized in monitoring scrambled federal channels.

"Think it will do any good?" Dwayne asked as he waited for someone in Texas to answer.

"In the next hour? Doubtful. Do it anyway."

Steele stared at the red dot mired in Tijuana.

Damn it, Joseph, call in.

40

IN DARKNESS, LANE STARED at the white-washed ceiling. Sweat ran cold on his ribs. The phone Joe Faroe had given him was under his pillow, along with an alarm clock Lane didn't think he would need anytime in the next century.

He was so wide awake his eyeballs burned.

He told himself he wasn't going to check the clock under his pillow again. But he did.

About two hours until Faroe called.

If he called.

Call me, he prayed silently. *I'm going postal here in the dark, thinking about—*

I won't think about it.
Won't.
Won't.
Won't.

His silent chant kept time with the waves piling against the beach, *chubasco* waves shouting the storm to come.

He hoped the tropical fury would wipe out the school.

Cigarette smoke and something sharper, more chemical, slid through the open window. The guards were just outside, laughing and talking among themselves.

Taking bets on whether Lane would survive the coming day.

Call me. Please!

41

The silence in the Escalade was thick enough to slice and serve on bread. Even with every window open, the SUV stank of sweat. Meeting with Hector did that to men, no matter how tough they thought they were.

Faroe and Grace sat close, close enough that she could use his body heat to warm herself. Whenever she started to say anything, he squeezed her silently.

Don't talk.

The vehicle finally stopped by the bright lights of the hotel where Faroe and Grace were registered. Faroe lifted her out and then turned toward Mustache.

Grace couldn't hear what Faroe said as he drew Mustache slightly away from the other gunmen, but she did see the exchange of something, palm to palm. As soon as Mustache climbed back into the Escalade, the driver shot out of the light like his tires were on fire.

"What was that all about?" she asked Faroe.

"Recruiting."

"What?"

"St. Kilda needs more contacts in Mexico."

"Spies."

Faroe shrugged.

"The lies and betrayals never end, do they?" she said quietly.

"There's plenty of lying and betraying to go around on both sides of the line."

Grace looked at Faroe. He'd let his game face slip. He was weary with something deeper than a simple lack of sleep. He handed the bellman a claim check for the car and waited silently, staring at the tips of his new boots.

"What happened?" she asked softly, stepping closer to him. "What was Hector so eager to show you?"

"A body that's going to hang from a free-way bridge sometime tomorrow morning. Only it isn't a body yet. It's mostly still the guy who laid that bomb down in Ensenada."

"We have to tell the—" Her voice broke. She let out a ragged breath. "Never mind. Old reflexes."

"Don't worry, *amada.* He'll welcome death."

Grace closed her eyes against the bright lights of the city.

"You leave anything at the hotel that you can't live without?" Faroe asked.

"The only thing I can't live without is my son."

42

"GOT HIM!" DWAYNE SAID triumphantly.

Steele took the phone. "Joseph?"

"Yeah."

"It's about time you turned on your damned phone."

"I've been talking to Hector Rivas Osuna. An interruption could have been fatal."

"Is Judge Silva with you?"

"Yes," Faroe said.

"Tell her to turn on her damned phone."

"Won't do any good. Her service ends near the border."

"Then get there fast," Steele said. "Ted left a message on her machine."

"What is it?"

"Your faith in St. Kilda is touching."

"Look, we just saw one man murdered and I met the next body to be hung from the freeway overpass, so excuse me if I'm not—"

"Who died?" Steele cut in.

"A guy who dissed Hector. Bang, bang, bang, bang, you're dead."

"Bloody wonderful."

"You're half right."

"Grace saw it?"

"Yes."

"How is she holding up?" Steele asked.

"Better than we have any right to expect. What is Ted's message?"

"He'll call her at Lomas at midnight. Find out who, what, or where Lomas is and call me back."

Steele punched out and stared at the red dot in Tijuana as if he could move it faster by sheer force of will.

43

Faroe punched the end button and drove quickly, closing in on the border crossing at Otay Mesa.

"Who, what, or where is Lomas?" he asked Grace.

She rubbed her face wearily, trying to stay awake. The adrenaline of being with a murderous madman had worn off, leaving her limp.

"Grace?"

"I'm reviewing a Lomas case, I know of at least five streets with that name, plus a town or two." She yawned. "Give me context."

"Ted left messages on your home phone

and your cell phone telling you to be in Lomas at midnight for his call."

She snapped upright. "Lomas Santa Fe. Our ranch. I haven't been there since I picked up Lane's computer. Ted had it with him while he was doing his kingmaking thing over ribs and beer, then he 'forgot' to return it to La Jolla."

"Turn on your phone. We might be close enough for you to get service. Listen hard to Ted's message. You know the man. Listen to what he doesn't say, how he breathes, what his voice is like."

Grace turned on her phone.

Nothing.

"How far is the ranch from here?" Faroe asked, accelerating.

The glow that was the Otay border crossing leaped closer.

"Even if you do the Nascar thing," she said, "we won't make it by midnight. Once we get over the border, it's at least forty minutes on I-5. The good news is that the Otay entry is closer."

Faroe punched a button on his phone and handed it to Grace. "Give Steele the location of the ranch."

While Grace talked, the Mercedes rocketed through the night, closing in on the dark and light-splintered chaos that was the border. She shut off the phone and handed it back to Faroe.

"We're almost there," he said. "Try your cell again."

She looked at the phone in her hand. "Nothing."

Planes on final approach to the Tijuana International Airport dropped down from the night and materialized in the runway lights. Just to the north, U.S. border patrol helicopters flew orbits over Spring Canyon, their spotlights stabbing down to the deep footpaths that braided the canyon floor.

"Lane should see this," Grace said.

"Why?"

"Add some artful wreckage and you have the opening of *T2*."

"*T2?*" Faroe asked as he pulled into the short line at the port of entry.

"The second *Terminator* movie. It begins in a world at war, pretty much like Tijuana, except that Tijuana is real. Don't tell me you've never seen *T2*?"

"I've lived it."

"Your choice."

"Your benefit."

"Win-win, huh?"

He would have laughed but it wasn't funny.

The cell phone in Grace's hand beeped. "Three missed calls." She punched in numbers. "Ted."

"Messages?"

"Just one." She retrieved it and listened with a growing sense of disbelief. "You slimy son of a *bitch*."

She hit replay and handed it to Faroe.

Ted's voice sounded cheerful, nonchalant.

Faroe wanted to throttle him.

"Hey, Gracie-girl. We need to meet real soon. It'd be good for everybody, especially for Lane. But it wouldn't hurt your career, either. I'll call you at Lomas at midnight and we can set it up. Ciao."

"Gracie-girl," Faroe said neutrally, handing the phone back to her.

"It's Ted's way of feeling superior." Her voice was even. Her eyes told Faroe that if he used that nickname, she'd clock him.

"Is he as smiley as he sounded?" Faroe asked.

"There was a lot of strain in his voice."

"Good. He deserves it. Is he lying?"

"I doubt it," she said. "He's serious when he's lying."

"Who's at Lomas right now?"

"This time of night? Nobody. We have a caretaker who does the grounds during the day, and a housekeeper two days a week."

"So you would be alone there, waiting for his call."

Faroe wasn't asking a question, but she answered anyway. "Yes."

"Nearest neighbor?"

"A quarter mile. They come and go, same as we did."

"Sweet," Faroe said.

His eyes said the opposite.

The car in front of them pulled through the port of entry. Faroe pulled forward and gave the customs agent a bland smile. The man looked bored and end-of-the-shift sleepy. Then he glanced down at his computer screen. His eyes widened and his manner suddenly changed.

"Where have you been in Mexico?" The question was sharp, meant to be intimidating.

"Tijuana, Ensenada, and back," Faroe said, meeting the inspector's eyes straight on.

"Pull over underneath that sign, the one

that says 'Secondary Inspection.' Don't leave your car, either of you. Someone will be along in a minute."

He frowned at Faroe, then reached for his phone as the Mercedes crept forward onto American soil.

"Now what?" Grace said, her voice anxious.

"The guys who followed us this afternoon probably put a border watch on us. Either they intend to pick up the surveillance again, or they just want to know when we crossed back."

"Does it never end?"

"Not for a while."

Not while you're breathing.

Faroe parked under the sign. He'd barely turned off the ignition before the inspector stepped out of his booth and trudged across the tarmac to them. He gave the interior of the vehicle a cursory glance, then said, "Okay, you can go."

Faroe hit the accelerator.

"He didn't even ask for papers, which means they already know who we are, or at least who you are," Faroe said. "How is this car registered?"

"To Ted's company until I get it transferred to my own name." She shrugged. "Just one of those details I haven't gotten around to."

"That might explain it," Faroe said, "but even so, the inspector let us off too easily. No long wait, no car search, no papers, no pat-down, no body cavity search. Just a short stall at the border while he checks our faces against the ID he called up on his computer."

"You suspect everything, everybody. Can't things just happen?"

"Not if you want to stay alive."

"We're in the U.S.!"

He gave her a sideways look and kept his mouth shut.

"Right," she said, angry with him, herself, and everything that had happened since Calderón had telephoned her about Lane. "What are we going to do about Ted's call? We're late."

"I don't think he's going to call."

"Then why would he want to make sure I'm at—" She stopped, swallowed hard, and said, "I don't like what I'm thinking."

"Good for you," Faroe said. "Your ever-lovin' ex has your cell number. He can call you at midnight no matter where you are. I think he just wanted to make sure you'd be there at Lomas, all alone, at midnight."

"He wouldn't have the guts."

"To do what?"

She shook her head. She really didn't want to go there.

"You don't think he has the *cojones* to kill you in cold blood?" Faroe asked.

"I know he doesn't."

"How about hiring it done?"

The coastal fog gave them a clammy embrace when they dropped down onto Interstate 5. At least Grace told herself that was why she felt chilled.

Faroe reached over the seat, snagged his jacket from the back, and dropped it in her lap.

"Put it on," he said. "And no, I don't think he intends to murder you. No benefit to him. If that changes, I'll change with it."

Grace pulled the jacket over her shoulders. "Should I feel good about that analysis?"

He glanced at the dashboard clock. Grace was right. At this speed they wouldn't make the ranch by midnight. He started checking the exit signs on the freeway.

"What are you looking for?" she asked.

"A nice anonymous motel. I'll drop you off, St. Kilda will have someone with you real quick, and I'll go to Lomas and do a little moonlight snake hunting."

"No." Grace's voice was low.

Faroe looked over, not sure he'd even heard her speak.

"No, you're not going to stash me in some nice safe motel," she said distinctly. "It would be like Ted to show up at Lomas instead of calling. If that happens, I want a little time with him." *So I can rip his face off.*

"That might be dangerous," Faroe said.

"Maybe for him but not for me. He keeps a nine-millimeter in his bedside table at Lomas. Last time I checked it was still there. If not, there's a fancy shotgun over the mantel that works just fine, and the birdshot is in the pantry with the caviar." She looked at Faroe. "Unlike you, I don't play against long odds for the hell of it."

Faroe threw back his head and laughed. "Damn, *amada,* Hector was right. You're hoping Ted makes a try for you."

Grace didn't answer. The longer she thought about what Ted had done to Lane, the colder her anger got.

Maybe I never climbed out of the gutter violence after all. Maybe it's still in me.

God, I hope so. I have to be like Faroe. Ruthless.

For Lane's sake. Lane, who didn't do anything to deserve this.

"Remember," Faroe said, glancing at her expression, "right now, Ted is worth more to Lane alive."

"How about wounded?"

"Are you a good enough shot?"

"Yes."

Faroe smiled. "Wounded works for me."

44

GRACE PULLED THE NOZZLE out of the gas tank, racked it on the gas pump, and waited for her receipt.

"Ready," she said.

"Almost done."

She watched while Faroe removed a translucent plate and loosened a lightbulb in the back of the SUV. He put the plate aside with the others he'd worked on.

"You drive," he said.

"Thank you, God," she said, sighing.

"Hey, I got us here on time, didn't I?"

"At slightly less than the speed of light," she muttered, climbing into the driver's seat.

Faroe slid into the back of the SUV and left the tailgate ajar. "At least I'm positive that nobody followed us."

"Is that good?"

"No. They should have been all over us like a rash."

"I had to ask, didn't I?" Grace turned the key and the big engine growled to life.

She turned onto the city street and drove in silence. After five minutes she turned onto a two-lane county road.

"You're sure Ted hasn't installed any security since the last time you were in Lomas?" Faroe asked.

"Yes. The summary of assets for the divorce was exhaustive."

"Remember the signals we discussed?"

"Yes."

Faroe shut up.

When Grace turned off the road into the long paved driveway, he looked over her shoulder. The dashboard clock read 12:04.

"If I'd been driving, you'd be on time," Faroe said.

Grace gave him a look in the rearview mirror.

He smiled, touched the nape of her neck

beneath her short hair, and heard her breath break. Her responsiveness made him want to haul her into the back with him for the kind of sex that would steam every window in the fancy SUV.

"As you approach that big oak up ahead," he said in a husky voice, "slow down to walking speed. When you hear the hatch close, pick up the speed again. Act like you're alone. Go ahead and get the weapon out of the bedroom, but keep the gun out of sight, somewhere he won't expect you to have it. He or someone else may be watching you from somewhere outside the house. If you see anyone, signal me."

"Where are you going to be?"

"Out in the brush, right behind anyone who's watching. I'll start well outside an ordinary surveillance perimeter."

Grace was still traveling at more than five miles an hour when she heard the faint whisper of fabric as Faroe stepped out of the back of the vehicle. In the dark glow of the taillights, she saw him come out of a running crouch and match the speed of the vehicle as he punched the button that automatically lowered and closed the tailgate. Then he slipped into the shadows of the big oak tree, vanishing into the spaces between moonlight and darkness.

Motionless, Faroe watched the Mercedes continue on up the gravel driveway to the deserted ranch compound. The chaparral lay on the coastal foothills in giant camouflage patterns, inky black and gray-green in the light of the moon.

He settled into the night. It was like going back to war again, where the choices were simple and the battle lines clear.

Infiltrate and exfiltrate, thrust and parry, win and lose.

Live or die.

I'll let Ted take care of the dying part, Faroe thought. *He has to be good for something, right?*

Silent, motionless, Faroe watched the taillights of the Mercedes flicker when she made the turn into the little traffic circle. The turnaround ran in front of the large California-style Tuscan villa. He bit back a laugh at some architect's idea of a ranch house. The stucco monster held the high ground overlooking the stables.

When Grace stopped, porch lights and several interior lights snapped on in welcome.

Motion sensors, right on time.

He watched her get out of the car and stretch like she'd gone a long time without a break from driving.

Okay. Nobody in sight.

She went into the house. Over the next several minutes, Faroe tracked her by watching lights come on downstairs and then on the second floor.

Nobody inside, either.

Faroe climbed soundlessly over a paddock fence beside the oak and headed for the stables a hundred yards away. He stayed in the shadows of the fence line and the cover of a head-high oleander hedge.

Something exploded under his feet.

Jesus, what—

A rabbit raced off, kicked out of its midnight nibbling by Faroe's boot.

It took thirty seconds for Faroe's heart rate to return to its normal measured pace.

He circled the stable quickly. Finally he reached a row of pencil cypress trees that burned like black flames against the moon-bright sky, defining the inland side of the property. He was about to slide into their cover and approach the house from the uphill side when he realized that he wasn't the only predator at work.

Cool night air slid down the slope toward him. He smelled the faint edge of recent, yet not fresh, tobacco smoke. Someone had been smoking nearby.

Faroe froze, waited, heard nothing.

He took a slow look around a cypress trunk. Thirty yards away, a figure materialized from the shadows of the tree line.

Someone was watching the house from the same spot Faroe had chosen to be his own observation post.

45

MOTIONLESS, FAROE RECALCULATED THE ODDS.

Not good.

But not surprising, either.

The man was dressed in some kind of night cammie suit. He had a long gun slung on his back, like he didn't really expect to need it. When he looked in Faroe's direction, moonlight sent a whisper-glow over the greasepaint that disguised the pale skin of the man's face.

A professional night predator, all decked out in the tools of his trade.

If the man had had his weapon trained on

the house, Faroe would have found a way to take him down. But the intruder was acting more like a bored guard than a paid executioner.

So whose setup is this? Who is screwing who, and with what tools?

Motionless but for the very slow turning of his head, always keeping the gunman in his sight, Faroe began a thorough visual inspection of the ranch compound. He paid special attention to the places he himself would have chosen to hide.

The man in the tree line quietly cleared his throat. A smoker's trait, unconscious, and deadly in the wrong circumstance.

Bad operational discipline.

But it suggested the dude was indeed relaxed. Even though Grace had already arrived, the main event hadn't begun.

Then what—or who—is the target?

Faroe identified two more hides, one in the brush at the edge of the clearing north of the house and another in the paddock area. He had just begun to examine the stable building itself when he noticed a brief green flicker in the partially open hayloft door.

An impatient sniper had just uncapped his starlight scope.

The telltale phosphorescence lit up his eye and the straight line of a watch cap on his forehead. He had spooled up his magical viewing device one last time, just to make sure it was still working properly.

All the bells and whistles, but their discipline needs a serious kick in the ass.

Faroe was familiar with the problem. It came from doing it too many times in practice and never doing it for real.

Okay. So we probably have some kind of government field office's special weapons team on a low-octane run, a step above routine drill, but not balls to the wall.

The only reason he'd managed to penetrate the operation so easily was that nobody had been detailed to watch the back side.

Too many dry runs.

Not enough wet work.

Faroe wasn't the only one to see the greenish glow. From down the tree line, he heard a quiet, edgy voice.

"Number Three, you're showing a light."

Instantly the cap went back on the starlight scope.

If Faroe had found himself in the middle of a St. Kilda operation, the team leader, the sniper, and the smoker would have been fired on the spot. The sniper should have known enough to keep his light capped, the team leader should have kept radio silence for anything short of life-or-death, and putting a smoker on the stalk was like sending up a flare.

The surveillance team scattered through the night around the Lomas ranch compound was made up of dudes earning a living, individuals of varying skill who were going through the motions, some more effectively than others.

Just people.

It was a simple truth that civilians had a tough time understanding. That and the fact that the government was armed by the lowest bidder.

Faroe lay back in the shadows, running scenarios in his mind. If Grace had been the target, the men would have moved in after she arrived—or been waiting in the house for her.

Are these Hector's men?

Doubtful. Even the Zetas mercenaries working both sides of the southwestern border spoke Spanish. If they'd hired gringos, it hadn't made a ripple yet.

Besides, the Zetas had done enough wet work not to be careless.

Did Franklin advertise in Mercs "R" Us?

Possible, but it wouldn't explain the feds following everyone—and then suddenly not following Grace.

The feds know she's going to be here. Does Ted know about the feds?

Headlights turned off the country highway and hit the driveway. The high beams flashed twice.

Near Faroe, the voice in the shadows spoke into a handy-talkie. "Primary is on the move, arriving in thirty seconds. Heads up. We don't want any surprises."

The green glow of the starlight scope appeared in the hayloft again.

Faroe watched the sniper sweep the grounds with his magic eye, prying into the darkness, covering the compound.

Covering.

Okay. Faroe let out a long, silent breath. *The weapons team isn't here to make an arrest. They're protecting an operation.*

The vehicle appeared at the end of the gravel driveway and swung around into the lighted traffic circle in front of the house. It was an oversize black SUV, a Suburban, but in the dark it looked a lot like the ominous Escalade Hector's gunmen used.

Must be a machismo thing.

And at night, with the lights off, black vehicles vanished.

The Suburban pulled past the front door and didn't stop until it found a place where the escape route couldn't be blocked. The driver was a professional trained in kidnap evasion.

"Primary, you're good to go," the radio voice said. "Make sure Franklin comes out last."

The headlights of the Suburban flashed again, proving that the vehicle was on the same radio frequency as the sniper and the weapons team. This was all for the benefit of one man.

Theodore Franklin.

Feds.

Bad combination.

Faroe slid back deeper into the shadows. If he showed himself now, the last thing he'd see in this life would be the green eye of the sniper's rifle.

The driver of the Suburban got out and searched the darkened compound. He muttered something and another man got out of the front seat. Both men were wearing dark windbreakers with bright lettering across the chest and back.

Law enforcement raid jackets.

The side door of the vehicle opened and a third man, heavyset and a little awkward, stepped down. The officers in the windbreakers fell in on either side of him and ushered him toward the front door.

Must be Ted.

The son of a bitch.

Franklin moved flat-footed, almost like he was in leg chains.

Behind him a fourth man slid out of the car. He wore a suit and carried a leather briefcase shiny enough to reflect moonlight. He walked like a man who owned the world.

One of the cops knocked firmly on the front door. The sound carried through the night. From Faroe's right came a voice from the team leader's radio.

"She's in the kitchen, headed for the front door right now."

Faroe was glad Grace didn't know that she was being tracked by a sniper's telescopic rifle sight.

The lawman was about to knock again

when the door swung open. Grace was out-lined in the hallway light. Obviously car registration wasn't the only detail she hadn't had time to take care of. She must have left clothes at the place because she was now dressed in dark slacks, a dark blouse, and flat shoes. She said something that Faroe couldn't hear.

"Mrs. Franklin, we're here on official business," a man said. His command voice carried clearly through the night. "It would be best if you cooperate."

Grace moved back and let them enter. As the second officer walked underneath the porch light, Faroe saw the lettering on the back of his raid jacket.

US MARSHAL

The door closed.

Well, that does it. This has gone from a goat roping to a clusterfuck.

Marshals weren't garden-variety cops. They protected courtrooms, served papers, transported prisoners, chased fugitives. And they administered a highly specialized program called "witness protection."

Franklin had found himself a mink-lined

hideout protected by the kind of bureaucracy that made an art out of delay.

But Lane had only a bit more than twelve hours to live.

All bets were off.

46

FAROE TURNED TOWARD THE officer in the camouflage coveralls. "Hey, you, over there in the trees. You're trespassing on private property. Come out with your hands up!"

The instant response was silence.

Then the officer slowly turned his head in Faroe's direction. At the same time, his right shoulder dropped.

He was sliding the assault rifle off his shoulder.

"Reach for that weapon and die," Faroe said flatly.

The man froze.

"Can you see him?" the man said into his radio.

The answer must have been negative because the man slowly raised his hands.

"We're federal law enforcement agents on official duty," he said. "Step out where we can see you."

"I don't care if you're aliens from the third galaxy over. You're trespassing and you're armed. I'm in fear of my life and I have every right to shoot you where you stand. Step backward out of cover so I can see you."

After a few seconds the man slowly straightened. Keeping his hands where they could be seen, he stepped backward out of his position. In the moonlight, Faroe could see reflective yellow letters on his back.

Another marshal.

"You see the lettering on the back of my coverall?" the marshal demanded. "That'll tell you who we are."

"How stupid do you think I am? You can buy anything on eBay. Keep walking backward toward me."

"You aren't being very smart."

"I aced target practice, which is all the smart I need. Back up."

Slowly the marshal backed up. When he was six feet away Faroe stepped out of the shadows, keeping the marshal between him and the barn.

"Tell your shooter in the hayloft to ease back on his trigger," Faroe said.

The marshal stood still but didn't say anything.

"Tell him."

"Hold fire," the officer said. He turned slightly, trying to get a look behind him.

In the half-light, Faroe could see the slender stalk of a radio microphone outlined against his cheek.

"Eyes front," Faroe snapped.

"We're federal officers. You're dipping yourself in deep shit."

"You're already up to your own lips in the stuff," Faroe said. "You and I are going to walk toward the house, where there's good light, and we'll let the judge sort out who's doing what and with which and to whom."

"You her bodyguard?"

"Give the man a prize. I'm walking in your shadow, so remind your boys about Ruby Ridge and what happens to snipers who take bad shots."

"He's the judge's bodyguard!" the marshal shouted. "Hold fire. We're going inside."

Faroe stayed close behind the marshal as they stepped out of the tree line and walked slowly across the front lawn. The skin at the base of his skull tingled as he sensed the gentle, giddy sensation of crosshairs intersecting there. He kept his right arm bent at the elbow, the posture of a man holding a gun.

Except he didn't have a gun and he sure didn't want anyone to know it until he was inside.

As the marshal reached the first step of the porch, the front door swung open. The marshal inside had been monitoring the radio traffic. He held a pistol close to his leg, ready to bring it to bear.

"Relax," Faroe said.

Then he stepped into the light and showed his empty hands.

"Oh, shit," the marshal in the coverall muttered.

"I won't tell if you don't," Faroe said. "I just wanted to get inside without being whacked by an eager shooter."

"Who are you?" the man in the doorway

demanded. "This is a federal crime scene. What are you doing here?" His windbreaker carried the name "Harkin" in yellow letters above a federal marshal's logo.

"Marshal Harkin, I'm representing the interests of an officer of the federal court," Faroe said clearly. "Her name is Judge Grace Silva. Do you have a warrant to be on her property?"

"You're under arrest for interfering with a federal officer, and that's just for starters."

Grace appeared in the hallway behind the marshal. She'd not only changed her clothes, she'd wiped off the streetwalker makeup.

"He's not interfering with anything," she said to the marshal in her best bench tone. "He's doing his job."

"Sneaking around in the dark?"

Her smile could have frozen fire. "When Ted demanded a meeting, at midnight, in a deserted house, I decided to bring somebody. Looks like Ted decided the same thing." Her dark glance raked the marshals. "Next time you ask for a command performance, tell me why in advance."

Faroe kept a poker face, but he was really glad Grace wasn't aiming all that power and scorn at him.

"Come in," she said to Faroe. "These are bona fide federal marshals. Apparently Ted is a federally protected witness, though no one will tell me what case he's a witness in."

Faroe walked into the house before the marshal could stop him. "Protected witness, huh? We used to call them snitches. They waste a lot of time before you get anything good."

Grace understood the message and sent one of her own. "I'm used to cutting through the bullshit."

Faroe nodded and gave her the lead. He might be hell on wheels in the shadows, but this was her world.

And she was good at it.

He followed her down the hallway and into a comfortably furnished living room that would have been called a salon if ranch houses had salons. Another marshal in a windbreaker stood in the middle of a large, magnificent Oriental carpet. His jacket bore the name "Tallman."

Ted Franklin stood behind Tallman, using him as a shield.

Faroe moved to one side. He wanted to see the man who had raised Lane and then given him to the Butcher of Tijuana.

Franklin was big, bulky, with the look of a man who liked alcohol too much and exercise not at all. He was wearing an expensive pinstripe suit and shiny loafers. His face was puffy, either from booze or lack of sleep. Both, probably. His eyes were bloodshot slits.

"Who's this guy?" Franklin demanded.

"You brought your friends to the party," Grace said. "I brought mine."

"Who is he?" Franklin demanded again. He turned to Tallman. "Make him show you some ID."

Tallman frowned. "You're not my boss, Mr. Franklin. Technically, you're not even a protected witness. We only agreed to go along on this visit as a courtesy. So until you and your attorney have concluded your plea negotiations, don't give me attitude."

Franklin looked like he'd been slapped. He straightened his shoulders and turned toward the fourth man, the one with the polished briefcase. He was coming down the stairs from the second floor.

"Tell them, Stu," Franklin said.

"Yes, Stu," Grace said coolly, "do tell everyone what this farce is all about."

Sturgis glanced around, saw a stranger, and kept his mouth shut.

Faroe looked at the man who must be Stuart Sturgis, lawyer to the criminally rich. He was in his late forties, clean-shaven, and sporting a two-hundred-dollar razor cut on his collar-length steel gray hair. He wore a two-thousand-dollar black silk suit with a black silk shirt and a white tie.

Mobster chic must be back in fashion.

"Did you find it?" Franklin demanded.

"No. Who's this?" he asked, looking at Faroe.

"Where is it?" Franklin snarled at Grace.

"Where's what?" she asked carelessly.

"The computer!"

"Computer? You mean Lane's computer, the one he used before he went to All Saints?"

"It's my computer," Franklin said in a rising voice. "I paid for it. Damn you, bitch, where is it!"

Faroe started for Franklin.

Tallman stepped between Franklin and Grace. "Judge Silva, we came here to help your husband retrieve some of his personal effects. If you could just help us, we'll be on our way."

"Legally," Grace said in her calm, cutting bench voice, "the computer doesn't belong to Ted. He gave it as a birthday present to our son. So even if you find the computer, you have no right to it. If that's all, gentlemen, I'm going to bed. It's been a long day."

Franklin shouldered his way around Tallman and towered over Grace. "Where's the fucking computer? So help me God, I'll break your neck if you don't—"

"Mr. Sturgis," Grace interrupted coldly, "would you define simple assault for your client? Or shall I?"

The marshal took Franklin firmly by the arm and turned him around. "Where is this computer supposed to be? I'll go look myself. If I find it, we'll let the lawyers sort out who it belongs to."

"In the bedroom at the end of the hallway on the right," Franklin said. "It's got to be there."

Tallman looked at Grace uncomfortably.

Faroe understood how Tallman felt. In the marshal's world, federal judges were gods. He really didn't want to piss one off.

"We have a warrant to seize the computer, Your Honor," Tallman said, producing a paper. "It's evidence in an ongoing investigation."

Grace read the paper with speed and care. She'd seen a lot like it. She gave the warrant back to Tallman. "Take any computer you find upstairs. But be quick about it. If I wanted to spend time near Ted, we'd still be married."

Tallman went up the steps two at a time. His footfalls sounded down the hallway.

Sturgis tossed his briefcase on a damask couch and sat down. He looked like he'd had a long day, too.

Grace went to a large cherry sideboard and opened a pair of glass doors. She pulled down a crystal decanter and began removing matching glasses from the shelf.

Faroe watched her. He seemed to be the only one in the room who could sense the rage and contempt beneath her outward calm.

"Drink, anyone?" she said.

"Please," Sturgis said. "Scotch."

Grace poured two fingers of golden liquid into a crystal glass and handed it to him.

Franklin's eyes followed the glass hungrily.

Grace lifted an eyebrow at him.

He looked away.

She poured another glass and stood in front of him. Franklin looked at her with hatred in his eyes. Then he snatched the glass from her hand and knocked it back in an eye-watering swallow.

Grace's smile lifted the hair on Faroe's neck. He reminded himself never to get between this woman and the welfare of her son.

"Poor teddy bear," she said with no sympathy at all. "What did you do that requires the services of the most expensive criminal litigator in California?"

47

"I'D RATHER BE CALLED the best, Your Honor," Sturgis said with a well-practiced courtroom smile.

"Your point is noted, Counselor, but I don't withdraw the characterization," Grace said without looking away from her ex-husband. "What are you charged with?"

Faroe watched, fascinated. This Grace was a far cry from the determined-to-be-bad public defender he'd met sixteen years ago.

Franklin started to speak.

Sturgis didn't let him. "We agreed that I would handle this, remember?"

Ted sucked down the last few drops of the

scotch. Ignoring Grace's disdainful look, he walked stiffly to the sideboard and poured another double.

"Technically, Your Honor, there aren't any charges yet," Sturgis said. "It is our position that there won't be any charges. That's part of what we're discussing with the authorities. Ted is a brilliant man, a genius. He may be in a position to offer certain unnamed federal authorities a great deal of help in understanding some of the, ah, complexities of international finance."

"So you're trying to negotiate a plea," Grace said. "Interesting. I thought you made it a point to fight to the bitter end of your client's resources. 'All or nothing,' isn't that your motto?"

"Sometimes the 'all' is pretty daunting." Sturgis notched up his courtroom smile. "That's what we're in the process of discussing, right, Marshal Harkin?"

Harkin made a gesture that could have meant anything. "Talk to the task force. Talk to the U.S. Attorney's office. Me, I'm just the babysitter."

Dressed in black, Grace prowled the hand-knotted carpet like a panther in an exotic cage. She stopped near the sideboard.

Near Ted.

If Ted had been in better shape, Faroe would have moved closer. As it was, he just enjoyed the show. When Grace wanted Faroe's input, she'd be the first to tell him.

"Task forces," she said. "U.S. Attorney's office. That sounds bad. How did a financial genius like you ever get roped into something so serious? Oh, wait, let me guess. Does it have something to do with your Mexican deals?"

Franklin turned his back on her.

"Tsk, tsk," she said. "I told you to be careful. It's a different system down there."

Plata o plomo.

"Was that it?" Grace said, turning to Sturgis. "Did Ted finally step out of all the gray areas into the black of dirty money? So much of it begging to be cleaned. So very profitable."

Franklin turned. "Listen, you—"

"Ted," Sturgis cut in. "Anything you say will jeopardize our negotiations with the government. These marshals aren't your lawyers. They could easily become your jailers. *Shut up.*"

Franklin looked from his lawyer to his ex-wife and then back again. "Get rid of them," he said, gesturing toward the marshals. "I need to talk to her."

Harkin came down the stairs empty-handed. "There's no computer anywhere upstairs that I can see under the constraints of the existing warrant. We could get a different warrant and search more thoroughly."

"This farce has gone on long enough," Grace said to Harkin. "I'd fight another warrant."

"Yes, ma'am, I figured you would."

Franklin slammed his glass down on the sideboard. Pieces of glass flew.

"Where is it?" he asked Grace shrilly, stalking toward her. "Where is the damned computer!"

"How would I know? You're the one who lost it, not me."

Faroe eased between Franklin and all the lovely sharp pieces of crystal.

Franklin jerked his hand toward the marshals. "Get rid of them, Stu. Right now!"

Sturgis drew Harkin into a corner and talked quietly with him for a moment. The marshal shook his head several times. Sturgis reframed his argument. Finally the marshal agreed.

"Give them some space," he said to his

men. "But everybody stays in the center of the room where we can see them. Agreed?"

Sturgis nodded.

As soon as the marshals couldn't hear them, the lawyer took a position on the rug, like a referee in a boxing ring. "Your Honor," he said, "Ted."

Faroe moved in beside Grace.

Sturgis frowned, then shrugged.

"Where's the goddamn computer?" Franklin demanded.

"If you want my help," she said, "tell me what's going on."

Sturgis acted like he was in a courtroom. "Judge Silva, the computer contains information that has great evidentiary value. You surely don't want to appear to be interfering with an important investigation, do you?"

"Shove it, Counselor," Grace said without looking away from her ex-husband. "I don't need lectures on how to manipulate the legal process. Talk to me, Ted. Does this have to do with Carlos Calderón and his colleagues in Tijuana?"

Franklin stared past her without answering.

"Actually," Sturgis said, "our position is that Calderón and his friends approached Ted, that he immediately sensed the impropriety of their intentions and began gathering evidence that would be used against them."

Faroe made a scornful sound.

Grace gave him a sideways look.

He put his poker face back on.

"So you were really kind of an undercover good citizen, is that it?" she asked her ex. "Was that before or after the task force investigators started hanging around Edge City Investments?"

"My client has not yet been charged with a crime, so his cooperation still has to be classified as 'willing,' Your Honor. We're reasonably certain our interpretation will stand."

"That's right," Franklin said roughly to Grace. "This is all going to blow over, trust me. I'm talking to people right now. Important people. One of two things is going to happen—either the case goes away completely or I become a hero. If you help me out, I can even guarantee your career won't be negatively impacted."

Grace gave her ex a look that had made more than one lawyer squirm. "I don't know whether I despise you more when you're being a politician or a crook. FYI, I don't give a damn about judgeships or who's who in the

Fortune roundup of rich men. All I care about is Lane. What about our son?"

Franklin looked away. "What about him?"

Faroe gently grabbed Grace's fist, the one she was going to clock Franklin with.

"We take the position," Sturgis said, "that your son's situation has nothing to do with the negotiations that are ongoing between my client and the government. Lane is just a rather troubled young man who is studying out of the country in a Catholic boarding school that is very stern about morals."

Grace looked at the lawyer like he was a bad smell stuck to her shoe. "Hasn't Ted told you about his little agreement with Carlos Calderón and Hector Rivas? Hasn't he told—"

Faroe squeezed her hand and interrupted. "I want to hear this. Where does Lane fit in this picture, Counselor?"

Sturgis shook his head. "We haven't mentioned Lane to the government. We think it might be wise if you refrained, too."

"You don't think the U.S. authorities want to know that an innocent boy is being held hostage in a foreign country in order to control his father's actions?" Grace asked in disbelief.

Franklin and Sturgis traded glances.

The lawyer turned his back, plainly stating that he wasn't any part of what happened next.

Franklin looked longingly at the glass he'd shattered on the sideboard. Then he sighed and faced his ex-wife.

"Why would Lane be involved?" Franklin said tonelessly. "We both know that he isn't my son."

Grace stared at him, too angry to speak.

"Nice work, asshole," Faroe said, his voice as neutral as Franklin's. "Not your DNA, so how could he be a part of this, right?"

"Who the hell are you?" Franklin said.

"The man who's trying to save your son's life. You should pray your knees bloody that I succeed." *Because if Lane dies, so do you.*

But Faroe wasn't going to say that in front of witnesses.

"I don't have a son," Franklin insisted.

"Tell it to the IRS," Faroe said. "You took all those tax deductions for a dog named Lane?"

Grace drew in a sharp breath. She knew Faroe better than anyone in the room.

And she was afraid.

"The point is," Sturgis said without turning

around, "that Lane's DNA puts a big hole in Grace's theory about Lane being a hostage."

"Right," Franklin said quickly. "If Carlos and Hector Rivas think they can control me by holding Lane, they've got the wrong hostage. Once they realize it, they'll let him go. No reason to hurt him, right?"

Franklin tried to meet Faroe's eyes but must have decided Grace would be easier.

Wrong again.

"I guess Mother Nature knew what she was doing when she didn't let you breed," Grace said.

"Don't give me that righteous act," Franklin said. "It's your life that's all lies."

Faroe still held Grace's fist but everything in him wanted to let her loose on Franklin.

And help her.

Later. When Lane's safe.

"Sturgis." Faroe's word was like a whip. "Turn around and put a muzzle on this mutt or get his lying ass out of here so that you and I can do some business."

"Listen, you son of—" Franklin began.

"Shut it, Ted," Sturgis said as he turned around. "This is going nowhere."

"Your problem, not mine," Faroe said. "As I

understand it, you really need that computer, right?"

"I knew the bitch was hiding it!" Franklin snarled.

Faroe gave him a look that penetrated the four shots of whiskey Franklin had knocked back.

"Your lawyer gave you good advice," Grace said. "Take it or go stand with your babysitters."

Franklin looked again at Faroe, then backed off and headed for the bar.

"Do you need the whole computer, or just some data from it?" Faroe asked Sturgis.

"The entire computer would be best, but there are some lists . . ."

"What kind?" Grace asked.

"Deposit lists showing movement of funds from one set of offshore accounts to another," Sturgis said.

"How are we supposed to recognize them from any other bunch of numbers that might be on the computer?" Faroe asked.

"The entire file is named 'Plaza.' It involves transfers from banks in Aruba and Panama to the Intercontinental Bank of Nauru."

"Where's that?" Grace asked.

Sturgis said, "Overseas."

"The South Pacific," Faroe said. "Its entire economy used to be based on bat shit—guano, to the tea party set. Then some bright schlub discovered the business of chartering international banking institutions. Now Nauru has more banks than it does citizens."

Franklin looked over with new interest. "You sound like you know your way around."

"Believe it," Faroe said, but it was Sturgis he was looking at. "So don't bullshit me and all of us just might get out of this alive."

The drink paused halfway to Franklin's mouth. He looked at Sturgis.

Sturgis was watching Faroe like a man who'd just discovered that guns weren't the most dangerous things in the room.

Faroe smiled.

It didn't make Sturgis feel better.

"If we find this file," Faroe said, "you'll work with us for Lane's release."

"Ah, we'd do what we could, yes," Sturgis said, "without, of course, admitting that Ted—"

"Wrong answer," Faroe cut in.

And waited.

"If you bring us that file, we'll do everything

in our power to see Lane safely into the U.S.," Sturgis said unhappily.

Faroe looked at Grace. "I'd get it in writing, but we don't have time to play legal games."

Lane had twelve hours to live.

48

GRACE SAT WITH HER head against the headrest, watching cars flow by in both directions, a steel river that began at one international border and ended at another.

Faroe hadn't tried to talk to Grace. She hadn't tried to talk to him. There was nothing to say.

The father was safe in federal custody and the son was waiting to be executed for his father's sins.

"Are they following us?" Grace asked Faroe finally.

"Not so far."

"Does the fact that you're doing ninety-eight have something to do with that?"

"Ninety-two, and I'm not the fastest car on the road."

As if to prove it, a Lexus rocketed by on their right, pursued by a beater with Baja California plates.

Faroe checked the mirrors. "When you took the computer to Lane, did you know?"

She froze. "What do you think?"

"You didn't know."

Her laugh was short and harsh. "I suppose I should be grateful for your trust."

"Actually Ted should be grateful there were witnesses back there. You would have cut him to bloody pieces with a broken glass."

"You weren't exactly sending him love notes."

"I was trying to figure out an appropriate death for him."

Grace gave Faroe a sideways look. "And?"

"Still trying." Faroe smiled grimly. "But no matter what, I'm going to be a gentleman about it. I promise you can have your pound of flesh first."

Grace smiled in spite of herself. *What am I going to do with you, Joe?*

She didn't know she'd spoken the words aloud until Faroe said, "Ask me tomorrow."

Her laugh sounded more like a sob.

He glanced at the dashboard clock. Steele should be setting down within the hour. At least there would be a safe place for Grace while Faroe went south.

"Do you think Lane knows anything about this file?" Faroe asked.

"He never said anything to me about Ted keeping files on the computer."

"I'll ask when I call Lane. If he could rig a wireless connection, I could suck that file right through the satellite phone."

"Lane knows all about wireless and 3G and a lot of other things that go right over my head."

"I'd sure like to see what Ted figures is his federal Get-Out-of-Jail-Free card."

"What good would that do?" Grace asked.

"I can't answer that until I see it, but I've got a real good idea. I think the Plaza file is just that—a list of all the black transactions Bank of San Marco did for Hector, Carlos, and the rest of the *narcotraficantes*."

"But that would implicate Ted. Why would he do that?"

"If he leads the feds to twenty or fifty or

whatever million bucks, they'll seize it, pat him on the back, and let him go."

"But—"

"That kind of money would pay for a lot of federal task forces," Faroe said, ignoring her interruption.

"You make it sound like law enforcement is a profit center for the U.S. government," Grace said tiredly. "I thought that was Mexico's specialty."

Faroe shrugged. "Governments are made of people. Some people are better than others and everyone has a price. Sometimes, like in most of Mexico, bureaucrats and politicians get rich directly. Others run the money through political parties or even bureaucracies. It all boils down to money and power and to hell with the meadow that's flattened while the elephants and donkeys dance for dollars."

"But—"

"You heard Ted back there, conniving with his lawyer and government agents to work out what amounts to a political solution to his large, personal legal problems. If that isn't a kind of corruption, what is?" Faroe asked.

"If you believe that, why bother?"

"I like meadows," Faroe said evenly. "I especially like the individual blades of grass. Like Lane. If I can keep the elephants from smashing him while they dance, that's good enough for me."

Silence grew.

Miles of it.

They were within sight of the helicopters circling the border when Grace said bitterly, "Shade upon shade of gray."

Faroe didn't answer. He didn't have to.

"So a rich, politically connected snake like Ted talks to the political types in Main Justice," Grace said. "He convinces them that it's in the best interests of everybody to let him pay an informal multimillion-dollar fine and slither off into his hole."

"Don't ask me to like it," Faroe said. "And don't ask me to pretend it doesn't happen."

"I won't. When you add the clever spinning of facts by a lawyer like Sturgis, Ted could end up looking like an upstanding citizen committing a selfless act of civic virtue. If Sturgis is good enough, they'll probably give Ted a presidential citation."

"Yeah," Faroe agreed, his voice tightening with anger. "And he's already on his way to flushing both you and Lane right out of the system."

"I can live without a judgeship—of any kind."

Faroe shot her a fast glance. No tears, no frowns, just the kind of determination that didn't know how to quit.

The only thing I can't live without is my son.

"Ted won't be able to explain away Lane's imprisonment," she said fiercely. "I won't let him."

"You're not going to like hearing this," Faroe said, "but I have to say it. By now, Ted and Sturgis are well on their way to painting you as a lying slut and Lane as a doper and a screwup who got himself in trouble in Mexico."

She took a sharp breath.

"Lane won't die a hostage," Faroe said, his words all the more terrible for the calmness of his voice. "He'll probably be an accidental overdose. If Hector doesn't stick a needle in the kid's arm, Sturgis will see to it that one is 'found' on the beach next to the body."

"Stop it."

"I'm trying to. But with Ted lawyered up and federally protected, we're holding the slippery end of a very shitty stick. Powerful people, whether politicians or crooks, don't like loose ends. Loose ends distract from the big, bright plasma-screen picture of reality that gets peddled all day, every day, on the news channels."

Grace looked over and at Faroe. In the flickering mercury-vapor lights of the freeway overheads, he looked like one of the Huichol death masks she'd seen in Lane's cottage.

"It can't be that easy to bury the truth," she said.

"It's easier. Bust some mutt with a few kilos of cocaine and watch your career soar. Get evidence that points toward one of Mexico's leading political families and watch your career tank. It isn't important to really do something about drugs—it's only important to *appear* to do something."

Without warning, Faroe took an off-ramp and sped down smaller and smaller roads. He pulled into the parking lot of Brown Field just as a helicopter leaped off the tarmac and headed out for Spring Canyon to shut off the flow of illegal aliens that neither the U.S. nor the Mexican politicians wanted to stop.

They just wanted to appear to.

"Were we followed?" Grace asked.

All Faroe said was "Time to call Lane."

49

CIGARETTE SMOKE CAME INTO Lane's room through open windows, along with gusts of warm, humid air from the storm that was inching closer to shore.

That's why I'm sweating.
Heat, not fear.
But his sweat was cold.

In the spaces between the cry of wind and waves, men's voices came from outside along with more smells of burning nicotine and something else, something Lane couldn't identify. If one guard wasn't smoking, the other was.

They were less than six feet from Lane's bed.

If Mom calls now, Lane thought frantically, *they'll know.*

Yet there was nothing Lane wanted or needed more than to hear his mother's voice and know that he wasn't truly alone.

The satellite phone beneath his pillow vibrated. Instantly he blocked any view from the window by diving under the sheet. He pushed the connect button.

And said nothing.

"It's Faroe," a man's voice said softly. "If you can hear me but can't answer, blow into the microphone. Once for yes."

Lane's breath sighed over the receiver.

At the other end of the line, Faroe's heart kicked with relief. "Good. Are you okay?"

Lane breathed into the phone again. Once.

"Is there anyone in the room with you?" Faroe asked.

Lane blew twice into the phone, then whispered, "Wait."

"As long as you want," Faroe said.

Sweating, Lane lay beneath the sheet, holding the phone until his hand ached from the pressure.

The guards' voices faded as they went on another tour of the cottage's perimeter.

"Okay," Lane said softly. "They're gone. It

usually takes them a couple of minutes to get back to the window."

"Has anything changed since we were there?" Faroe asked quickly.

"No," Lane said, keeping his voice so low it barely transmitted. "Father Rafael came to see me. He said he thought things would be okay. Do I trust him or not?"

"Until we find out a little more, treat him as an unknown quantity," Faroe said. "But if things come unstuck, use your own judgment. He might be the best option you have. Do you understand?"

"Yeah," Lane said. "Is Mom there with you?" The question was tentative.

"She's here," Faroe said carefully. He didn't want the boy falling apart on the phone. Or Grace.

"Good," Lane said. "I just didn't want her to be alone right now. She worries a lot."

Faroe smiled even though his throat ached. "Do you have access to a file called 'the Plaza' on your hard drive?"

"That's Dad's file," Lane said, his voice suddenly cautious. "He trusted me with it."

It was about the only way Lane had connected with his father in years—showing him how to use the computer.

"I know," Faroe said. "He told us about it."

"You saw Dad?" With an effort, Lane kept his voice low. "Tonight? Is he coming to get me before"—*Hector kills me*—"the deadline?"

Faroe wondered how Lane had found out, then decided it didn't matter. What mattered was keeping Lane from panicking.

"Ted showed up in Lomas Santa Fe, at the ranch," Faroe said carefully. "He wanted your computer. He wanted the Plaza file."

Lane listened for the guards, heard only the wind and waves. "So?"

Sitting in the SUV, Faroe wondered what to say. *How do you explain to a kid what a self-serving piece of shit his father is?*

"I don't have enough time to explain it to you," Faroe said evenly. "Can you trust me on this or do you want to hear it from your mother?"

Before Lane could answer, Grace leaned forward and said, "Tell Joe everything you can. Please. It's our only way to help you."

Back at the cottage, the strain in Grace's voice made Lane's eyes tear. He swallowed hard. "Okay."

"Is it a big file?" Faroe asked.

"No, but it's encrypted."

"How?"

"Do you know what PGP is?"

"Pretty Good Privacy," Faroe said.

"Yeah. I taught him how to do it. He's got the key. I don't."

Shit. But all Faroe said was "So you can't read it."

Lane closed his eyes and sweated cold. His mother's voice had told him more than her words. "Please don't be mad. It's Dad's file. He asked me to keep it for him, to make sure nothing happened to it."

"And now I'm asking you to break that confidence," Faroe said.

"I don't know what's right. If it's Dad's, if he needs it . . ."

Faroe cursed silently but didn't lean on Lane. Nor did he ask for Grace to take over. Lane was having a tough enough time surviving without being caught in a tug-of-war between his parents.

"I respect what you're saying," Faroe said softly, "but until I know exactly what's in the file, I can't tell you what's at stake. All I know is that file is the only leverage we have to get you out of All Saints."

"What about Dad? Isn't he coming for me?"

"I'm sorry."

Faroe listened to the silence for what seemed like an eternity.

Finally Lane drew a shaky breath, then another one. The third time his breath didn't break. "So it's betray Dad or die? Is that what you're saying?"

"I'm saying that your father never should have put that file on his son's computer. He never should have signed his son into All Saints. He never should have touched Hector Rivas Osuna's dirty business."

Lane's eyes widened. He knew who Hector was.

Everyone in northern Mexico knew who Hector was.

"Are you saying D-Dad is a crook?" Lane asked, his voice barely a whisper.

"I believe so," Faroe said, "but I can't prove it until I see that file. Is there enough charge on the satellite phone to send the file to your mother?"

"No. I'll decrypt it. Then . . . well, then . . ." *I'll know something I don't want to know.*

But not knowing meant that he would die in less than twelve hours.

"Lane?" Faroe asked.

Lane grabbed what he did know and held

on to it like a rope tossed to him across muddy floodwaters. "PGP is an old commercial program. It's good enough but not great. I've got a couple sample keys and a hacker friend told me about a trapdoor in the program. I might be able to squeeze through it."

Faroe drew a deep breath. "Can you do that with what you have at the school?"

"Sure. All I need is time."

"What about the guards?"

"The Chicharrones Brigade already think I'm hiding under the sheet playing with myself. They laugh about it."

Faroe bit back raw words of frustration. "Go for it, son. How's the charge on the phone?"

There was a muffled sound before Lane said, "About a quarter."

"Shut it down. Save it for another call in four hours. Unless your situation changes radically—then you call right away. Want a quick word with your mom?"

"Just—tell her I love her. If I hear her voice I'll—"

"Okay, I understand. She sends her love. So does your dad."

"Then why doesn't he come get me?"

He's too busy saving his own ass.

But all Faroe said was "Be careful."

Lane punched the end button, shut down the phone, and hid it under the pillow again.

Voices drifted in through the window. The guards were laughing and talking about the bets that had been placed on how Hector would kill Lane.

So far no one had put money on simple execution.

50

ANOTHER BORDER PATROL HELICOPTER leaped from the tarmac of Brown Field and swung sharply off into the darkness over Spring Canyon. Searchlights probed the tangle of brush where coyotes, feral dogs, smugglers, bandits, and sweating illegals hid. A mile away, along the south edge of Spring Canyon, the lights of Tijuana's Colonia Libertad washed in a glittering tide against the steel wall of the border. The night was alive with fear and hope.

Grace and Faroe stared out the windshield, waiting for Steele's plane to land. The airfield in front of them was pools of darkness and strips of light. Thin fingers of mist curled around the pedestal lights at the edges of the hardstands.

A group of people came out of the night and raced across the asphalt runway, disappearing into the darkness on the other side.

"What was that?" Grace asked, startled.

"Illegals," Faroe said. "Ghosts in the night. They disappear and then reappear a thousand yards or a thousand miles away. By dinnertime those runners could be in Chicago or New York or Atlanta."

"You really enjoy the shadows, don't you?" Grace asked.

"It's the only place I've ever felt completely alive."

She made a sound that could have been a laugh. "Completely alive, huh? In other circumstances I'd be insulted, or at least disappointed."

"In other circumstances, I'd tell you that we met and loved in that shadow world. Best thing that ever happened to me."

"And the worst," she whispered.

"That too. Have you figured out which hurts most?"

She made that sound again, half laugh, half sigh, all sadness. "No."

"Neither have I."

Off to the east, above Otay Mesa, a pair of powerful lights appeared in the darkness—an aircraft on a straight-in final approach.

"Steele," Faroe said.

An oversize buslike vehicle that had been parked on an isolated tie-down area started up its diesel engine. Running lights and interior lights snapped on.

At almost the same moment, another vehicle drove through the perimeter gate and headed for the bus. As it passed under a light on the front of a small hangar, Faroe got a good look. It had the unmistakable profile of an armored messenger truck. He punched his speed dial and within a few seconds was speaking with a St. Kilda communicator.

"Is someone supposed to be meeting Steele?" he demanded.

Grace could hear the distant, disembodied voice on the other end of the phone line. He sounded amused.

"Okay," Faroe said, snapping the phone shut.

"And?" Grace asked.

"Looks like Steele has been rounding up the usual suspects and then some."

Faroe started the Mercedes and joined the

odd caravan that was assembling on the hardstand.

Ambassador James Steele came down the ramp in the arms of a mammoth linebacker of a man named Harley. Steele rode with his arm around the bodyguard's neck. He was dressed in a newly pressed suit, a clean white shirt, and a perfectly knotted tie.

Faroe and Grace met Steele at the bottom of the ramp. Three men got out of the idling diesel bus, which doubled as traveling quarters and a rolling command post. Faroe didn't know any of the three, but they all moved like former Navy SEALs or special ops of some stripe.

One of the men pulled a gleaming, tricked-out wheelchair from the motor home's baggage compartment. A few swift motions positioned the chair and activated its electronics. In the glare of the jet's landing lights, Steele looked down at the unconventional wheelchair for a long moment, examining its tubular frame and cutaway alloy wheels.

"Have I mentioned that I'm not into racing?" Steele said acidly to Harley.

Harley deposited the Ambassador on the seat, arranged his legs, and made some adjustments to the seat and controls. "I've been jonesing to get you into this one for months. Now stop pouting and pay attention. This is the joystick."

"Oh my God," Steele said through his teeth.

"Forward is forward, back is back, and side to side are self-explanatory," the big bodyguard-nurse explained.

"I'm still not racing anyone," Steele retorted.

But as he fiddled with the joystick, he didn't quite conceal his pleasure at how responsive the machine was. Not as good as legs, but better than whatever else was in second place.

"If I can only teach this contraption to talk politely to me," Steele said to Harley, "I can fire you."

"Not until you teach it to wipe your ass, too."

Steele laughed, then looked at Faroe and Grace. "You look like you could use some sleep, Your Honor. I have legal meds if you need them."

"So far, so good," she said.

"Don't be shy," Steele said. "They're part of every special ops survival kit, and those people are trained within an inch of their lives.

You aren't. You don't want to be staggering tired when you need to be alert."

"She'll think about it," Faroe said before Grace could answer.

"And so will you," Steele said to Faroe.

It wasn't a suggestion.

"Before I debrief you," Steele continued, "there's someone you must meet."

They watched as Steele turned the chair smartly and rolled across the asphalt to where the idling armored car was parked. As the Ambassador approached, the side door of the truck swung open and a slight, white-haired Mexican in a business suit stepped down. The Mexican moved with a flat-footed limp and a stiffness in his upper body that spoke of old injuries.

When the two men met on the hardstand and shook hands, the Mexican bowed stiffly at the waist, a courtly gesture that was old-fashioned and completely natural. They spoke together in the shadows between the hard glare of headlights and landing lights. The smell of cigarette smoke drifted over.

"Who is it?" Grace asked quietly.

"If it's who I hope it is, Lane's chances just went up. I'll gladly sit in a smoke-filled room to pick that man's brain."

Steele and the other man crossed the asphalt to stand in the shadows near Grace and Faroe.

"Allow me to introduce Dimas Quintana Blanco," Steele said, "one of the foremost journalistic chroniclers of Tijuana's *narcotraficantes.* Señor Quintana has agreed to advise us in an informal way on our problem."

Faroe offered his hand. "A genuine honor, señor."

"It is mutual," Quintana said with a small smile. "I won't ask your name, because I know you by too many as it is."

Faroe's smile flashed in the shadowed night.

Quintana took Grace's hands in his own and bowed. "Judge Silva, I am profoundly sorry to hear of your troubles."

"I didn't expect to be discussing them with a journalist," Grace said bluntly.

"Don't worry," Faroe said. "The Rivas Gang already has offered Señor Quintana silver or lead. He chose lead. Ten years ago, ROG assassinated his business partner. Three years ago, they tried for him."

Grace's stomach clenched. It was one thing to hear vague rumors of Mexican journalists, cops, and judges being shot because they refused to go along with ROG.

It was quite another to look at the dark eyes of the man whose life had been scarred by lead.

"In Tijuana, any honest journalist has a target painted on his back," Quintana said calmly, dropping his cigarette to the ground and crushing the ember with his heel. "Fortunately, ROG's gunmen are cowards as well as bad shots. We survive—very carefully, yes, but we survive. Whatever information I have, I will give to you with greatest pleasure."

51

STROKE AFTER STROKE OF lightning raked across the sky, turning night into a blinding network of white against black. Thunder was immediate, continuous explosions that rocked the night. Rain came down like the end of the world.

"Yes!" Lane laughed out loud as guards raced for cover. "Bring it! Send those *cabróns* running to cover."

Since the nearest permitted shelter was fifty feet away in another cottage, he wouldn't have to worry about his guards peering in his windows and wondering what he was doing under the sheet or in the closed, locked bathroom.

For a few seconds more Lane enjoyed the storm washing across his face, its taste wild and sweet.

Like freedom.

Then he closed the windows, pulled the curtains, and took his computer into the bathroom, where there was both privacy and an electrical outlet. The last thing he wanted was to run out of juice just when he hacked into the file.

If I hack it.

No. When. I've hacked harder security.

But he'd been younger then. He hadn't believed in death. That, and the guards, broke his concentration.

Pretty Good Privacy was turning out to be pretty good indeed. The first sample key he'd played around with hadn't gotten him very far. As in headfirst into a stone wall, locked up, reboot, and try again. And again.

And again.

The cigarette smoke and jokes and catcalls from the open windows hadn't helped. But now all he had was the heady freedom of the storm and the computer itself, something he was comfortable with.

Something he was good at.

Something that didn't constantly taunt him that he was scheduled to die at twelve-thirty this afternoon.

52

"So," STEELE SAID, SUMMARIZING the debriefing, "in less than forty-eight hours you've managed to get on the wrong side of both the lords of the Tijuana underground and the United States government. Even for you, Joseph, that's impressive. Now what?"

Señor Quintana hid a smile behind his neatly trimmed mustache and goatee.

"We need some muscle on standby," Faroe said.

"Three ops are already aboard, not including Harley," Steele said, pointing around the interior of the motor coach. "Wood is the armorer, ex-SEAL with good sources of supply, fluent in Spanish. Jarrett and Murchison are communications cross-trained, also fluent in Spanish, and Murchison is a medic. Dwayne is working on a helicopter and pilot."

"Problems?" Faroe asked.

"Only that you wanted an Aerospatiale."

Wood smiled in approval. "Fast helo, that."

Faroe looked at the two men and one woman—Murchison. They had the relaxed yet ready posture of people accustomed to being sent to strange places at strange times to do jobs that may or may not be legal. And to do them quietly.

"Okay," Faroe said to the ops. "You three take the chopper down to All Saints at first light. No matter what I tell you, or what sat photos and web site stuff you have, nothing beats seeing it yourself."

All three nodded.

"Pleasure to work with someone who understands that," Wood said.

"I learned it the hard way," Faroe said dryly.

"At least you learned," Murchison said. "That's why I went private. Some bosses never learn."

Grace looked at the other woman and told herself Murchison wasn't flirting with Faroe—which was true. Then Grace told herself she didn't care—which wasn't true.

Maybe I need some of those wake-up pills after all. I keep forgetting why I think I want to keep Faroe at arm's length.

Don't I?

Faroe turned back to Steele, answering the question his boss hadn't quite asked. "I want an Aerospatiale for more than speed. The American Coast Guard uses them for search and rescue. The Mexican navy might not be so quick to fire on us if they think it will be the opening shots of World War III."

"Then you've decided that force is the best option?" Steele asked.

Grace went very still. She'd learned enough about St. Kilda to know that force was an unhappy last resort in kidnap situations.

"I hope not," Faroe said, "but I'd be a fool not to be prepared."

"Outline your other options," Steele asked.

Faroe looked at Grace. "Judge, I need you to be alert. Harley will show you a place for a quick nap."

She stared at Faroe for a long time. Then she shook her head. "If I have to, I'll use Steele's meds."

"The more I tell you, the more vulnerable you become when this is over."

"What about you?"

"I'm used to it. I need you strong. Trust me."

"The last time I did that, you told me to get the hell out of your life."

"If things go wrong now, wake-up meds won't save your job," Faroe said bluntly. "Ignorance will."

"Ignorance?" Grace laughed. "I'm complicit in a bombing in Ensenada. I saw a man murdered in Hector Rivas's Cash-and-Carry Bank and House of Horrors. I lied repeatedly and with great pleasure to agents of the United States government. Right now, just what part of *ignorance* do you think applies to me?"

"Okay. Point taken. But this is going to get ugly," Faroe said. "I don't want it to get ugly all over you."

"Too late." She toed off her flat shoes. The recessed lighting inside the vehicle showed dark spots against her golden brown skin. "I still have that murdered man's blood on my feet."

Instantly Harley got up, went to the sink, returned with a wet cloth, and knelt in front of Grace.

"Thank you, but it won't change anything," she said to Harley. Then she looked at Faroe. "Will it."

Faroe opened his mouth, closed it, and ran his thumb over her cheekbone. "I'm sorry."

She turned her head, brushed her lips over his thumb. "Why? You didn't do it."

Steele watched them, eyes narrowed, face expressionless.

Grace turned to him. "You made the trip for nothing, Ambassador. Joe and I aren't going to bloody each other." *Yet. But tomorrow? Well, tomorrow is another day, isn't it?* "It's also too late to separate us. You need Joe. You need me. If we break your rules by being together, well, we'll just have to be your exception, won't we?"

Steele almost nodded.

And almost smiled.

The expression on the Ambassador's face made Faroe wonder what he'd missed.

53

LANE SWIPED AT HIS EYES, telling himself it was sweat, not tears, that kept blurring his view of the computer screen. He really wished he believed it.

Another bout of thunder made the cottage tremble.

He noticed the sound only because it meant that his mouthy guards wouldn't be catcalling from the windows. His stomach growled and cramped with hunger.

He ignored it.

He couldn't take a chance on eating drugged food. After he was free, he'd eat a double-sausage pizza as big as a coffee table. He'd bury his face in the spicy sauce and—

After.

But first he had to hack his way into his father's file.

The second sample key wasn't any better than the first had been. He must be screwing up something because he was light-headed and scared and hungry.

Focus, Lane told himself fiercely. *You can do this in your sleep and you know it. It's just a matter of concentration and time.*

Concentration he didn't have.

Time that was sliding away.

Suck it up.

Just. Suck. It. Up.

Lightning burned through the little bathroom window. Lane didn't notice it, or the thunder that followed. He was staring at the computer screen, his fingers poised over the keyboard.

Shaking.

54

GRACE AND STEELE SAT at the motor coach's built-in dinette. Across from them, Faroe and Quintana conferred over a map of Baja California del Norte, orienting the journalist on All Saints School.

In the background the three operators checked firearms and ammunition, set the defaults on cell phones and pagers, and inventoried the equipment that had already been laid aboard the coach. Their movements were economical, quick, and relaxed. They slid through the small space between Steele's wheelchair and the cupboards with the casual grace of the physically fit. Every time they passed, they looked at the map, noting anything new that had been added by Quintana or Faroe.

Grace was getting more and more nervous. Everyone was paying way too much attention to what everyone agreed was the most dangerous option.

Brute force.

She put her hand over the map. Both men glanced up at her.

"I know I should shut up and let you do your thing," she said, "but I can't. I have to be certain we haven't overlooked some other way to get Lane free."

Faroe put his hand over hers and curled their fingers together. "What angle do you think we're missing?"

"Politics."

"Whose?"

"Start with Hector," she said, looking at Quintana.

"Hector smokes enough crack to put an elephant on the moon," Faroe said.

Quintana lifted his thin shoulders in an elegant shrug. "May he smoke too much and die soon."

"Someone else will take his place," Faroe said.

"It is the curse of American drug habits feeding Mexico's political corruption," Quintana said.

"Somehow I can't see Hector running for president," Grace said. "And that's the kind of politics I'm talking about."

"Very few *traficantes* care about politics," Quintana said, "except to understand who to buy in order to be left alone. *Traficantes* have no interest in a director of public works, or a provincial secretary of education. They are only interested in the police. As long as they control the police, they are safe."

"Don't forget the people who appoint men to direct the police," Steele said.

Quintana sighed and looked like a man who wanted a cigarette. "Important appointments are made in Mexico City. That is why men like Hector Rivas own jet aircraft that depart weekly with millions of gringo dollars headed for the corrupt bosses in our national capital. There was a time when the national power structure was as addicted to those weekly payments as Hector is to his cocaine. That is how one president ended up in exile and his brother in prison."

"But it's better now?" Grace asked.

Quintana hesitated. "At the highest levels,

it is better or at least more discreet. But the corrupt relationship between trafficking and law enforcement still remains. Hector Rivas is the boss. Four of his nephews participate in the daily activities of payoffs and corruption. Several nieces are said to be involved."

"What about Hector's own children?" she asked. "Does he have any?"

"*Sí.* It is not well known, but they are in the United States with their mother. He loves them very much. We know he visits them often, but we don't know how. No one sees him crossing the border."

"They live in the U.S. so they can't be taken hostage," Grace said bitterly.

"It is a way of life," Quintana said.

"It must be," she said. "Carlos Calderón acted like it didn't matter that his son was enrolled at All Saints."

"Oh, it matters. Many million times it matters." Quintana pursed his lips. "Think of the narco dollars as a river. The river flows out into the desert and disappears into the ground. But down there, beneath the surface, everything still flows, yes? Underground rivers."

Grace nodded.

"Then, hundreds of miles away, the water

surfaces again. Carlos Calderón is where the dollars reappear. He is not a *traficante,* he is a facilitator, one of the principal links between the *traficantes* and the *politicos.* That is politics."

"Is it something we can prove?" Grace asked.

Faroe shook his head. "We don't have time for courtroom proof."

"But we have time to mount an attack that could get Lane shot?"

"Contingency planning only." He released her hand, pushed back against the seat, and rubbed his face wearily.

"Can't we leverage Carlos's political need to have a clean public image into a way to help Lane?" she insisted.

Faroe reached for a cup of coffee and emptied it in three long swallows. "We don't have enough time to convince anyone who matters."

"But—"

"Your ex is trying to save his ass by handing a U.S. federal task force a gift-wrapped, high-level money-laundering case," Faroe said impatiently. "Whatever he says about Calderón is tainted. Lane is hacking his way into the closest thing we might have as proof of Calderón's complicity. The money trail. That's what Hector wants, and he wants it enough to kill."

Steele fiddled with the joystick on his wheelchair and closed in on a cup of coffee. "Why would Ted Franklin put that information on a teenager's computer?"

"Because he didn't trust his own accountants," Faroe said. "But he still needed a record of money transfers, passwords, accounts, and the banks that hold them. All the hundreds—thousands—of details that go into money-laundering buttloads of money."

"Where is the money due to surface?" Steele asked.

"As the funds to purchase the bank Ted peddled to Carlos, who peddled it to Jaime, who talked his uncle into buying his very own personal laundry," Faroe said.

Grace looked at Quintana. "Do you know anything that would give you leverage over Hector?"

"Short of a sawed-off shotgun?" Faroe muttered.

Quintana smiled rather grimly and concentrated on Grace. "Do not waste your son's life trying to reason with ROG. They kill because they can."

"Listen to him, Grace," Faroe said. "How many drug murders a year in Tijuana?" he asked Quintana.

"Perhaps five hundred, *más o menos.* These are savages. You cannot bargain with them. You can only stop them with overwhelming force."

"And before you think of going to Ted's senatorial buddy," Faroe said to Grace, "think about this. At the end of the twentieth century the U.S. investigated Mexican money laundering. Investigators posed as drug traffickers and implicated a number of Mexican bankers. A classic sting. The Mexican bankers were lured to Las Vegas and arrested. Want to guess what happened?"

"No. Yes. Tell me."

"Within three days, the entire Mexican political establishment closed ranks. American drug agents in Mexico were threatened with arrest, or worse. Our ambassador was recalled. The American attorney general apologized publicly about our outrageous conduct."

"Why?" Grace asked flatly.

It was Steele who answered. "Mexico treated the entire matter as an attack upon its national honor. The administration in

Washington, in its effort to avoid upsetting the fragile Mexican financial structure, acquiesced. It takes no great genius to imagine what a well-placed and powerful man like Calderón could do if he felt seriously threatened by a U.S. senator."

Grace looked at Quintana. "What if you threatened Calderón with exposure?"

"I can attack a known *traficante* like Hector Rivas and survive. There is an element of public theater in my coverage that ROG understands and often enjoys." Quintana smiled thinly. "But even my armored car and my dozen bodyguards cannot guarantee my safety or that of my family and employees if I attack the Calderón family. I am sorry."

Grace looked to Steele. "Aren't there any politicians here or in Mexico who would be willing to help?"

"That was my first thought," Steele said.

"And?" she asked.

"I rejected it."

"Not enough time," Faroe said. "Not enough secrecy. That's why you came to St. Kilda, Grace."

Steele nodded. "Sometimes the only swift, sure way to untie a knot is with a sword."

"However . . ." Faroe said. He looked at

Quintana. "Do you know where Hector's family is in the U.S.?"

"One. A daughter. Yes."

"We should explore that," Faroe said quietly.

For a moment there wasn't any sound but that of the diesel generator powering the vehicle's lights.

"No." Grace's voice was emphatic. "Joe always thinks in straight lines. Isn't there some indirect way? Doesn't Hector Rivas have an enemy who wants to get even, someone who would help us?"

"Hector has killed all his enemies and many of his friends," Quintana said.

"You're saying that there isn't a single person in northern Mexico who wants Hector and his gang stopped and could help us do just that?" Grace said.

Quintana thought for a moment. "Perhaps, yes, perhaps. Ascencio Beltrán."

"Beltrán?" Faroe asked. "El Tiburón?"

The Shark.

"You know him?" Quintana asked.

"He was a major marijuana smuggler sixteen years ago. Then he dropped out of sight. Some say he was killed. Some say he was in jail."

"He is alive," Quintana said. "He is living in the only place in Tijuana that Hector Rivas does not control. It is the place no one controls. La Ciudadita."

Faroe smiled oddly. "The little city within the city. I'll be damned."

"What is La Ciudadita?" Steele asked.

"The street name for the federal prison at La Mesa, in south Tijuana."

"Will El Tiberón help us?" Faroe asked.

Quintana's shoulders shifted in a shrug. "He might, but first you must convince Sister Maude."

"Who is she?" Grace asked.

"The unsainted saint of La Mesa," Faroe said. "Will she see me?"

"Us," Grace said instantly.

"You don't want to see La Mesa Prison," he said, his voice flat.

"Haven't we had this conversation before? What does *want* have to do with any of this? Sister Maude might feel better about your intentions if you have a woman with you."

"She's right," Steele said. "There are times and places where men alone just can't get the job done."

Quintana said, "I will call Sister Maude."

What Faroe said made Grace wince.

55

IMAGES POURED INTO STEELE'S computer, bounced from the helicopter to the satellite and back down to San Diego. Steele took one look at the photos and reached for the scrambled cell phone.

Grace answered it on the first ring. "Joe's driving fast and needs both hands to flip off people who get in the way. Can I help?"

Steele smiled. The more he saw of Grace, the better he liked her. Balls and brains were a tough combination to beat.

"Tell Faroe that the situation has changed at All Saints," Steele said.

"Lane?" she asked, her voice raw.

"Not directly."

At the other end of the call, Grace sagged with relief.

"What?" Faroe shouted so Steele could hear him.

Grace held the phone to Faroe's ear.

"Wood is sending me digital photos from the helicopter," Steele said. "Overnight, the soccer field grew a full crop of tents. Armed personnel are all over the place like ants on honey."

"So Hector owns the army, too?"

"Do you believe in coincidences?" Steele asked dryly.

"Not that one. How many soldiers?"

"Too many. Any extraction of Lane would have to be extremely quiet. Softly, softly, catchee monkey, and mind the fangs and claws."

"The chopper is too loud," Faroe said. "We might fake an emergency landing, but we'd have to shoot our way out. The Aerospatiale isn't built for that."

"Wood and Murchison are examining water extractions. Jarrett and you could infiltrate wearing the uniform of the day. We would provide sniper coverage, of course, but if we used it . . ."

"It would all go from sugar to dog shit real quick," Faroe finished.

He braked, hit the horn, and swerved around an idiot doing fifty in the fast lane while shaving and flossing his teeth.

"Can you cover the place from real-time satellite photos?" Faroe asked.

"If you don't mind spending thousands of—"

"Spend it," he cut in. "It's on me. Can you get enough resolution for individual ID?"

"Not unless they look up and wave on command."

"Is Lane's sat tracker still working?"

"Yes," Steele said. "He hasn't moved."

"Let me know if that changes. Anything else?"

"Your final option isn't much of an option anymore."

56

THE GUARD IN THE visitors' parking lot carried a pistol and charged Grace and Faroe ten dollars because they arrived in a Mercedes. The guard at the visitors' gate carried a pump shotgun and charged them another twenty dollars because they were gringos.

The courier waiting for them inside the gate was unarmed and he refused a tip altogether.

"Por El Señor," he said.

For the grace of God.

The courier was wearing an Oakland Raiders cap and a Metallica T-shirt, and had the shy dignity of an altar boy.

He ushered them down a long, narrow alley lined with doors made from steel bars. From inside, hidden by the shadows, prisoners stared at them with glittering eyes. Several of them made smooching and sucking noises when they saw Grace.

She ignored them.

"Muy peligroso," the courier warned them.

Very dangerous.

"Only if you let them out," Faroe said.

An inmate hissed at him.

The air smelled of raw sewage.

"Breathe through your mouth," Faroe said in a low voice to Grace.

"So I can savor the taste? This makes Terminal Island and Lompoc look like day spas."

"You asked for it."

She walked around a cloudy puddle that had gathered on the ground near what must have been a cracked septic line. "It's a learning experience."

"Only the first time. Whatever happens, eyes front and just keep walking like you've seen it all a dozen times before and weren't impressed."

"Like you?"

"Just like me."

The courier led them out of the alley and into the main prison yard. It was as big as a large city block. Even this early in the morning, the space was crowded. Groups of men leaned against walls or gathered near the ratty palm trees, smoking and talking and waiting for something to happen. Anything.

The concrete walls around the courtyard were three stories high. Guards with shotguns and assault rifles prowled the catwalks wearing tan uniforms, sunglasses, and baseball caps.

There weren't any guards in the main yard. The inmates were on their own.

A group of children were choosing sides for a schoolyard game, but there was no school inside La Mesa Prison. The tallest of the children proudly held a soccer ball. It was so scuffed and worn that its leather covering was the same color as the soil of the courtyard.

One of the kids spotted the outsiders and whistled an alarm. The entire group broke and ran toward the gringos, shouldering and elbowing to get close. They shouted in Spanish and thrust out their hands, palms up, demanding or pleading for money.

Grace hesitated.

"No," Faroe said, taking her arm. "Nothing."

"But—"

"Remember," he cut in. "You've seen it all."

"They're children," she said in a low voice, keeping her eyes front. "Why are they in prison?"

"They were born here."

The courier looked over his shoulder at them.

"Hurry up," Faroe said.

They walked quickly toward a small building huddled on one side of the main yard. The makeshift church was built of unpainted concrete blocks. A rusty cross made out of rebar was wired to the wooden front door.

When they reached the little church, Faroe loosened his grip on Grace's arm and spoke in a voice only she could hear. "Remember, *amada,* you're inside the prison but outside the pale. Tijuana is San Diego's Indian country. La Mesa is Tijuana's Indian country."

"Odd place for a church."

"Wait until you see the mother superior."

The courier knocked softly on the wooden door, pushed it open, and gestured for them to enter. Inside, rows of battered wooden benches faced an altar dominated by a dark-skinned plaster Christ with *indio* features, a massive crown of thorns, and a blood-drenched torso. To one side a serene, un-usually beautiful Virgin Mary smiled her blessing down from a niche in the concrete-block wall. The niche was crowded with burning candles. The air was thick with their sooty smoke.

A white-haired woman in an ankle-length straight skirt and a blue zippered sweatshirt knelt at the altar rail. After a few moments, she rose and turned toward Grace and Faroe. Tall, very well built beneath the modest clothes, the woman was striking. She had the high cheekbones and large, almond-shaped eyes of a cover model. Those eyes were blue, very dark against the frame of white hair that once had been blond.

Grace glanced once more at the shrine. The other woman clearly had been the inspiration for the painting of the Virgin.

"Good morning, may God bless you," the woman said in clear, unaccented California English. She came down the aisle between the benches, moving gracefully toward her visitors. "I'm Sister Maude."

Her handshake was firm and her smile

gracious. She dismissed the courier and invited them into her quarters at the rear of the chapel. A propane gas ring burned beneath a teakettle. She poured hot water into three chipped, cracked mugs and added powdered coffee. She put the mugs out on a table, gestured to the mismatched chairs, and sat down facing her guests.

"Dimas Quintana warned me you don't have much time," Sister Maude said. "How can I help you? You may speak freely here. This is a house of God."

Faroe looked around with the eyes of a man who didn't trust much on earth and less in heaven.

"Excuse my bluntness," he said, "but we've had mixed results with some of God's representatives here on earth."

Sister Maude studied the two of them over the rim of her cup. "The church is a human institution, as well as a holy one. There are errors. There are sins. There are realities that require even the most devout of Christians to conceal their full intentions from the worldly forces that work to see God and his believers fail."

For several moments, Faroe studied Sister Maude, who was studying him in return.

"We have to trust somebody," Grace said.

Sister Maude's smile made her look a decade younger. "God's message is that, precisely. What is your problem, *señora*?"

"My son is being held prisoner."

"Here?" Sister Maude asked, surprised.

"No. Close to Ensenada, at All Saints School."

"Hector Rivas Osuna is holding him," Faroe said, watching the nun closely.

At the mention of Hector, Sister Maude's serenity vanished. "Him," she said, the word a curse on her tongue. "I often wonder why God has not seen fit to include Hector Rivas in our La Mesa congregation. He has many enemies here. I doubt he would last one night. Then I would gladly wash his body as I have so many others." She sighed. "And I will say my rosary a hundred times for that uncharitable thought."

"I know a priest who treats Hector Rivas with great respect," Faroe said. "This priest has even agreed to act as Lane Franklin's jailer. Father Rafael Magón."

The nun turned her head as though to spit on the floor. Then she shook her head. "God's will be done. Father Rafael Magón ministers to monsters. As long as traffickers give suitable amounts to the church, he permits traffickers to mount shrines to the saint of *traficantes,* Jesús Malverde, and Santa Muerte, the demon saint."

"Magón isn't the first," Faroe said.

"No. God's ways are beyond my understanding." Sister Maude bowed her head briefly. "Some of the men and women who come to this chapel are as much pagan as they are Christian, so I must make allowances for their uneducated beliefs. But Father Magón is beyond belief. He ministers to those who murdered a great man of God—Cardinal Ocampo."

Grace frowned. "I've heard that name."

"He was the cardinal of the borderlands, all of them, from sea to sea," Sister Maude said. "He was assassinated in the Guadalajara airport in '93."

"Why?" Grace asked, shocked and not hiding it.

"Cardinal Ocampo had begun denouncing *traficantes,* particularly ROG. Hector Rivas arranged his murder."

"I remember the . . . incident," Grace said carefully.

"It was investigated thoroughly," Faroe said. "Both the government in Mexico City and the church in Rome cleared ROG of any wrongdoing. In fact, the federal police determined that the cardinal's death was accidental, a case of mistaken identity."

The nun's hands trembled with anger that was human, if not charitable. "A cardinal in a limousine mistaken for a rival trafficker? They open the door and pump fourteen bullets into the cardinal's red robes by *mistake*? That is murder." She straightened and looked Faroe in the eye. "But sometimes the church must bend to government pressure. Hector Rivas goes free and even takes communion." She crossed herself quickly.

Faroe knew enough history to be certain that the church didn't bend easily.

Or for long.

Sister Maude took Grace's hands in her own. "If Hector Rivas has your son, I will pray for you. Beyond that, I can't help."

"You can introduce us to Ascencio Beltrán," Faroe said.

"Are you sure?" Sister Maude asked, shaking her head. "If Hector Rivas is the devil, Ascencio Beltrán is his chief rival in hell."

Faroe smiled. "May the enemy of my enemy lead a long and fruitful life."

57

When Grace walked through the prison alley again, she was braced for whistles and catcalls.

Not one rude sound came from the men.

Whatever these inmates had done outside the wall, they respected Sister Maude. Men took off their ball caps when she walked by. Some inmates approached her shyly, kneeling by the bars and asking her blessing.

Faroe and Grace followed the nun out of the main yard and through a gate watched by two burly men wearing designer exercise suits and high-crowned Stetsons.

"Welcome to Shangri-la," Faroe said softly

to Grace. "Private apartments for the dudes who can afford it or who have the raw physical power to hold on to real estate without paying rent."

They followed Sister Maude into another alley with a dozen wooden doors opening onto it, like an auto court without a parking lot. The ramshackle buildings were made of corrugated plastic sheets and plywood. Makeshift plumbing dripped water and sewage. Electrical cords looped from apartment to apartment like orange and yellow spaghetti. At the far end of the alley, a man sat on a three-legged stool.

There was an assault rifle across his knees.

"That's the first La Mesa guard I've seen down here," Grace said.

"He's not a guard. He's a prisoner," Faroe said. "The guards own the top of the walls but the yards belong to the inmates."

"That's a form of prison management we haven't tried in the States."

"You'd be surprised."

Sister Maude led them to the front door of a two-story hooch with a television antenna on the front corner. She knocked and waited. After a moment, a scowling man came to the door. He had reddish hair and a wide scar that ran from the corner of his mouth to his forehead.

She spoke to him in Spanish, gesturing to Faroe and Grace.

He said he would ask *el jefe* and closed the door.

It popped open a minute later. The red-haired man invited them inside. The interior of the apartment was clean and well furnished, a surprise after the slapdash exterior. A large-screen plasma television hung from one wall. The screen showed a Mexican soap opera whose leading lady was in real danger of falling out of her tube top and breaking an ankle on her four-inch spike heels.

A gray-haired man with a big belly and a face that looked like it had been flattened with a two-by-four sat in a leather recliner, staring at the television.

The man with the red hair disappeared down a short hallway that led to another room.

"*Jefe* Ascencio," Sister Maude began.

The man in the recliner held up his hand. In a few moments the screen faded and a commercial came up.

"Begging your pardon, Sister, but I had to

see what kind of hellish problem my poor Amelia would find herself in," Beltrán said wryly. "Those poor, sexy ladies always have a big problem at the end of each episode, as if they believe we watch for more than the moment her top slips down."

He looked past her to the two Americans. He glanced at Grace and dismissed her. Then he looked at Faroe and grunted.

"Some gringos are very brave," Beltrán said. "Or did you think I would forget you, you son of a bitch."

Faroe smiled. "Not likely, *jefe*."

"You two know one another?" Sister Maude asked.

Beltrán pursed thick lips and nodded. "He is the reason I am here."

"Hey, we offered you Terminal Island and you ran south," Faroe said.

Beltrán chuckled thickly. "The gringo prisons up there are much cleaner, it is true, but the warden down here, he is very understanding. So are the guards. I pay and they let me live and work as I wish."

"Work?" Faroe asked. "I thought Hector Rivas had run you out of smuggling."

"Rivas!" The old man turned his head and spat in the direction of a wastebasket. "That bastard has tried to kill me three times. I have one of his bullets in my head and another in my left kidney."

"Hector Rivas is our enemy too," Faroe said. "He has taken this woman's son and threatens to kill him. We ask for your help."

Beltrán scratched his belly through a gap in his loose shirt. "Why would I help you? You are no friend of mine."

"I'm the enemy of your enemy, and sometimes that's enough," Faroe said.

Scowling, Beltrán gestured toward the leather sofa that sat at a right angle to his recliner. "I will listen but don't expect more."

Grace and Sister Maude settled onto the sofa on either side of Faroe while he gave a quick sketch of the kidnap, deliberately leaving out what Franklin had that Hector wanted.

"*Aiee, chingón.* Hector Rivas. He kill a boy as quick as a man. I have lost much to that son of a bitch. He owns the police, he owns the *politicos,* he has an army, he has the load cars and the tunnels, all the plaza, at his disposal. Most of all he has Jaime, the real brains. No balls, but . . ." Beltrán shrugged.

"Tunnels?" Faroe asked casually. "The Chinese ones?"

"Tunnels?" Beltrán said, smiling like a cat. "I know nothing of such things, the eighth wonder of the underworld, ROG's great secret."

"The Chinese tunnels were shut down a long time ago," Faroe said.

"*Sí,* but Jaime built them again."

"You mean the one the DEA shut down a while back?" Faroe asked. "The one that was good for forty tons of cocaine?"

"That was one of them, yes. A half mile long. It goes from a pottery warehouse in Mexico to a farmer's barn in Campo, on the other side."

That was one of them.

Faroe was glad his game face had had a lot of practice. "Too bad they found it. A blocked tunnel doesn't help me kill Hector, so it doesn't help you get out of La Mesa alive."

"There is another tunnel," Beltrán said.

Grace looked at her hands and prayed as she hadn't since she was thirteen years old.

"Is it open?" Faroe asked.

"Like the plaza, yes, it is open." Beltrán grinned, showing off some gleaming stainless steel teeth. A rich man's smile, because only the rich in Tijuana could afford a dentist.

"Where is it?" Faroe asked.

"Ah, that is the mystery."

"The men who built it know where it is."

Beltrán's smile was darker this time, shaded with something close to respect. "So quick. You would make a good *jefe.*"

Faroe waited.

"ROG found a small village of hard-rock miners, brought eighteen of them in under guard, and used them to construct two tunnels," Beltrán said. "Later he killed the men."

Sister Maude crossed herself and murmured, "Eighteen souls."

"Innocents," Beltrán agreed.

"Even for Hector," Faroe said, "that's a lot of bodies to hide in the desert all at once."

"You remember the massacre three years ago, the men in the mountains east of Ensenada?" Beltrán asked.

"They were members of a tiny *ejido,* a communal settlement," Sister Maude explained to Grace. "Armed men stormed the village at night, rounded up all the men, and murdered them with machetes and machine guns. No one knew why. It was just assumed they were smugglers or marijuana farmers."

Beltrán shook his head. "They were miners, all of them."

"The men who dug the two tunnels," Faroe said. "Makes sense, if you're Hector Rivas."

Again, Beltrán smiled in approval. "When the first tunnel was discovered, Hector thought someone had talked. To protect the remaining tunnel, he sent men into the village. The executioners were sloppy. One miner survived."

"That's quite a story," Faroe said. "Too bad I can't verify it unless I talk to the survivor."

Beltrán laughed with delight. "If you get tired of being poor, I would make you my second-in-command. But I need much money to introduce you to this miner. For me, for my courier, and for the poor miner, you understand."

"Do it," Grace said quietly.

"How much, *jefe*?" Faroe asked.

"A million dollars. American, of course," Beltrán said. "Cash, you understand."

"A million dollars?" Grace laughed sharply. "That's crazy."

"A million dollars is not much for a life, when it is your own—or your son's."

"Only drug dealers have that kind of cash," Grace said.

"Or money launderers," Faroe said.

"I don't have access to Ted's accounts."

She looked at her watch and tried to swallow the bitterness clawing up her throat. "Even if I did, I couldn't raise that much cash in less than six hours."

Faroe took her clenched hand in his own and gently straightened her fingers.

"The meeting with the miner must be arranged immediately," Faroe said to Beltrán. "He must give me complete and detailed information about the tunnel. To sweeten the deal, if I get the chance, I'll throw in Hector Rivas. Dead."

Beltrán thought about the terms, then nodded his acceptance. Even if Hector killed the boy, there would still be money up front that Beltrán would keep.

A lot of money.

"*Sí,*" Beltrán said.

Faroe reached into his shirt pocket and pulled out a small packet. Skillfully he undid the folds of paper and held it out toward Beltrán.

Diamonds gleamed and shimmered with every breath Faroe took.

"*Hijo de la chingada,*" Beltrán said softly, almost reverently. Then, without taking his eyes off the sparkling stones, he called, "César, ¡*andale!* Bring your loupe."

Beltrán took the open jeweler's packet with an ease that said he was used to handling loose stones. He stared down at the shimmering band of white fire gathered like pay dirt in the seam of a gold miner's pan.

The redheaded man with the scar came to the doorway of the living room. *"Sí, jefe?"*

"Are these real?" Beltrán asked.

César looked at the dozen stones in the fold of the paper. His eyes widened. He licked his lips unconsciously, then looked first at Beltrán and then at Faroe.

"Wow!" César said in unaccented English.

"I paid more than a million for that packet in Ciudad del Este," Faroe said. "I know diamonds. Do you?"

"Oh, he knows," Beltrán said. "He used to be a cat thief, cat burglar, whatever you call them. Before that, he was a jeweler."

César took the diamonds over to a window, pulled up the shade, and carefully laid the paper on the sill. He picked up one of the stones and held it to the light. The stone was big enough that he could handle it with stubby, massive fingers that looked more suited for strangulation than finesse.

"You have a good eye," César said, going through the stones with the speed and precision of a professional. "If these came from Ciudad del Este, on the Triple Frontier, they were probably mined in Brazil or are smuggled goods from somewhere else."

"What are they worth?" Beltrán asked. It was the only thing he cared about.

César shrugged. "It's all about demand." He handed the packet back to Faroe. "But you'd have to be a complete burro not to get a million American for these in Hong Kong."

Beltrán started to say something, remembered Sister Maude, and said something else instead. "I am in prison in Mexico. How can I expect to turn that pretty pile of glitter into money in Hong Kong?"

"If you can arrange multikilo hashish shipments from here, you can convert those diamonds into cash," Faroe said evenly.

Beltrán pursed his lips and traced his mustache with his forefinger.

Faroe tapped the jeweler's parcel and waited.

Beltrán traced his mustache again.

Faroe started to put the packet back into his pocket.

"I will call the miner," Beltrán said, holding out his hand. "No guarantees."

Faroe had expected something like this.

He opened the packet, selected three of the stones, and cradled them in his palm.

"Here's the deal, *jefe*," Faroe said. "You work on thirds. A third now, a third when you deliver the miner, and another third when we locate the tunnel to our own satisfaction. The miner gets the three smallest stones, two when he tells me about the tunnel and one when we locate both ends of it. Since he knows you're involved, I'm sure the miner won't lie to me."

Beltrán pursed his lips, shifted his belly a bit, and finally reached for the diamonds in Faroe's hand.

"The miner lives in the mountains," Beltrán said. "I can get a message to him, but the nearest phone is three kilometers from the village. If he agrees, I'll call you."

58

FAROE AND GRACE CROSSED back over the line into San Ysidro and headed west on Dairy Mart Road into the marshy bottomlands of the Tía Juana River. The silence in the car didn't bother either of them.

Then she sat up straight and shook her head.

"What?" Faroe asked.

"I'm sorry. But I've got to say it. What's to prevent Beltrán from keeping the diamonds you gave him and blowing you off?"

"Greed," Faroe said. "Beltrán wants the rest of the payoff. He doesn't get it unless he delivers this miner."

"He could double-cross you."

"Beltrán?"

"Yes."

"I'm not a fool, Grace. Neither is Beltrán." Faroe smiled coldly. "He likes his brains right where they are, in his skull. And he wants Hector dead so bad he sweats thinking about it."

"Are you really going to kill Hector for Beltrán?"

"Not unless I have to." Faroe looked in the mirrors automatically. Nobody in sight.

Time to start worrying.

"But knowing how that smart son of a bitch Hector works," Faroe added, "he probably won't leave me any choice. That's one hard, efficient dude."

"You sound like you admire men like Hector."

"Admire? No. They're filth with a swagger. But respect? That's a different matter. Hector and men like him are modern warlords. They grab survival with both hands and use it to club any rival to bloody surrender."

Grace grimaced.

"Civilization is all about not having to confront warlords on an everyday basis," Faroe said. "But just beneath the pretty veneer, survival is always about the strong and the quick and the mean."

She wanted to argue.

She couldn't. She'd seen too much in the past day that supported his words.

A mile north of the spot where the stinking little channel of Río Tía Juana flushed into the ocean, Faroe turned into a small, decently maintained trailer park that had far more vacancies than rentals. The fencing that surrounded the park had gaps you could ride an elephant through.

"What's this?" Grace said.

"A trailer park."

She gave him a sideways look that burned.

"That St. Kilda owns," Faroe added, smiling.

"It doesn't look like a profit center."

"It isn't. The previous owner went bankrupt because the nightly traffic in smugglers and illegals scared the tenants. The few people who live here now make it a religion not to notice anything. Period."

"Convenient."

"St. Kilda owns a lot of small, shabby properties like this around the world in places where borders meet, either formal national borders or the less formal ones on the slip face between chaos and civilization."

"Today this is a command post," she said, looking around, "and tomorrow a field that needs mowing."

"Actually, the illegals keep it pretty well flattened."

"You could repair the fence."

"We do, like clockwork."

Grace looked at the ragged fence. Her mouth flattened. "Are you sure this is southern California, U.S. of A.?"

"Dead sure."

Quintana Blanco's retread Brinks truck and two other motor coaches were parked close to Steele's coach.

The helicopter crouched in one corner of the park. Next to it was a ground-start unit whose batteries were being recharged by extension cords from the RV utility stands.

"Guests?" Grace asked tightly.

"Command and control in Steele's coach, armory and bunkhouse for the standby crew in one of the new coaches and intell in the second."

"Intell?"

"I asked for somebody who can monitor the juicier frequencies on either side of the border, *federales* and state judicial police down south along with some of the freqs that I guessed are being used by ROG's operators, FBI, DEA, and border guards on this side."

"You know the radio frequencies that ROG uses?"

Faroe parked and shut off the Mercedes. "I described the equipment I saw in the safe house, and St. Kilda's tech figured out what bandwidth they use."

"Don't they scramble it or something? The FBI certainly does."

"Sure, but that doesn't stop guys like Randy, it just slows them down. And even scrambled traffic can be useful. It tells us there's something going on, even if we don't know exactly what it is."

"All this in the hands of a bunch of private operators," she said. "It ought to bother me."

"But it doesn't, does it? Not anymore."

"I don't know if that's good or bad."

"Let me know when you figure it out." Faroe draped his hands over the wheel and stretched his shoulders. "And while you're figuring, keep in mind that St. Kilda Consulting isn't at war with the forces of civic order. It's just that we can do things governments can't or won't do for reasons that those governments just as soon the world never knew."

"You mean like my ex making a farce of law enforcement and justice?"

"Yeah."

She sighed. "Is it really that simple?"

"It's always that simple and never that easy. Why do you think that the United States has such a difficult time shutting down the narcotics traffic?"

"According to the head case I had in my courtroom a few months ago," she said, "it's because the CIA and the FBI make part of their annual budget by pushing heroin and crack in ghettos and barrios."

"Was he wearing a tinfoil helmet to keep aliens out of what passed for his mind?"

"She, actually. And she wasn't, but it would have been an improvement over her hair."

Faroe shook his head. "Crooks and politicians love conspiracy theories—it keeps the masses entertained and their eyes off the bottom line."

"Which is?"

"If we shut down the *traficantes,* we take a huge risk of turning Mexico into a failed state, like Afghanistan or Somalia, except those countries are half a world away and we share one hell of a long border with Mexico."

"Speaking of tinfoil helmets and wild ideas . . ." Grace muttered.

"I wish tinfoil would get the job done. I've seen reputable estimates that more than half of Mexico's economy depends, directly or indirectly, on drug money. It's the great multiplier, creating jobs at home because there's money to spend. Without the money from illegal workers up north and drug money everywhere, Mexico's economy would implode. A failed economy equals a failed state."

Faroe turned and looked at Grace, trying to see what she was thinking. Whatever it was, she was thinking hard.

"Shutting down the smugglers," he said, "would lead to the collapse of the Mexican banking system, the Mexican political system, the Mexican economy. The dudes who run things in Washington, D.C., understand macropolitics, and that is macropolitics to the third or fourth power."

She let out a long breath. "Keep talking. This time I'm listening. Really listening."

"Think about the fact that the Clinton administration shut down two different investigations that led straight into the heart of the Mexican banking system. One was a banking and money-laundering investigation that implicated about a dozen of Mexico's biggest banks. The other was a long-term effort to document the ties between Mexico's power elite and the drug lords."

Grace thought about Calderón. "What did Mexico do?"

"It threatened to start shooting American investigators as invading terrorists unless the U.S. backed off. We backed off real quick. All the presidents since then have made the same choices, only a lot more quietly. Nobody, north or south, is going to derail Mexico's economy, and every politician you put a microphone in front of is dead set against drugs and indignant as hell if anybody suggests otherwise. You've seen Hector's money rooms. You do the math."

"In the courtroom it's called 'complicit behavior.'" She stared at Faroe. "You aren't the complicit type."

"I'm not a government with a government's problems. Neither is St. Kilda Consulting. That's why we don't have to call failure a 'deferred success.'"

She laughed softly, raggedly, drew a broken breath or two, and forced herself not to look at her watch.

"Ready?" Faroe asked quietly.

"As in 'Ready or not, here it comes'?"

"Yeah."

"I'm working on it."

"That's what I love about you," Faroe said.

"Work ethic?"

"Guts."

"Guts?" She gave a crack of laughter. "I'm so scared my hands shake if I don't clench them together."

"And yet you keep on doing what has to be done. That, *amada,* is my definition of guts."

59

THE MOTOR COACH WAS more crowded than it had been before dawn. Quintana Blanco was seated at the dinette table, speaking in low, sharp Spanish on a cell phone and taking notes on a legal pad. Harley was seated across the table from him, talking quietly into another phone.

A new operator had taken over in the cramped little kitchen. He was building a dozen sandwiches on a long counter that looked like a short-order cook's prep table. The new op had the lean, weather-burned look of a hunter or a cowboy. His gaunt face was buffered with a salt-and-pepper beard.

He sliced open packages of meat, cheese, and bread with a double-edged dagger. He had the same focus and economy of motion that the other operators did.

"Do you have any clumsy people in St. Kilda?" she asked Faroe.

"Clumsy ops don't last long enough to get disenchanted with government service, drop out, and join St. Kilda."

Steele was conducting a briefing in the rear salon of the motor coach. Three more operators had squeezed into the small space. Two were strapping, muscular men whose lats and pecs bulged beneath snug T-shirts. The third was a woman in her late twenties with long brown hair pulled back into a ponytail. The big men deferred to her without hesitation.

She was the one being briefed by Steele.

When she glanced up and saw Faroe, for an instant her face softened. Then the moment passed and her look of calm competence returned.

"Hey, Joe, how's it?" she said quietly.

"Hi, Mary," Faroe said. "Glad you're here. You, too, Ciro, Jake. Grace, this is Mary. She's the coldest sniper in the can. Ciro and Jake here spot for her and provide cover."

Mary rolled her eyes. "From you, I suppose that's a compliment."

She offered Grace a handshake that was strong and at the same time restrained.

"I'm not sure I've ever met a sniper, male or female," Grace said.

"Maybe you've never needed one before." Mary's smile was as confident and gentle as her handshake.

Steele said, "Joe forgot to mention that Mary is also an honors graduate from UCLA, physics and literature, and she quit the U.S. Army when they wouldn't let her train in her chosen specialty."

"Sniping is an old boys' club gig," Mary said.

"The bench used to be," Grace said.

"Step by step," Mary said, grinning. "We'll get 'em yet."

"Go, sistah!"

This time it was Faroe who rolled his eyes.

Steele folded the topographic map he'd used in the briefing. "News?"

"Nothing since I called you," Faroe said. "We're still waiting for Beltrán to call."

"He gave that thug a third of a million dollars in diamonds," Grace said, "with the promise of twice that amount if and when."

"Don't worry," Faroe said. "It won't show up on your bill."

"That wasn't what I was worried about," she shot back.

"Money is just money, but was it a wise investment?" Steele asked.

"Our final option is pretty much fucked," Faroe said. "This is the only other dog in the race that Hector doesn't own, so I'm backing it."

"A real dog," Grace said.

"Do you have a better idea?" Steele asked her before Faroe could.

"No," she said starkly. She closed her eyes. "I—no. I'm sorry. It's just that Beltrán should have called by now."

Faroe slid one hand into her hair and pulled her gently against him. "You have nothing to apologize for, *amada.*" Because she was right. "Yes, he should have called. A three-legged dog could have made it from the telephone to the village and back." He looked at Steele. "What about you? You have a better dog to put in this race?"

Steele smiled oddly at both of them. On

another man it would have been affection. With Steele it was hard to tell.

"The intelligence monitors have picked up a lot of traffic," Steele said, "all scrambled, all on the bands used by the Rivas satellite cell phones. Randy is very impressed by their encryption program. It has three levels that we know of. He's working on the fourth. From the language he's using, it's hard going."

Faroe said something foul in Spanish under his breath and added, "Not good."

"No, it isn't. If we had more time—"

"We don't," Faroe cut in.

Steele nodded. "Something has changed just in the last hour or so, but we haven't the faintest idea what it might be. So if you intend to make use of this miner and his intelligence, you'd better be quick about it."

"Anything on the law enforcement bands?" Faroe asked.

"The Bureau and the DEA are scrambled," Harley said. "Traffic volume seems routine but who knows? There are a few local agencies whose freqs are in the clear. Cahill heard what sounded like a surveillance convoy calling out street grid coordinates in Chula Vista. There's something cooking but we don't know whether we've got the elephant by his tail or his trunk."

Grace turned inside Faroe's arm and faced the other people. No one mentioned the tear tracks on her face.

"See if somebody can figure out what frequency the *federales* use in Tijuana," Faroe said. "They're the key. Hector owns them."

"We're all over it," Harley said. "Nothing definitive or you'd know it already."

"Fine, sorry, forget I mentioned it." Faroe reined in his frustration, the knowledge that the last hours of Lane's life were racing away and Faroe was helpless to do anything but take an assault rifle down to All Saints and die with him. "If there's traffic, there's action. Let me know when you know."

Grace put her hand over his, pulling herself closer to him. She didn't need to be a mind reader to know what he was thinking.

She was thinking it too.

Lane.

Seconds racing.

Minutes gone.

Less than five hours and counting down.

Too fast.

Not enough time.

60

LANE HEARD THE NEW guards arrive, heard just enough of their conversation to know that he was being taken away. He dove for the satellite phone and hit the button that automatically connected him to Faroe.

One ring.

Answer it.

He grabbed his computer and ran for the bathroom.

Two rings.

Be there. Oh, God, please be there!

He locked the door behind him.

Three rings.

He turned on the shower.

Just like always. Nobody but Mom to—

"Faroe," said a voice.

"They're moving me," Lane whispered.

"I can't hear you over the background noise. Pitch your voice low and don't whisper."

"They are moving me," Lane said, struggling with his voice and his fear.

"When? Where?"

"As soon as I get out of the shower. I don't know where, but I got it! I cracked that sucker bigger than shit. It was so sweet. I had this old beta tester's code key and they used it almost verbatim in the 8.0 version."

In San Ysidro, Faroe put together enough of the rush of words to understand. Lane had hacked the file. "Good job! What's in the file?"

"A bunch of numbers, bank names, and dollar amounts. Greek to me. Here, I'll read you some. There's a January eighth date, then Bank of Vanuatu, a ten-digit number, and the figure, two million three hundred thousand, to *Sparbuch* . . ."

Faroe closed his eyes, visualizing the data. Ted Franklin had used a blind overseas account to transship a hefty sum of money, then converted it to an Austrian savings passbook account.

". . . followed by another sixteen-digit number," Lane said. "Do you want me to read the number to you?"

The *Sparbuchen* were anonymous. Period. Creating new accounts was difficult, but existing accounts were still as protected from money-laundering investigations as they ever had been.

"I don't need the number yet," Faroe said. "How many entries are there?"

Lane juggled the phone between his ear and his shoulder while he wiped steam from the shower off the computer screen. "About sixty. No, more like seventy. Some of them look like duplicates."

He glanced over his shoulder. The guards were shouting for him to come out.

"Give me a minute to dry off!" he yelled back at them in Spanish.

Then he punched a button on the laptop keyboard.

"Lane, what's happening?" Faroe asked.

The keyboard popped up slightly.

"They're getting impatient," Lane said.

Someone began hammering on the door with something harder than a fist.

Lane grabbed the computer's hard drive.

Wood splintered.

He pushed the hard drive into one of the many deep pockets in his cargo shorts and fastened the Velcro tab.

Wood groaned and popped.

He slammed the keyboard back in and shoved the gutted computer beneath a pile of damp towels. The charging cord stuck out like a flag. He yanked the cord out of the wall and buried it with the computer.

The door shuddered on its hinges.

"I'm coming!" Lane shouted, turning off the shower with one hand and reaching for the bathroom lock with the other.

The door burst open, shoving Lane backward. He tripped and went down. The satellite phone flew against the toilet, then bounced against the shower curtain and into the bathtub.

Kicking, cursing, and slinging punches, Lane tried to get free of the hands reaching for him. Something hit him on the cheek. His head roared and things went fuzzy.

A deep male voice snarled commands. Then the man picked up the phone.

"*¡Dígame!*" he ordered.

Faroe didn't.

"Who you talk?" the guard shouted at Lane in English.

"His name is Ivegot Thedrive!" Lane yelled toward the cell phone.

Something connected with his head.

The world exploded into a nasty shade of red, then faded to the kind of black Lane had never seen before.

61

FAROE STARED AT THE handset. It took every bit of his discipline not to throw the phone against the wall.

Grace felt the rage tightening the muscles in his body. She spun toward him. "Lane? Is it Lane?"

"He's okay," Faroe said quickly, despite the sound of fists hitting flesh he'd heard. Some of those blows had undoubtedly been scored by Lane. He was a tough, wiry kid well on his way to becoming a man. "The guards are onto the phone. They turned it off. They're moving him somewhere."

"Is the phone with him?" Steele asked.

"Would you leave the phone with him?" Faroe asked sarcastically.

Steele didn't bother to answer.

Someone from the back of the bus said, "Sat phone hasn't moved from previous location."

Faroe looked like he'd rather have been wrong about the phone. "Put someone on the real-time sat photos."

"There are too many groups of people on the school's grounds to be certain we have Lane," Steele said. "The resolution simply isn't that good."

"Do it anyway."

Grace watched Faroe. He looked calm, yet she sensed the waves of rage and frustration radiating from him. Suddenly he spun and hit the wall with his fist. A shudder went through the heavy motor coach.

No one said a word.

Everyone but Steele and Grace retreated to the far end of the motor coach, giving Faroe some room.

"Talk to me, Joseph," Steele said quietly.

"If they get Lane away from All Saints, they'll drag him down that rathole called Tijuana, and we'll have hell's own time finding him," Faroe said.

What he didn't say was that Lane would already be dead if and when they did find him.

Faroe didn't have to say it aloud. It echoed in the silence that followed his words.

"We have one helicopter, one sniper, and two lightly armed shooters," Steele said finally. "Even if we had three times that much firepower, I still wouldn't allow an air strike on a school where an army company is bivouacked."

The look on Faroe's face told Grace that Steele wasn't saying anything Faroe didn't already know.

"Lane cracked the security on Ted's file," Faroe said. "I was right. He ran between fifty and a hundred million dirty dollars through some offshore business accounts and then parked it in some clever little Austrian passbook savings accounts. Nobody's going to find it without the file, not even Ted."

"In other words, the computer is the key to a huge amount of narco dollars," Steele said.

"It was," Faroe said.

"But now?"

"Now it's time to look at our hole card."

"Which is?" Steele asked.

"Father Magón."

"So you trust him," Grace said to Faroe.

He smiled thinly and turned away.

"Joe?" she asked.

"When you're down to your hole card," Faroe said, "trust is the least of your problems."

62

Father Magón was dressed for the soccer field rather than the confessional. Loose shorts, black T-shirt, and athletic shoes.

Maybe that was why the soldiers ignored him.

"What are you doing?" he demanded in colloquial Spanish. "That boy is a student here. You have no right to—"

"Get out of our way," one of the soldiers shouted back.

Lane was slung over a big soldier's shoulder like a sack of beans, held in place by a large hand. The man's other hand held a school duffel hastily stuffed with clothes.

The boy's eyes were open, furious. There was a cut on his cheek that was already swelling into a bruise.

Magón stood in front of the soldier who was carrying Lane and said loudly, "Lane, are you hurt?"

The boy said something that sounded like ". . . hell no . . . rat bastard pussies . . ."

Two soldiers grabbed Magón and jerked him away.

"Where are you taking him?" Magón demanded.

The soldiers just kept on walking.

Magón started to follow.

One of the guards turned around and leveled his assault weapon at the priest. "Stay out of this. It has nothing to do with the church."

Magón waited until the soldiers were out of sight before he turned and ran into the cottage. Some of Lane's clothes were scattered around. The bed was a tangle. The bathroom door was smashed, hanging drunkenly by a single hinge.

The priest locked the front door and went to the bathroom. Towels lay in a damp pile. The mirror was a haze of cracks and splinters. The shower curtain had been torn off the rod.

There was a cell phone tangled in the curtain.

Magón picked up the phone, studied it, and hit the button that redialed the number of the most recent outgoing call.

"Who is this?" a male voice asked instantly.

"A man of God," Magón said, recognizing Faroe's voice but not knowing if it was safe to speak openly.

"Father Magón?" Faroe asked.

"Yes."

"You should carry your cell phone with you. Right now it's ringing and kicking me into voice mail. Is Lane okay?"

"A little bruised, but not really hurt. He was cussing out the soldiers while they carried him off."

In San Ysidro, Faroe leaned against the counter and almost laughed. "I hope they don't understand English slang. Do you know where they're taking him?"

"I asked. They ignored me. I pushed. They pointed an assault rifle at me. All I know for certain is that no helicopters have left the school."

"Vehicles?"

"Momentito."

Magón walked to the front of the cottage, which overlooked the long, sweeping road leading up to the school.

"Three Suburbans are leaving now," Magón said. "I would guess Lane is in one of them."

"Can you get into Lane's cottage without being seen?"

"I'm inside it now."

"Go to the bathroom. Lane was using the computer when he called me from there."

Magón walked quickly back to the bathroom. He shook out the shower curtain.

Nothing.

He stirred the towels with his foot. He connected with something solid and ripped aside the towels.

"I have it," he said into the phone.

Faroe smiled like a shark. "Is it running?"

"No. The screen is blank."

"Can you turn it on?"

Magón juggled the phone and the computer. He hit the start-up button. Nothing happened.

"It's not working," Magón said. Then, "Wait. I see a power cord."

Faroe waited impatiently while the priest fiddled with the cord.

"It's not starting up," Magón said. "The

cord is in the wall and in the computer, but nothing happens when I press the start button."

His name is Ivegot Thedrive!

"Look at the keyboard," Faroe said. "In the top row of function buttons, above the row of numerals, right in the center, there is a transparent button."

"I see it."

"That releases the keyboard so you can get inside. Push it."

Magón pushed.

The keyboard came free.

"Lift the keyboard and look inside," Faroe said. "Tell me if you see any loose wires or missing pieces."

Magón removed the keyboard and studied what was left. "I know little about the interior of computers."

Faroe waited, reminding himself to breathe.

"There is a loose connection in the lower right-hand corner," Magón said. "It could have been part of a module that has been removed."

Shit.

"Well, that adds a real gloss to this cluster," Faroe said. Then he grinned. "But good for Lane anyway. Did he get to take any luggage?"

"A small duffel."

Faroe blew out a breath. He'd have to assume that Lane still had the hard drive.

Assumption is the mother of all fuckups, and she has many children.

He'd just have to hope that none of those bastards were his.

"Do you remember an incident a few years back," Faroe asked, "when men were executed in the mountains south of you?"

"I remember several such incidents, regrettably."

"The dead men were from your birthplace, or close by. They were miners, not *narcotraficantes.*"

"I know the incident. They were Pai-Pai, indigenous communal farmers. Many of them worked their own small gold mines. Seventeen of them were lined up and murdered. No one knows why."

"Hector Rivas, your favorite parishioner, murdered them to protect a secret."

Magón turned his head and spat on the bathroom floor.

"Yeah, I thought so," Faroe said. "You're undercover there. A spy for the church."

"Spies and priests don't live in the same world."

"Some of them do. You, for instance. I'll bet you're gathering a case against ROG as the murderers of Cardinal Ocampo."

"God doesn't need my help. He already knows the guilty parties. They will pay their penalty on Judgment Day."

"But the earthly church is a different matter," Faroe said, ignoring Magón's words. "The earthly church has to survive in this cruel, nasty, brutal world of ours. Survival goes to the swift, the strong, and the mean. The earthly church has survived on all three counts."

"What is the point of this?"

"I could call Hector and blow your investigation right to hell."

"Why would you help Hector Rivas Osuna?"

"He wouldn't live long enough to enjoy it. Neither would Calderón or Ted Franklin. Are you listening, man of God? If Lane dies, none of you will have to wait for Judgment Day. I'll punish sins of commission *and* omission. Do you understand?"

"I understood that since the first time I saw you with Lane," Father Magón said finally. "I would help if I could. I can't. The boy is beyond the reach of anything but my prayers."

"I have something for you to do while you pray."

"What?"

"Take a little helicopter ride with me to Pai-Pai country. If not, I'll drop a dime with Hector."

Magón's breath sighed across the phone. "I suppose I don't have a real choice. But I do ask that you keep me out of this as much as is possible. The cardinal's death is not insignificant."

"Neither is Lane's. I'll do my best to keep your skirts clean. Go to the Mission San Isidro."

"The church just off the Transpeninsular Highway?"

"No. The ruins. The site of the original church. The place where your church spent a hundred and fifty years trying to separate the Pai-Pais from their native religious beliefs. Be there in half an hour."

The phone went dead before Magón could ask why.

63

AS SOON AS FAROE disconnected with Magón, Steele said, "Ascencio Beltrán called your cell. It rolled over to mine."

Faroe would have asked how long the rollover connection had been in place, but he had more urgent things to worry about. "Number?"

Steele hit the send button and handed over the cell phone.

"While I talk to him," Faroe told Grace, "get Sturgis to give us a direct number for Ted."

"Why?" she asked.

Faroe was already speaking Spanish with Beltrán. The man had been so eager to talk that he answered his own phone rather than stepping Faroe through a bunch of flunkies.

"When do I meet the miner?" Faroe asked.

"It is not that easy," Beltrán answered.

It never is.

"How hard is it going to be?"

"The miner is in a little town called El Alamo," Beltrán said.

A little town called Cottonwood. Sweet. There can't be more than a thousand places with that name.

"Where's that?" Faroe asked.

"In the Trinity Valley."

Better.

"I've been there," Faroe said. "It's a good place to find miners."

"Only if they wish to be found. The man I spoke of does not wish to be found, even by me."

"Did you spook him?"

"No. I worked through cousins of cousins. He is very frightened. He spends most of his time praying in various village churches."

"So he's devout."

"*Aiee,* he could teach kneeling to a nun."

Faroe almost smiled. "I've got a helicopter. Do you have a contact who could meet us close to town and take us directly to the miner?"

"There's a dirt airstrip on a small mesa about a kilometer south of the town."

"Marijuana transport?" Faroe asked.

"Of course. The villagers, they are used to hearing helicopters and planes and such. The miner will not worry. My man will expect to be well paid."

"I'll bet. No one in Trinity Valley wants to be seen with a gringo who might be DEA."

Beltrán laughed. "It is good to work with someone who understands."

"Your man will be well paid. So will the miner." Faroe glanced at his watch and did a quick mental calculation. The Aerospatiale was about to be put through its paces. "Tell your man we will be there in an hour."

"Agreed. May we drink a toast over Hector's grave."

"Works for me." Faroe punched out and said clearly, "Any movement on the sat phone I gave Lane?"

"Negative" came from the back of the bus.

He looked at Steele. "Tell them to rev up the chopper."

Steele hesitated. "We haven't had time to

set up the usual cover for the helicopter. You'll have to fly under the radar the whole way."

Faroe nodded. He hadn't expected anything else. He hit the redial button on Steele's phone, memorized Beltrán's number, and entered it into his own phone for future use. As Faroe worked, he heard Grace's voice. The edge in it told him that Sturgis was stonewalling.

". . . the point is that we have something that Ted wants more than he wants his next birthday," she said.

"I'll be the judge of that," Sturgis said.

"I'm the judge, remember? I gave you a number to call. Now I want Ted's direct number—"

"Impossible."

"—or you can explain to Ted why you booted a chance to get your hands on Lane's computer," she finished, talking over the lawyer.

"The legally constituted members of the task force won't be happy when they find out you're interfering with their investigation. I'd be surprised if you aren't facing some federal charges. Unless you work through me, I'll make certain that no member of the San Diego federal defense bar will touch your case with fire tongs."

"Promises, promises," she said sardonically. "Do you want the documentary history of Ted's wire transfers or not? At the rate Ted's burning through brain cells with alcohol, I doubt if he can remember half the transactions."

"That's not your problem."

"It's not yours, either. It's Ted's. If he can't deliver the narco bucks to be seized, the feds won't let him walk."

"You have the files?"

"Yes," Grace lied without hesitation. "You and the feds aren't the only ones interested in the files. The *traficantes* who put up all the money want it back."

"Ted will get it to them."

"Not if the feds seize it."

Faroe came and stood close. Grace tilted the phone so that he could hear the lawyer's side of the conversation.

"Look, the money isn't the problem here," Sturgis said. "Ted could come up with fifty million in a heartbeat."

"The same can be said of the *traficantes*," Grace shot back. "But Hector doesn't want to look like a burro in front of his buddies, so he wants a very specific fifty million bucks. The feds want their high-level money-laundering case at least as much as they want the money. No transaction records, no case. Are you still with me?"

"Yes," the lawyer said unhappily.

"For that reason, and that reason alone, Ted should be willing to help us retrieve the computer. Lay aside the fact that Lane still thinks the world of Ted, loves him, and doesn't know why he's been abandoned." The look on Grace's face said that she wasn't laying it aside, that Ted would pay. "We all get our onetime opportunities to make up for how we've screwed the pooch. This is Ted's. So give me his damn number."

"The alternative?"

Faroe took the phone. "If Ted decides to cut a deal with one side or the other that leaves Lane out, Ted is a dead dude walking. And so are you."

"Are you threatening me?"

"Hey, you're listening. Give the son of a bitch a cookie."

"I thought all you professional security types were cold and dispassionate," Sturgis muttered.

"I am. That's why I'm alive and you'll be looking over your shoulder."

"Christ, man, lighten up. Under other circumstances, I might like you. I certainly could find some work for you."

"Ted's number," Faroe said. "Now."

"I can't. Professional responsibility to my client and all that."

"Say hello to hell for me."

"Wait! I'll call Ted. I'll tell him you have the files. It's up to him whether he calls the number Grace gave me or not."

"Ted calls in the next five minutes or he's out of the game."

"But—"

Faroe punched out of the conversation.

"Well, Your Honor," he said roughly to Grace, "you got your way. You are now finally and fully a party to what may become conspiracy and murder in the first degree. How does it feel?"

Without a word she got up and disappeared into the back of the coach. Faroe followed as far as the salon, which was now empty. He grabbed a sandwich from the platter on the counter and made short work of it.

As he was chewing the last bite, she came back with her purse and sat down on the couch next to him. She lifted the flap of the heavy leather shoulder bag and produced a clean black steel semiautomatic pistol. She checked to make sure the safety was on, then reversed the pistol and presented it to Faroe, butt first.

"It's fully loaded," she said, "and there's a round in the chamber."

64

FAROE SLIPPED THE SAFETY on Grace's gun and pulled the slide on the Browning just enough to confirm her warning. He reset the safety and released the magazine from the butt of the gun. The round brass shells of a dozen cartridges gleamed through the side slot of the magazine.

"You shouldn't keep them stacked like this," he said. "The magazine spring gets fatigued under a full load. The last two rounds might not mount properly."

"How many bullets does a good shot need?"

A corner of his mouth kicked up. "You

won't mind if I have Harley tune this thing up?"

"Not if you get me a smaller gun in return. The Browning has always been too heavy for me."

Faroe hit the intercom on the coach and asked for Harley. The bald bodyguard appeared from the part of the bus reserved for Steele.

"Look this over," Faroe said, handing him the Browning. "Grace has been keeping the magazine fully loaded. She needs a smaller gun."

Harley gave her a quick look. "You qualified with this Browning?"

"FBI all the way," she said. "If the gun was going to be around the house, I wanted to know how to handle it."

"Wish more people felt like that," Harley said. "Let me see your hands, please."

She held up both hands, palm out, fingers splayed.

"I've got just the thing," he said. "I'll be right back."

"What?" Faroe asked, looking at Grace's expression.

"Just surprised that you agreed to carry a gun."

"And I'm surprised I'm letting Harley get you a new one."

"Guess we just keep surprising each other."

"Yeah." Faroe rubbed a knuckle gently along her chin. "If—when—Ted calls, I want you to talk to him."

"I'm not sure I can be civil to him."

"Hey, at least you're not sure. I flat know I wouldn't be."

She almost smiled. "What do you want me to say?"

"Tell him that if he wants the computer files, he'll have to look Lane in the eye to get them. We'll arrange the time and place and let him know where and when. And get a callback number in case our trace can't."

The satellite cell phone on Faroe's lap rang. He glanced at the caller ID and shouted over his shoulder, "Harley, have communications trace this. Get on it *now.*"

"Yo!" came from somewhere inside the bus.

Faroe mounted the phone in a cradle, turning the unit into a speakerphone.

"I'm guessing it's Ted," Faroe said to Grace. "I'll try to stay out of it."

The phone rang for the third time.

"Keep him talking until we have a trace," Faroe added.

He punched the button on the phone and leaned back, inviting her to speak up.

"Hello," she said.

"Grace?" Franklin asked. "I thought this number belonged to someone called Joseph Faroe. Let me talk to him."

"When it comes to Lane, Joe and I speak with one voice."

There was an empty silence on the line, then unpleasant laughter.

"So he was your shack job before we were married?" Franklin said. "Tell him thanks for leaving his get in my—"

"We've been around this track before," Grace interrupted. "I was faithful after we were married, which is more than you can say."

"And that's supposed to make up for all the years, all the support, all the money I lavished on you?"

"In the beginning I more than earned my share. I never asked for the rest of it. Not even for all that political currency you spent to get me appointed to the bench. That was your idea, not mine." She smiled thinly. "And guess what? You won't be able to use my judicial status to your benefit anymore. I resigned."

"What?"

Faroe wanted to ask the same question.

"Resigned, quit, stepped down, *adiós, muchacho,* I'm history," she said. "I faxed a letter to the presiding judge an hour ago."

She glanced sideways at Faroe to see how he was taking the news. He looked like a man who'd just gotten a fist to the gut. She had a feeling it would be a while before he let her out of his sight again—especially to go to the bathroom that was next to the fax machine.

"Is it because they put your circuit court appointment on hold?" Franklin asked quickly. "That's just a temporary—"

"No," she cut in. "Having Lane held hostage reminded me about what's important and what's crap. Being a judge because somebody corrupt pulled wires is crap."

"Get real," Franklin said. "Life is all politics, all of it, right down to this criminal case. That new director of the FBI belongs to the Dinosaur Party. He won't take guidance from the White House on anything. But he's going to come to heel shortly. Trust me on this. Then this whole mess will all go away. Even the Mexicans will sign off on the deal Sturgis and I are putting together."

"Mexicans?" Grace asked. "By that you mean Carlos Calderón and Hector Rivas Osuna?"

Franklin laughed. "I mean Mexico City, Gracie-girl, the top tier of government. They can't afford to have an international airing of one of their most influential bankers' dirty linen. Carlos has lots of juice in Mexico City, and damn near as much in Washington, D.C."

"Washington? What does that mean?"

"Former Senator Ben Carson, that's what it means. When he decided not to run for the Senate again, it was because he was set to become Grupo Calderón's registered lobbyist. He's on the payroll to the tune of about a million bucks a year. He takes care of Calderón's business just fine."

"What about Hector?" Grace asked. "He's the one with a gun to Lane's head."

"Hector Rivas Osuna? Bad news, there. He's a real liability. Some of his own are going to take him out."

"Will that be before or after he executes Lane?" she asked acidly.

Faroe winced. Her voice could have taken the hide off an elephant.

"Don't be hysterical, Gracie-girl," Franklin

said. "Hector's not going to kill the boy. It would be bad for business. Jaime's a businessman."

Grace glanced at Faroe and gestured toward the phone. She was pale to the lips and her fingers were curled into claws.

Faroe shook his head and mouthed, *Not yet.*

"Jaime may be a businessman," she said, "but Hector gives the orders. He's perfectly capable of killing Lane just because you dissed him. Hector is an irrational crackhead and he's the most powerful man in Tijuana."

"That's like being the biggest turd in a septic tank," Franklin said. "He's nothing."

"The king of the cesspool is holding our son. Hector is a family man. He can't imagine a father who wouldn't move heaven and earth to save his boy."

The sound of ice swirling around a glass came clearly over the speakerphone. Then the sound of Franklin swallowing once, then again. It was followed by a faint, musical tinkle, ice cubes floating in a crystal glass. He drank, sucked noisily on an ice cube, spat it back into the glass, and sighed.

"I'm sorry as hell that Lane is in the middle of this," Franklin said finally. "He's a nice enough kid, but even if he had my DNA, I still couldn't help him. Maybe his real dad could do something. He looked like a nasty piece of business."

Grace tried to speak. Nothing came out.

He's a nice enough kid, but even if he had my DNA, I still couldn't help him.

Faroe leaned toward the speakerphone. "Yeah, you sure are sorry. You're as sorry a piece of shit as I've ever scraped off my boots."

Franklin sounded like he had just swallowed wrong. He sputtered and gasped and coughed.

"Faroe? You've been listening?"

"To a coward writing off a kid? Yeah, I heard every word."

"You expect me to apologize for the truth? Hold your breath, asshole."

"Apologies from cowards are worthless. I wouldn't use yours for butt wipe."

"Hey, you—" Franklin began hotly.

"Shut up," Faroe said in a lethal voice.

Silence.

"Now listen like your sorry life depends on it," Faroe said, "because it does. I have every file you hid on Lane's computer. The boy is good. He saved the FBI the trouble of hacking into those files. He did it himself."

The sound of Franklin's shocked gasp was very clear. "You're lying."

"Account numbers in Vanuatu and *Sparbuchen* in Vienna."

Silence.

A long swallow.

A whispered "Shit."

"If we can't cut a deal with you," Faroe said, "those files go straight to the feds and we collect a ten percent bounty for finding laundered drug money."

"Those are *my* files!"

"Do you think the feds care? Once we give them the files, the feds don't need you. Next thing you know, you're in Lompoc and some bull is calling you sweetie and using your fat ass for a punchboard."

Silence.

The sound of a man swallowing.

Ice clinking.

Liquid gurgling.

"While you're drinking too much," Grace said bitingly, "think about this. If we don't get Lane back in good working order, I'll tell Hector Rivas Osuna that you've been talking to the feds."

Faroe smiled. "Good idea, *amada.* Then Ted wouldn't have to worry about being someone's prison bitch. Hector has shooters in Logan Heights. If I don't get to Ted first, they will. Either way, he's dead meat."

More swallowing.

More ice clinking.

"Suck up something more useful than booze," Grace said coldly. "Suck up some guts."

"Fuck you," Franklin said.

"She has," Faroe said.

The silence spread.

"Okay, okay," Franklin said. "She was useful but that's over. What do you want from me?"

"Be ready to go south on very short notice," Faroe said.

"Oh no. No way. I'll cooperate, but I'm not going into Mexico."

"You'll do what we tell you to do," Faroe said. "If we're lucky, none of us will have to leave U.S. soil."

"What about the FBI?" Franklin asked anxiously.

"String them along for a few more hours."

"But—"

"Do it or die," Faroe said ruthlessly. "Your choice."

"I—God—okay. Okay. I'll do it."

65

THE HELICOPTER DARTED STRAIGHT into a green-brown hillside bowl, then banked sharply and flared over a flat landing spot just outside a rectangle of crumbled walls. Sun-bleached grass inside the ruins flattened in the prop wash as the pilot skidded the machine to a hovering halt twenty-five feet above the ground, then began to settle stiffly to the ground.

Faroe let out a breath. He was glad that Steele had talked Grace into staying in San Ysidro in case Franklin or even Lane called again. The whole flight had been fast and furious.

And low.

Really low.

They'd been flying nap of the land to avoid Mexico's air-control radar.

So far, so good.

A black Toyota Forerunner was parked in the shade of a scrubby oak tree near what once had been the front door of the mission church. Dressed in jeans, a guayabera, and a broad-brimmed Panama hat, Father Magón leaned against the front fender of the truck. Holding on to his hat with one hand, he turned his shoulder to the prop wash.

"He looks more like a *campesino* than a priest," the pilot said.

"I should have told him to wear his cassock. But he knows what I want, and he knows the Pai-Pai. He must have thought civilian clothes would get the job done quicker."

The pilot eased down on the power. The heavy blade spinning overhead slowed, but it still was going fast enough to cut through a man's skull.

Faroe undid straps, set aside the noise-canceling earphones that allowed pilot and passengers to communicate, and popped open the door. A moment later he was on the dry, dusty ground, running out from under the chopper's deadly, whirling umbrella.

"Glad you showed up," Faroe said, shaking Magón's hand. "Let's go. We're on a short clock."

As soon as both men were strapped in, the chopper leaped for the sky.

Faroe tapped his headset, signaling Magón to put his own on.

"One of Beltrán's men, a cousin of a cousin of a cousin," Faroe said, "will meet us. He knows the local dialect."

"So do I," Magón said. "As you guessed, I was born in the village. But Hector doesn't know that. He thinks I'm a *chilango* who pissed off a cardinal."

Faroe smiled.

"You really think this miner will risk his life to help you?" Magón asked. "Because if Hector finds out about this, we're all dead."

"True fact," Faroe said dryly.

He dug into the hip pocket of his jeans and pulled out a chamois drawstring bag the size of his palm. Gently, shielding the contents as best he could from the helicopter's rough ride, he opened the drawstrings.

Then he spilled a thin stream of white fire into his palm. The gems caught the late-afternoon sunlight before Faroe made a fist over them. He held his fist out to the priest, who automatically opened his own hand.

Faroe dribbled twelve diamonds one by one into the priest's palm. Most of the stones were pea- or bean-sized. One was as big as a man's thumbnail.

"They are real?" Magón asked.

"As real as death. Five hundred thousand Yankee dollars in very portable form. Here, take the bag. You'll need it to keep the stones corralled."

"But why are you giving the diamonds to me?"

"They'd frighten a poor miner even more than the prospect of death. You're not intimidated by wealth. Take those, convert them into cash, and help the families of the seventeen men who were killed, and the one who survived."

"And in return?"

"The tunnel."

Narrow-eyed, Magón glanced from the stones to Faroe.

"Don't worry, *padre.* I didn't kill anybody for them."

"The thought had occurred."

"No blood on these so far." Faroe's smile

was thin. "Not that church jewels have always been clean."

Magón shook his head sadly. "You are indeed a cynic."

"A realist. So how about it? Will you persuade the miner to help?"

Magón looked at the diamonds for a long time. "El Alamo has no well. That would be a good place to start." He looked at Faroe. "You are very generous. I'm sure the miner could be persuaded for much less. Perhaps you are not as much of a *realist* as you think."

Faroe didn't answer.

The priest tilted his hand so that the morning sun fell on the stones, turning them into fire. Then, slowly, he poured the stones back into the chamois bag, tied it securely, and pushed it deep into a pocket of his jeans.

"I will do what I can," Magón said.

"That's all anyone can ask. Even God. Did you bring a dog collar? It might comfort the poor bastard we're asking to risk his life."

"No collar. Just this."

Magón reached inside the neck of his cotton shirt and pulled up the heavy gold chain he wore around his neck. A splendidly baroque gold crucifix hung from the chain. The cross was almost as big as his hand.

"The gold in this cross was mined in El Carrizo a century ago. It is well known among the Pai-Pai. One of their martyred leaders wore it. He was my great-grandfather."

Faroe looked at the antique crucifix and hoped it would be enough.

66

BELTRÁN'S COUSIN OF A cousin of a cousin was a thin man named Refugio. He met them at the dirt runway in a black Dodge crew-cab pickup that gleamed despite a coating of back-road dust.

Faroe recognized the smuggling type, if not the individual. Refugio had the blunt, hard features of an Indian. The two halves of his mustache didn't meet on his upper lip. Wispy hair curled down to both corners of his mouth. He was dressed *jalisqueño* style—cowboy boots, jeans, a wrangler's shirt, and a sweat-stained Stetson with a single tassel on the back brim.

He carried a Colt semiautomatic pistol, cocked and locked.

The slab-sided barrel was thrust through his ornately tooled leather belt, but outside the waistband of his jeans. The pistol was as much a part of Refugio as his hat, and worn just as casually.

Faroe shook hands in the gentle style of Mexico rather than the firm, you-can-trust-me gringo style. But when he spoke in Spanish, he was as direct as any Yankee.

"We have very little time to save a boy's life," Faroe said, urging everyone toward the truck. "What can you tell me about this miner?"

"His name is Paulino Galindo," Refugio said. "He is a very frightened man. He lived most of the last year in an old mine shaft. I brought him food but only recently convinced him it was safe to move to the house where I am taking you."

"So you and Beltrán have been holding this trump card for some time," Faroe said.

Refugio smiled. "But of course. Paulino is a symbol to the people here. They know what he has endured. We find it useful to have the support of the village because many of them grow fine sinsemilla marijuana."

"Yeah," Faroe said. "I can see how Beltrán would want to keep his sources happy."

Refugio looked sideways at Magón. "Are you truly Father Magón? Should I talk of these things outside a confessional?"

"Yes, I'm Father Magón," the priest said. "And I do not judge any of these people harshly. They are simply trying to survive in the leftover places of a world owned by the wealthy and the powerful. For the poor, it has always been that way."

"I am happy you have come," Refugio said. "Paulino trusts nothing but the church, not even me. You will be the key in his lock."

Faroe sure hoped so.

As Magón settled into the truck, he fingered the gold cross around his neck. It had been worn by others before him and had taken on the patina of their sweat. And his.

The ride was short and bumpy. Galindo's house was hidden a hundred yards off the road in a grove of dusty green oaks. The house looked like a fortress built of round cobbles from a nearby stream bed. The stones had been cemented together into thick walls with very few windows. More like rifle slits than real windows.

They parked a hundred feet away and approached on foot. Faroe noticed that Refugio made enough noise for a mariachi marching band. Obviously the man didn't want Galindo to think that enemies, rather than friends, were approaching the stone fortress.

Even so, the barrel of a long shotgun covered every step of the path they walked.

"Paulino, it is Refugio," he called out in the local dialect, which was a creole of Pai-Pai and Spanish. "I bring a priest for you. See his cross?"

Magón held the cross up.

The barrel wavered, then withdrew.

After a few moments the heavy wooden door swung open. A small, stoop-shouldered man wearing dirt-caked jeans and a World Cup soccer T-shirt stood in the doorway. He had a full head of dusty black hair and hands full of a shotgun. He stared at the strangers for a long moment, particularly at Magón's cross.

Finally Galindo set the shotgun aside.

Refugio embraced the little miner in the Mexican style, then introduced Faroe by name and Magón by his honorific, *el padre*. Galindo's glance never lifted from the crucifix that hung around Magón's neck.

The disbelief and awe in his eyes told

Faroe that the miner recognized the cross as something more than a symbol of Christian faith.

Galindo talked quickly to Refugio.

Even before Refugio could translate the dialect into a more understandable form of Spanish, Magón lifted the heavy chain from his neck and handed the crucifix to the miner. Hesitantly, Galindo took the cross. He held it in the morning light, then slowly turned the crucifix over to examine the small maker's marks on the back.

Galindo whispered a few hushed words, crossed himself, and looked at Refugio. "I hear of this crucifix."

Magón nodded, not waiting for the translation. His creole was rusty, but it was his birth language, not easily forgotten. "I am from these mountains. Your grandfather probably found the gold that was beaten into this cross."

Faroe understood just enough to be grateful for Refugio's running Spanish commentary. It told Faroe that he could trust Beltrán's man, at least when it came to translating.

Reverently, the miner lifted the crucifix to his lips and kissed it. Then he returned it to Magón with a torrent of words.

"He tells me that since I am from these mountains, I know how dangerous they are," Magón translated for Faroe. "Now that you outsiders know his secret, the rest of the world may soon know, too. Then he will have to leave, maybe go to some godless place like Chile, where men die in the copper mines from the acid in the air."

"Tell him that I understand his fear," Faroe said. "Tell him that I am afraid for my own son, who has only hours to live."

Magón put his hand on Galindo's shoulder and spoke earnestly to him for several minutes. Faroe caught some of it. Refugio filled in most of the gaps.

The rest became clear when Magón pulled out the chamois bag and spilled diamonds into Galindo's hand.

Refugio gasped what could have been an oath or a prayer.

"I told Paulino that these would belong to him and to the seventeen families who suffered a loss," Magón said in English to Faroe. "I promised to help them turn the stones into a new life here, one that doesn't have to revolve around fear."

"Did he believe it?"

Magón shrugged. "Perhaps."

"Did you?" Faroe asked.

"At least as much as he does."

"Then tell him this," Faroe said. "If he shows us both ends of the tunnel, I'll do everything I can to make sure that Hector Rivas Osuna doesn't live to find him."

"*¿Aquí?*" Galindo asked in Spanish. Then, surprisingly, in rough Spanglish. "Here? *En México? Nunca.* No, no, *hombre.* It no happen."

"That's why we need the tunnel," Faroe said. "To get Hector out of Mexico."

Galindo looked confused.

Magón translated Faroe's words.

The miner looked shocked, then laughed with delight. "*Hijo de la chinga— Aiee, lo siento, padre.* I so bad mouth."

Magón almost smiled. "We can pray for forgiveness together, Paulino. I, too, believe Hector is the son of a great whore."

Refugio snickered.

Galindo looked at the diamonds, then at Faroe, and began speaking earnestly.

Magón translated. "Señor, I will help you. In God's truth, I would pay you those diamonds to rid Mexico of this evil devil Hector."

Smiling, Faroe shook the miner's hand and

said, "As soon as we find the tunnel, the diamonds belong to you and the families of the men who built it."

Galindo talked quickly to Magón, who turned to Faroe. "He says that he is but a poor miner. He can't draw or read maps, so how can he help you find the mine?"

"Ask him if he's ever ridden in a helicopter."

A moment later Magón said, "He hasn't."

Faroe smiled slightly. "Then he's going to have quite a story to tell."

67

HARLEY TOUCHED THE TINY electronic bud in his ear and turned to Steele. "It's Mary. We got trouble."

"What and where?"

"Right here. FBI in raid jackets."

Grace turned from her cell phone. She'd spent the last ten minutes assuring her boss and his boss that she meant every word of her resignation. "Excuse me," she murmured. "I have to go."

She hung up just as someone knocked on the door of the bus.

"FBI," said a man's voice. "We can do it easy or we can do it hard. Open up, Steele."

"Do you have a warrant?" Harley shouted.

"Want us to get one?"

Harley looked at Steele.

Steele mentally categorized the visible contents of the coach. Nothing illegal. Even so . . .

"Put away all papers. Shut and lock every door, every drawer, every cupboard," Steele said. "Tell everyone in the other motor coaches to do the same and not to open up for anyone without my direct order or a warrant."

Grace stuffed everything that was out on the counter into a cupboard and slammed it shut. The traveling lock clicked, ensuring that even if the ride got bumpy, the cupboard would stay closed.

Harley talked into his spidery headset while he put away everything but food. The ops in the back of the coach shut doors with themselves on the inside. Dead bolts slammed home, leaving nothing but the salon and the kitchen in open view.

"Do you want to wait in my suite?" Steele said to Grace.

She smiled thinly. "Not a chance. I know the letter of the law. I'll make sure they behave."

Steele laughed softly. "I do like you, Ms. Silva."

"Grace, and it's becoming mutual."

A fist banged on the door again. "Open up, Steele, or I'll be back with warrants that will put your ass in prison."

Harley opened the door and stood in the doorway, filling it. "Good morning, gentlemen, ma'am. ID, please."

The request was gently stated.

And Harley looked like a mountain ready to fall all over the three agents if they didn't act civilized.

One by one they took out ID.

Harley looked everything over. "Supervisory Special Agent Cook. Agent González. Agent Daily. Nice raid jackets. Looks really sweet over your business suits."

Cook pocketed his ID and started up the steps.

The other agents hung back.

Harley didn't move.

"Get out of the way," Cook said impatiently.

"Ambassador Steele," Harley said without looking away from the short FBI agent. "Are we inviting them inside?"

"It will be quite crowded with three more

people in here," Steele said from behind Harley. "Is that necessary, Agent Cook? Indeed," he added too softly for the other two agents to hear, "at this point is it even advisable?"

Cook narrowed his eyes. This wasn't the first time he'd tangled with St. Kilda Consulting. He hadn't learned to love them, but he'd learned they could bite.

Power was power, with or without a badge.

"Wait in the car," Cook said to the other agents. "No point in crowding. Yet. I'll let you know if that changes."

"What about the others?" González asked.

Cook glanced around the park. Agents in task force raid jackets waited in cars, blocking the exit to the park.

"Tell them to stand down. For now. When the warrants come through, let me know."

González didn't say anything. She knew as well as her boss did that it was more like *if* than when. Even with a task-force-friendly judge, their probable cause was thin.

As in transparent.

Harley stepped aside.

Talon Cook walked inside the coach. The first thing he saw was Judge Grace Silva,

Ms. No-Nonsense Nutcracker herself, in person, watching him with hawk eyes.

The cherry on the cake of this cluster.

"I'm sorry to see you here," Cook said to her.

"I'm sure you are." Grace's smile was all teeth as she looked at the movie-star-handsome agent. Unfortunately he suffered from short man syndrome, which took about forty points off his considerable IQ. "Tell me, Agent Cook, just what basis in law you have for threatening Ambassador Steele with warrants and arrest in order to gain entry into his private motor home."

"We have a warrant for the arrest of one Joseph Faroe."

Grace didn't even blink. "For?"

"Interfering with a task force investigation."

She held out her hand.

"The judge hasn't signed it yet," Cook said. "We're expecting it to come through at any moment."

"And what is the basis for this purported warrant?" she asked evenly.

Cook didn't answer.

"I thought so," she said, glancing at Steele.

He just smiled.

"Obviously we have something you want, whatever that might be," Grace said. "You have something we want. That's the traditional basis for a negotiation. Have a seat, Agent Cook."

68

THE HELICOPTER CAME IN from the north and circled the eastern edge of Tijuana like an American border patrol aircraft slightly off course. The pilot made slow orbits over the hillside slums and shantytowns of Colonia Libertad.

Galindo sat in the front seat, next to the pilot, looking a little dizzy from the circling. Faroe looked over his shoulder, orienting him to the aerial view of reality while Magón translated. Galindo had never been in an aircraft, much less in an aerobatic helicopter. He was having a hard time sorting out perspective.

Finally he spotted a crowded highway intersection.

"There, I remember," he said over the intercom in rough Spanish. "We travel on that when they bring us to the warehouse."

Ahead of them lay the patterned ground lights of the Tijuana airport looking sullen beneath a haze of jet exhaust, heat, and humidity from the storm circling over the Pacific. Beyond the airfield was the fenced and plowed border.

Faroe touched the pilot on the shoulder and pointed to the industrial buildings behind the airport perimeter fence.

"Then it has to be in there, right?" Faroe asked in Spanish.

Galindo nodded quickly. "Yes. Yes. I remember the noise. Big jets shake the ground and we dig deep."

"Let's have a closer look at those buildings," Faroe said. "Maybe you'll remember the shape of a door or windows or something."

"That's restricted airspace," the pilot said in English over the intercom. "Unless you want to dogfight the Mexican air force, we can't get any closer."

"I think I see one of your status lights flashing red," Faroe said.

The pilot looked at the status lights. Green. He ducked his chin, staring at Faroe over the top of his aviator glasses. Then he shrugged. "Sure. Why not? It's not my bird."

He fingered the dials of his radio and brought up the airport tower frequency.

While the pilot argued with the air traffic controller about just how urgent a need the helicopter had to land, Galindo stared at the ground, trying to recognize something, anything, that would identify which building might be hiding the entrance to the tunnel.

"Look," the pilot said to air control. "I have a status light flashing red every time I get above sixty feet. I don't know if I can make it over the border. I can declare an in-air emergency, land, and then we'll all spend the rest of the day doing paperwork, or you can just give me clearance to fly straight and low for Brown Field."

After a supervisor was called in, the pilot got clearance for a shortcut to the border.

"Going down," the pilot said over the helicopter intercom. "Look sharp. This card can only be played once."

The helicopter passed over the field, then

dropped to about thirty feet above the taxiway that led to the warehouse area.

"Slow down and let Galindo have a good look," Faroe said. "It's got to be on this side of the airport, somewhere close to the border fence."

The pilot slowed.

Magón talked urgently with the miner, who kept shaking his head and staring anxiously at the hangars and industrial buildings. Then Galindo started talking rapidly in creole, pointing to one of the warehouses.

"That's it," Magón translated. "He recognized the printing on the roof."

The helicopter flew slowly over a large sheet-metal hangar with four twin-engine executive jets parked in front. From the look of it, part of the hangar also served as a warehouse.

Faroe read the sign painted on the roof. "Aeronáutico Grupo Calderón. I'm shocked, dude. Just totally shocked. Who'd a thunk?"

The pilot snickered.

"Is he sure?" Faroe asked.

"They transported him in vans with curtains," Magón translated, "but he remembers that name on the side of the vans."

"Gotta love advertising," Faroe said. "And

there's how they got rid of the dirt." He pointed to the fake hills and raised landscaping that surrounded the building.

Magón was quiet.

Too quiet.

"You didn't know about that nasty little alliance between the drug trade and Grupo Calderón?" Faroe asked.

"I knew there was a relationship," Magón said, his voice thick with disgust. "I didn't think it was this close."

"It's so close that I don't know who's pitching and who's catching. Ask Galindo about the entrance on this side."

"The tunnel entrance is at the back, on the left, in a big supply closet," Magón said.

"What about the other end of the tunnel?"

Magón didn't have to ask Galindo. The miner was already pointing toward another industrial sheet-metal warehouse a quarter mile away, on the other side of the border.

"It must be that building there," Magón translated. "He can give you distances and compass directions from memory. They had to be very precise to come up in the right place on the other side."

Faroe touched the pilot on the shoulder and gave him a thumbs-up. "Take us home."

Magón kept translating. "The other entrance is in a bathroom in the manager's office of that building. Galindo was in charge of the calculations. He only missed by one meter over a distance of six hundred meters."

Faroe's eyebrows rose. "Then he can find both entrances again, right?"

Galindo nodded eagerly. He understood Spanish a lot better than he spoke it.

Faroe called Steele to tell him they'd caught a break.

No one answered.

Frowning, he tried again.

Still no answer.

The helicopter picked up speed, then dropped off the radar as soon as the terrain allowed. Soon waves were rushing by beneath. Just beneath. The pilot circled back into U.S. airspace at wave-top height and settled onto the sandy RV park north of Imperial Beach.

Faroe started swearing under his breath when he spotted the extra cars through the flying sand caused by the prop wash. He thought about keeping everyone aboard and running for it.

He didn't.

There was no time to run and no place to hide.

"Everybody out," Faroe said.

Galindo and Father Magón stumbled to the ground, shielding their eyes from the sand.

"That's it," the pilot said as Faroe jumped out. "I'll get away with that stunt once. But if you don't start checking in with customs and immigration, there will be F14s from Miramar waiting to shoot you down."

"Thousands of Mexican peasants make it across the border every night," Faroe said.

"They aren't flying helicopters."

Faroe slammed the cockpit door.

Instantly the chopper lifted off the sand just enough to fly back out to sea, below the radar. Everyone turned their backs on the gale of sand and air. The grit from the prop wash hadn't even settled before a black Suburban raced up. The two people who jumped out had FBI written all over them.

No wonder Steele wasn't answering his phone.

69

"NICE OF YOU TO give us a ride to the motor coach," Faroe said as two agents ran up.

Agent González and Agent Daily didn't smile.

"ID," Daily said curtly.

"Last time I checked, this was the United States," Faroe said to him. "So why don't you show me some ID first?"

"Read my raid jacket," Daily retorted.

"Want to read mine?" Faroe asked. "I've got quite a collection. Gotta love eBay."

Magón bit back a smile.

González flipped out her badge holder.

"Who are you and where did you come from?"

"You may not know it, but we're on a real short clock," Faroe said. He gestured toward the vehicles parked across the exit. "Who's in charge of all these boys and girls?"

"Agent Talon Cook," she said.

"Ah, good old Short Order. Take us to him."

Agent Daily coughed. "Are you Joe Faroe by any chance?"

"Does it matter?" Faroe asked.

González pulled out a two-way. When Cook picked up, she said, "We've got three unidentified males, two probably Mexican nationals—"

"Don't bet on it," Magón said, smiling.

"—and one six-foot-plus, dark-haired, green-eyed American with attitude who's got the moves to back up his smart mouth."

"Faroe," Cook said, disgusted.

"Hey, Short Order," Faroe said loud enough for the radio to pick it up. "Still hangin' tall?"

Daily coughed again.

"Bring the son of a bitch to Steele's coach," Cook said.

"What about the other two men?"

"Pat them down and keep them with you. If you find any weapons, cuff them."

"What about the chopper?" González asked.

"You see any numbers on it?"

"No."

"Then what chopper are you talking about?" Cook asked sardonically. "Get Faroe over here."

"You want him patted down?"

"Oh yeah. I really hope he's carrying. Then I'll have his ass in prison."

"Hold your breath, darlin'," Faroe called out.

What Cook said was illegal over U.S. airwaves.

Daily coughed again.

"Better take something for that," Faroe said, holding his arms out and taking a wide stance. "Might be contagious."

"Smart-ass," Daily muttered.

Faroe winked.

While Daily patted him down, Faroe congratulated himself on leaving Grace's Browning in the motor coach with Harley. A lot of times, a weapon was just more trouble than it was worth.

This would have been one outstanding example.

Daily patted down the other two men,

found only the antique gold crucifix, and looked at Magón curiously.

"All clean," Daily said into his two-way.

"Bring Faroe" was all Cook said.

70

Aɢᴇɴᴛ Cᴏᴏᴋ ᴏᴘᴇɴᴇᴅ ᴛʜᴇ door while Faroe was still a step below the doorway, which put the men on a fairly even footing.

"Well, well," Cook said. "Look who's going back to prison."

Faroe took the last step up.

Cook held his place long enough to give a hard push.

Faroe had been expecting it. He didn't budge.

The FBI agent smiled. His teeth were perfect and white, his hair curly and black, his body fit and muscular. He would have been pretty if his eyes weren't like ice.

Faroe knew for a fact that the FBI agent was deadly in unarmed combat.

Too bad Cook can't get over being short. It makes life hell on everyone over five feet six who gets close to him.

"You playing doorstop today?" Faroe asked.

Cook turned just enough to let Faroe inside.

Grace got up and came to Faroe with questions in her eyes.

He nodded slightly.

She was so relieved she sagged against him. He put one arm tight around her, tucked her into the banquette, and slid in beside her. He knew Cook would feel better looking down on him.

"Since when do you hang with felons, Judge?" Cook asked.

"They come through her courtroom all the time," Faroe said. He leaned close to Grace and breathed in her ear, "We're in." Then he looked at Steele. "Any warrants?"

"They're working on it," Steele said dryly.

"What are *we* working on?" Faroe asked.

"Oh, you're all lawyered up," Cook said. "Your lawyers are talking to ours, and we're talking to each other. But hey, I don't have my legal dictionary and I can't remember the U.S. Code sections that cover interfering with a federal officer, impeding a federal investigation, and—oh yeah, violations of the Neutrality Act. I love that one. Is it a capital felony, Judge?"

"Since I've already called corporate counsel," Steele said, "I was just suggesting that Agent Cook discuss those matters with him."

"I don't talk to lawyers," Cook said. "I leave that to the U.S. Attorney."

"You don't talk to lawyers?" Faroe said. "Then how do you cut a deal with the likes of Ted Franklin?"

"Franklin's not a defendant, which is a hell of a lot more than I can say about you. You're going down like you did last time, only this time you ain't coming out."

"Turn down the volume," Grace said flatly. "You don't have any warrants. You don't have any probable cause. You don't have anything but a badge that's so heavy it's a wonder you can stand up straight."

Both Faroe and Cook looked at her in surprise.

"I've had a gutful of your bullshit," Grace said evenly, staring at Cook. "We don't have the time, I don't have the patience, and you don't have the authority. Either get back on topic or get out of St. Kilda's bus and off its property."

Steele rubbed his mouth and looked bland, but his eyes actually twinkled.

Faroe looked at Grace like he'd never seen her before. And he hadn't. Not this Grace, the one who would go toe-to-toe with a supervisory special agent and rip his face off.

"And the topic of the day is . . . ?" Faroe asked into the shocked silence.

"The FBI's fabricated case against St. Kilda," Grace said, "which we've already shot down. We were just opening the topic of Ted's computer files, without which no one has a case against Hector Rivas Osuna and Carlos Calderón. No files means no one seizes fifty million dollars along with the kind of headlines that advance careers."

"Fifty million, huh?" Faroe asked.

Grace nodded.

"A lot of money" was all Faroe said.

Apparently the task force didn't know there could be twice as much money. Faroe saw no need to point it out.

"Did you get to the part where the task force's mismanagement of their informant could well cost the life of a U.S. citizen, Lane Franklin, presently a prisoner in Mexico?" Faroe asked.

Cook stared at Faroe without blinking. No surprise there.

"No, we were closing in on that issue when the chopper landed," Grace said. "But Cook's expression tells me he already knows and doesn't give a damn."

"He will," Faroe said.

Cook shrugged. "You cooperate with us, get me the files, and I'll make a call to the school. The kid will be on the next flight home."

Grace went still. "Let me make sure I heard you correctly. The FBI is willing to use a child as—"

"I didn't say that," Cook cut in.

She turned to Steele. "Did you hear Supervisory Special Agent Cook offer to trade Lane's freedom for the computer files?"

"I do believe I did," Steele said. "Shocking to think the American government is complicit in the kidnapping of an American child."

"We didn't kidnap anyone," Cook said impatiently. "The Mexicans didn't kidnap anyone. The kid is a screwup who is in school in

Mexico until his father signs him out. That's not kidnapping, that's old-fashioned discipline."

"Nice story," Faroe said. "Only Lane isn't at the school anymore. Mexican *federales* dragged him out and took off with him. Want to look at the sat photos?"

"We lost him in Tijuana," Steele said quietly.

"I figured you would," Faroe said, but his eyes never left the FBI agent.

Cook didn't want to believe what he was hearing.

"Yeah," Faroe said, nodding. "Your snitch Ted lied to you. Want a hankie?"

"Prove it," Cook said flatly.

Faroe glanced at his watch. "In less than three hours, Hector will kill the boy. How about the kid's head in a box? That enough proof for you? But, oh, yeah, if that happens, you can kiss the files, your career, and your handsome ass good-bye. Lane is my biological son."

Cook's eyes widened. He looked at Grace, at Faroe, and back at Grace.

"Yes," she said. "Ted is Lane's legal father. Joe is Lane's biological father."

"He knows?" Cook asked.

"Lane? No," she said. "Ted knows. He has for years."

"Judas Priest," Cook said, raking a hand through his black curls. "You mean Ted is lying about that school?"

"He put Lane in All Saints as a hostage to ROG. At the time, I didn't know it was more than a school." Grace hoped her tears didn't show, but knew they did.

So what? I can cry and still get the job done.

"Man, in two years running this task force, I thought I'd heard it all." Cook blew out a hard breath. "I have kids of my own. I'd kill anyone who . . ." His voice dried up.

"But if your kid was in Mexico," Faroe said, "you couldn't do shit. How many times have you gone south without ROG knowing exactly what you're doing and where you're doing it? For that matter, how many times have you been able to go south of the line with your own pistol on your belt?"

Cook's mouth flattened. "You know the answer."

"I sure do. One inch south of the razor wire in Spring Canyon, you lose ninety-five percent of your authority," Faroe said. "It's been that way for fifty years. But I have a way to tweak things just long enough to make you a hero."

"A hero is a dude with his head so far up his butt he can't see the light of the oncoming train."

"Spoken like a true FBI bureaucrat," Faroe said. "You ever heard the saying, 'Faint heart ne'er fucked the fair maiden'?"

"I've heard it from guys who thought they could catch lightning in a bottle."

"So you're not interested in Hector Rivas Osuna?" Faroe said.

"Hell yes, I want to take Hector out of the game," Cook said roughly. "You see the reward posters wallpapering the port of entry? Five million bucks. No federal agent can collect that reward, but I don't care. I just want that narco asshole in an American prison."

"Even if you come up with those files," Grace said, "you're still a long way from getting your hands on Hector."

"We'll get him," Cook said.

"Which century?" Faroe asked. "He's been indicted in the United States for six years. He's still king of the dunghill down south. What's one more piece of paper calling him Supercrook? He frames them and hangs them in his bathroom."

"Realistically," Grace said, "all Ted can give you is the fifty million dollars in his files, correct?"

"I take the long view," Cook said.

"My view doesn't go past twelve-thirty today," Faroe said coldly. "Work with us and you'll get the files, the fifty million, and good old Hector *on this side of the line.*"

"Don't tell me, let me guess," Cook said sardonically. "You're going to put on a stretchy blue bodysuit and a red cape, grab Hector, and shove him through a hole in the fence."

"Close enough," Faroe said.

"When we took custody of the dudes who killed Kiki Camarena that way, the American judges crapped in their robes," Cook said. "Sorry, Your Honor."

She shrugged. "I resigned from the federal bench this morning."

Cook started to ask something, then thought better of it.

"What I'm going to do," Faroe said, "won't ruffle the feathers of any except the most irrational of federal judges."

"What's your plan?" Cook demanded.

"I'll grab Hector on this side of the line, where he'll be caught in the commission of a federal felony."

"Superman you might be," Cook said, "but you ain't Santa Claus. I know Santa Claus. He's a fat guy with a big red suit and elves."

Faroe waited.

"No hole in the fence?" Cook demanded.

"Just a hole in the ground. Hector's tunnel."

Cook's eyes widened. "Who told you about the tunnel? Who was it? I'll bust his ass right out of the agency."

"I heard about it south of the line."

"Where is it?"

"The tunnel?" Faroe asked.

"Shit, yes, the tunnel!"

"Do we have a deal?"

"Deal? What deal?"

"You produce Ted Franklin at the time and place of our choice. We'll give you Hector Rivas Osuna and his tunnel."

71

FAROE GRABBED A SATELLITE phone in one hand and gestured with his head at Grace.

"Excuse me, gentlemen," she said to Steele and Cook. "You don't need me for the nitpicking."

She stood and walked away from finalizing the last details of the informal deal she and Steele were hammering out with Cook. When she caught up with Faroe, he was knocking on the door to Steele's suite.

"Harley, it's Joe," Faroe said. "Let's trade places."

A moment later the door opened and Harley walked out. Grace and Faroe went into the suite and locked everything up behind them.

"I still can't believe you got the feds to give St. Kilda any funds they seize over fifty million," Faroe said in a low voice.

"There may not be any. Ted is lying slime. Hector is worse. But no matter how much is in the fund, St. Kilda will get the reward for Hector and you'll be repaid for—"

"I don't want it."

She gave Faroe a dark, level look. "You'll get it anyway. It's the least I can do for dragging you back into the very world you wanted to escape."

He shrugged. "Somehow that doesn't seem important to me anymore."

"Then what is?"

"Lane." Faroe pulled Grace into his arms. "You. Us. We've got a lot of sorting to do, *amada.* Once Lane is safe, I want a chance to see what we have going."

"Yes."

He looked at her. "Just that easy?"

"Easy? *Us?* Bite your tongue. Never mind. I'll do it."

He took the playful kiss, deepened it, and didn't let go of her until they were both breathing too fast.

"Hold that place in your mind," he said huskily. "We'll go back as soon as we can."

She licked her lips. "And here I thought you were going to let me play with your cell phone again."

Faroe laughed, hugged her hard, and stepped back before he changed his mind about letting go of her. "You can hold that place along with the other one. Right now we have Hector to deal with."

"How?"

"Father Magón gave me some numbers for Hector. I'll call the first one and you take it from there."

"Why?"

"Hector underestimates women. It's a cultural attitude that goes bone deep. It gives us an edge."

Grace looked at the phone like it was a snake. "What are my talking points?"

"First, we have Ted sacked up and ready to chat with Hector about the missing millions."

"That should get Hector's attention."

"Second," Faroe said, "the price of that conversation is Lane, alive and well, *on this side of the line.* We won't go south to do this deal. If Hector wants the money, he has to come north."

"He won't like it."

"He'll take it. He doesn't have any choice. Third, it happens now. We do the high-noon thing at the border. Hector chooses the place."

"Got it. What part of the plan aren't you telling me?"

Faroe blew out a hard breath. The drawback to a smart woman was that she was smart.

"Hector wants the meeting for obvious reasons," Faroe said.

"Money."

"Yeah, but he also wants to kill Ted."

Grace's eyelids flinched, but all she said was, "Can he kill Ted and not kill everyone else who's there, including Lane?"

Faroe smiled the kind of smile that wasn't reassuring. "You learn fast, *amada.* I'm betting Hector will try to kill everyone, including Ted's FBI handlers if they insist on going into the tunnel with him."

"What will you do to prevent Hector from killing everyone in sight?"

"You'll be the second to know."

"That's not good enough."

"It's the best I can give you," Faroe said. "I've designed a trap that Hector can't refuse—he'll use his tunnel to bring Lane north and kill Ted. But Hector doesn't know what we know."

"Which is?"

"A paranoid warlord on crack will think he can set up the exchange in his warehouse over on Otay Mesa, kill everybody who's there just for shits and giggles, and run back south like the weasel he is."

"From here, Hector's plan looks good," Grace said bluntly.

"His plan will only work over my dead body."

"That's not funny."

"At least if I die," Faroe said, "there will be a good reason. I'm not sure I can say that about some of the other times I nearly bought it."

Grace looked at him for a long time. Then she closed her eyes and told herself that if she could play showdown poker with the head of a federal task force for fifty million dollars, she could do it with the Butcher of Tijuana for her son's life.

Couldn't she?

Faroe waited for one of the longest ten counts of his life. When he couldn't take anymore, he said, *Amada? You okay?*

"No. Call Hector."

"You sure?"

"Just do it!"

Faroe punched in the number, hit the transmit button, and held out the phone.

Grace took it and began counting rings.

On the fourth ring, a male voice said, *"Bueno."*

"I need to talk to Hector Rivas," she said in English.

"¿Quién habla?" the man demanded.

"Grace Silva."

"What you want?" the man asked.

"Hector knows what I want. If he wants you to know, he'll tell you. Get him."

Faroe waited.

And waited.

And waited.

Just when he thought Hector wouldn't take the bait, Grace began talking.

"Hello, Hector."

"Ah, Your Honor, how strict you are," Hector said in Spanish. "Poor Fernando is whipped. He takes such good care of your son, too."

"He'd better. Without a live and healthy Lane, you'll never see your hundred million again."

Hector made a rhythmic, juicy sound.

"Put Lane on the line," Grace said.

"No *es* possible," Hector said in Spanglish, loudly, like a man trying to get through to a very dim person.

She grimaced. His words were a little slurred, a little hissed. He'd been drinking as well as smoking. "It's very possible. If I don't have proof of life, you don't have Ted's files."

"The boy, he fine. Take my word."

"And here's a hundred million. Take it to the bank."

Hector laughed out loud. *"Aiee,* a ball-breaker."

He shouted an order in Spanish.

Grace hit the mute button. "He thinks I'm a ball-breaker. He's telling someone to bring Lane."

Faroe's grin was a hard slice of white.

She released the mute just as Lane's voice came on.

"Mom?"

"Are you okay?" she asked quickly.

"Yeah, I guess so. They even brought me a Big Mac for dinner. Whoopee."

"Do you have everything you need?" she asked carefully.

"Uh," he hesitated, then understood what she was asking. "Yeah, I've got everything I need. I'm— Wait a minute. I wasn't done!"

"You see?" Hector asked in Spanish. "Your son is good. Now, where is your husband?"

"You mean my ex?" she asked. "Last time I saw Ted, he was folded into a car trunk, in handcuffs and leg chains and with a gag in his mouth. Joe Faroe is nothing if not thorough."

Faroe laughed silently.

"Que bueno," Hector said, chuckling. "You bring him to me right now and I give you Lane."

"No."

"¿Qué?" he asked sharply.

"I'm not going to do business with you in any part of Mexico. That is not negotiable."

"I so sad. You no trust Hector."

"Yes, it's sad, and it's not going to change," Grace said crisply. And her fingernails dug into her palms. "You pick a place on this side of the line for the exchange. You have two hours to set it up."

"Ah, you worry I kill the boy after noon."

"I think you're too smart to be that stupid," she said. *Especially if you lay off the booze and crack.* "The problem is Ted—we can't keep him in the trunk forever."

Hector laughed so hard he choked. *"Aiee. Such a woman! But I no can cross the border."*

"If tons of marijuana can, you can. You have millions of reasons to."

"Do you have the information?" Hector asked in rapid-fire Spanish. "The banks, the transactions, all the numbers—you understand?"

"I understand. We have what you need. Faroe, ah, persuaded Ted to talk."

"These records, you truly have them?"

"The records will be present at the exchange." She gave Faroe a cold, lawyerly smile.

There was a humming silence.

Grace's nails dug deeper into her hands.

Faroe pried apart her left hand and rubbed the scarlet crescent marks.

"Do you know the Otay Mesa crossing?" Hector asked.

"Yes. I know the Otay crossing," she repeated so that Faroe would know.

He closed his eyes in relief or prayer.

"We trade there," Hector said in Spanish.

"Bring Ted Franklin. I will hear from his lips the truth of the records. You understand?"

"Yes. Ted will be with me. Where, exactly, do we meet?"

"I will call you. And, *señora*?"

Grace's heart stopped, then beat faster. "Yes?"

"Joe Faroe will be with you and Ted. No one else."

"Joe? I hadn't planned—"

Hector talked over her in rough English. "Faroe come or no deal. I want that smart gringo where I can see him. *¿Claro?*"

"Very clear. He'll be with me."

Hector hung up.

So did Grace.

"Did I just hear you promise that I'd be with you?" Faroe asked.

"Yes. Is that a problem? He's obviously going to use the warehouse just like you said."

"Yeah, but I hadn't planned to be there with you."

Surprised, Grace asked, "Where were you going to be?"

"At the Mexican end of the tunnel, sneaking up on Hector."

Silence.

"What's Plan B?" she asked.

"I'm working on it."

Faroe went to find Father Magón. If anyone had a direct line to Carlos Calderón, it
would be the Vatican spy.

72

Lane sat in a broom closet and thought about playing soccer—with various heads used for the ball. His recent nomination for butthead of the hour was Fernando Díaz, one of Hector's endless stream of nephews. Or maybe they were his bastards.

They sure had the attitude for it. The thought of kicking some of them right between the goalposts kept Lane from focusing on the steady throb of his bruised face and the fact that his bladder was so full his back teeth were floating.

And then there were all the seconds ticking away into minutes and minutes into—

Don't go there.

Don't think about it.

Think about kicking Fernando in the balls.

Lane was real tired of Fernando whispering through the door, telling him all about how he was going to be dog food by twelve-thirty.

Dad won't let that happen.

Will he?

Lane wished he had more confidence in his dad, but he didn't. This would be just one more in a long line of moments when his dad let him down.

Hey, the good news is that it will be the last time.

Lane tried to laugh.

It sounded too much like a sob.

He went back to running his fingertips over the mops, brooms, vacuum hoses, and dustpans that were hanging on the walls, waiting to be used. If he was some slick ninja, he'd break off a broom handle and go through the *vatos* outside like a one-man demolition derby.

But he wasn't a ninja and he had too much sense to pretend otherwise.

No point in dying before he had to.

"Hola, niño," Hector said, opening the door to the utility closet.

Lane squinted against the sudden light. His heart filled his throat, beating like a captive bird.

"You okay?" Hector asked.

Oh, sure, I'm just frigging fantastic, locked in a closet waiting to die. And Hector's breath could kill scorpions at twenty feet.

"I could really use a bathroom," was all Lane said.

With surprising strength, Hector pulled Lane to his feet and pointed to a door across the hall.

"Don' be long," Hector said around the cigarette stuck in the corner of his mouth. "You daddy, he wait."

"Dad? He's coming here for me?"

"You go. Then we go. *Andale, niño.*"

Lane was so relieved he nearly wet himself. He could hardly believe that his father was really going to come through for him.

"Dad?" he asked.

"Sí, sí," Hector said impatiently. *"¡Andale!"*

Lane hurried across the hall. With every step he felt the slight weight of the hard drive in his pocket.

73

FAROE AND GRACE WENT back to the main salon in time to see Steele and the FBI agent cautiously shaking hands across the table.

"Supervisory Special Agent Cook has agreed to an arrangement that will ensure complete FBI control of events in their jurisdiction," Steele said, weighing his words with the care of the ambassador he once had been. "His surveillance and weapons teams will cover the exchange, with full authority to shut the operation down if he, as field commander, decides it's too dangerous."

Faroe went still and deadly. "Shut it down?

Dangerous? All he's worried about is Franklin getting a bullet in his fat ass."

"Right now," Cook said, "I'd put a bullet in him myself. Snitches. Jesus. I hate the slimy rocks they live under. I've already told Ted and his attorney that they'll cooperate to the fullest or any deal for immunity we might have in the works is DOA." He looked at Grace. "I wish you'd come to me instead of St. Kilda. It would have been cleaner."

"When it mattered, I didn't know you existed," Grace said. "But even if I'd known you by your first, last, and middle name, I'd have gone to St. Kilda Consulting. They represent my interests and only mine."

Cook's mouth turned down at one corner. "After working on the Calderón task force for two years, if my son was a hostage, I'd think about going to St. Kilda myself. And kiss my career good-bye."

Faroe poured himself a cup of coffee from the urn on the kitchen counter and turned to Cook. "But you still have to play the game like your badge trumps everything, right?"

"Operational control? Is that what's chapping your ass?" Cook asked. "You know that I have to go to my bosses with clean hands.

That means operational control on this side of the line."

Faroe took a drink of coffee and waited for what he wanted to hear, or all bets were off.

"But that doesn't mean I give a rat's hairy ass what goes on at the other end of the tunnel," Cook said. "If you want to shoot Hector between the eyes and drag him into the United States by his hang-downs, go for it. Just don't tell me about it ahead of time."

That was what Faroe wanted to hear.

"Deniability," he said, saluting Cook. "It's the major reason St. Kilda exists. You've got it. But we have a problem."

"Just one?" Cook said acidly.

"Hector wants me where he can see me on this side of the line," Faroe said.

"Do you think he suspects a trap?" Steele asked while Cook was still processing the possible meanings of Faroe's words.

"No. He just doesn't trust me unless he can see me."

"Smart dude," Cook said. He looked at Steele. "Can any of your other people handle the job down south?"

"No," Faroe said instantly.

"What?" Cook demanded. "You got a clone I don't know about?"

"No, but now that this is officially a federal case, I won't put St. Kilda operatives into a situation that could cost them their lives or their freedom."

"Hey, look," Cook said. "I told you I'm not going to ask what your ops might do on the other side. Ain't my jurisdiction. Ain't my problem."

"You can promise immunity all you want," Faroe said, "but it's up to the director, the AG, and a mixed batch of judges to keep your promise."

Cook didn't look happy, but he didn't argue. "The Ambassador told me what happened to you sixteen years ago."

"Then you know why I don't trust the system, and why I won't have any more St. Kilda ops on your record as players."

"So you're planning to call off the southern end of the operation?" Cook asked.

"I didn't say anything about anything. All I want from you is a ten-foot ladder and size twelve running shoes."

Cook looked at Steele. "Is he for real?"

"He ran the fifteen hundred meters in college," Steele said. "He still runs it."

Grace wrapped her hand around Faroe's arm. "What are you going to do?"

"I'm certainly not going to tell you in front of Cook because it might just possibly maybe could involve illegal reverse entry."

She blinked. "What?"

"Jumping over the border fence while headed south," Faroe said. "That's just not the way things are done on Otay Mesa. Trust me on this."

Her lungs ached with the screams she was holding back.

Holding your breath won't help anyone.

Breathe.

"All right," she said. "What do you want me to do?"

He smiled slowly. "Things that are still illegal in some states."

Grace didn't know she could laugh until she heard herself. Some of the tension gripping her eased.

Until she looked at her watch.

Breathe.

74

FAROE, GRACE, AND STEELE sat in the shadows beside the St. Kilda command center, watching. Unlike the *chubasco* that had drenched Ensenada and then blown on up the coast, the storm gathering in the trailer park had yet to break.

Faroe didn't know if the clouds or the task force would cut loose first.

A pair of dark blue FBI buses, a mobile command center, and at least a dozen undercover sedans and trucks had joined the St. Kilda motor coaches in the small park. Weapons teams in Kevlar helmets and blue coveralls prowled with undercover investigators from the Rivas task force and command officers from a half dozen local, state, and federal agencies.

Alpha males and a few tight-lipped alpha females walked stiff-legged, waiting for the signal to kill or die.

"This pretty much defines a Mongolian goat-fuck," Faroe said. "It reminds me why I left government service. Too damn many servants."

Steele smiled. "Be proud. You've started a wildfire that is burning asses all the way to Washington, D.C. My last phone call was from the attorney general's chief aide, wondering what in the name of J. Edgar Hoover we were doing by injecting ourselves into a federal investigation of the highest priority."

"What was your answer?" Grace asked.

"I told him that several St. Kilda operators had agreed to act as confidential informants for the task force in expediting the arrest of the Mexican national who is number three on the FBI's ten most wanted list. I also pointed out that the Justice Department regularly relies on evidence gathered by private investigators."

"Did that make him feel all warm and squishy?" Faroe asked.

"I didn't ask about the state of his under-wear," Steele said.

"All he wanted was deniability for the AG if something goes wrong," Grace said.

"Precisely," Steele said. "He also reminded me that confidential informants are not per-mitted to perform actual law enforcement du-ties."

"Meaning?" Grace asked.

"No guns," Faroe said, flipping the satellite phone end over end. "No boots. No badges. Those toys are reserved for sworn agents of the United States."

"No guns, huh?" she said.

"Cross our hearts and hope to die," Faroe said.

"That's a grim saying," she muttered.

"So I promise not to shoot anybody inside the United States," Faroe said, launching the satellite phone again. "Under the United States, that's a different matter." He looked at Steele. "Did you really refer to me as a CI?"

"Confidential informant. It's just a descrip-tion."

"So is shit. And that's how agents think of snitches. Oh, excuse me. CIs."

Faroe spun the phone upward again.

At the top of its arc, it rang.

He grabbed the phone, punched a button, and said, "Faroe."

"*Hola,* asshole," Hector said. "You know El Rey Mexican Foods warehouse at Otay?"

"I can find it."

"Bring Franklin, the ball-breaker, and you. One hour."

"We'll be there. But before anything happens, I'll need proof of life. Be ready to let us see Lane and talk to him."

"She jus' talk—"

"We talk to him before we give you the files or there's no trade. *¿Claro?* And we hand the files to you personally. I don't trust any of your men with the information and neither should you."

Hector laughed. "*Sí,* gringo. You listen."

"I'm listening."

Faroe concentrated, repeated back seven numbers, and waited for confirmation.

The line went hollow.

Lane punched out the call on his end. "That was Hector. The exchange is set for the warehouse of El Rey Mexican Foods, just like we hoped. I've got the front door code."

"When?" Grace asked.

"One hour." He looked at Steele. "Where are the kids?"

"Right where you wanted them, in the weeds at the border," Steele said. "Mary is still lobbying to go over the fence with you."

Faroe shook his head. "Not this time." He whistled shrilly through his teeth. "Yo, Cook! You've got less than an hour to get to an Otay warehouse and infiltrate your shooters."

Cook waved and started shouting orders. People began running like their feet were on fire.

Faroe stood up and headed for the beach.

"Where are you going?" Steele asked.

"I need a few minutes away from the hive."

75

GRACE FOLLOWED FAROE THROUGH the wind and stinging grit until she stood just behind him on the beach. Distant thunder blended with the relentless pounding of storm surf. Salt spray and a foretaste of rain stole light from the air, turning morning to evening. There was no horizon, simply the wild blending of sky, sea, and storm.

"Am I part of the hive?" she asked above the wind.

Without turning away from the sea, Faroe held his hand out. "I'm thinking about Lane."

She laced her fingers through Faroe's hand.

"I'm thinking about the time I didn't have with him," Faroe said, gripping her hand. "The first time he walked, the first word he said. I'm wondering if he was like the toddler I saw in Peru, who pointed at the surf and said 'laughing water' and then he laughed with it. Joy. Innocence. Openness. The things Lane had to lose to survive."

Grace didn't say anything. She simply held Faroe's hand.

"Then I think about all the other times I wasn't there," Faroe said. "The first time Lane got bloody protecting someone smaller. The first time he sucked it up and didn't cry because crying didn't get the job done. The first time his voice broke. The first time he looked at a girl and felt like his skin was too small."

Grace told herself the cool moisture on her face was salt spray.

"Now Lane is as old as a lot of the soldiers in too many of the regular and irregular armies around the world," Faroe said. "More innocent maybe—until forty-eight hours ago."

She lifted his hand and put her cheek against it.

"I'm used to violence, to death," Faroe said. "Not indifferent to it. Just not surprised.

I can accept that I won't see the next sunset, but not Lane. *Not Lane.* And there's damn little I can do to prevent it. So damn little. So I have to trust in greed and violence, because they're reliable weapons and innocence isn't." Faroe's fingers tightened, then slid away from her grip. "So be it."

"Can you forgive me?" Grace asked, feeling cold, watching the coming storm with eyes that didn't see.

Faroe skimmed the back of his fingers over her cheeks, her tears, her wind-tangled hair.

"The 'honors' were about even on both sides," he said. "So yes, I forgive you for knowing I wasn't what you needed all those years ago. Have you forgiven me?"

"Yes," she said.

For an instant his fingers clenched. "Now all I have to do is forgive myself."

She made a sound that could have been laughter, but wasn't. "Same here."

His hand slid out of her hair and to his belt, where the satellite phone was holstered. He started to punch in a number, then stopped.

"Go talk to Steele, *amada.* I'll only be a few minutes."

"Does this have to do with Lane?"

"Yes."

Grace didn't leave.

Faroe didn't ask again.

76

CARLOS CALDERÓN HELD HIS scrambled cell phone like he expected it to slice open his hand.

In a way, he did. Opportunity was like that.

It cut both ways.

The phone beeped.

He crossed himself and answered it. *"Bueno."*

"This is Faroe. Is this Carlos Calderón?"

"Yes. I have been expecting your call."

"Listen carefully, because I'll only say this once. You and Jaime want Hector Rivas Osuna out of the game. I've arranged for that to happen."

"How?" Carlos asked, almost afraid to hope. "It can't come back to me."

"It won't. All you have to do is tell Jaime to take Hector to the Tijuana warehouse, wait for him to be out of radio range, and then pull everyone out. Just leave Hector and don't lock up behind him. I'll do the rest. Do we have an agreement?"

"That's all? Just leave him?"

"That's it."

The satellite connection hummed.

North of the border, Faroe waited.

And prayed.

"It is done," Carlos said.

77

TED FRANKLIN WAS COMING down off his drunk, which meant that he swung between surly and frightened.

When Cook approached with handcuffs, Ted freaked.

"I'm not wearing those things! No way! You crazy?"

"Settle down," Cook said. "It's part of the act. You're supposed to be Faroe's prisoner, remember?"

"I said I'd go with him—I didn't say anything about cuffs!"

"It isn't a choice," Cook said.

Before Franklin could do anything but

gasp, Cook had the man's hands behind his back and the cuffs on tight.

Franklin started sobbing.

Jesus, Faroe thought. *He's going to have a total meltdown before he even sees Hector.*

Faroe elbowed his way into the circle of agents around Franklin.

"Give me the key," Faroe said to Cook.

Cook hesitated, then handed it over. "Personally, I'd rather bitch-slap some sense into him."

"Take a ticket and get in line." Faroe unlocked Franklin's cuffs, but left one of them attached to his right wrist. "Ted. Yo, TED!"

Franklin blinked and focused on Faroe.

"This is an act," Faroe said distinctly. "These are props." He held the open cuff in Franklin's face and pointed to the chain. "See that link? It's weak. All you have to do is give a good solid yank and it breaks."

Cook turned away so that Franklin wouldn't see him smile.

The other agents did the same.

Franklin tried to focus on the chain, but he couldn't see through the tears.

Faroe had counted on that.

"It will break?" Franklin asked.

"Yes. I'd show you, but we've only got one pair of fake cuffs. So relax and remember it's an act."

"An act," Franklin repeated. He took a few ragged breaths and wiped his face on his shirtsleeve. "Do I have to?"

"Hector expects to see you in cuffs, so that's what we'll show him," Faroe said. "But we know better. We know you can get free anytime you want, right?"

A few more broken breaths, another swipe of arm over nose, and Franklin said, "Uh, yeah."

"Ready to play your part?" Faroe asked.

". . . yeah, I guess."

"Okay. I'm going to cuff you, but I'll keep your hands in front this time. Ready?"

Franklin swallowed and stood up straighter. "Okay."

Faroe had the handcuffs back on before Franklin could blink.

Or change his mind.

"What's going to happen?" Franklin asked in a rising voice. "I should know. I have to know!"

With a muttered curse, Cook turned back to his reluctant snitch. "Like I told you the last twenty times you asked, you, Grace, and

Faroe are going to meet Hector in a warehouse up on Otay Mesa in about forty-five minutes. You listening this time?"

Franklin nodded.

"The warehouse has a tunnel that leads to another warehouse south of the line," Cook continued in a monotone. "That's how Hector will bring Lane north. It's the only way he can cross north without risk of discovery."

"A tunnel," Franklin said. "Why can't you come along, you and a bunch of armed men? It would be safer."

"Because Hector isn't a fool," Faroe said. "He'll have men watching the warehouse. If too many people go in, the deal's off, Lane dies, and if you're really lucky, you go to prison for money laundering. If you're not lucky, Hector has you killed before you go to trial." *Assuming I don't drop you first.* "Any questions?"

Franklin shuddered. He shook his head.

"To keep everyone alive," Faroe continued with false patience, "we have to make it look like I grabbed you and am willing to trade you for Lane. That's why the weapons teams from the Bureau will have to hang way back in the weeds, waiting for our signal."

"But when Hector knows it's a trap, won't he try to kill everyone?" Franklin asked.

Cook's eye-roll said that the question had come up before.

Repeatedly.

"He won't get the chance," Cook said, giving an impatient glance to his watch. "We're running out of time."

Faroe started to turn away, then stopped. "Here, let me help you get into the act."

"What?" Franklin said.

Faroe gave him a short, sharp right cross followed by a left uppercut that ripped along the side of Franklin's face.

It was over before Cook could stop it.

Blood trickled from the left corner of Franklin's mouth and from his nose and the ugly welt on his cheek. Automatically he reached up to the wounded areas.

"I'm bleeding!" Franklin said.

"That's the whole idea," Faroe said. "Smear the blood around on your white banker's shirt. You have to look like you put up a good fight but got your clock cleaned. And it has to be real, right down to the shocky look around the eyes. Hector knows exactly how a man who has been beaten looks."

Franklin stared, then touched his own bloody face and wiped his hands on his shirt.

Faroe patted him on the shoulder. "Lookin' good. Keep it bleeding, or I'll have to pop you again." He looked past Franklin and the agents and spotted Grace. "Motor coach," he said to her.

She caught up with him just as he got to the motor coach.

"You lied about the cuffs, didn't you?" she asked.

"Yeah."

"Did you really have to hit him?"

"Yeah."

"You enjoyed it."

"Yeah. You have a problem with that?"

She sighed. "Not as much as I should."

The same hand that had opened up Franklin's cheek stroked gently down Grace's. "We'll get through this, *amada.* But first, we have to wire you for sound."

She opened the door to the coach. "Cuffs on Franklin and a body bug on me. Lord."

"That's how the weapons team will know when to hit the front door. I'd wear it, but I'm going to be in another country."

"Once I put it on, they'll be able to hear everything I say?"

"That's the idea."

"Then I'd better say it now."

Grace grabbed Faroe, pulled him close, and said against his mouth, "Come back to me, damn you. Promise me."

Faroe sank into the kiss, grateful that he had a way not to make promises he couldn't keep.

78

Rain came down in drenching curtains blown apart by gusts of wind. The windshield wipers beat like a frantic heart.

No, Grace thought. *The wipers don't care. They're just machines doing a job.*

It's my heart that's frantic.

She was swimming through a mercury landscape laced with dull diamonds where industrial lights tried to penetrate the stormy gloom.

Franklin sat in the backseat, saying nothing.

Faroe drove the Mercedes slowly along slick streets lined with square, windowless import-export warehouses and used-car lots surrounded by sagging chain-link topped with coils of razor wire. If there were any employees around, they were tucked inside away from the weather.

"It reminds me of a war zone," Grace said. "Fortresses without windows and stockades without prisoners."

"Close enough," Faroe said. "This used to be rye fields and tumbleweed, but even then it was crisscrossed by smuggling paths and pockmarked by foxholes. The border patrol had to come out here once a month to shoot the packs of feral dogs that crossed over every night from Mexico to hunt."

"They shot dogs?"

"Rabies. Distemper. You name it, the feral dogs had it. Shooting them was the only way to keep them out of San Diego."

Grace couldn't disagree, but she didn't like knowing about it.

"There it is," Faroe said.

She leaned forward and saw a boulevard sign: EL REY MEXICAN FOODS. The sign was in front of an oversize tilt-up slab building that backed up to the border fence. Except for a faint light in one of the interior rooms, the building was dark.

The warehouse was barely a block west of the Otay port-of-entry buildings.

Grace looked at the front of the building, where the offices would be.

Nothing moving.

"It looks deserted," she said uneasily.

"It probably is," Faroe said. "Galindo did a little touch-up work after the tunnel was finished. He said Hector always made sure no employees were around when the tunnel was being used. Even the family members who humped the drugs through the tunnel only knew the one end of it."

Faroe slowed and turned into the darkened parking lot beside the warehouse. "Galindo should have guessed what Hector planned for the tunnel rats. Dead men tell no tales."

"So he killed the miners," Grace said, shaking her head. "Hector makes the feral dogs look sweet."

"That means he'll try to kill us," Franklin said in a rising voice. "He will!"

"Take it easy," Faroe said. "The place is already surrounded by a dozen of the best sharpshooters and fast-entry troops in the business."

He braked to a quick stop in the parking lot and shut off the headlights.

"I don't see them," Franklin said. "I don't see anyone!"

"Neither will Hector, until it's too late," Faroe said, looking around. "I'll bet there are at least two in that Dumpster over there by the back door and another one or two under that oleander hedge along the back of the property."

Franklin made an unhappy sound. "But they can't see us when we're inside."

"With the transmitter that's wired to Grace's bra," Faroe said, "the FBI will be able to hear someone break a sweat a hundred feet away."

Static popped twice through the speaker of the small handheld radio on the console beside Faroe.

"What was that?" Franklin asked sharply.

"One of the assault team keyed his microphone," Faroe said. "It's the standard silent signal that a transmission was received." He picked up the radio and clipped it to his belt next to his phone. "When I go south, you'll be in communication with the backup team via Grace's bra."

She shot him a sideways look.

He smiled. "So just holler if things go wrong and the Bureau powder monkeys will blow every door on that box and come down on Hector like acid rain. They want that bastard bad enough to taste it."

"I thought they were after the money," Franklin said.

"They'll take that and be glad," Faroe said. "It might just cover their expenses plus the five million they'll have to fork over for the capture of Hector."

"You really expect to collect on that?" Franklin asked.

"St. Kilda will collect. It might keep Steele happy for a whole week."

"But—" Franklin said.

"Later," Faroe interrupted. "Now it's quiet time."

He drove a slow circle around the square, blank warehouse, checking concealment spots and potential countersurveillance locations. The place looked abandoned, but there were more than twenty federal agents within a hundred yards.

And there were three St. Kilda operators facedown somewhere in the rows of the strawberry field that lay between the warehouse and the border fence.

The only sign of the surveillance team was a faintly glittering puddle of broken glass just outside one of the warehouse's rear doors. Someone had used a silent pellet gun to break the glass housing on the automatic light inside. More than once, Faroe had done the same kind of thing for the same reason.

He pulled up in the dark shadows of a ten-foot-high oleander hedge and watched a border patrol Suburban cruise slowly by on the dirt road immediately adjacent to the twelve-foot boundary fence. The vehicle slowed even more, then stopped. The driver lowered his window and peered through the rain at the field.

Damn, Faroe thought. *He must have spotted a movement.*

Faroe leaned over Grace's breasts. "Which mutt forgot to tell the border patrol that there's an operation going down here?"

Static popped from the radio on Faroe's belt.

Message received.

The border agent opened his door and stepped out. Obviously he was taking a better look at the rain-swept field a hundred feet away. He stepped off the roadway, an agent on the way to flush a band of illegal immigrants.

Then the man stopped and reached for his belt radio.

"Yeah, Cook," Faroe said against Grace's shirt. "Hector probably has someone watching from the other side, so tell the border patrol to haul ass out of here like he just got a hot call on Dairy Mart Road."

The border agent held the radio to his face long enough to acknowledge. Then he tossed the radio back into the truck and climbed in. The red and blue lights on the roof snapped on. The green and white vehicle left a rooster tail of mud as the agent raced down the boundary road in the direction of Chula Vista.

"Good job," Faroe said. He nuzzled against the transmitter. "Thanks."

Grace took a startled breath. Then she smiled.

"Okay, Central," Faroe said, his lips less than a half inch from her shirt. "We're going to the warehouse now. We'll be inside in about thirty seconds. I'll play it loose until I make sure that nobody's waiting. And we'll need a sound check to make sure the body bug works inside the walls. Do you copy? Pop once."

A single burst of static whispered from the radio on his hip.

"Did you get the inside wired for sound?" he asked.

Another pop.

"Remember," Faroe said to Grace and Franklin, "there are TV cameras inside the warehouse, so expect Hector to be watching."

"Can he listen, too?" she asked.

"Galindo didn't know about any microphones, but we can't be certain. The task force will be listening for sure, even if your wire shorts out." Faroe pointed to the warehouse. "The rathole is in the washroom beside those offices. Knowing Hector, he's probably got shit smeared on it to blow out the noses of customs dogs."

"Sweet," Grace said.

"That's our Hector."

Faroe let the vehicle coast silently across the blacktop to the side door. He shut off the engine. Silence built around them.

"You have that thing Harley gave you?" he asked Grace softly.

"Yes."

"Remember *when* to use it?"

"What are you two talking about?" Franklin demanded.

"The gun in my purse," she said.

"They gave you a gun? Why didn't I get one?"

"It didn't go with the handcuffs," she said.

Franklin slumped back against the seat.

"Stop worrying about all the ways I can screw up," she said to Faroe. "I know the rules of engagement. I do nothing unless someone is in immediate danger of being killed. But if things fall apart, I won't stand by and scream. I'll start shooting and save the screaming for later."

Faroe's radio popped once. He smiled. "Dead or alive, just like the posters said?"

"Exactly like that."

Faroe breathed against her neck. "Don't say anything you wouldn't want to appear in an after-action report."

"I'm just stating the obvious," Grace said. "Hector is an old-fashioned fool. He doesn't think women are a personal threat. I'll have a better chance of getting a shot at him than all the ninjas in the parking lot."

"Are you a good shot?" Faroe asked.

"From six inches who isn't?"

"Don't do anything to make Hector mad," Franklin said nervously.

"I was thinking more like dead," she said.

"Uh, Cook, you'd better back up that real-time tape and start over again," Faroe said, pulling out his shirt to cover the radio.

A single pop.

Faroe reached for the door handle. "Show-time."

79

IGNORING THE RAIN, FAROE got out of the Mercedes, opened the back door, and dragged Franklin roughly out.

"Hey, watch it!" Franklin said.

Faroe's response was another snake-fast blow to the corner of Franklin's mouth.

Grace made a low sound but didn't say a word. She just shut the door behind her and waited in the rain for whatever came next.

"Let it bleed," Faroe said softly to Franklin.

"No more," Franklin said, "or I'll—"

"You're lucky I don't gut you for what you

did to Lane," Faroe cut in. "Shut up and count your blessings."

Franklin's eyes showed white in the rain-washed gloom.

Faroe shoved.

A stumble, a lurch, and Franklin was on his way. He staggered over to the concrete slab that was the threshold of the warehouse and stood numbly in the broken glass of another neutralized security light. If he noticed the rain, he didn't show it.

Blood ran red, then pink, down his face to his no-longer-white shirt.

Grace didn't try to shield herself from the rain. She waited while Faroe punched a seven-digit combination into the electronic sentry that controlled the door.

The bolt released with a sharp metallic snap.

Faroe swung the door open, went in low, and felt around until he found a light switch. From the ceiling thirty feet overhead, bright lights blazed on, dividing the warehouse into pools of light and darkness.

Nothing moved.

He looked around slowly, twice, then waved Franklin and Grace inside and closed the door.

The huge warehouse was so empty it echoed. Toward the front, a half dozen wooden pallets stacked with cases of a popular brand of canned Mexican chilies made a backdrop for the front offices. Toward the rear, where the doors were locked and wired to alarms, another half dozen pallets loaded with canvas sacks of pinto beans and rice were lined up as a screen in front of another small suite of offices. In between was more than a hundred feet of nothing but concrete floor and thirty-foot metal ceiling.

Faroe counted four closed-circuit television cameras on wall mounts positioned to cover the entire interior of the warehouse. Red status lights burned on each camera, a warning that they were transmitting to a control center.

The camera mounted above the warehouse door swiveled to follow Faroe's movement. He pulled Grace close and breathed down her blouse.

"Transmitter check."

The radio on Faroe's belt beneath his shirt popped twice.

"I'm going off the air," he told Grace's bra.

Two more pops.

Faroe kissed her fast and hard and deep. She kissed him back the same way.

Then he turned his back to the closest camera, reached under his shirt, and switched off the radio. He walked toward the sand-bagged defensive position that had been created by pallets of beans and rice.

Except for the soft drumroll of rain on the roof, the place was silent.

The offices were empty.

The door to the bathroom was locked.

Unless there was somebody already inside the bathroom, the warehouse was deserted.

"Anybody home?" Faroe called out.

Silence.

Pulling his cell phone off his belt, he punched in numbers as he walked back to Grace and Franklin.

"No noise," he said to them.

He punched the send button and listened for the telltale sounds of another phone ringing somewhere in the warehouse.

Silence.

After two rings, Hector answered. His voice was slurred, like he was loaded.

Good news and bad news in one, Faroe thought grimly.

"We're in the warehouse," Faroe said. "No-body's home."

"We close, *pendejo*." Hector chuckled.

"Put Lane on."

"You give me Franklin with the files."

It wasn't a question.

"With my blessings," Faroe said.

"You have him?"

"You're looking at the TV displays, what do you think?" Faroe said impatiently. Then he said to Franklin, "Wave to the cameras."

Sullenly Franklin lifted his cuffed hands toward the nearest camera.

"Now put Lane on," Faroe said.

"I no like orders. I am *el jefe*."

"You're in charge the moment I see you and the kid," Faroe said. "Until then, we're just two men bullshitting over the cell phone."

Over the invisible link that reached up to a communications satellite in space and back down six hundred feet to the south, Faroe heard a moist noise as Hector sucked on a Mexican cigarette and drew the cocaine smoke into his lungs.

Enjoy it, Faroe thought. *With a little luck, it will be your last.*

"Okay," Hector said, his tongue thick. "You

talk to Lane. Then I send Jaime. If he like what he see, we make next step."

The connection rattled hollowly for a moment, then Lane's voice came over.

"Mom, Dad?"

"It's Joe," Faroe said. "You okay?"

"I guess." Lane's voice sounded shaky. "At least I, uh, have everything I left with."

"Got you. Can Hector hear me?"

"I don't think so."

"Watch your mom. Don't take your eyes off of her. Okay?"

"Yeah."

"Do what she tells you to do," Faroe said. "Don't pay any attention to your dad. Just your mom. Got that?"

Lane started to say something, but his words turned into a sharp cry of pain.

"Don' worry, gringo," Hector said. "He jus' fine. I show him manners, tha's all."

Faroe's grip on the cell phone made his knuckles white. "Send in your man."

He looked at his watch and started counting.

80

FOR WHAT SEEMED LIKE an eternity, Faroe, Grace, and Franklin stood in the glare of the overhead lights. By Faroe's watch, the eternity was only one minute and forty-nine seconds.

Faint sounds, metal on metal, muffled.

Fifteen seconds.

A toilet flushed.

"Who will it be?" Grace asked under her breath.

"Jaime," Faroe said. "Hector has to send someone he trusts, someone who already knows both ends of the tunnel. That means family. With people like Hector, blood is all that counts."

And blood is what screws them every time.

Faroe would have felt sorry for Hector if the man hadn't earned a slow death fifty times over.

The doorknob of the bathroom squeaked.

The bathroom door swung open. Jaime Rivas—blow-dried and splendid in an Italian suit and loafers without socks—strolled out of the darkened room, zipping up like he'd just finished filling a urinal. In his left hand he carried a silver-plated semiautomatic pistol.

Jaime never took his eyes off Faroe.

"*Hola,* Jaime," Faroe called out. *"¿Qué pasa?"*

"Shut up," Jaime said. "I don't like to chat as much as my uncle does."

When Jaime was ten feet away, he snapped his pistol up to eye level and stared over the sight into Ted Franklin's face.

"You stupid son of a bitch," Jaime snarled. "I ought to whack you right now."

Franklin made a primal sound of fear.

"You kill him and nobody is happy," Faroe said. "Especially Carlos Calderón."

Jaime stared through the pistol sight at the patch of skin between Franklin's eyes. "Where's the file?"

"It's on a hard drive, *pendejo*," Faroe said. "All decrypted and ready to go."

"Show me."

"No."

"What?" Jaime's face flushed.

"You heard me," Faroe said. "Hector gets the file, not you. You don't like the deal, complain to him."

Jaime lowered the pistol an inch. The muzzle now stared at Franklin's pale, trembling mouth. "Where is the hard drive?"

"When we see Lane, you see the hard drive," Faroe said. "That's the deal."

Jaime turned his head and stared at Faroe. The look in Jaime's eyes made Grace want to step backward.

"Tell Hector the deal is ready to go down," Faroe said.

Jaime switched the pistol until it was pointed at Faroe's face. "Hector won't mind if I kill you."

Faroe looked bored. "Calderón will. He wants that hard drive. You start whacking people, you don't get it. *Claro,* homeboy?"

Jaime turned the gun on Grace. "Give me the file and she lives."

"Shoot her and you die," Faroe said. "Now stop jerking off and go tell Hector to bring Lane."

A slow, thin smile changed Jaime's mouth. "You are a very clever man, gringo. I give you that."

Jaime lowered the pistol and pointed it again at the floor. He stared a long time at Grace's face, trying to read her expression. She hadn't flinched under the gun and she didn't flinch under his eyes.

"Hector likes you," Jaime said. "He'll fuck you before he kills you."

Grace just looked at Jaime.

"My uncle will be here in a few minutes," he said.

Jaime turned and strolled back across the warehouse to the bathroom. He glanced over his shoulder at Faroe. "I see you soon, gringo. Look for me."

The bathroom door slammed behind him.

Faroe let out a long breath. "Keep your gun handy, *amada*."

He turned and walked swiftly toward the front door, sliding silently through light and shadow, light and shadow, until there was only darkness.

"What do I tell Hector?" Grace called after him.

"That I went out for a smoke."

81

BY THE TIME FAROE ran across the parking lot he was well on his way to being wet. He ignored it. He'd be a lot wetter before he got dry again.

Cook, wearing green and brown cammies and carrying a matte-black submachine gun, stepped out of the hedge. Another operator in a ghillie suit lay on the ground, a backpack radio in front of him. He was listening to what was going on in the warehouse.

Grace was saying something to Franklin. Faroe couldn't make it out, but he knew it was her voice.

"Sounds muddy," Faroe said to Cook.

"Not on a headset." Cook pulled a flat combat radio set from the cargo pocket of his cammies. "That Jaime is a real piece of work. For a minute there I thought we'd have to go in before Hector showed."

"Jaime was just testing. Life would be a lot easier for him if he had the files rather than Hector or Uncle Sam."

Cook stepped behind Faroe, slid the radio's clip over his leather belt, and fed the cable and earpiece over his shoulder. Faroe hooked the receiver over his ear and slipped the clear plastic earpiece into place.

"Volume is on your right, squelch in the center on top," Cook said.

"I know. St. Kilda field-tested these things before they were delivered to the Bureau."

Faroe turned the volume dial and after a second heard the ragged sound of Ted Franklin breathing quickly, shallowly. His fear came across in each ragged breath.

"Relax," Grace said. "Joe knows what he's doing."

Faroe tapped the earpiece and nodded to Cook. "Good to go. What about the tunnel?"

"You should get reception when you cross over to this side of the fence, but I won't guarantee anything before that."

Faroe nodded.

"If we have to blow the doors," Cook said, "I can't guarantee anyone's safety."

"No shit."

Counting off seconds in his head, Faroe ran toward the border fence.

82

FAROE SLOGGED THROUGH THE strawber-
ries and leaped the shallow ditch separating
the field from the dirt road that ran along the
fence. Through sheets of rain he saw what
looked like ghosts. He ran toward them. The
hollow metallic sound of an aluminum extension ladder being laid against the heavy
chain-link fence told him he was heading the
right way.

Mary and two other St. Kilda operatives
were trying to brace the bottom of a long ladder that barely reached to the top of the border fence. A long-barreled bolt-action rifle
with a telescopic sight hung upside down

across Mary's back. It was a sniper's rifle, .50 caliber, capable of dropping elephants before they heard the shot.

Everyone but Faroe was dressed in cammies that shed rain.

"I told you I was going south alone," Faroe said, reaching for the ladder.

"Wait," said one of the ops. "It's sliding like a bitch in this mud."

Mary gave Faroe an angelic smile. "I'm using the fence as a benchrest. I've got your back."

Faroe watched the ops struggle to place the ladder securely in mud that was slicker than snot. "A fifty-caliber round will go halfway to Ensenada."

"Not if I don't aim halfway to Ensenada," she said. "I won't fire unless I have a clear shot and see that you need it."

Faroe gave up on keeping Mary out of the game. "Did you see Lane?"

"Just a peek through the scope, when they took him inside. Handsome kid beneath the bruises."

Faroe's mouth flattened. "What about a Mexican wearing long hair and an Italian suit?"

"He ran a squad of gunmen around the

perimeter of the Tijuana warehouse half an hour ago," Mary said. "A few minutes ago the gun handlers got in some SUVs and split."

"So far, so good." Faroe smiled darkly. "After this goes down, if you get Jaime in your sights, drop him. He's not as mean as Hector, but he's a whole lot smarter."

"Will do. Jaime is still over there, sitting in a black Murano with another man. Here." Mary pulled a pistol from the ballistic nylon holster she wore and handed the weapon butt first to Faroe. "It's cold."

He nodded, checked the round in the chamber, and shoved the pistol in his belt, butt forward.

Like Hector.

Faroe took two steps up the ladder.

It slipped.

While the ops cursed and threw their weight against the ladder, he kept going.

The last rung of the ladder was tangled in the razor wire that looped along the top of the barricade fence.

"Leather gloves," he called down.

Within seconds the ladder shivered under the added hundred and twenty pounds of female sharpshooter.

"Here," Mary said, passing up a pair of gloves. Then she saw the top of the ladder. "Wait! Let me get canvas or something to throw over the loops. They'll tear the hell out of you."

"No time."

Faroe yanked on the gloves. Like his borrowed running shoes, they were a little small. He pried apart two loops of wicked wire, then eased up the ladder and stepped through the separated coils with their razor-blade edges and barbs.

"Joe, you can't—"

"I have to."

Straight ahead, brace yourself on the coils, one foot on the top of the barrier fence, then over and into thin air.

No sooner thought than done.

Except the razor wire collapsed, then lashed back at Faroe as he leaped. He twisted in midair and landed hard in the mud. He made himself push past the wrenching fall, forcing himself to breathe, to move, to stand.

Pain stabbed, telling him what he already knew: he hadn't dodged enough of the razor wire. His right sleeve was wet with more than rain.

"Oh, man," Mary said. "You're cut bad. Stay down until I—"

"No! That's an order."

Quickly Faroe checked the cuts for the deadly pulse of arterial blood. So far, so good.

He took off running.

83

"I DON'T LIKE THIS," Franklin said.

"Nobody asked you to," Grace said.

"I'm getting out of here. I'm a sitting duck!"

"You'll be a dead one if you run."

The tone of Grace's voice made Franklin turn and look at his ex-wife. She had her back to the nearest camera. She was holding a gun.

It was pointed at him.

"You're kidding," Franklin said.

"You're all that stands between Lane and death." She flicked off the safety and took up slack on the trigger. "You gave him as a hostage to the Butcher of Tijuana. What makes you think you should live and Lane should die?"

"I never meant—"

"I don't care what you meant," she cut in ruthlessly. "I have to deal with reality, and reality is that you're a money launderer to murderers, and a coward who put a boy on the firing line to save your own ass. I'd feel more compassion for a rabid dog, but I'd kill it just the same."

Franklin looked at Grace's eyes, the flat line of her mouth, and the darkness around her eyes from tension and lack of sleep.

She gestured slightly with the gun. "Sit on the floor behind those bags and stop whining. When Hector comes, don't show yourself and don't talk unless I tell you to. Do you understand?"

"You're crazy."

"My gun is quite sane."

Without a word Franklin walked away from the only safe exit, across an expanse of cold concrete cut by circles of light and pools of black, and sank down in shadows behind burlap bags of rice.

Grace hid the gun behind her purse and faced the camera again.

84

FAROE GRINNED DESPITE THE blood dripping down his right arm and pooling in his leather glove.

You tell him, amada. *He'll never underestimate you again.*

And neither would Faroe.

He clamped the gloved fingers of his left hand over the deepest slash on his arm and kept running south. The airport runway lights glittered in the rain like a beacon. He sprinted across the cement between planes and ducked under the eaves of an anonymous building. Breathing deep and steady, he searched through the rain for sentries around the Grupo Calderón warehouse and hangar.

A black car was idling in front of the Grupo Calderón building, the same kind of SUV Mary had seen Jaime driving.

The lights flashed once.

I see you soon, gringo. Look for me.

Headlights flashed again.

Faroe pulled his pistol and ran toward the vehicle. The driver's electric window slid down. There was a man in the passenger seat.

"So, you came alone," Jaime said, ignoring the drawn gun.

"One riot, one ranger," Faroe said. "How many men does Hector have with him?"

"None. He doesn't want any witnesses. Even me."

Faroe hoped Jaime wasn't lying, but didn't count on it.

The passenger leaned forward. It was Carlos Calderón. "I want that money!"

"Sue the U.S. government," Faroe said. "All I promised you was Hector."

"The hangar is open," Jaime said. "The bathroom is—"

Faroe was already running. He knew where the tunnel entrance was.

He was inside the hangar before Jaime left the parking lot.

The wooden door of the lavatory stood ajar at the back of the hangar. The floor and the toilet were filthy. The cubicle stank. The mirror over the tiny sink was flyspecked and grimy. It reflected a man who looked like he'd been used to mop up a bloody murder scene.

Faroe shoved the stinking toilet to one side. The stool was connected to a concrete waste pipe by a section of flexible hosing that leaked and dripped. There was a puddle of raw sewage in the bottom of the hole that was the mouth of the tunnel. The metal rungs of a ladder were shiny with foul moisture.

No point in worrying about gangrene in a few days when I'm likely to be dead in a few minutes.

As soon as he dropped below floor level, he lost radio contact.

85

GRACE STOOD BESIDE THE door of the warehouse bathroom and listened to the noises that welled up from the open hatchway. Everything was clear, distinct, almost too loud. She heard footsteps drawing closer, followed by a muffled cry.

Lane!

Then came Hector's voice, surprisingly close, cold.

Deadly.

"Stop here," Hector said. "Shut up. If you good, I good. You bad, I fock you mother and you father and you. Then I kill *todo el mundo*. *¿Claro?*"

The sound Lane made was a growl of fear and anger.

Grace gritted her teeth against the scream clawing to get out of her throat.

Hurry, Joe. Lane needs you.

I need you.

I'm not nearly as good at this as you are.

Silently she backed away from the bathroom door where light spilled out brightly. Holding the pistol against her thigh, she walked quickly through separate pools of light and ribbons of darkness. She stopped near the back wall of the hangar, where pallets cast dark shadows. Seventy feet of empty darkness and vertical tunnels of light separated her from the bathroom.

She turned sideways, keeping the gun out of sight.

From inside the bathroom came the hollow ringing sound of someone climbing a metal ladder. The black muzzle of a heavy-bore semiautomatic pistol rose up out of the floor. The weapon was equipped with a black device mounted like a sight on top of the barrel. A pencil-thin beam of red light reached out. Wherever the beam touched, a bullet could instantly follow.

Hector's black hair appeared at the mouth of the tunnel. He stuck his head up slowly, eyes glinting, like a rat coming out of a sewer.

The red light lanced out across the emptiness, piercing the cones of light, a red finger that touched first Grace, then the shadows and spaces behind her.

She thought about shooting Hector, but the range was extreme, the pistol unfamiliar, and Hector could have left someone down with Lane, a gun at his head.

"Where is my son?" she demanded.

Her voice carried clearly through the warehouse.

Hector climbed out of the tunnel and pointed his heavy black pistol at her. The red light danced in her eyes, then came to rest on her collarbone.

"Where is Faroe?" Hector asked.

"He didn't feel like hanging around waiting for you to kill him."

"He leave you?"

"Yes."

Hector shook his head. "You no have good luck with men."

"I've noticed."

"Where is Franklin?"

"You'll get him when I get my son."

Hector walked into the warehouse with a faintly dragging step. Using the laser beam, he checked out the stacks of cartons and piles of red stone pots. Satisfied that no one was hiding there, he walked toward Grace.

The red dot settled on her breast.

"Maybe I kill you now," Hector said. "Then Franklin. And the boy."

Has Jaime already killed Joe? Grace thought. Then she shoved the thought away. She had to stay calm.

For Lane.

Hector kept coming toward her, flashing in and out of darkness like a ghost.

Fifty feet. Forty feet. Thirty.

Twenty.

Grace turned fully toward him and assumed a shooting stance. Reflected light slid over her dark pistol like water. "You'll be the first to die."

Hector grinned and kept walking. "You shoot good?"

"Yes."

She centered the black blade of the pistol sight just south of Hector's shiny belt buckle.

He chuckled, stopped, and lowered his pistol. "*Basta.* Enough."

"It's not enough until Lane appears here. Unharmed."

"Where is that burro Franklin? I see him on TV, but no more."

"He's here. Where is Lane?"

Grace's pistol didn't waver.

Hector shook his head. "Ah, *señora,* Judge, I no like this. You demand too much."

Pistol at his side, he took one step, then another, staring past Grace, trying to see into the shadows.

There was just enough light for him to see her finger taking up slack on the trigger.

He stopped. "You tough, you know?"

"No closer" was all she said.

Hector gathered his shoulders in an exaggerated shrug. "I no like orders from a woman."

"Then consider the orders from the gun, not the woman," Grace said.

"*Aiee,* such a ball-breaker." He laughed. "I get Lane. You get Franklin. But if it go bad, the boy die first."

"Nothing will go bad. You want Ted. I want Lane. End of negotiation."

Hector dropped his chin and glared at her. "I no believe Faroe leave you. He is here, *escondido,* to kill me."

"Joe Faroe wants Lane alive more than he wants you dead."

Hector shook his head.

The pistol Grace held felt like it weighed fifty pounds. Cold sweat trickled down over her ribs. *Joe, where are you?*

Hurry!

"Joe is Lane's biological father," Grace said roughly. "That's why Ted gave Lane to you as a hostage. It didn't matter to Ted."

Hector's eyes glinted. "This is true?"

"As true as death. Joe and I won't double-cross you for any amount of money. We want our son alive and well."

Hector glared at her, then he spat in disgust. He dug a Marlboro pack out of his shirt pocket with his free hand, shook loose a cocaine-laced cigarette, and took it out with his teeth. He put away the pack, dug a lighter out of his jeans pocket, and struck a flame.

The movements were ritualized, including the deep breath full of cocaine smoke he drew into his lungs. A shimmering haze of pleasure and power swept through him.

"We do it the gun's way," Hector said. "This time."

He walked back across the concrete to the bathroom and disappeared down the hole.

TIJUANA
MONDAY, 12:23 P.M.

86

IGNORING THE PAIN THAT jolted through his
arm every time his feet struck the ground,
Faroe ran down the long tunnel. He dismissed
the trail of blood flung from his slashed left
calf and his right arm. A man could bleed a
lot and still function if he wanted to bad
enough.

Faroe wanted to.

The single strand of overhead electrical
wire blossomed every hundred feet with a
bare lightbulb. The lighting might have been
primitive, but the walls were expertly shored
with timbers. Wherever the miners had struck
loose soil, the walls were lined with sheets of

plywood to hold back the dirt. The footing was irregular, humped up with rocks and dirt.

The only sound Faroe heard was his own breathing—deep, harder than he wanted, and better than he had any right to expect. He was losing too much blood.

About every hundred yards, he ran past service rooms, narrow little chambers with a ceiling just high enough for a man to stand erect and repair the blowers that brought air down to the tunnel. He was reaching the last of those chambers when he heard Hector Rivas cursing as he climbed down a metal ladder.

Faroe flattened himself into the tiny service area, forced himself to breathe lightly, and eased his head forward just enough to see down the last hundred feet of tunnel.

Hector.

Lane!

For an instant, relief loosened Faroe's knees.

There was a gag tied across Lane's mouth and his hands were cuffed in front of him around the metal ladder.

So near.

And way too far for a pistol shot.

Not when he was shooting wrong-handed, light-headed, with an unfamiliar gun. Surprise was his only hope. If he crept close enough, he could put a bullet in Hector's head.

A head shot was the only sure way to save Lane.

And Faroe had to be certain, because one shot would be all he got. For that level of certainty, he couldn't be more than thirty feet from Hector.

So Faroe waited, breathing shallowly despite the aching of his lungs. Sweat cooled, but not the hot slide of blood down his right arm and into his left shoe.

87

HECTOR'S SHOVE SENT LANE stumbling back into the dirt wall of the tunnel. He sat down so hard his handcuffs clanged against the ladder.

Lane hardly noticed. He was still reeling from the conversation he'd just heard echoing down from above.

Joe is Lane's biological father. That's why Ted gave Lane to you as a hostage. It didn't matter to Ted.

This is true?

As true as death. Joe and I won't double-cross you for any amount of money. We want our son alive and well.

Lane wondered if his mother was lying.

And he was afraid she wasn't.

It explained too much. Answered too many questions. And turned his world upside down all over again.

"Don' move," Hector ordered.

Lane didn't.

Hector laid his pistol down on an overturned barrel and dug in his pocket. Then he hauled Lane to his feet and unlocked one of the handcuffs.

Lane ripped his gag off with his free hand and coughed. "Water."

Hector ignored Lane and slapped the open cuff on his own left wrist. Metal clicked as the cuff closed, binding the boy to him. Hector picked up his pistol, shoved it into his waistband, and turned to Lane.

"You fight me, you die," Hector said. He jerked his head toward the ladder. "Go."

One-handed, Lane started fumbling up the ladder. He felt Hector's breath against his bare calf as the Mexican climbed after him.

88

GRACE HAD JUST FINISHED checking that Franklin was still hidden behind the pallets when she heard scuffing sounds from the bathroom. Quickly she walked to where she'd stood before and raised the pistol into shooting position. She was sixty feet from the bathroom, much too far for a shot, but it was the only place where she could watch both Franklin and Hector.

Her heart soared when she saw Lane's head.

And sank when she realized that he was cuffed to Hector.

I'll have to get close to shoot. Very close.

Six inches.

She doubted Hector was that foolish.

Hector crowded out of the hole behind Lane so quickly that the boy tripped. Using the handcuffs and a casual strength that shocked Grace, Hector levered Lane right into the line of fire from her pistol.

"Mom!"

Using the cuffed hand, Hector backhanded Lane. "Shut up."

Forcing herself to keep the pistol steady, she spoke urgently to Lane. "Do as he says. It's almost over. Soon you'll be free."

It cost every bit of Grace's strength, but she kept the pistol steady.

Trip again, Lane. Go down hard and fast. Stay down.

Please, God.

Joe, where are you?

Are you even alive?

Hector laughed at Grace as he strode away from the bathroom, closing the distance between them. "Now you take my orders, yes?"

She drew a hidden breath and sighted

past her own son's head, letting Hector see the deadly black eye of her gun.

He slowed, then stopped ten feet from her.

"Unlock Lane," she said.

"Give me Franklin."

"Not until Lane is free."

"How I know Franklin is here?" Hector said.

"Speak up, Ted."

Silence.

She glanced in the direction of Franklin's hiding place. He had a look of terror on his face.

"Say something," she snarled, "or I'll shoot you myself."

"Dad?" Lane asked, not able to stop himself. "Did you really come for me?"

The sound Franklin made wasn't a word.

Hector pointed his pistol in the direction of Franklin's voice. The bloodred laser beam probed the shadows.

Franklin saw the light, made another throttled sound, and shrank from the beam.

Grace sensed as much as saw a movement in the bathroom. Silently, slowly, like a bloody ghost, Faroe rose up out of the hole in the floor. His right arm was covered with blood. There was a gun in his left hand.

The wrong hand.

Dear God.

Grace's eyes locked with Faroe's. He jerked his head to one side, warning her not to give him away. Instantly she shifted her glance.

Dragging Lane, Hector was walking toward Franklin's hiding place, getting farther away from her and Faroe with every step.

"Stop!" Grace shouted.

She took several steps toward Hector, hoping to distract him from Faroe.

Hector swung his pistol. The red dot of death settled between Grace's eyes.

"Let Lane go," she said, ignoring the red beam. "Now."

"No," Hector said angrily. "Franklin!"

Twenty feet away, Grace kept her pistol aimed at Hector's face and wished to hell Harley had given her a pistol with a laser sight. Hector was using Lane as a shield.

Six inches.

Maybe even twelve.

How close do you have to be, Joe?

But that was one question she couldn't ask.

"The instant you get Franklin," Grace said, "you'll kill everyone to protect your tunnel. Turn Lane loose. Now!"

One second.

Two.

Three.

Four.

With a sound of terror, Ted Franklin snapped. He broke cover, racing for the door, for freedom.

Hector whipped his pistol toward the sound. He fired once while the laser spot was still moving.

The sound was deafening.

The laser spot settled on Franklin's fleeing back. Hector fired twice more. Franklin landed facedown and didn't move.

While the shots echoed Faroe was running, had been running since the instant the red dot left Grace's forehead.

Now the dot was swinging back toward her.

Knowing he was too far away to be certain of missing Lane, Faroe yelled to distract Hector.

Hector spun toward the unexpected attack. For an instant he was shocked by the sight of a blood-soaked man running toward him, sighting along the pistol he held in his left hand. When Hector recognized Faroe, the Mexican snapped his cuffed arm over his hostage's head and yanked Lane close. Even as Hector started to point the pistol at Lane's head, he saw that Faroe was alone.

Eyes wide with horror, Lane saw that the bloody man running toward them was Joe Faroe.

With a flick of his wrist, Hector pointed the laser spot at Faroe's left side and fired.

Faroe took the shot, spun around, and kept on coming.

The red dot settled on Faroe's head.

Lane sank his teeth deep into Hector's arm, lashed out at his gun hand, and threw himself to the floor.

Hector's shot ricocheted wildly around the hangar.

Grace's shot didn't. Hector was dead before he hit the cement.

Faroe smiled even as his world went black.

So long, Hector. See you in hell.

89

IMMEDIATE FAMILY ONLY
NO MORE THAN TWO
VISITORS AT A TIME

LANE LOOKED AT THE sign on the heavy wooden door of the intensive care unit, then at his mother.

"Maybe I should wait out here," he said.

"It doesn't get any more immediate than you and Joe," Grace said.

"I'm still having a hard time getting my mind around it."

"The fact that your biological parents are

human, and your legal father is all too human?"

"Uh, yeah."

She gave Lane a hug even as she regretted the new lines of tension around his eyes. He looked—and was—years older than he had been a month ago.

"It's okay," she said. "Most kids don't have to deal with their parents being people until they're twice your age. Most adults never have to go through what you did. And in case I haven't mentioned it, I'm very proud of you."

"Ambassador Steele said the same thing. So did Cook."

"So will Joe, if he's awake."

So would Ted, if he wasn't such a jerk.

But he was, and two bullets in the back hadn't changed that. When she and Lane had gone to see Ted in the next room over, he'd pretended to be asleep.

"I know this isn't easy," she said. "There's a lot to sort out, for all of us. Life has . . . changed."

Lane made a sound that could have been a laugh. "Ya think?" Then he hugged her hard. "Sorry. I didn't mean that the way it sounded. You walked away from your career and risked your life for me. I love you, Mom. I just wish I'd known."

"About Joe?"

"Yeah. I guess. I don't know."

She almost smiled. "Sometimes Joe affects me the same way. But you should know that I love him very much."

"I already figured that out." *When you ran past Dad and cried all over Joe.*

Lane still didn't like to think how he'd done the same thing just as soon as he'd taken the key from Hector's pocket and unlocked the cuffs.

It's not that I don't love Dad.
It's just that I don't like him.

"I like Joe," Lane said. "Hell—heck—I'm not the first kid to have two fathers, right? How does he feel about it?"

"Joe?"

"Yeah."

"Ask him."

Grace opened the door, saw that Faroe was sitting up, and went quickly to his side. He was pale and his mouth was tight with pain. The bullet had missed all organs, but it had ripped a hole in the rest. She kissed him gently, then took his left hand and cradled it against her cheek.

"You look like hell," she said.

"You don't." Faroe slid his hand around her neck and urged her down for a better kiss. "You smell like heaven. Want to break me out of this joint?"

Lane cleared his throat.

"He knows," Grace said as soon as Faroe released her mouth.

"Then he shouldn't be surprised to see us kissing." Faroe held his good hand out to Lane. "How about a left-handed shake?"

Awkwardly Lane took Faroe's unbandaged hand.

"Thanks for saving my life," Faroe said, squeezing and releasing his son's hand.

Lane stared. "What? I didn't do anything."

"You yanked Hector off-balance before he could kill me, and then you got out of the way so your mother could do what had to be done. Your quick thinking saved her life, too. And Ted's." *Cowardly piece of dog crap that he is.* "How does it feel to be a hero?"

"I was scared as hell—uh, heck," Lane admitted.

"Hell works for me," Faroe said. "That's how scared I was."

"Really?"

"All the way to the soles of my feet."

"Then I guess it's okay to be scared," Lane said, his tone half questioning.

"I'd be worried about your brains if you weren't." Faroe smiled. "I'm not worried."

Lane's answering smile was shy but real.

For the first time since the violence in the warehouse, Grace allowed herself to hope.

"Has Steele been in to see you?" she asked Faroe.

"Last I checked, we weren't related, and the head nurse is a real dragon."

"Do you think that would stop the ambassador?" Lane asked. "Wheelchair or not, the man's a full-on bulldozer."

"Good point. Yes, he came to see me," Faroe said to Grace.

"You didn't sign anything, did you?"

Silently Faroe held up his heavily bandaged right hand.

"What did you tell him?" Grace asked.

Faroe gave Lane a sideways look. "She grill you like this about homework?"

Lane snickered. "Always."

Faroe shook his head. "I told Steele that after I married you, you would be available to negotiate the terms of our future, if any, with

St. Kilda Consulting. If you don't marry me, I won't have a future worth negotiating, so the point is moot."

Lane looked at his mother's flushed cheeks, tear-bright eyes, and dawning smile. "I'm going to check out the cafeteria," he said.

"You don't have to," Faroe said.

"Yeah, I do," Lane said. "Or do you need me to close the deal with her?"

"You're okay with the idea?" Faroe asked Lane.

"Of you and Mom?"

Faroe took Grace's hand. "Yes."

Lane gave his mother a one-armed hug and headed for the door. "It'll be weird, seeing her happy, but I'll get used to it. And she won't have so much time to worry about me."

The door closed behind Lane.

"That's one hell of a kid you raised," Faroe said. "I've known a lot of men who would be a wreck after what Lane went through."

"He's not over it yet. There will be nightmares."

"Like you had?"

"Yes."

"I've had my own," Faroe said. "Still do."

"Tell him that someday. He admires you."

"For screwing up?" Faroe asked, disgusted.

"For saving his life. And mine. You set yourself up to take Hector's bullets so that I could get close enough to shoot him without endangering Lane."

Faroe sighed and leaned more heavily into the propped-up pillows. "Does that mean you'll marry me?"

"Only if you start practicing left-handed with a pistol."

He laughed, winced at the pain, and settled for a smile. "Pistol practice. Guess that means we're staying with St. Kilda?"

Grace smiled. "It's a good thing you're already lying down."

He gave her a sideways look. "Why?"

"Steele has been grooming you—and now wants to groom us—to take over St. Kilda Consulting when he retires."

"You're shitting me."

"Nope."

Faroe didn't know what to say.

"Before you say yes or no, think about this," she said. "If we sign with St. Kilda, the contract will be retroactive to a week ago. In other words, neither of us will have to pay St.

Kilda for any costs incurred in saving Lane."

Faroe whistled softly. "Steele must be feeling generous."

"Not quite." Grace smiled like a lawyer. "There's the five-million-dollar reward for Hector Rivas Osuna, plus anything in excess of fifty million dollars that might be recovered from Ted's files. If we were free agents, the money would go to us."

Faroe was quiet for a long time before he said, "You dropped the hammer on Hector. It's your call on the reward."

"And the rest?"

"They say that blood washes off gold, but I don't know if there's enough water on earth to clean Ted's money." Faroe sighed and shifted on the bed, trying to get comfortable. "Again, it's your call. You and Lane had to live with the mutt. But damn, I wish that Hector had been a better shot."

She smiled grimly. "I've already started the process to remove Ted from any legal guardianship of Lane. Talon Cook said he would personally guarantee that Ted doesn't cause any problems over it."

"Is Ted going to do hard time?"

"Stu has the morals of a reptile, and he's

as clever as they come in manipulating the law for his clients—until their money runs out. So I guess we'll just have to hope that Ted's money runs out before he walks."

"Lane's alive," Faroe said. "That's what matters."

"You really don't care about the money, do you?"

"You'll negotiate a good salary—"

"And bonuses."

"—for us with Steele. We won't starve. And if we don't sign the contract, the task force will be squeezing us to give information on St. Kilda Consulting. Steele might grate on me from time to time, but bureaucracy grates on me all the time."

Grace grinned. "Steele loves you too. He wants to be your best man."

"What!"

"Harley says you'll look *fabulous* in a white tux."

Faroe closed his eyes. "That's it. We're eloping."

"You sure? Lane hinted he'd love to give me away."

Faroe opened his eyes. "You wearing a tux, too?"

"I was thinking about that red outfit I picked up in Mexico."

"Only if we elope."

Smiling, she leaned down and kissed him. "Two white tuxes it is."

was supposed to have used. It was a quite mad way to do it. He couldn't hope to get away with it. Sooner or later he was going to have to account for the boys not being there. As far as he knew he had a long reign in front of him. No one has ever been able to think why he should have chosen so difficult and dangerous a way when he had so many simpler methods at hand. He had only to have the boys suffocated, and let them lie in state while the whole of London walked by and wept over two young things dead before their time of fever. That is the way he *would* have done it, too. Goodness, *the whole point* of Richard's killing the boys was to prevent any rising in their favour, and to get any benefit from the murder the fact of their deaths would *have* to be made public, and as soon as possible. It would defeat the whole plan if people didn't *know* that they were dead. But Henry, now. Henry *had* to find a way to push them out of sight. Henry *had* to be mysterious. Henry *had* to hide the facts of when and how they died. *Henry's whole case depended* on no one's knowing what exactly happened to the boys."

"It did indeed, Brent; it did indeed," Grant

said, smiling at counsel's eager young face. "You ought to be at the Yard, Mr. Carradine!"

Brent laughed.

"I'll stick to Tonypandy," he said. "I bet there's a lot more of it that we don't know about. I bet history books are just riddled with it."

"You'd better take Sir Cuthbert Oliphant with you, by the way." Grant took the fat respectable-looking volume from his locker. "Historians should be compelled to fake a course in psychology before they are allowed to write."

"Huh. That wouldn't do anything for them. A man who is interested in what makes people tick doesn't write history. He writes novels, or becomes an alienist, or a magistrate—"

"Or a confidence man."

"Or a confidence man. Or a fortune-teller. A man who understands about people hasn't any yen to write history. History is toy soldiers."

"Oh, come. Aren't you being a little severe? It's a very learned and erudite—"

"Oh, I didn't mean it that way. I mean: it's moving little figures about on a flat surface.

It's half-way to mathematics, when you come to think about it."

"Then if it's mathematics they've no right to drag in back-stairs gossip," Grant said, suddenly vicious. The memory of the sainted More continued to upset him. He thumbed through the fat respectable Sir Cuthbert in a farewell review. As he came to the final pages the progress of the paper from under his thumb slackened, and presently stopped.

"Odd," he said, "how willing they are to grant a man the quality of courage in battle. They have only tradition to go on, and yet not one of them questions it. Not one of them, in fact, fails to stress it."

"It was an enemy's tribute," Carradine reminded him. "The tradition began with a ballad written by the other side."

"Yes. By a man of the Stanleys. 'Then a knight to King Richard gan say.' It's here somewhere." He turned over a leaf or two, until he found what he was looking for. "It was 'good Sir William Harrington,' it seems. The knight in question.

There may no man their strokes abide, the Stanleys dints they be so strong [the treacherous bastards!]

Ye may come back at another tide,
methinks ye tarry here too long.

Your horse at your hand is ready, another day you may worship win

And come to reign with royalty, and
wear your crown and be our king.

'Nay, give me my battle-axe in my
hand, set the crown of England on my
head so high.

For by Him that made both sea and
land, King of England this day I will die.

One foot I will never flee whilst the
breath is my breast within.'

As he said so did it be—if he lost his
life he died a King."

" 'Set the crown of England on my
head,' " said Carradine, musing. "That was
the crown that was found in a hawthorn
bush afterwards."

"Yes. Set aside for plunder probably."

"I used to picture it one of those high
plush things that King George got crowned
in, but it seems it was just a gold circlet."

"Yes. It could be worn outside the battle
helmet."

"Gosh," said Carradine with sudden feeling, "I sure would have hated to wear that

crown if I had been Henry! I sure would have hated it!" He was silent for a little, and then he said: "Do you know what the town of York wrote—wrote in their records, you know—about the battle of Bosworth?"

"No."

"They wrote: 'This day was our good King Richard piteously slain and murdered; to the great heaviness of this city.'"

The chatter of the sparrows was loud in the quiet.

"Hardly the obituary of a hated usurper," Grant said at last, very dry.

"No," said Carradine. "No. 'To the great heaviness of this city,'" he repeated slowly, rolling the phrase over in his mind. "They cared so much about it that even with a new régime in the offing and the future not to be guessed at they put down in black and white in the town record their opinion that it was murder and their sorrow at it."

"Perhaps they had just heard about the in-dignities perpetrated on the King's dead body and were feeling a little sick."

"Yes. Yes. You don't like to think of a man you've known and admired flung stripped and dangling across a pony like a dead an-imal."

"One wouldn't like to think of even an enemy so. But sensibility is not a quality that one would look for among the Henry-Morton crowd."

"Huh. Morton!" said Brent, spitting out the word as if it were a bad taste. "No one was 'heavy' when Morton died, believe me. Know what the Chronicler wrote of him? The London one, I mean. He wrote: 'In our time was no man like to be compared with him in all things; albeit that he lived not without the great disdain and hatred of the Commons of this land.' "

Grant turned to look at the portrait which had kept him company through so many days and nights.

"You know," he said, "for all his success and his Cardinal's hat I think Morton was the loser in that fight with Richard III. In spite of his defeat and his long traducing, Richard came off the better of these two. He was loved in his day."

"That's no bad epitaph," the boy said soberly.

"No. Not at all a bad epitaph," Grant said, shutting Oliphant for the last time. "Not many men would ask for a better." He handed over the book to its owner. "Few men have earned so much," he said.

When Carradine had gone Grant began to sort out the things on his table, preparatory to his homegoing on the morrow. The unread fashionable novels could go to the hospital library to gladden other hearts than his. But he would keep the book with the mountain pictures. And he must remember to give The Amazon back her two history books. He took them out so that he could give them to her when she brought in his supper. And he read again, for the first time since he began his search for the truth about Richard, the school book tale of his villainy. There it was, in unequivocable black and white, the infamous story. Without a perhaps or a peradventure. Without a qualification or a question.

As he was about to shut the senior of the two educators his eye fell on the beginning of Henry VII's reign, and he read: "It was the settled and considered policy of the Tudors to rid themselves of all rivals to the throne, more especially those heirs of York who remained alive on the succession of Henry VII. In this they were successful, although it was left to Henry VIII to get rid of the last of them."

He stared at this bald announcement. This placid acceptance of wholesale murder. This simple acknowledgement of a process of family elimination.

Richard III had been credited with the elimination of two nephews, and his name was a synonym for evil. But Henry VII, whose "settled and considered policy" was to eliminate a whole family was regarded as a shrewd and far-seeing monarch. Not very lovable perhaps, but constructive and painstaking, and very successful withal.

Grant gave up. History was something that he would never understand.

The values of historians differed so radically from any values with which he was acquainted that he could never hope to meet them on any common ground. He would go back to the Yard, where murderers were murderers and what went for Cox went equally for Box.

He put the two books tidily together and when The Amazon came in with his mince and stewed prunes he handed them over with a neat little speech of gratitude. He really was very grateful to The Amazon. If she had not kept her school books he might never have started on the road that led to his knowledge of Richard Plantagenet.

She looked confused by his kindness, and he wondered if he had been such a bear in his illness that she expected nothing but carping from him. It was a humiliating thought.

"We'll miss you, you know," she said, and her big eyes looked as if they might brim with tears. "We've grown used to having you here. We've even got used to *that*." And she moved an elbow in the direction of the portrait.

A thought stirred in him.

"Will you do something for me?" he asked.

"Of course. Anything I can do."

"Will you take that photograph to the window and look at it in a good light as long as it takes to count a pulse?"

"Yes, of course, if you want me to. But why?"

"Never mind why. You just do it to please me. I'll time you."

She took up the portrait and moved into the light of the window.

He watched the second-hand of his watch.

He gave her forty-five seconds and then said: "Well?" And as there was no immediate answer he said again: "Well?"

"Funny," she said. "When you look at it for a little it's really quite a nice face, isn't it?"

About the Author

ELIZABETH MACKINTOSH used two pen names during her writing career: Josephine Tey, who was also her Suffolk great-great-grandmother, and Gordon Daviot. She was born in 1897 in Inverness, Scotland, where she attended the Royal Academy. Miss MacKintosh later trained for three years at the Anstey Physical Training College in Birmingham, then began her teaching career as a physical training instructor. She gave up teaching to keep house for her father, who lived near Loch Ness, and pursue her writing. Her first book was *The Man in the Queue* (1929), published under the Gordon Daviot pseudonym, and it introduced the character of Inspector Grant, familiar now from the Tey novels. The author wrote chiefly under the signature of Gordon Daviot from 1929 to 1946, during which time her works included the play *Richard of Bordeaux* (1933), which ran for a year with John

Giclgud in the lead part. The first of the Josephine Tey mysteries, *A Shilling for Candles*, was published in 1936 and was eventually followed by *Miss Pym Disposes* in 1947. Also included among the Tey mysteries are *The Franchise Affair* (1949), *Brat Farrar* (1949), *To Love and Be Wise* (1950), *The Daughter of Time* (1951), and *The Singing Sands* (1952). Elizabeth MacKintosh died in London on February 13, 1952.